Heart of Shadows

ALSO BY PHILIP G. WILLIAMSON

Moonblood

HEART OF SHADOWS

Philip G. Williamson

LEGEND

Published by Legend Books in 1994

1 3 5 9 10 8 6 4 2

First published in the United Kingdom by
Legend Books Limited
20 Vauxhall Bridge Road, London, SW1V 2SA

An imprint of Random House UK Limited

London Melbourne Sydney Auckland
Johannesburg and agencies throughout the world

First published in Great Britain in 1993 by
Randon House UK Limited

Typeset by Deltatype Ltd, Ellesmere Port, Cheshire
Printed in England by Clays Ltd, St Ives plc

ISBN 0 09 931451 7

CAVEAT: THE BOOK OF THE BEGINNING

MANY NATIONS, DYARCHIM among them, elected long ago to deny the existence of the original Myth of the Earliest Days. So profound is the fear of its message that all references to the Myth in any other than the approved, most recent version (which itself predates history) have been expunged. The Dyarch Old Texts, written more than four thousand years ago, acknowledge the approved version as the original. Knowledge of any other version is forbidden by Dyarch law, upon pain of death.

This law is not widely known, for good reason. The existence of the law in itself admits the existence of that which it is denying. Nevertheless the law must exist in order that civilization's course may be maintained without deviation or upheaval.

Traveller, be conscious, then: to read what follows will place you outside the law in those lands where such knowledge is suppressed. To speak of what you have read will almost certainly place you in a position of grave personal danger.

But to *understand* is to tear through the veil of the past and look upon the world anew.

... *and she cast him from her, believing that he must perish but knowing that for the remainder of his days he would be bound to search fruitlessly for that which was taken from him.*

And she took herself away in anguish and sorrow, for all she had striven for had been in vain. She languished alone for a thousand long years, reviled by those whom she had loved, until at last she died.

But he did not die. He became like the daemons, immortal and wicked, a hollow creature given to depravity and grotesque mischiefs. He stalked the earth alone, seeking, ever seeking, feeding upon others, taking pleasure in their forms, delighting in their pain.

And it is said that he is still upon the world, and there are folk steeped in darkness and evil who worship him and seek to help him find his fullness.

But she, who gave him life, who loved him and brought forth their children, she who was forced to cast him from her ... she is gone forever.

Extracted from the Forbidden Myth.

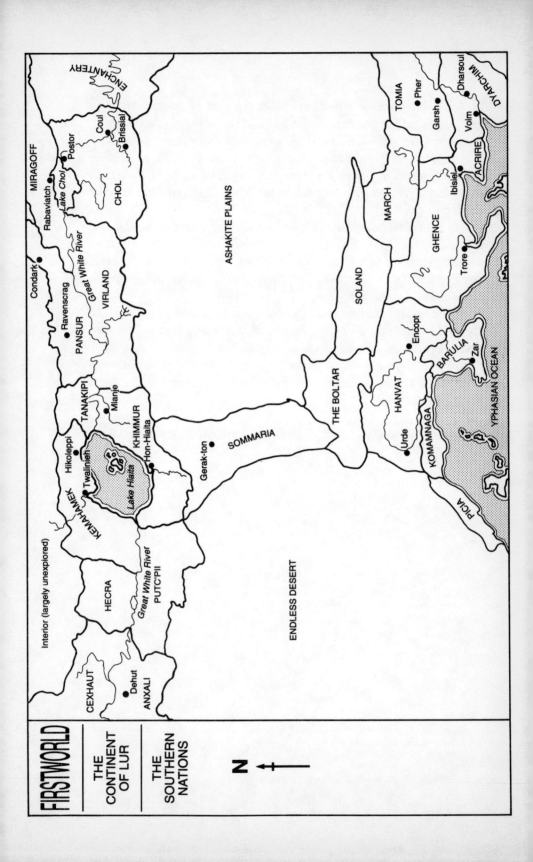

PART ONE

I

'*LEAVE IT!*'

Edric's voice cut through the warm, enclosed air with a harsh sibilance. The others looked up in surprise. Edric's face was wild.

'My friend, Edric, what is the matter?' Master Frano stood firm and unruffled. In the torchlight a half-smile hovered quizzically upon his lips. 'Leave it? Surely you are not serious? Yet if you are not, I have to say this is an inappropriate moment to introduce humour.'

Edric had backed away a step, fear in his eyes. Edric, who in just hours would be dead, looked now as though he had seen a premonition of his end. His face gleamed palely, his dark hair sweat-stuck to his forehead. His eyes were wide, reflecting the flames of the two torches which were all that illumined the breathless subterranean chamber.

'We must leave it!' he repeated, his voice breaking. 'We shouldn't be here. It is not our place. And this . . . *thing!* Can you not feel it?'

'I feel the anticipation of a weight of coin in my pouch when Master Frano divides up the profits of this venture,' replied Gully, the former soldier, now Master Frano's lieutenant. 'And now, with the addition of this, I expect my pouch to be all the heavier.'

They all stared at the object embedded in the rock behind the false wall. Gully hefted his pick. 'C'mon lads, the sooner we get it free the sooner we can be out of here.'

'*No!*' Edric shook his head from side to side, taking another step back, his hands held before him as if warding off something unseen and menacing. 'We must leave it! I feel it, it is unnatural!'

Master Frano moved to place his hands upon Edric's shoulders. 'Edric, if you feel so strongly about this, leave us. Join young

Sildemund outside with the wagons and await us there. You will receive your share, have no fear about that.'

'I want nothing of this!'

The unmistakable edge of authority crept into Master Frano's voice. 'We will discuss it later. But for now, if you will not help us, leave us to get on with the task of freeing this great gem and exploring the remainder of this place.'

'It is no gem!' protested Edric, transfixed by the strange stone they had partially uncovered. From what was so far visible it appeared roughly oval in form, smooth, though asymmetrical. It was perhaps the size of a sheep's bladder, deep reddish in hue, lined with broken, irregular bands of a darker colour, and streaked with thin filaments of yellowish-white. To Edric's eyes the colours seemed unfixed, pulsing infinitesimally, as though the stone was imbued with some weird life-force. Enclosing it was a strange, cage-like structure, made up of dirty, whitish bars of unidentifiable metal. There was something engraved upon the front of the cave, a twisting, serpentine emblem, badly cracked and eroded so that it could not properly be made out.

'It is no gem!' he repeated, and gazed wretchedly into Master Frano's face. 'I tell you this: we must not disturb it. I cannot say how I know this, but I know it as surely as I know that I stand here now. We must leave it and go.'

The others watched; one or two exchanged nervous glances.

'You are unwell still, Edric. Your fever has not yet left you.' Master Frano spoke deliberately loudly. His hands exerted pressure upon Edric's shoulders, propelling him gently but determinedly back. 'Begone now. Wait for us above. We will join you as soon as we are done here.'

Edric retreated with a tormented expression. At the base of the crumbling, rough-hewn stair which led to the entrance of the grotto he hesitated, one foot upon the lower step. He seemed torn, on the verge of one last appeal, but Master Frano had ordered his men back to work and none now glanced Edric's way.

One hand to his head, Edric climbed the stair into the dying light of afternoon. Twenty paces away Master Frano's son, Sildemund, was preparing a meal over a fire beside the two wagons.

They had come upon this place an hour or so ago, by accident as they perceived it, and as it provided adequate cover and a view of the surrounding land Master Frano had chosen it for the night's camp.

Two days earlier, en route for the border crossing which would take them out of Tomia back into their homeland of Dyarchim, they had stopped for the night at a wayside inn. There they learned of increased activity by both Tomian and Dyrach guards at the border crossing point. All travellers seeking to pass between the two countries were being searched in a manner far more thorough than was usual.

Speculation in the inn's common room was of a link with the siege of Garsh, a remote Tomian hill-town, the enclave and virtual prison of a community of religious cultists. Tomian troops had recently surrounded the town, denying ingress or exit to anyone. There were rumours of a massacre, though nothing substantive.

A second line of conjecture – which may still have been linked with Garsh – held that the border guards were on the lookout for an escaped murderer. Tales were told of a couple of particularly grisly murders and the theft of a considerable amount of money, but no one really knew, and the guards themselves were apparently tight-lipped. Plainly, however, they were searching for someone or something considered to be of great importance.

This was a blow for Master Frano.

He was a trader, Frano Atturio, from the port city of Volm, situated at the mouth of the river Tigrant on Dyarchim's southern coast. He regularly travelled this road, carrying merchandise between Dyarchim, Tomia and Ghence, and on occasion travelling further afield into Barulia, Hanvat and even Sommaria. He dealt mainly in silks, spices and sundry exotica brought from the far southern lands across the blue Yphasian Ocean, which came to Dyarchim on fat, wallowing merchantmen with billowing sails of yellow, blue or red. The ships were crewed by nimble sailors with ebony skin, short of stature, who spoke in an incomprehensible tongue and were prepared to sell their cargoes at favourable prices.

Over the years Master Frano had built up a profitable business. He had gained a reputation for reliability and honest dealings among his numerous clients. That certain of the goods he chose oft-times to carry were deemed over-exotic in the eyes of the authorities was no deterrent. There was a ready – if not open – market for such merchandise, and prices paid could be handsome.

Well-concealed compartments in his wagons ensured that contraband would be revealed only to be most assiduous of searches. And the border guards were easily persuaded to look the other way in return for a small gift of liquor, narcotics or a trinket or two for their wives or sweethearts. Master Frano was not alone in practising his trade to its fullest extent, and though on rare occasions he had been obliged to hand over slightly larger gifts than intended, he had never encountered serious difficulties.

But the situation now appeared grave. More than one of the inn's clients reported arrests of merchants on both sides of the border. Goods had been impounded and the offenders were held in chains or, in the case of those arrested in Dyarchim, escorted under guard back to Dharsoul, the Dyarch capital.

Such arrests were almost unheard of. Two, or perhaps three times a year, by clandestine arrangements between customs and the Merchants' Guild, a merchant, chosen by lot, and in collaboration, would be 'uncovered' while passing through border control. Any illegal goods would be confiscated and the 'criminal' would receive a significant fine, paid secretly out of Guild funds. He would then be released, within two days at most.

By this means everyone was kept happy: the merchants, because international trade could by such means carry on unhindered; the guards, because the bulk of the impounded goods would be circulated among them at temptingly low prices; and not least the authorities, who were able to demonstrate that justice was being seen to be done, while at the same time reaping profit from the unofficial sale of the confiscated goods.

So whatever was afoot at the border now was plainly of no little import. The last time there had been any such restrictions was more than a decade ago, at the time of the Dyarchim rebellion. There had been scandal and corruption in high places then, and a violent uprising against the Crown. For a time the country had seemed close to civil war, though it was impossible to know exactly what was going on. Understandably the borders had been virtually closed until the rebellion was put down. But this . . . this was something quite different.

Master Frano had cursed freely, and pondered his options,

which appeared bleak. He could not risk arrest. The goods he carried were of substantial value. Discovered, they would earn him heavy tolls at least, and likely an uncomfortable spell in prison, not to mention loss of revenue. But short of taking a long detour, adding as much as two weeks to his journey time, there was no other route back to Volm.

It was Gully who had come up with the answer. A former battalion scout with the Dyarch army, he knew of a way through the hills which would avoid the border crossing. It was a circuitous route, but not impassable for the wagons. He was confident he could lead Master Frano's party safely over the frontier, to rejoin the main Volm road inside Dyarchim with a time loss of no more than three days.

So they had set out from the inn at daybreak, travelled for several hours, and in lonely countryside safe from prying eyes Gully had directed them from the road into Tomia's parched wildlands.

Now they were past the frontier, had advanced without mishap, and were making their way down through the hills towards the Volm road. A landslip in a canyon through which they would have passed forced them to make another detour, but fortunately Gully had been forewarned of this by a customer at the inn with whom he had spoken briefly. Gully thus took the party via a route suggested by the fellow, which skirted the canyon some distance before they approached it, and added only a few more hours to the journey.

It was here that they had come upon the ruin – if ruin it was. To begin with they were not aware that anything had ever stood there. Time, perhaps aided by the hands of men, had erased almost all traces of anything other than the work of nature. Master Frano simply spotted the low, flat-crested knoll from a distance – a basalt extrusion from some forgotten volcanic shift, now overgrown. He sent Gully foward to investigate. Gully returned and reported a gentle slope on the knoll's lee-side, and a suitable plateau at the crest, well covered with dense pines and massive boulders.

It was after they had established camp that Picadus, one of Master Frano's party, had remarked casually upon the regular shape of the clearing in which they rested. Moments later, after half-hearted investigation, he had pointed to what he perceived as regular impressions and rises in the ground.

'A building of some sort once occupied this area,' he declared.

'Look, this is the line of a wall. And here, a break for an entrance, and the grounds level rises. I'll warrant there were steps where this slope is.'

The outlines Picadus indicated were so vague as to be almost indiscernible, and the others showed scant interest. But then Dervad, gathering wood for a fire at the edge of the clearing, startled a huge buck rabbit from its rest. The rabbit bolted into a scrub of myrtle, and took refuge in a hollow beneath a boulder. The men gave chase, thinking to sup on rabbit stew that evening.

The bolthole proved larger than was at first thought. No amount of probing with sticks and poles could discover its limit, nor encourage the quarry out. So the men took picks and spades and began tearing at the edges of the hole, determined to flush the rabbit into the open.

Within a minute of furious work they had enlarged the opening sufficiently to make it plain that they were standing at the entrance of some kind of hidden grotto. And Picadus, staring into its black depths, pointed out the narrow stone steps rudely hacked out of pitted rock and ancient soil, which led down into the earth.

Master Frano, who until now had taken no part in the operation, became intrigued and ordered that the entrance be widened further. It was quickly discovered that the natural rock around the opening would permit entry only in single file. Master Frano had torches brought and, leaving his son, Sildemund, to tend the camp, led the way into the gloomy orifice.

Their initial search uncovered nothing except a musty cavern, formed by nature, apparently untouched in ages. It was of no great size. They thought at first that it was unoccupied, then something shot out from concealment and came at them low and fast, glimpsed only as a brownish blur in the dark.

The men leapt willy-nilly, in terror of their lives, with yells and shrieks of alarm. Dervad badly grazed an elbow on the cavern wall. Then the foe was identified; the big buck rabbit, forgotten in the excitement of the discovery of the cave. Their fear gave way to shouts of relief, sheepish laughter and curses as the rabbit fled up the steps to freedom.

The laughter relieved the tension that had built up as they had descended into the cavern. At Master Frano's bidding they explored the furthest angles of the grotto.

A word from Picadus brought the others rushing to his side. His torchflame had revealed a gaping crevice lined with glittering walls. Diamonds! Gems! They crowded forward eagerly, but their hopes were dashed as Master Frano pronounced the find to consist of nothing more than common quartz crystals.

Disappointed, they searched on until presently Master Frano shook his head. 'There is nothing here, lads. It is just a natural cave. But no matter.'

'Those steps are not natural,' Picadus protested. 'They were hewn by some person long ago to give access to this secret place. It had a use of some kind. There must be something here.'

'Perhaps it was the home of a hermit.'

'Perhaps, but I tell you, a building stood outside. And if that was so, then why make steps into a cave outside if not for some secret purpose?'

Master Frano raised an eyebrow. 'Is this not a case of "putting the cart before the horse"? I would imagine that our hermit, or whoever it was, lived here in this cavern first and built a more comfortable home outside, in which he subsequently took up residence.'

'We should not leave until we are absolutely sure that there is nothing to be found,' persisted Picadus. He took up a spade and began to dig at a mound of rubble in one corner of the cave. The others watched for a minute until he ceased, streaked with sweat, staring angrily at the hole he had made.

Beneath the rubble was solid rock, nothing more.

On a whim or out of frustration, Gully took his pickaxe and struck hard at the cavern wall. Surprisingly, instead of merely chipping the hard rock the head sank deep. Gully frowned, then wrenched the pick free. As it came out of the wall it brought with it great flakes of mortar or stucco and a shower of smaller stones.

'The torch!' Gully cried. He leapt to the wall, examining it with eyes and hands. 'A false wall!' he yelled, wheeling. 'Someone has closed this area off with rubble and sealed it with mortar, painted to resemble the natural rock!'

Master Frano was at his side, his eyes bright. 'Tear it away!'

The men set to. Within seconds a large aperture was opened, revealing a deep recess in the rock large enough for two men to step into standing abreast.

Before them now was solid rock, but in the middle of it something gleamed dully, reddish in the flame light – a strange, smooth crystal or stone, held in a cage which was sunk into the rock itself.

Less than half an hour after Edric left the grotto Master Frano and his men emerged and joined Sildemund at the wagons. Dusk was closing in. The evening was warm and the watery sun had almost settled behind the distant hills.

'Well, Sildemund, is supper ready?' demanded Gully, sluicing his hands and face from a water barrel. 'What have you done for us?'

'It's ready, Gully. Bread and soup of vegetables, with a little ale. Sadly, brave and skilled huntsmen, we are without fresh rabbit meat to add substance and flavour to the soup. That big bunny showed rare ingenuity. It is no shame on your part to have been outwitted by such a clever beast.'

'Enough mouth, boy!' retorted Gully, and cuffed him playfully about the head with a wide, calloused hand. He leaned over the pot and proceeded to ladle soup into a battered tin dish.

Master Frano settled himself beside his son. 'Where is Edric?'

With a tilt of his head, Sildemund indicated a motionless shape huddling under a blanket beneath one of the wagons behind him. 'He's in a queer mood. Won't eat or drink. Says he wants to be alone.'

'You were right, it's the fever,' said Picadus. Two weeks earlier, in Ghence, Edric had been struck down by Blue Estuary Fever. For several days he had been in a state of almost unrelenting delirium, exhibiting the common symptoms of the disease: prophetic babblings accompanied by vivid hallucinations, visitations and visions of doom.

Frano nodded to himself ruminatively. 'He was always the sensitive one.'

'What happened, Father?' asked Sildemund, tossing back his long light brown hair from his face. 'He was shaking when he came back up. He worried me. What did you find down there?'

'This,' Frano produced from his satchel a bulky package bound in rough cloth. He unwound it and displayed the oddly formed red stone held in its close shell of curved metallic bars.

Sildemund bent close. 'What is it?'

'I don't know. It is not ruby or opel, nor pyrope, almandine, spinel, corundum, quartz or any other stone known to me.'

'Is it valuable?'

'If nothing else its rarity must surely pronounce it so. But I cannot assay it. At home I will endeavour to free it from this container and turn it over to someone more familiar with rare gems than I.'

Master Frano wrapped the stone again and replaced it in his satchel.

'Is that all you found?' enquired Sildemund.

Gully chuckled. 'That and a frantic buck rabbit!'

'Then what was it that so upset poor Edric? I've never seen a face so white.'

Master Frano cast a backward glance over his shoulder, at Edric curled in the shadow. 'As Picadus says, it must be that he still suffers from the fever.'

They finished their meal. Picadus brought forth his cittern and a song or two was sung. Then, with the night watch set, the men retired.

The party rose at daybreak. Sildemund made breakfast as the others packed the wagons and fed and watered the horses and harnessed them for travel. Master Frano, with a slightly troubled look, approached Gully.

'Where is Edric this morning? I do not see him.'

Gully glanced around the camp and shook his head. 'His blanket is still beneath the wagon, but I have not seen him,'

Frano summoned Dervad. 'Yours was the last watch. Did you see anything of Edric?'

Dervad nodded. 'He was up before dawn, pacing back and forth, very agitated. I asked him what was the matter. At first he ignored me. He made off as if to leave the camp, then seemed to change his mind. Again I tried to discover what was troubling him. This time he replied, "I have to make my peace. I must apologise for what you have all done". But he sat down then by the fireside and seemed calmer. I returned to the watch and have not seen him since.'

'He was awake most of the night,' said Sildemund, standing at his father's side, 'I heard him muttering to himself.'

Master Frano nodded. He cast an uneasy glance in the direction of the hidden cave entrance. 'Back to your tasks, lads,' he said, and strode towards his wagon. Climbing inside, he located his satchel and satisfied himself that the cloth bundle was still there. To reassure himself fully he removed and unbound it. The red stone had not been taken.

He rejoined his son outside. 'Bring a torch and come with me.'

Master Frano walked to the edge of the clearing, to the boulders which concealed the cavern entrance. He stood there for a moment, gazing down the rude stair into the musty dark. When Sildemund arrived he took the torch from him. 'Wait here.'

Master Frano descended, his free hand gripping the hilt of his short sabre.

Two minutes later he returned, haggard-faced, climbing the steps as if the effort cost him dear. 'Go to the wagon,' he ordered in a subdued voice. 'Bring a sheet of good strong cloth, and something to bind it with. Then – but not until you have delivered it to me – go discreetly to Gully. Have him come here with a stretcher. On no account alert the other two. Do you understand?'

Sildemund nodded and was gone. Though he could barely contain his curiosity, he knew from his father's face and manner that this was not the time for questions.

By the time Gully arrived in the cavern, stretcher over one shoulder and Sildemund at his back, Master Frano had wrapped Edric's corpse securely in the cloth Sildemund had brought. On his knees, he was binding it now with cord. He left the upper part loose so that he might reveal Edric's face, at least, to his companions. It was the torso that he did not want anyone to see.

Gully stopped short in shock. 'What happened?'

'I don't know.' Master Frano rose wearily. 'I found him here. His chest . . . He must have somehow fallen heavily onto a sharp rock or something.' He looked sorrowfully at his lieutenant. 'This is a terrible day. I have known Edric a long time. He was a good man. Ah, Gully, you know this is the first time a man has died in my employ. It grieves me sorely.'

Both Gully and Sildemund stood in stunned silence, hardly able to take in what they were witnessing. Master Frano looked towards the entrance to the cavern. 'We must bury him, outside. In this heat we could not hope to carry his body home with us before. . . .' He left the sentence unfinished.

The grave was dug in silence, at the edge of the clearing, well away from the cave. Master Frano stood sombrely beside the body as the men worked. He seemed almost protective of it, as if afraid that, were he to move away, someone, out of curiosity, might decide to undo the cloth binding to take a look at the corpse.

Edric was lowered carefully into the earth. With a leaden heart Master Frano recited a few well-chosen words and the grave was filled. Ten minutes later, each immersed in his own thoughts, they climbed aboard the wagons and mounted their horses.

Master Frano rode beside his son, and as the wagon rumbled slowly over the rough ground towards the distant Volm road, his thoughts returned again and again to what he had seen in that cavern, the sight he had been at pains to keep his men from seeing.

No fall could have done that to Edric's body. His chest had been smashed as if with terrific force. He would have needed to have dropped forty feet or more onto a single jagged rock to have caused so much damage. And the wound itself did not seem appropriate to a fall.

Master Frano closed his eyes tightly, trying to dispel the image in his mind. The cavity, bloody and filled with soil and grit. And Edric's heart. . . .

Master Frano made a choking sound. Sildemund glanced his way with concern. 'Are you all right, Father?'

'Yes, yes.' He averted his face. It was not his son's question that upset him. It was the body again, lying on the ground before him, the chest cavity agape. And again he felt the sickness and the disbelief. Yet he had seen it, and he had not been mistaken. He had made doubly certain, for he had doubted himself even then.

Distressing as it was, it was not what he had seen that had most disturbed him. It was what he had not seen. That which had not been there. There was no explanation, yet he was forced to accept it.

It had gone.

The heart.

Where was Edric's heart?

2

THE FOLLOWING DAYS, after returning to Volm, Master Frano's time was largely taken up with matters of business and related affairs. Edric had left a widow and two young children who now lacked ready means of support. Master Frano, deeply affected by Edric's death, took pains to ensure that they were not left wanting.

He had acquired a modest degree of wealth over his lifetime, but Master Frano Atturio was not given to extravagance. He employed a minimum of household staff and kept his basic retinue small. Stubborn at times, possessed of an acute eye for business and the ability to drive a difficult bargain, he was also a man who inspired loyalty among his employees. He was unusual if not unique in that he supplemented the basic wages of those who regularly accompanied him on his business travels with a small percentage of his overall profits. By this means he had gathered a faithful cadre of workers who would defend his reputation and honour to the last. If there was a need for extra hands he would hire on a salary set in accordance with local Guild regulations, but this he would almost invariably supplement with unofficial gifts for work well done. It assured him an ever-ready pool of workers, if at times generating tensions with his business rivals. That he went to some considerable personal cost to take care of Edric's family surprised no one. Had any remarked upon it in his presence he would have dismissed it as simply a duty.

The day after his return home a heavily freighted carrack from the south seas hauled into port. Master Frano went straightway to the quayside to haggle over goods. He had storage facilities there, and commerical premises, *M'Atturio*, in the town centre close by, which occupied the ground floor of the home where he lived with his family.

His son, Sildemund, was sixteen, a strapping lad, tall with fair-brown hair, a little heavy around the waist, but strong and broad of shoulder. Sildemund had demonstrated intelligence and decisiveness, and to Frano's satisfaction had many times shown himself trustworthy, responsible and eager to aid his father. Adventurous within limits, wily when the need arose, yet of a cheerful and engaging disposition, he also displayed a good head for commerce. One day, Master Frano hoped, Sildemund would take over the business, continuing in his father's family name, and to that end Frano had instructed him in all aspects of his affairs.

Frano, only four years off sixty now, entertained no illusion as to his capacity to continue for many more years at his current pace. The lengthy, often arduous journeys to Tomia, Ghence and elsewhere had long ago lost their glamour. They tried his strength and will these days, and with each trip his desire for the next diminished. He anticipated the day when he might hand over that side of the business to a trusted and capable captain, leaving himself free to remain at home and concentrate on the shop and imports.

In a year, Master Frano thought, perhaps two, he would give Sildemund his first opportunity to lead a trip into Tomia. If all went well, he would think seriously about enrolling his son as a full partner.

Ilse, Master Frano's wife, had died three years earlier. It had been a bitter blow. Ilse was a good and kind woman, hard-working, devoted to her family. Frano missed her dreadfully, even now. Their daughter Meglan, Sildemund's twin, did what she could to take her dear mother's place. She worked diligently in the house and shop and took much of the book-keeping off her father's hands. But Meglan was an unconventional child, not best suited to the role she had cast for herself, no matter her willingness and effort. Her father had come to accept that Meglan's heart and future lay elsewhere.

Precisely where was less easily determined. Meglan was matur-ing into an auburn-haired beauty, slight of build but long-limbed and well proportioned. In the last couple of years she had attracted a flow of Volm's young notables, eager to escort her to fêtes, balls and functions. Yet she held herself somewhat aloof, showing little enthusiasm for the life they offered, and consorted with none on a regular basis. Her temper, when aroused, could be fiery. On more than one occasion Master Frano had witnessed some sorry young hopeful exiting the house in full rout with his tail between his legs.

To an experienced eye the signs of Meglan's dissatisfaction with her lot were plain. Since Ilse's death she had tried hard to conceal it, feeling bound by family duty and the love of her father and brother. Among her female friends she seemed to have no intimates or confidantes – indeed she saw them infrequently and professed herself uninterested in the submissiveness and petty frivolities of their lives. Frano worried, for there was at times a fire in Meglan's eyes, and a wilful, headstrong side of her nature, a quiet rebelliousness, so far contained. Such traits did not enhance the prospects of a woman in Dyarch society.

At the first opportunity Master Frano set about seeking expert opinions on the strange red stone. He had found, somewhat to his surprise, that the bars which contained the stone could be bent aside without great effort. In the grotto they had been inflexible: Gully, levering with his pick, had failed to budge them. But now, in his study, attempting to analyse the metal of the bars, Frano discovered a hitherto unnoticed flaw in one. Prising with the handle of a hammer he was able to part two of the bars. He thus removed the stone and left the cage in his room.

Frano went first discreetly to a friend, a lapidary named Jerg Lancor who had premises on Volm's market square. Lancor traded in fossils, stones, crystals, gems and precious metals. He had links with the Algefud, the master gem-cutters of the Endless Desert, whose expertise in crafting the most magnificent jewels and gems was legendary. Lancor was perhaps Volm's major authority on precious gems.

Lancor made sweet tea, then seated himself at his desk and unwrapped Master Frano's stone.

He spent several minutes examining it, with eyeglass then fixed lens. He turned it over in his hands, muttering to himself and tugging at his short grey beard. He directed light onto it through a prism to gauge its reflective and refractive properties. As Master Frano patiently sipped his tea Lancor took books from shelves and studied their pages intently. He stared long and hard at the stone as if by this means he might elicit information that by all other methods appeared to be eluding him. At last he shook his head with a sigh.

'I'm sorry, Frano. It shames me to admit it, but I can tell you practically nothing about this item, other than the fact that it is like nothing I have ever come across.'

'But surely you can at least identify the type of stone?' said Master Frano.

Jerg Lancor raised his hands in a gesture of submission, 'I cannot. It is plutonic, I would venture, but unusually dense. It's smoothness I would normally attribute to the hand of nature – I suspect it has passed long ages beneath the sea. Except . . .' He frowned, cocking his head with a puzzled expression, then went on. 'The whitish viens here on the surface are almost certainly a form of calcite, but the stone itself . . .' He took a small crystal from a tray upon his desk and held it up between finger and thumb so that it sparkled in the light. 'This is a diamond. Now watch.'

Master Frano bent forward and peered as Lancor put the edge of the diamond against the red stone and drew it across as if to score a line upon its surface.

'You see, no mark.'

'That is rare, is it not?' enquired Frano.

'Rare? It is extraordinary! I cannot say positively without further examination, but this stone appears to be harder than diamond itself, as hard perhaps as fabled adamant!'

'Then it is valuable?'

'I did not say that. The fact is, I cannot put a value on it. You might say that it is worth whatever anyone is willing to pay for it. Where did you get it?'

'From a travelling merchant I met on the Ghence road. I was struck by its unusualness.'

'Did you pay a high price?'

Frano shook his head. 'He was willing to trade it for virtual sundries.'

Lancor studied Frano's face for a moment, then turned back to the mysterious stone. 'Note these dark shadow effects across the red. They are extraordinary also. I can trace no distinction in make-up between the dark and the red, though they cannot be identical in all respects. The dark bands give an odd illusion of being unfixed, though plainly they are wholly bonded. It is queer to stare at them. I could almost swear that they shift slowly, a most disconcerting trick of the eye.'

He blinked, tugging at his beard again. 'I would have said that it was ancient beyond telling, but. . . .'

'But what?'

'I am confounded by it.' He held it up in his two hands. 'It is unusually heavy. And cold, so cold. Despite its appearance I feel there is something not quite natural about it. I am sorry, Frano, I can tell you nothing more.'

Lancor returned the stone to Master Frano, who wrapped it and replaced it in his satchel.

'There are others you might ask,' Lancor said, sipping his tea then, finding it cold, setting the cup aside. 'Though here in Volm I suspect you will find no one who can add to my account. In Dharsoul there is Kemorlin, who is more knowledgeable than I. Should you feel inclined to make the journey you will probably find him in the souk; he has a home nearby. Mention my name. There is the university also. And, as you know, there are interesting folk from far afield to be found in the capital. Perhaps you will have more luck there.'

Frano next took the stone to the office of Volm's most eminent banker, Gotif Aldhem, who handled many of Master Frano's affairs. Aldhem was a short, dumpy, pink-faced man with overflowing buttocks, who ushered Frano into his private office with an air of being both pleased to see him and simultaneously wishing him away so that he might apply his talents to other, weightier matters.

'I am sorry to call upon you without an appointment like this, Master Aldhem,' Frano apologized as he seated himself before the banker's wide desk. 'It is good of you to see me.'

'Not at all. It is always a pleasure. Now, how can I be of service?'

'I merely wish . . .' Frano produced the stone, wrapped in its cloth, and displayed it to the banker's eyes. '. . . to show you this and ask your opinion. I am trying to ascertain its value.'

The banker's eyes widened. He leaned forward, made to lift the stone then, with a frown, seemed to change his mind. He withdrew his pudgy fingers almost guardedly, without touching the object. 'Where did you get this?'

Master Frano repeated the story he had told Jerg Lancor.

Aldhem listened, a curled forefinger raised to his upper lip. He seemed a touch ill at ease, though being a busy man he was perhaps concerned that his time was being wasted.

'I'm sorry,' he said. 'I really am afraid I'm unable to help. I have never seen its like, and could not begin to estimate its value.' He frowned at the stone again, then stood. He fluttered his fingers towards the object, still failing to touch it. 'Perhaps you would take it away now.'

'Of course.' Frano immediately wrapped the stone and returned it to his satchel. He eyed the banker, whose gaze never left the stone and who seemed quite discomfited. 'Is something the matter, Master Aldhem?'

Aldhem started. 'What? Ah, no. No. I am a little stressed, I think, perhaps slightly under the weather. The recent storm. I feel . . . You know, sometimes I feel oppressed by the sadness and hardships of the world. It is as though they lay a weight upon my heart.'

Frano gaped at him in astonishment. Never in his life had he known the banker speak in such a manner – and they had been acquaintances for almost forty years. Aldhem was an obsessively private man. He had no interests outside of his work. He did not socialize, other than from professional necessity. When he and Frano met they spoke exclusively of business and finance. This outburst of emotional candour was completely out of character.

Gotif Aldhem recollected himself and grew embarrassed. He touched his forehead, shaking his head. 'I mean . . . that is, well, simply that – ah, ha-ha! – simply that . . .' At a loss, he moved quickly to the door and opened it. 'I am sorry, Master Atturio. I wish I could have been more helpful. Ahem. You must call in and take lunch with me soon.'

That evening Master Frano sat alone in his study, gazing pensively at the red stone which rested before him upon his desk. In the light of three wax candles its predominant colour was a deep blood red, varying to liver or murrey. It seemed to hold a barely discernible inner glow, remote and uncomforting, yet in an unsettling way, intimate. Far from being discouraged by his failure that afternoon, Master Frano was becoming more and more intrigued by his find.

In Volm there were one or two other persons whose advice he

would seek in regard to the stone. Realistically he held little hope that they would have more to tell than Jerg Lancor or Gotif Aldhem, but he would visit them on the morrow all the same. If they could add nothing to the precious little he had so far, then on the following day he would travel inland to Dharsoul.

It was not a prospect he particularly relished at the present. Dharsoul lay more than twenty leagues away, on the banks of the Tigrant. Travel upriver was slow. Unpredictable currents, land-slips and shifting mudbanks made ferries unreliable. The road was a more practical proposition, but the thought of several more days on horseback or wagon held no attraction. Frano was weary and sore. He had planned, upon his return to Volm, to rest a little. There was plenty to keep him occupied here, but he had the luxury of his own comfortable bed at night, and the company of family and friends.

But this stone. . . .

He would take Jerg Lancor's advice and look up Kemorlin, and perhaps seek out a professor at the university and any other learned folk in the city who might throw light on the mystery. If he did not tarry he could be back home well within the week.

As he mulled these things over there came a soft knock at the door. Meglan entered. She moved up quietly beside him and put her arms around his shoulders and kissed his grey head.

'Supper's ready, Father.'

'I will be right there.' Master Frano took one of her hands in his and held it tenderly. He turned to look into her face. As often happened, he was struck by Meglan's likeness to her mother. Dear, sweet Ilse. She should have lived. If things had only been different. She had been just forty, and her disease was not a killer if treated in good time. But she was a woman and by law doctors could not attend to her before their male patients. A virulent outbreak of dark scale in the city had added to the problem. The hospital was quarantined; no doctors were able to free themselves for several days. By then it was too late for Ilse. She had died a week later.

Frano tried not to dwell on it. It did no good; this was simply the way of things. Now, seeing Meglan's face beside him, feeling the tenderness of her kiss and the warm pressure of her arm, he was transported back twenty years and more, to his courting of Ilse and their early years together.

Meglan saw the look. 'You think of her?'

'I see her.'

She smiled sorrowfully and pressed her cheek to his grey head, holding him. Presently she straightened, pushed back her long hair from one side of her face and tucked it behind one ear. 'Come on now, it's time to stop working. Sil's closing the shop; we are ready to eat. What are you doing, anyway?' Meglan's eyes fell on the red stone. 'What is this?'

'Something I brought back from Tomia.'

Megan leaned forward to inspect it more closely. 'It is a strange thing.'

'Do you like it?'

She was moving around the desk, her fingertips touching the wooden surface, circling the stone. Her eyes were intent, her brow knitted. 'I don't know. I don't think I do.'

'Oh? Why is that?' enquired Master Frano, feeling a small twinge of disappointment, and even unease.

'There is something about it – the way these dark bands filter into the red. And the yellow strands on it surface. . . . Is it valuable?'

'I truly don't know.'

'It is like a heart,' declared Meglan, her eyes absorbed in the stone.

At these words Mater Frano felt a chill.

'A heart?' His voice stuck in his throat. In his mind's eye he was back in the grotto, staring down at a corpse.

Meglan bent low that she might better inspect the object. 'Yes. Its form, its colour. I see a bloody heart. A heart turned to stone.'

To cover his confusion Master Frano heaved himself erect and began clearing things from his desk. He made to blow out the first of the candles.

'It is unappealing,' Meglan said. Her tone had altered, was filled with unbidden emotion. 'And cold.'

She straightened slowly and her fingertips went to her lips. In a small voice she said, 'Oh.'

Master Frano turned to look at her. With shock he saw that her eyes had filled with tears. They glistened like living diamonds in the candlelight, and tumbled down her cheeks.

'Meglan, my darling, what is the matter?' He hastened around the desk to her.

For some moments she could not speak. When she did it was to say, in a small voice. 'I don't know. I felt suddenly so sad. It must be thinking of mother.'

She shook her head and dabbed at her eyes with a handkerchief Frano gave her. Glancing at the red stone she disengaged herself from her father's embrace and moved towards the door of the study. 'Father, hurry now. Join us downstairs so that we can eat.'

Master Frano gazed at the stone with troubled thoughts, then wrapped it quickly in its cloth, placed it in a cabinet, and followed her out.

3

THE FOLLOWING MORNING Master Frano's plans were thrown into disarray by an incident in the town centre.

He had just come out of the shop of a local goldsmith, the last among those persons in Volm whose advice he sought in regard to the stone. Prior to the goldsmith he had shown the stone to the merchant captain of the south-seas carrack moored in the harbour, and then to the president of the Merchants' Guild in Volm. None of these men was able to provide him with fresh information, and he was therefore resigned to a trip to Dharsoul.

He mulled over this as he crossed the busy market square, intending to take refreshment in the cool of a nearby taverna. He would leave in two days. That would give him the time today and tomorrow to conclude one or two pressing matters at home.

As he entered the taverna Master Frano became aware of a fracas inside. Voices were raised but Frano, entering from bright sunlight, could make out little as he stepped into the shade of the interior.

Someone came hurriedly out, barging into him in the doorway. Frano was knocked backwards. He collided with the doorjamb, lost his footing on the step and fell. His knee twisted as he careered face forward onto the dusty ground. Writhing in pain he caught a glimpse of a figure swathed in a dark burnous, peering down at him for a second then hastening away.

Moments later he was surrounded by people trying to help him to his feet. Among them was Dervad, whose hand was cut and bleeding, though Master Frano was in too much pain just then to notice. Unable to walk, Master Frano was carried through the narrow streets to his home, while someone ran off to alert his physician, Doctor Sibota.

Master Frano lay upon his bed, his knee swollen and throbbing. Meglan fussed over him, applying a cold compress to the knee and gently bathing his hands which he had severely scraped in trying to prevent his fall. Sildemund was out, but Dervad had accompanied Frano home and waited beside him, his own hand bandaged by Meglan.

'What was the argument about, Dervad?' asked Frano through his pain. 'And what happened to your hand?'

Dervad was uncertain. 'It all happened so quickly. This man was asking questions in the taverna – about you, I think.'

'About me?'

'He wanted to know of merchants who had returned to Volm in the last few days. I asked him his business and he said he wished to interview a merchant who had come across the wildlands, possibly – he thought – in order to avoid the border control posts. I got a bit wary at this and didn't venture anything. But I asked him what his interest was. He said he would only discuss his business with the merchant in question. Then he produced some coins, and said he would pay for the name of the man he sought.'

'What was his name?'

'We didn't get that far. I didn't even get a good look at him. He kept his hood up and the dust-scarf wrapped around the lower half of his face.'

'Working for the customs, do you think?' mused Frano. 'I wonder how they knew.'

'I don't know, but he was a sneaking type and his manner left a lot to be desired. A few of us got annoyed when he showed his money. Figured he was customs, yes. Working undercover. Except he wasn't exactly subtle in his approach. Anyway, one or two of them crowded him a bit, just to make it plain to him that he wasn't welcome. That's when he fixed me with a stare. It went right through me. I've never seen a look like that. "You work for him, don't you?" he said. I didn't reply. He said, "Tell your employer there is a matter of urgency to discuss. Tell him it is *this* urgent". Then I felt a terrible pain in my hand. He'd stabbed me! I didn't even see it! And before I could react he'd gone.'

Megan looked anxiously at her father. 'Who is this man, Father? Do you know?'

'I can honestly say I don't. Nor do I know what it is he wants. Perhaps it isn't me he is looking for. Certainly he didn't stop to introduce himself.'

'But did you leave the road and travel across country?'

'We did.'

'Then it *must* be you.'

'Others may have taken a similar route. There are unusual restrictions at the border just now.'

'But he knew Dervad to be your man.'

'It could have been a guess. Or somebody may have pointed Dervad out. You are sure you did not mention it yourself, Dervad?'

'I didn't say a thing,' Dervad looked thoughtful. 'Master Frano, it did occur to me—'

His thought remained unexpressed, for at that moment Doctor Sibota arrived. He was a tall, stiff fellow with oiled black hair which he wore in twin plaits at the nape of his neck. He cast his eyes proprietorially over Frano, and said in a tone of frank censure, 'Well, Frano, what have you been doing this time? You are too old to be cavorting the way you do.'

'Me? I was simply trying to sit down to enjoy a quiet drink!'

Sibota grunted, set down his case and examined his patient at some length. Eventually he pronounced the knee badly sprained with the possibility of a fractured or dislocated patella, or even a fracture of the joint itself. 'I won't be certain until the swelling has reduced and I can examine you more closely. Until then you must keep this leg completely still.' He turned to Meglan. 'Be sure not to let him leave this bed.'

'For how long?' demanded Master Frano.

'I shall examine you again tomorrow, but I can say without a shadow of a doubt that you will not walk for at least ten days, and if there is a fracture it will be longer than that. Months, possibly.'

'Impossible!'

Sibota ignored him. 'You may be able to get about with the aid of sticks after a few weeks, though I forbid you to leave the house.'

'Out of the question!' Frano fulminated, and again was ignored.

'I shall return directly with binding, splints and some embrocation. In the meantime, do not move that leg!'

'Attend to Dervad before you go, would you, Doctor,' Meglan asked. 'He has been stabbed in the hand.'

'Stabbed?' Sibota frowned and shook his head. 'Let me see?'

He took Dervad's hand and unbound the dressing, which showed the stain of blood. He looked closely at the wound. 'This is a nasty cut. With what were you stabbed?'

'A knife, I think. I didn't see it,' said Dervad.

'The blade was foul.' Sibota spoke to Neena, the elderly housekeeper, who stood clutching her hands by the door. 'Bring clean hot water please.'

This was done and the doctor carefully cleaned Dervad's wound, then applied an astringent from a jar in his case which made Dervad clench his teeth and caused his eyes to water.

'You must come with me to my surgery,' said Sibota then, bandaging the wound again, 'This requires stronger anti-infectants than I carry with me.'

The next morning, confined in bed, his leg in a splint, Master Frano breakfasted with Meglan and Sildemund. While they ate he told his son of the decision he had, with difficulty, arrived at during the night.

'I am entrusting the red stone into your care, Sil. I wish you to take it to Dharsoul. Seek out Kemorlin, and if necessary others whose names or titles I shall provide you with. Ask their advice. I need to know what this article is, and whether it has value. I curse the fact that I cannot go in person, but I rely upon you to act wisely and judiciously in my stead.'

Sildemund was visibly excited by the prospect, swelling with pride at the trust his father was placing in him. 'Have no fear, Father, I will do as you bid, to the letter, and I will guard the stone and your interests with my life.'

Master Frano reached out and laid his bandaged hand upon his son's. 'Sil, your life is of infinitely greater importance to me than those things. Consider that your priority, and let everything else follow in its natural course.'

Sildemund grinned. 'Done.'

'Gully and Picadus will accompany you,' Frano said. 'They know the road and the land, and are more experienced than you in the ways of the big city. Heed their advice, lad, and trust them. They are good and reliable men.'

'I know it well, Father. I will be pleased and reassured to have them at my side.'

Meglan spoke. 'Father, can I not go too? It is a long time since I hve seen Dharsoul, and the experience will benefit me also.'

'You, Meg? My darling, who then will look after your poor invalid of a father?'

'You have Neena, and the other staff. You do not need me.'

Old Neena, the housekeeper, had been with the family since before the children were born. Indeed, she had become virtually one of the family. But Master Frano was not to be swayed. 'No, Meg. I'm sorry, but I do need you here. Until I can shift my carcass again I am virtually helpless. Somebody has to run the day-to-day affairs of the business.'

'Then let Sildemund stay and I will go in his place. I am as competent as he. I can perform any task that he can.'

'Aye, that may possibly be so. Yet two things stand in your way, neither of which lie within my sphere of influence. The first is that you are a woman. And a very young and – for all your competence – inexperienced woman at that. If I know anything of the kind of people we are to be dealing with in Dharsoul, and as a man I believe I know much, you will not be taken seriously. You may even find yourself endangered. Yes, yes! I accept your protests! I do not disagree. But you must accept that what I say is true. I simply state the facts, and they are what they are, immutably.'

'And what is the other thing?' asked Meglan, quietly seething.

'The second point is that I have already witnessed the effect a mere glimpse of this unusual stone can have on you. Who is to say what it would do were you to carry it on your person for several days?'

'It was far more than a glimpse, Father.'

'Do you offer that as your defence? The fact is that you were gravely disquieted. I have seen the stone render similar effects upon others. It does not affect me that way, nor Sildemund. Therefore, though I would far rather go in person, as I cannot Sil is best qualified to take my place.'

'But at least I have awareness of the stone's qualities!' Meglan cried, 'Who knows, it may yet be wreaking an effect upon you and Sildemund without your being aware of it! Look at what has already happened!'

For an instant Master Frano was lost for a response, this being something he had not considered. He wondered at his fascination with the stone, his attraction to it. Could it be exerting an imperceptible influence upon him?

No! He banished the thought, irked with himself and with Meglan for suggesting it.

Sildemund was frowning. 'What are you talking about?'

'There is something in this stone,' began Meglan. 'It has a bad quality.'

'Silence!' fumed Master Frano. 'There is nothing in it. It is a stone, that is all, a strange and mysterious artifact, but it has no power.'

'How can you say so—'

'Enough! I have made my decision. Sil, send out immediately for Gully and Picadus. Have them rendezvous with you here. I wish you to leave as soon as you are able.'

Sildemund departed. Meglan was looking at her father penetratingly and Master Frano found himself unwilling to meet her gaze.

'Why not have Sil sell it in Dharsoul?' she said. 'Be rid of it.'

'I shall sell it when I have ascertained its value to my satisfaction.' Frano experienced a pang of conflicting emotion. There was profit to be had from this stone, he was sure. At the same time he was vaguely aware of an unfamiliar feeling deep within him, a faint acquisitiveness, an as yet undefined reluctance to give the stone up. 'That is the time to sell, and not before.'

An hour later the horses were packed and saddled. Gully and Picadus waited outside as Sildemund said farewell to his father and sister.

'Remember, act wisely and keep safe,' said Master Frano, warmly embracing his son. 'Heed the advice of Gully and Picadus – but listen: they do not know that you carry the stone, nor your real purpose in Dharsoul. It is better that you keep it that way. They will not ask questions, so do not volunteer information. They will guard you with their lives. Go well, my son, and return home soon.'

Sildemund straightened. 'You can rely upon me, Father.'

He turned and took his sister in his arms. He held her firmly, kissing her head. 'Dear Meg, I shall miss you. I am sorry we will be apart again, so soon. But I will be home in a few days. While I am gone, I charge you with our father's welfare.'

Meglan drew back. 'I should be with you.'

'No, you should be here, with Father.'

'Do not be impetuous, Sildemund. Stay free of danger.'

Her brother smiled. 'Have no fear.'

She kissed him hard. 'Go safely!'

Sildemund left the bedchamber. He said goodbye to Neena downstairs and went out to mount his horse, pulling up his hood to shield him from the fierce heat of the sun and wrapping his dustmask over his face. Meglan followed him to the front door, and stood with old Neena who dabbed her eyes with a handkerchief. Sildemund waved, the thrill of anticipation and adventure tingling in his breast. With his two companions he set off for the Dharsoul road.

'There is a man to see you. A Mister Skalatin.'

It was evening, Meglan. closing the shop, had been startled by the presence of a swathed figure standing motionless in the dusky shadows close by the door.

'Skalatin?' Master Frano roused himself from a light doze. 'Skalatin? I know no one of that name. What does he want?'

'As I said, to see you. He will convey nothing of his purpose to me – I am, after all, only a flittering maiden. He insists you will know what it is about.'

Her father frowned. 'Well, he is mistaken.'

'Father, he insists that you will most definitely wish to talk to him. His manner is cold and forceful. He is. . . . I don't like him.'

'Where is he?'

'I had him wait downstairs.'

'You had better show him up.' Master Frano eased himself into a more comfortable position on the bed.

Meglan hesitated as she went to the door. 'Father, there is something unsettling about this man. He is not pleasant. Be careful.'

Frano smiled indulgently. 'Child, you fuss too much over me. Do you think I am so ingenuous?'

'No, but you are confined here, and immobile.'

'You believe Mister Skalatin intends me harm?' Frano's smile became pronouncedly sceptical.

'Don't mock me, Father. I don't know what he wants, but I do not like him.'

'I am not mocking – but neither am I as helpless as you might think.' Master Frano withdrew his bandaged hand from beneath the sheet. In it he held a gleaming, curved-bladed dagger. 'Do not worry for me, Meg. Show this visitor up, please.'

The visitor entered moments later, with Meglan just behind. Master Frano thanked his daughter and she retired. But as she went she did not quite close the door of the bedchamber. She made her way quickly downstairs to the scullery, took up a long kitchen knife and concealed it in the folds of her skirts, then crept back up the stairs. Halfway up she took up a position where, hidden in the dark, she might overhear everything that was said in her father's room.

Master Frano surveyed the stranger, who had placed himself near the end of Frano's bed, just beyond the fullest glow of the candles, so that he was largely in shadow. He stood perfectly still, almost as if inanimate. He was of about average height, tending to slightness in build. He wore a dark burnous and kept the cowl up, thus preventing Master Frano from making out much of his face.

What he could see was not pleasing to the eye. Cadaverous features. Unusually pale, a sharp, bony chin, tight, narrow mouth like a pale gash. The eyes, hidden in shadowed sockets, reflected darting pinpoints of light. One hand was clutched close to Skalatin's throat, showing knobbly white knuckles and pale, thin fingers. Master Frano was in little doubt that this was the man he had glimpsed that morning, who had knocked him to the floor in the doorway of the taverna.

Meglan had the measure of this man: he was a danger. He had stabbed Dervad in the hand. Frano gripped the hilt of his dagger beneath the cover, but his bandaged hand throbbed with pain, his palm had begun to sweat, and he wondered how firm his grip would be were he forced to use the weapon.

'What do you want?' he said without warmth, 'Are you here to express regret, to offer reparation for the injury and inconvenience you have caused?'

Skalatin appraised him in silence for a moment. His voice, when it came, was a subdued rasp, quite without emotion. It carried an accent that Frano could not place. 'I come merely as the representative of another.'

'What other?'

'One who is prevented from coming in person.'

'And what does this person want?'

'You know the answer to that, surely?'

'I do not.'

'You have taken something that is not yours. It is the ancient property of another, who desires it back.'

'I do not know to what you refer.'

Skalatin gave a sigh, with a sound like the scrape of sand over bones. 'I believe you do, and I would prefer not to play games. Rather than waste time, then, I shall shall state the obvious. The article to which I refer is the red stone which you removed from its resting place. I have come to collect it.'

'It was buried, hidden, in unclaimed wilderness. It is rightfully mine, therefore.'

Skalatin's voice took on a hardness. 'It is not yours. The one I speak of will have it back.'

'You have proof of ownership?'

'You are tiresome, old man. Let me tell you that patience is not a virtue in which my client is prepared to indulge. However, that is not to say that generosity is absent.' Skalatin brought from beneath his burnous a leather pouch which he tossed onto Master Frano's bed. The pouch landed heavily, with a dull chink, and from its open neck spilled coins.

'Fifty gold crowns,' said Skalatin. He raised his hand to his mouth and gave a dry cough. 'That is the price my client will pay to recover property that is already his. No questions. Give me the stone now and the money is yours.'

Frano stared wide-eyed at the money. It was a small fortune. In a year of dealing in contraband over international borders he could hardly hope to make as much in clear profit.

'It is a more than generous sum,' said Skalatin, 'for believe me, the one I speak of need pay nothing at all.'

Frano looked back at him, irked in equal measure by both his manner and the shadows that seemed to collude with the man to obscure his face. 'Your client must be a very wealthy man.'

Skalatin gave a shrug of one shoulder, but said nothing.

'Why is he so anxious to regain the stone?' Frano asked.

Skalatin made a gesture of impatience. 'It is of no matter to you! Do I believe this? Do you truly hesitate? I had not taken you for a complete fool!'

Frano spoke carefully, his throbbing fingers curled more tightly around the dagger hilt. 'I do not have the stone. That is to say, it is no longer here.'

'Then where is it?' Skalatin's whole body shuddered, his dry voice rising with an almost palpable anger that made Frano's skin crawl.

'That I am not presently prepared to say.'

'Then you are a fool!' Skalatin bent forward and snatched up the leather pouch. A portion of his face entered the candlelight. Frano glimpsed sallow, stretched, broken skin like decaying parchment, a nose and cheek that seemed scarcely more than bone. Then the face was back in shadow. 'I have already said that patience is not my client's greatest virtue. Take heed, old man, the price you will pay for non-compliance will be harder than you can bear. Be sensible, then, I shall return on the morrow, and you will trade me the stone then.'

Skalatin turned before Master Frano could muster a reply, and swept from the room.

Outside he came upon Meglan who, unprepared for his sudden exit, had had no time to move from the stairs. Skalatin halted and gave a low chuckle. He leaned close to her, and she involuntarily drew back, pressing herself against the wooden panel of the wall behind. She found herself looking into his eyes – or rather, into the darkness that hid his eyes. She glimpsed a cold, distant glitter in a blackness that seemed to howl.

Meglan uttered a sob of fear. Skalatin's hand rose to caress her cheek, clawlike, its touch dry and wintered. She was filled with revulsion, yet lacked the power to resist him. The reek of his breath so close brought the image of rotting corpses to her mind; its sound was like something dragged across an infinity of pain.

'Chi-ld,' he breathed. 'So-o beautiful. Oh yes, you are per-fect.'

There was a thud upon the wooden floor between them. The knife that Meglan had held in her skirt had dropped from her hand. Skalatin chuckled again. He lowered himself and tugged it free, clasped the handle in his fist, then held it up before her face. Meglan saw, or thought she saw, a sudden brief flicker in the cowled dark of his eyes. He thrust forward. The blade ran past her cheek and plunged deep into the wood panel behind her.

Skalatin levered the blade up and down. Meglan heard, close in her ear, the tortured wood fibres splintering, sundering. Skalatin's lips were beside her other ear, his chuckle vile and intimate. He inhaled, slowly and deeply, in such a manner that she felt something was being drawn out of her. As if confirming this he made smacking sounds with tongue and mouth. He gave a low grunt, a breathy sound, then pushed himself away, pulled his cloak about him, and passed on down the stairs.

Meglan remained frozen where she was until she heard him leave the house, his footsteps passing beyond earshot as he entered the street. Retching with fear and revulsion she ascended the remaining stairs with trembling limbs and entered her father's room.

4

'YOU MUST DO as he says!' Meglan implored. 'He is a devil! He is not human!'

'Patience, Meg. You are overwrought.'

'Overwrought? Overwrought? Father, this man has insulted, injured and menaced you. He has stabbed Dervad. What more do you need? He is *dangerous*, and you worry because I show an emotional response?'

'I am thinking more about what this means. Skalatin is a felon, quite possibly a madman. I could have him arrested, it would not be a problem. But I am reluctant to take that step. He comes to us with a generous offer, claiming to be the representative of some anonymous personage even more mysterious than he. Who can his client be, I wonder. And why, why is he so anxious to regain this stone?'

Meglan, seated beside the bed, raised her fists before her in sheer exasperation. 'Father, we do not care who or why! He offers good money in exchange for the stone. Take it, then, and be rid of that hateful object.'

'Hateful? Truly it has disturbed you, but I find nothing hateful in the stone itself. And plainly its value is high – possibly higher than I had imagined. If Skalatin's client is willing to offer fifty crowns on his first contact, I would wager he could be persuaded to increase it to seventy without great effort, or even eighty. A hundred perhaps!'

Meglan vented a small scream. 'What is the matter with you? This is not a man to haggle with. Take the money! Give him back the stone! Please, let us be done with it.'

'You forget, Meg, I no longer have the stone.'

'You should not have sent Sil away with it! I will go after him. If I ride swiftly I will catch him before he reaches Dharsoul. You somehow stall Skalatin until we return. If I go now we could be back in a couple of days. Protect yourself; employ bodyguards. When Skalatin sees that you are sincere he and his client will surely be persuaded to wait a short while longer.'

Master Frano shook his head. 'Sildemund is already ten hours gone. You could not leave before morning, and even then the road is dangerous for a young woman alone.'

'I will take guards.'

'No! You would not catch him. He will not be long at Dharsoul. By the time anyone reached him he would be preparing to return anyway.'

'Something might delay him at Dharsoul. At least if he is warned he will return immediately.'

'I have said no, Meg. Besides, Skalatin's interest makes me all the more intrigued to discover what Sildemund can learn about the stone.'

'Oh Father, can you not see how unwise this is? Skalatin will return in the morning. What will you tell him, then?'

'I shall explain that I am expecting the stone to be returned to me. I will not say where it is. I will ask him to wait a while longer.'

'And if he will not accept that?'

'Does he have a choice? It is the truth, after all. What can he do? He may be villainous, but we are ready for him now.'

Meglan stared long and hard at him, a tumult of emotion in her breast. 'He is capable of worse than villainy. I sense it. He is wicked. I do not wish you to become his adversary.'

'Calm yourself, Meg. You worry too much. I will not oppose him. I shall simply endeavour to negotiate, as is my nature. If Skalatin is unwilling then I will acept his fifty crowns and give him the stone as soon as I have it back. Now, I am tired and it is getting late. Perhaps you would be good enough to plump my pillow and extinguish the candles so that I might sleep.'

Meglan did as she was asked. When she had gone Master Frano lay for a long time in the dark, stroking his grey whiskers, deep in thought.

Midway through the morning Doctor Sibota called again, as he had promised he would, to check on Master Frano's progress. The swelling of Frano's knee had reduced slightly but Sibota was still unable to fully determine the extent of the injury.

'There could well be a fracture, it remains impossible at present to say. Keep applying cold compresses, and keep the foot high, on pillows or some other support. Now, your hands.' The Doctor unbound Frano's hands, inspected them and declared his satisfaction. 'The healing process has begun. I am relieved to see it. You are more fortunate than your man. His wound shows signs of severe infection.'

'Dervad?'

'That blade had been steeped in filth or some kind of pernicious agent.'

'How serious is it?' asked Frano with concern.

'I am doing all I can to contain it, but it has advanced more rapidly than I could have anticipated. I am striving to prevent an eating sore. If putrefaction sets in he will be lucky to lose no more than the hand.'

'Lose the hand? Spare neither effort nor expense, Sibota. Charge your account to me, but do not let him come to harm.'

The doctor bathed and dressed Frano's hands with clean linen, then departed. An hour later Meglan came taut-faced into Frano's room. 'Skalatin is back. He is downstairs.'

Frano pushed himself into a sitting position. Despite himself his heart had begun to pound. 'Send him up.'

Meglan hesitated. 'Would you rather I told him we do not have the stone at present, and ask him to return?'

'No, just send him up.'

Skalatin entered, dressed as before in a dark burnous. Though the light was better it did not help, for his face was obscured, the lower half concealed by a filthy black dust-scarf. He strode provocatively to the end of the bed and stood looking down at Master Frano.

'Well?' came the surly, dry rasp. 'I hope you have considered well during the night, and come fully to your senses.' The gelid glitter of his hidden eyes darted, taking in the room. 'Yet I do not see the stone. Where is it?'

Despite himself Master Frano was nervous. He cleared his throat. 'I do not have it at present. I am, however, doing all I can to secure it again quickly.'

Skalatin made a sound of comtempt. 'Where is it?'

'It is currently on its way to me.'

'That is not good enough!'

Without warning Skalatin stepped suddenly forward and climbed up onto the bed. He stood erect, brutally kicking aside Master Frano's injured leg. Frano cried out in pain. Skalatin paid him no heed. He lowered himself onto his haunches, straddling Frano's legs. Thrusting his torso forward he slid up on hands and knees until his masked face, with its loathsome sallowness, hovered just inches above Frano's.

Frano, in outrage and fear, struggled to draw his dagger from beneath the cover. His assailant tossed his head like an enraged beast, emitting a guttural snarl. One clawlike hand shot out from beneath the burnous and seized Frano's wrist, gripping with a force that paralyzed. Frano gasped with the pain, and his knife slipped from fingers that were suddenly limp.

Skalatin's hand shifted so that it covered Frano's. He increased the pressure of his grip, his strength exceeding the human, slowly and deliberately squeezing Frano's injured hand.

Frano cried in helpless agony. The putrid vapour of Skalatin's breath assailed his nostrils, burrowed into his lungs, insinuating itself deep inside him, entering his blood, violating him. He struggled, gagging, choking, weak as a child in Skalatin's power.

Skalatin gave a grunt. He eased the pressure on Frano's hand a little. Frano, gasping, looked into those dreadful eyes, drawn into their void, into something eternally distant, lifeless, beyond the grasp of human emotion.

'Old man,' Skalatin slowly rasped, 'I warned you that my client is not patient. Do I have to demonstrate the price you will pay if you attempt to thwart him? You will not bear it!'

His mouth dry with terror, Frano took a few gasping breaths, then managed to find his voice. 'I will get the stone! It will just take a little time!'

With a contemptuous gesture Skalatin released him and sat back astride his middle. His voice grew calm, weighted with menace. 'I will return. You will have the stone.'

He got down off the bed. As he did so there was a crash. The door flew open, slamming into the wall behind as Meglan rushed in. She held a kitchen knife high in one hand.

'*Get off him!*' Without a thought for her own safety she hurled herself at Skalatin.

Skalatin stepped towards her with a swift, fluid motion, deftly blocking her knifehand with one forearm. His other hand flew out, almost casually, ramming into Meglan's chest. As she staggered under the blow his fingers curled around the neckline of the embroidered caftan she wore. He twisted the material, hoisting it high, lifting her virtually off her feet. Meglan's face turned puce as he held her on her toes. Her hands clawed at his wrist, her windpipe blocked by the knot of her clothing in his fist.

'*No! Leave her!*' Master Frano called out, struggling to rise from his bed.

Skalatin let out a harsh, scoffing sound. With the same hand he yanked Meglan completely off her feet. Effortlessly he swung her around and cast her across the room. She slammed into a wardrobe and folded to the ground.

'*Meg!*'

Before her body had even settled Skalatin, unconcerned with her fate, had swivelled to face Master Frano. He raised his arm and targeted the old man with a minatory finger. 'Your man is marked. He will show you the price.'

Then he was gone.

Master Frano dragged himself from the bed and across the floor to where his daughter lay motionless. 'Meg! Meg!'

He loosened the clothing at her throat then slapped her cheek, sobbing with terror at the sight of her limp form. To his relief her eyes opened, rolled, closed again. She gave a moan. Master Frano took her in his arms and held her. 'Meg, my darling, my baby. It's all right. Oh, don't be afraid. He has gone. It's all right now.'

Meglan forced herself back to awareness. She cast her eyes quickly around the room, then clutched her father as her body shuddered with relief and fear.

'Are you hurt?' said Frano.

She gave a slow shake of her head, then gingerly stretched her limbs. 'Not seriously. Some bruises, and my throat. . . . Are you? What did he do to you?'

'I am all right. Don't worry.'

'Oh Father, what is he? He cannot be a man!'

'Don't worry, we will be rid of him soon.'

'Why did you bring this stone to us? I knew as soon as I saw it that it was evil. Where did you get it?'

Master Frano held her head against his breast and said nothing. After a while Meglan disengaged herself from his embrace and stood. There was the sound of a footstep outside the door. Meglan spun around with a grasp, then sagged with relief as Neena came into the room. At the sight of the two of them the old housekeeper gave a cry of alarm, her hand flying to her mouth. 'What has happened?'

'It's all right, Neena,' Frano said, mustering a show of calmness. 'We had a misunderstanding, that's all.'

The absurdity of that statement brought a sharp burst of laughter from Meglan. She stifled the sound, feeling herself rising towards hysteria.

'Who was that man?' said Neena, bewilderment on her face. 'He stormed out. He stared at me so . . . so . . . Oh, what has he done to you?'

'Neena, it is nothing. Go back to your duties, please.' Frano extended a hand to his daughter. 'Help me back to my bed, Meg. I must lie down.'

'I will send for Sibota,' said Meglan as, with her help, her father settled himself into a seated position on the edge of the bed.

Frano shook his head. 'There is no need.'

'Father, what are we going to do?'

Frano, taking deep, laboured breaths, hung his head in despair. 'I will give him the stone.'

'But you don't have it! It will be days before Sil returns.' She ran her hand through her hair, thinking rapidly. 'I will go, Father. I must. I will find Sildemund and bring him back immediately.'

'No! I forbid it! I will explain again to Skalatin that he must wait a little longer. I will hire guards so that next time he comes he will find us well protected. If necessary I will even agree to part with the stone without payment. That will assure him of my sincerity.'

'I hope so. Oh, by the soul of Yshcopthe, I hope so.'

'Now, help me back. I want to rest.'

But rest was impossible. Even as his head touched the pillow Master Frano's mind worked furiously, probing through his shock and fear, seeking to find some clue to the mystery that confronted him.

But his fear remained uppermost, and with it the implicit menace of Skalatin's last words. What had he meant: '*Your man is marked. He will show you the price*'?

Before the day was out Frano would know the answer to that.

The remainder of the morning and much of the afternoon passed without great incident. Meglan took charge of the shop, and sent Frano's assistant out, first to recall Doctor Sibota to tend to her father, and then to hire bodyguards. Sibota arrived within the hour, and only minutes later three stout fellows armed with shortswords and knives, and clad in padded leather jerkins, were stationed within the house, two at Franos's door and the third in the shop with Meglan.

Doctor Sibota was thorough, but brusque. 'You have suffered no more damage, Frano, though you've plainly had a shock. What in the name of all devils are you up to?'

Frano was absorbed in his own thoughts and did not reply. Sibota made ready to depart.

'There is something here that you are unwilling to discuss. I sense. Whatever it is, plainly it is not pleasant. Ah, yes, I know, it is not my place to ask, nor necessarily to know. But I am your physician and your health is my concern, and whatever it is that you are currently involved in, it plainly does not enhance your well being.'

Frano merely grunted as though he had really not heard, then, rousing himself somewhat, said, 'How is Dervad?'

'I am concerned for him. I have kept him at my surgery so that I might monitor him. I think I may have no choice but to operate, probably today.'

Frano's eyes settled with foreboding upon the doctor. 'You mean amputate? His hand?'

'I cannot guarantee that it will be only the hand. The purulence has spread like nothing I've seen. I expected it to slow down, perhaps to reverse, but it has not.'

'Then what are you saying?'

'I am anxious to return to him now. If its progress is not stalled within the next hour or two, I will operate while the light remains good. I am sorry, I fear I will have to take off his arm.'

Was this what Skalatin had meant? *Your man is marked.* Dervad had been cut by a poisoned blade, deliberately, indiscriminately. He was an innocent. He had no part in this. He had simply accompanied Master Frano, dutifully, as he was paid to do. If anyone was to pay it should be him, Frano, for he was the one who had brought the stone back to Volm.

Was this the price?

'Does Dervad know?'

Sibota nodded gravely. 'I had to tell him.'

'How did he take it?'

The doctor hesitated, wishing to spare Frano's feelings, then said simply, 'Not well, but he understood.'

Master Frano felt that a gulf had opened within him, into which he was plummeting with sickening speed. Yet at the same time, everything had slowed, the moments cruelly drawn out so that he might fully experience the anguish he felt.

Dervad. Poor, good Dervad.

And Edric!

A groan escaped Master Frano's mouth.

'Frano, are you all right? You have turned very pale.'

Frano nodded weakly. 'Go. Tend to Dervad. Do everything you possibly can.'

Lying there, helpless and for the most part alone, Master Frano was at the mercy of his thoughts. And they were not merciful. They tormented him without cease, accusing, reminding, demanding, narrowing. He broke out in a fevered sweat, then collapsed suddenly into uncontrollable shivering. He wept silently, berating himself for his foolishness, then reminding himself that it was not, on the face of it, foolishness to have taken the stone.

Anybody in his position would have done the same.

But Edric had known. He had understood something.

But then Edric had had Estuary Fever. He had been delirous.

Meglan had perceived it, too. And the banker, Gotif Aldhem.

But by then the deed was done. The stone was in Volm. It was too late.

The stone. The stone. What was this cursed thing? And how could he get it back quickly to Skalatin?

Master Frano's tortured musings were interrupted unexpectedly by the sound of footsteps outside. The door of the chamber opened. Meglan stood there, ghastly-pale. Doctor Sibota was with her, holding her. She was hunched, her whole body tensed in shock. Indeed, it was plain that without Sibota's support she might have lacked the strength to stand.

They came into the room, Sibota's eyes were downcast. Meglan's focused glazedly upon her father. Master Frano could not tell how much time had passed since Sibota had left. It did not seem long. He had not slept, nor even dozed. It was still daylight outside. Surely it was less than an hour?

'What is it? What is the matter?' he cried, reeling from a shock that had yet to come.

At first nobody answered: both seemed stricken by some cursed compulsion to silence. Then Sibota, who himself was oddly grey and showed all the signs of being in a state of shock, said in a quiet, shaking voice, 'It is Dervad.'

Frano stared, not daring to let himself understand. 'Dervad? Is he— Is he—'

'He died,' said Sibota, a modicum of strength returning to his voice, mingled with – what was it? Accusation?

'Died?' Master Frano groped for words. 'But was it such a difficult operation?'

'It was not the operation,' replied Sibota. 'He died while I was out. While I was here with you.'

'Oh. Oh, no!' Frano shook his head in profound distress, the tears starting to his eyes. 'Did the poison spread so quickly?'

Meglan was sobbing, unable to stop herself. Sibota, still holding her shoulders, said, 'You still do not understand, Frano. It was not the poison. Dervad has been murdered, horribly murdered, while I was out.'

Now the blow struck Master Frano like a hammer. He gaped, his jaw sagging wide. Of its own accord a frail arm lifted before him, warding off what he knew with certainty would come next.

'I returned to my surgery,' went on the doctor, struggling to remain calm, 'to find Dervad's body upon the floor. His blood covered the floor and walls. His chest had been torn open, frenziedly, as if by some crazed beast. His—' Sibota gulped. 'His chest had been filled with broken glass and potshards – my own medicine vials, smashed to pieces. And his . . . his heart was gone, had been wrenched from his body and could not be found.'

Meglan gave a great cry. She wrested herself free of Sibota's grasp and fell in tears upon her father, grasping his shoulders, shaking them.

'Father, you will tell me now! What is all this about?'

Master Frano could only shake his head in horrified stupefaction. She shook him harder, unable to prevent her actions. 'Tell me! Tell me! How did Edric die? What happened when you found that stone?'

But her voice was a distant roar, an echoing scream that formed the walls of Frano's mind. And he was falling, falling, faster, and faster still. He fell forever into a deepening, never-ending abyss, where all was darkness, pain and ceaseless torment.

And he heard his own voiceless scream, joining the cacophony that was his daughter's.

'Oh by all the spirits of Moban who created us, *what have I done?*'

5

DUSK WAS FALLING, the sky streaked with pink and purple. In Volm the evening's long shadows had been absorbed into the greater gloom, though a few of the highest towers and rooftops still reflected the dying sun. Meglan rode out at a canter, a pair of guards accompanying her. She passed beyond the last of the houses into the open countryside, where the distant hilltops were kissed by the late tints of rose-gold light.

She had made the decision that afternoon: she would defy her father and set out after Sildemund. It tried her conscience, and she knew she would have to leave without telling Master Frano, but there was no other way. Meglan was terrified. The day had brought horrors like nothing she had ever known. Her greatest fear was not for herself, but for what consequences any further delay in returning the stone to the evil Skalatin might precipitate for Master Frano.

The arrival of the city militia had prevented her immediate departure. Their captain, Gosbedah by name, a gaunt, stooping, fish-eyed fellow, with breath that reeked of cheap wine, wanted to question her and Master Frano over Dervad's death. His men searched the house. It was plain, at least initially, that Master Frano was not above suspicion.

'You have been injured?' Captain Gosbedah eyed Frano's bandaged leg and hands.

Frano was glazed-eyed, his voice a murmur, though he some-how – in an attempt to deny his feelings to himself – managed to summon a note of disgruntled and inappropriate humour. 'Knocked flat by a lummox.'

Gosbedah requested details. Frano supplied them, but omit-ted to mention Skalatin by name. He had, however, already spoken of Skalatin in regard to the visits to the house. Meglan

wondered whether the omission was deliberate, or whether Frano
was simply too disoriented to recall.

Gosbedah, standing beside Frano's bed, nodding to himself,
turned around as if to speak to one of his men. He seemed to lose
his balance and toppled. His weight came down upon Frano's
knee, eliciting a sharp cry of pain from Frano.

'My apologies, sir! I am so clumsy!' Captain Gosbedah righted
himself. 'Plainly the leg is very sensitive.'

'The bone may be broken!' Meglan spoke sharply.

The captain continued to address Master Frano, whose teeth
were clenched against the pain. 'I am so sorry. I wonder whether I
might just ask your daughter to unbind the dressings on your
hands for a brief moment.'

Meglan stared at him in disbelief. 'You think— You did that
deliberately! By the spirits, you think my father murdered
Dervad!'

Gosbedah concentrated upon Master Frano, saying blandly, 'I
do not know who murdered him. That is what I am here to
ascertain. Now, if I could just see your hands.'

Frano was inclined to obstinacy, but Meglan, her cheeks
burning, said, 'Do as he asks, Father. You've suffered enough
tortures already.'

Gosbedah stood motionless as she removed the bandages. He
leaned forward and examined Master Frano's hands dis-
passionately, then nodded. 'Plainly you are quite debilitated by
your injuries.'

'He could not have left the house. There *are* witnesses.'

'Quite so. I shall interview them presently.'

'You mean he is still under suspicion?'

Gosbedah again adressed Master Frano as though Meglan had
not spoken. 'I am satisfied that your condition would have
precluded such a ferocious assault on a man considerably younger
and stronger than you. I do have a few more questions, though, if I
may.'

Gosbedah asked about Doctor Sibota, whose innocence was
also in question. Frano's replies seemed to persuade him that there
would be no useful purpose served by arresting the doctor. The
captain was less than happy with the circumstances, however, this
being the second man in Frano's employ to die within days. He

questioned Frano thoroughly on the particulars of Edric's death. Only now did Meglan learn details of what had occurred in the ancient, hidden ruin, for Master Frano had remained mute to her earlier pleas.

Still, Frano's answers were not entirely clear. He was in shock, even the captain could perceive that. He confirmed that Edric had died the same violent death as Dervad, that he had found the body and that there had been no witnesses.

Gosbedah scratched his nose thoughtfully. 'The suggestion is, then, that whoever or whatever killed him has followed you here. We might further surmise that it is this same fellow whom you say has terrorized you and your daughter. Skalatin, is his name? Either him or the client he has referred to.'

Frano blinked in weary concurrence.

'You say he claims that you have something which belongs to him, but you deny that this is so?'

A vague nod. Meglan stared in dismay at her father, but he avoided her gaze. Why was he not mentioning the stone? She was tempted to tell Gosbedah, but something – perhaps family loyalty – prevented her.

'We will need to exhume the body,' declared Gosbedah. 'To verify the details you have given me. Will you accompany us?'

'How can he?' demanded Meglan.

Gosbedah eyed her askance, clearly irritated by her manner. Frano spoke in a weak voice. 'I doubt that I could find the place again. It is deep in the wildlands. You would need to speak to Gully. He will know the way.'

'And where might I find him?'

'He is away at present on business with my son. He should be back in three or four days.'

'Ah well, it will have to wait then.' Captain Gosbedah sounded relieved, as though the prospect of a long ride to dig up a corpse in hot, arid countryside held little attraction. He glanced across at Meglan, and his eyes dropped to the light emerald chiffon fichu she had knotted loosely around her neck. He extended a hand and gently eased aside the material. 'This discolouration of your throat and neck, presumably it is the marks left by the assailant, Skalatin?'

Meglan nodded, swallowing.

'Plainly it was an exceedingly violent assault.'

Gosbedah asked a few more questions, spoke briefly to Neena and the guards Meglan had hired, then left with his men.

Having seen him out, Meglan climbed the stairs back to her father's room and seated herself beside him on the bed. 'Now, Father, you will tell me exactly what happened when you found that stone.'

Frano looked at her for a long time. She was shocked at how old he appeared. She was ashamed, for she was adding to his distress, but she had to know. 'If you will not speak to me, Father, I shall have to go to Captain Gosbedah and tell him that you are concealing the truth. You may have good reason for keeping something from him, but after what has happened you cannot possibly justify keeping me in the dark.'

So, wearily, tearfully, Frano related the events of that evening, and his discovery of Edric's mutilated body the next day.

'But why have you not mentioned this? Why not tell the captain about the stone?'

'I don't know!' Frano threw his head from side to side. 'There is something . . . I just could not . . . I fear for the consequences if Gosbedah should claim the stone and further prevent Skalatin from regaining it.'

Meglan sat with him a while longer, gently holding his injured hand. She felt that there was still something that he had not disclosed. Perhaps he could not. Perhaps he did not even know himself.

The stone. She shivered. Her father's secretiveness might be rooted in its subtle, malign influence, or the influence of its unprincipled master.

She already knew that she would go after Sildemund; she was waiting for her father to doze so that she might slip away. Neena entered, bringing medicinal tea for Frano. He was drowsy. Leaving Neena with him, Meglan slipped out to make preparations.

She saddled her horse, a sleek, sturdy, three-year-old grey filly named Swift Cloud, then went back indoors to pack essentials and arm herself. She changed into hose, boots, light tunic and burnous. She strapped a dagger and light sabre about her waist, and took a bow and quiver of arrows for the saddle-pack. She was not a fighter, though she had spent many hours watching the youths on the military training grounds, and when Gully had taken young Sildemund through basic weapons practice Meglan had insisted that he teach her too.

Gully, at first chiding, later confessed himself not unimpressed. Meglan had shown resourcefulness and spirit, and on one or two occasions, angered or frustrated by Sildemund's superior strength and overall ability, she had resorted to unorthodox methods and actually bested him in armed combat.

Sildemund, his pride wounded, and in some pain, had complained of unfairness.

'Surely the object is to win, brother?' Meglan had retorted, pleased with herself. 'Trounced by an enemy in true combat, would you cry "unfair!" as he took your life?'

Gully had roared with laughter at that, and Sildemund had hobbled from the field, clutching throbbing parts, his education – Meglan hoped – more complete for the experience.

But now she felt self-conscious and fearful. That *had* been play, for all its ardour. The idea that she might actually have to use in earnest these weapons that were belted around her slim waist – use them against skilled men or beasts that would do her harm – sent a chill through her innards.

She returned her mind to the task before her. Almost certainly Sildemund would reach Dharsoul before her. But by leaving now she could at least – she hoped – find him quickly and hasten his return, saving perhaps as much as two days that he might otherwise spend in the captial. She had to. Skalatin had made it plain that he would not wait long before exacting another terrible price.

Meglan hired a couple of guards, fellows well known to her, capable weapons-men and trustworthy. She took money from the shop to enable her to hire fresh steeds along the way, for she intended riding without stopping for sleep. Perhaps that way there might even be a remote chance of catching Sildemund before he reached Dharsoul.

Neena informed her that Master Frano was asleep. Meglan felt her resolve slipping. She did not want to leave her father.

'Where are you going, garbed like this?' cried Neena anxiously, and Meglan took her into her confidence.

'. . . Say nothing to Father until he asks, as he will surely do. Then tell him simply that I have gone after Sildemund and will return soon. Nothing more.'

She embraced Neena, who clutched at her, reluctant to let her leave. Meglan freed herself, went outside and mounted Swift Cloud. Neena stood weeping in the doorway. Meglan cast a last glance up to her father's window, where a faint yellow glow of candlelight was visible, then she put her heels to Swift Cloud and rode out into the encroaching night.

Within an hour she knew the folly of her action. She had imagined that by the light of the moon she would be able to make fair progress through the night. Although she did not know the road well, she did know that it was well maintained, following the course of the River Tigrant for many miles, and carrying much traffic throughout the daylight hours.

But outside Volm the night closed in rapidly. There was nothing to mark the way ahead and the moon waned, a slender sickle which cast no appreciable light. Engulfed in darkness, Meglan and her two guards were forced to slow to a walk. One of the guards, named Jans, took the lead, leaning low from his saddle and peering ahead to try to make out the way.

Even this quickly became impracticable. The dark swallowed everything and Meglan had to rely for guidance solely upon the sounds made by her companions and their steeds. It had grown cold, the heat of the day dispersing quickly and a bitter breeze coming down out of the hills. Jans, backed by his companion Eldan, voiced concern: even at this slow pace there was a serious risk of a horse stumbling and going lame, breaking a leg or, worse, wandering unwittingly right off the road, perhaps to pitch itself and its rider down the steep, invisible bank into the river.

Meglan was not yet to be deterred. 'We cannot stop. Dismount if you must, and lead the way on foot, but we must keep going!'

Jans did so, none too willingly, but it failed to help. He was literally feeling his way forward with his feet. There was nothing to be seen bar the millions of clouding stars far overhead, and the occasional bulky outline of an outcrop of rock against the sky. It was impossible.

'Mistress, I will continue if that is your wish, but it will not help us,' Jans said. 'To advance this way is to make no advance at all.

What small progress we might make will count for little. Even should we avoid an accident, by morning we will be too exhausted to make good use of the day.'

'He is right, Mistress Meglan,' said Eldan. 'An ant will make better progress than us tonight.'

Meglan felt thwarted; alone she would have shed angry tears. But she accepted that she must heed the two men's advice.

She gave the word to stop, and they cautiously led their horses from the road, away from the river side. Meglan walked with her hand extended before her, feeling for obstacles. She felt rough grass beneath her feet and heard the rustle of bushes as the wind passed through. Then they were beneath trees. They tethered the horses to a bush. Meglan removed Swift Cloud's saddle, then, too fretful to eat, wrapped herself in blanket and burnous and lay down to a night of fitful sleep.

6

FAR AHEAD ON the Dharsoul road Sildemund and his two
companions, Gully and Picadus, had made better progress.

Knowing nothing of events at Volm they had travelled at a
steady pace, unhindered, without particular haste. On the first
night they lodged at a caravanserai beside the way. They moved
on at first light and stopped only briefly at a wayside inn at
midday, to rest their horses, fill their bellies and wash the dust
from their throats with good ale.

Sometime after leaving the inn, as they broke out upon a
parched and dusty plateau, Gully reined in his mount and pointed
into the shimmering distance. They were in a lonely region of
barren hills and ragged gulches and canyons called Dazdun's
Despair. According to legend Dazdun had been one of the godlike
enchanters who long ago had battled over Firstworld. Through a
ruse plied by the infamous Arch-Enchantress Yshcopthe, Dazdun
was dispossessed of his magical powers. He was said to have
wandered aimlessly, though in circles, upon the earth. Such was
his desolation at having been reduced to the status of a mere
mortal that his passage brought about corruption and distortion
of the land, rendering it infertile and hostile to life.

Certainly Dazdun's Despair was an arid and inhospitable
region, though the description would apply equally to much of the
Dyarch hinterlands. The road had abandoned the riverside some
miles back, where sudden cliffs reared and the Tigrant coursed
through places where men could not follow. The way took a
tortuous path, never straying far from the edge of Dazdun's
Despair. Once through the Despair, Dharsoul lay less than a day's
ride away. Gully was confident of reaching the capital well before
nightfall on the following day.

Sildemund had squinnied his eyes to see what it was that had caught Gully's attention. At first he saw nothing. The sky was near-white, blindingly bright. The landscape stretched away, a wilderness of blasted yellow and brown rock and earth, all folds, crags and craters, bearing nothing but the hardiest of scrub.

Then he saw a movement. He craned forward in the saddle. His heart began to beat fast. Yes, there!

Two hundred paces away grey shapes moved slowly in disorderly procession up a steep bare hillside. They were four in number – no, five! The fifth had just emerged from the shadow of a hump of rock. They rolled and bounced without discernible aim, as though without volition of their own.

'Hill-ghosts?' Sildemund was filled with fearful wonder.

'Aye,' Gully sat easily in the saddle, his eyes now scanning the road ahead.

Sildemund continued to observe the strange procession until the last ghost had disappeared over the brow of the hill. He turned to Gully, his eyes bright and wide with excitement. 'That is the first time I have set eyes on a hill-ghost.'

Gully nodded, and gave a grin.

'You have encountered many, I suppose, Gully?'

'Not so many. They are uncommon things.'

'And you, Pic, have you seen a hill-ghost before?'

Picadus, who was in a sombre mood, nodded and said merely, 'Once or twice.'

Sildemund scanned the distance in the hope of one last glimpse of the strange things, but to no avail.

'Have you ever been attacked by one?'

Gully shook his head. 'They are not hostile as such – at least, I have never known them to be.'

'But I have heard stories—'

'Aye, there are stories. But in my experience hill-ghosts are aimless, insentient things. They go whither they are blown, like smoke. If they contact you they can cause harm or disorientation, but contact is haphazard as far as I know. They do not knowingly or purposefully seek us out.'

He patted his horse's neck, as the creature had grown a touch restive, seeming to sense the proximity of the ghosts. He gazed ruminatively into the distance. 'It is unusual to find them here. In the hills of the Boltar or Soland, aye, and most especially on the fringes of the Endless Desert. But here, in Dyarchim? I've never seen one, and know of no one who has.' He turned his big frame to Picadus. 'Have you, Pic?'

Picadus shook his head as though the subject held no interest for him.

Sildemund thought to hear the faintest sound coming from beyond the hill. Yes! A distant, melancholic piping, an eldritch lament like nothing he had ever heard. He listened in fascination, feeling strange tingles along his skin.

'It's their song, Gully! It's the song of the hill-ghosts!'

Gully smiled at his excitement, and his own ears picked up the haunting beauty of the melody-less voices. The song of the hill-ghosts was said to be capable of casting a spell on men's minds, entrancing them, causing them to do things that in ordinary circumstances they would not do. Listening now, as he had before on occasion, he could believe it possible. The distant, unearthy song affected him. In closer proximity he might have found himself enchanted by its strange properties.

'What are they, Gully? The hill-ghosts, from where have they come?'

Gully shook his head and swept a lock of long fair hair from his brow. 'Some say they are elemental things, ages old, formed of dust and vapour, others that they are the ghosts of strange beasts long gone. Others believe them to be weird creations of the Enchanter Wars. We don't know.' He clicked his tongue and urged his mount on. 'Come, we should not tarry.'

They rode on along the edges of Dazdun's Despair. Sildemund was alert, still hoping for another glimpse of the hill-ghosts, but he saw nothing and the strange song was quickly lost to his ears.

As they rode they passed wagons or carts and the odd pilgrim or wayfarer heading in the opposite direction. They stopped briefly to exchange news, and learned that there had been bandit activities reported some way to the west of Dharsoul.

'If that is so it may be wise tomorrow to seek company,' Gully remarked.

As evening began to close in they made camp in a dry gulch close to the roadside. Sildemund built a fire and cooked bacon and waybread, which they ate with watered wine. Gully suggested that Picadus take out his cittern. Sildemund especially wanted Picadus

to compose a ballad about the hill-ghosts. But Picadus, unusually, was not in the mood. They pressed him and he became
irritable. When they asked what was bothering him he declined
to reveal his thoughts. Mystified, they left him to himself and lay
down to sleep.

The following morning dawned hot and without a breath of a
breeze. Under Gully's direction the three waited beside the road,
rather than ride on unaccompanied. An hour passed and a couple
of wagons appeared in the distant haze, accompanied by four
armed men on horseback.

As they drew closer Gully stepped out and hailed them. The
wagons halted forty paces away. There was a brief consultation
between the guards and a bearded man seated beside the driver,
who by his garb gave the impression of some wealth. Two of the
guards rode cautiously forward.

'Why do you call us?' asked one.

'Greetings!' declared Gully. 'Are you bound for Dharsoul?'

The guard surveyed him with narrowed eyes. 'Perhaps. What is
it to you?'

Sildemund noted their mistrust. They were well armed; he
wondered at the wisdom of stopping them.

'We are bound there too,' Gully replied. 'For security we should
perhaps ride together. We hear tell of bandits somewhere on the
road ahead.'

The guard looked dubiously into the distance. 'Wait.'

He and his companion turned their horses around and trotted
back to the first wagon.

'Tell your master that I am Sildemund Atturio, son of Master
Frano Atturio of Volm,' Sildemund called after them.

The men conferred briefly with their employer. They rode back.

'Our master wants nothing of it. Your name is unknown to him.
Off the road now, so that we can pass.'

'I implore you to reconsider,' said Gully. 'The way ahead may be
dangerous.'

'We have considered enough! You may be cutthroats yourselves, in collusion with those you claim lie ahead. We will take
our chances. Now, let us pass.'

Reluctantly the three moved back to the side of the road. The
wagons rumbled forward, the guards nervously fingering their

weapons. The bearded merchant cast them a single impersonal glance as he passed, but did not speak.

'Do not follow in our immediate wake,' warned the first guard as they rode away.

Gully kneaded his neck with the palm of his powerful hand and watched them until they had passed beyond sight. 'Nothing for it, lads, we must continue alone. Best wait half an hour, though. They were too edgy. If they spot us in their rear they may give us trouble.'

They sat in the shade of a wild fig. Gully leaned with his head against the trunk, his eyes closed, humming to himself. Sildemund watched the road, but no travellers passed. Picadus kept his own counsel, a frown of troubled concentration knitting his brow. Presently they set off again.

An hour passed and they met no one upon the road. They came to an intersection where the way branched northward in the direction of Tomia. Unofficially this intersection was recognized as marking the end of the region called Dazdun's Despair, though the land remained harsh for some miles more.

Half a mile past the northern road Gully raised his hand and once more brought them to a halt. Sildemund did not have to ask why, he had already spotted the plume of dark smoke curling skywards on the road ahead. The source could not be identified, for the road was obscured by rising land and massive clumps of rocks.

'What do you think it is?'

Gully pushed back his hair, squinting into the distance, the sun full on his brown face. 'I'm not sure.'

The area they were in was one of sparse scrub, dotted with the occasional stunted cypress or uncultivated olive tree. A harsh, rubbly plain gave off to one side; to the other, a little way off, a long, sheer scarp rose.

Gully was watching the rocks that flanked the road ahead. 'Did you see anything? A movement by that turret of rock?'

Sildemund shook his head. 'Perhaps it was a wild goat.'

'Perhaps, but I am not happy. We will advance with caution. Keep your eyes peeled, and have weapons ready. Pic, watch the rear. *Pic!* Snap out of it!'

Picadus looked up as if the effort cost him.

'I sense danger, Pic. Watch our rear!' Gully spoke gruffly.

Sildemund looked anxiously at Picadus, who barely nodded. Gully clenched his jaw. 'You too, lad. Picadus seems to have little concern for his life today.'

They advanced, the road descending, entering the shadow between two boulder-crowned elevations. They kept single file, Gully at the fore, then Sildemund, with Picadus a few paces behind. Sildemund glanced up, scanning the towering boulders, then swivelled to check the rear. Picadus was also looking back, but seemed hardly interested in what he saw.

They rounded a bend. Ahead lay the burning hulk of a wagon. Three bodies littered the road. Sildemund recognized the merchant who had earlier declined their offer of company. He lay on his back, plagued by flies, his mouth open, blood from a mortal wound on his chest clogging the dust. The two others were guards, arrows studding their bodies.

Sildemund heard a low groan off to his left. Beside a boulder a guard knelt – the same man they had spoken to at the roadside. His hair was matted with blood. One hand rested upon the boulder for support; he stretched the other towards them, his mouth open but soundless. He seemed unable to walk, or even see.

Gully's eye were still on the surrounding rocks. He gave a cry. Something flew past Sildemund's unprotected head and embedded itself in the dirt beside the road. A second missile raised dust on the road in front of his horse.

The horse shied. Sildemund brought it under control. More arrows were raining down. He saw figures among the rocks. Three, four, more.

'Back!' Gully yelled. Already he had loosed two arrows at the men in the rocks. Sildemund yanked upon the reins, jerking his horse around, and spurred it into a gallop. Picadus, a little slower, had his sabre drawn. There were whoops and shouts. More men were leaping down from the rocks towards the road.

Sildemund bent low, urging his mount on. He glanced behind him, saw Gully close by, loosing arrows as he rode. Picadus, his lips set in concentration, had wheeled his mount around and was following close in their wake.

But now, fifty paces back along the road, mounted men bore down upon them wielding sabres or slim lances. Sildemund cried out to Gully. Gully pointed to the right. 'Off the road! We will try to outpace them!'

They veered their mounts onto the rough, swerving between huge boulders. A bandit leaped from an overhang into Sildemund's path. Sildemund, his sabre drawn, slashed at him. The man jumped back, and Sildemund's blow missed. As the brigand recovered his balance he was cut down by Gully.

On the gallop, Sildemund re-sheathed his blade. They broke out onto the rocky plain. More bandits were coming at them now from the right, several on horseback, forcing them to veer left. Caught between converging groups they could take only one course, out further into the wild.

They weaved between scrub and rock, their path taking them upwards. Foam flew from the mouth of Sildemund's horse. He urged her on with anxiously whispered words. The footing was treacherous and he could not give her her fullest speed. Even so her passage was becoming laboured on the incline.

He risked a look behind. Their pursuers had not gained on either side, but were riding on a course that would bring them together a little way behind Sildemund and his companions.

The ground steepened, then they broke out onto the lip of a low ridge. Beyond Sildemund saw the world of Dazdun's Despair laid before him. The land shimmered in the heat-haze, all dark scars and ragged declivities, with occasional small black clots of stunted trees, stretching as far as he could see beneath a blinding yellow-white sky.

They followed the crest of the ridge, the only way they could go, taking them back in a vaguely westward direction. Sildemund was dismayed to see the bandits divide again into two groups. One followed their path, climbing the slope to the ridge. The other galloped along the base of the slope, keeping a course more or less parallel to theirs. Gradually, being on less exacting terrain, the second group was gaining ground.

Sildemund and his companions were outnumbered by at least five to one. He peered ahead, trying to descry the path. Were they heading into a cul-de-sac? Would they be forced back down, directly into the path of the second bandit group?

Gully pointed, grim-visaged, sweat gleaming on his cheeks. The land rose steeply ahead of them, all loose, rotten earth and shale. The three urged their mounts upwards.

The earth slid beneath Sildemund's horse's hooves. She stumbled, struggling to find a hold on the unsure slope. Both Gully and Picadus had pushed a little way ahead, their mounts having found better purchase. Sildemund's horse found her footing, and thrust on gamely on the firmer ground.

Then suddenly she stumbled again and went onto her knees. Sildemund was pitched violently forward. He was almost thrown, but managed to cling on. But now, as she rose, his mount's rear legs gave way and he, throwing himself back at the same time to counter the initial forward motion, slid over her haunches.

He landed off-balance and sat down hard. Out of control, he rolled and skidded down the slope.

There were great whoops from the bandits behind. Sildemund managed to arrest his motion and scramble frantically upwards, but he was on shale and earth that was little more than powder, and he made scarcely any ground.

Sudden panic rose in his breast. He heard air through a horse's nostrils as death bore down on him from behind. He twisted, that he might face his assailants, groping for his sabre. The closest bandit was almost upon him, his mount struggling up the slope, his sabre raised. The man's eyes gleamed, his teeth bared in a grimace of savage triumph.

He leaned low and struck. Sildemund rolled. The blade sighed past his head. With a wild yell the bandit was off his horse and leaping down upon Sildemund. Sildemund's sabre had caught in his scabbard. He wrestled to free it. The bandit was over him, lofting his sabre in both hands. Sildemund knew a moment of sheer, mind-numbing terror, waiting for the blade to slice through his flesh and bone.

There was a flurry of movement. The bandit staggered, throwing back his head. Blood blossomed suddenly on his tunic. Behind him Gully stood, yanking free a bloody sabre.

'Up!' yelled Gully, thrusting the dead man aside before he could even fall. The others were almost upon them. 'To the rocks!'

Sildemund grasped at bushes and rocks, gasping, hauling himself upwards to a tumble of boulders a few yards higher. Picadus stood there, blankly staring down. His bow hung loose in his hands.

'Shoot, damn you!' Gully roared, and Picadus half-heartedly raised the weapon.

Gully grabbed Sildemund by the scruff of the neck and dragged him the last couple of paces into the rocks. There was no time to catch their breath. The bandits, seven of them, were almost upon them again and Picadus had not let fly a single shaft. Further down, the second group had begun its ascent. Sildemund felt his spirits plummet. His reprieve had been brief. They were hopelessly outnumbered.

He was aware of sounds in the distance: the muted drum of hoofbeats; the blare of a horn. Grabbing the sabre, ready to defend himself, he saw the second group of bandits suddenly curtail their ascent of the slope. They veered away, to gallop back along the line of the ridge.

On the plain below, emerging from behind a bluff, there came a cloud, flecked with glints of bright metal. Sildemund heard the faint jingle of harness. His heart fell again as he identified yet more riders.

'Soldiers!' Gully, his bowstring taut, shifted his eyes to squint down onto the plain.

Sildemund peered hard. He saw banners in the dust, red, gold and blue. About forty mounted soldiers were pounding towards the slope, racing to intercept the fleeing bandits.

'The Queen's men! We are saved!' Gully's bowstring snapped. He flung the bow aside and drew his sabre. He let loose a great yell and leapt from the rocks at the nearest bandit.

Sildemund went after him, his sabre free; for all his exuberance Gully was still outnumbered.

The bandits were in disarray. Seeing their companions on the run and a detachment of Dyarch troops turning to ascend the slope, their one thought now was of escape. Gully's sabre bit into the flank of the nearest, who spun his horse around with a bellow of pain and made off without retaliation, clutching his wound.

Sildemund lunged at another, but he too wheeled away and was gone, his mount kicking dust in its wake. Sildemund went sprawling head first and slid helplessly down the slope on his belly, his mouth filling with dust and grit. He thudded into a jutting rock and came to a halt. He climbed to his feet, coughing.

Gully arrived at his side, laughing, and threw an arm around his shoulders. 'Never mind, lad. It was a good try! You'll get your bandit next time!'

Sildemund spat muck from his mouth. They stood together and watched the Dyarch troops pursue the enemy along the ridge.

Five soldiers split from the chase and walked their mounts to the base of the ridge. Sildemund, Gully and Picadus led their horses down to meet them.

Sildemund addressed their leader, a tall, broad-shouldered fellow with long dark hair confined by a flowing white silk fillet, stained by sweat and grime. The lower half of his face, like those of his men, was covered by a heavy cloth faceguard, which helped keep the dust from mouth and nostrils. He wore a lightly laminated surcoat, elaborate in design and of high quality, which marked him out as a man of status, quite possibly a noble. His eyes were lustrous blue beneath dark brows.

'Sir, I would thank you. Without your intervention we would surely have died here today.'

The officer surveyed him with a keen and searching gaze. 'Whither are you bound?'

'Dharsoul, sir, where I have business to conduct in the name of my father, Master Frano Atturio of Volm.'

'We are returning to Dharsoul.' The officer unclasped his faceguard and let it fall to the side. 'Ride with us, if you wish. The remainder of your journey, at least, should be trouble free.'

The main body of his troop was returning at a leisurely pace across the plain beneath the end of the ridge. The officer was swinging his horse around. From behind Sildemund came Gully's voice, raised in exclamation. 'My lord! Prince Enlos!'

Sildemund turned. Gully had dropped onto one knee, his head bowed. Picadus, with a somewhat bewildered expression, was following suit. Gully signalled with eyes and hand for Sildemund to do likewise.

Sildemund turned back to the horseman. He saw the arresting, begrimed features of a man aged perhaps twenty-five or six. The skin was brown and weathered, the jaw strong. His mouth was wide, perhaps too wide, with full, deep ruddy lips set now in a quizzical smile. He sported a neatly trimmed black moustache which drooped to the edge of his jaw. The nose was straight, the brow broad and intelligent. The eyes, alert and appraising, had a vaguely perturbing quality, for while they penetrated they also held a veil over his thoughts, and in doing so implied unknowable aspects to his character. A small scar in the shape of a perfect cross was set high upon his left cheek.

Sildemund was at first too stunned to react. Then he sank like his companions to his knee, stuttering, 'S–sire! Please forgive me! I could not have known it was you.'

Prince Enlos's eyes glowed with amusement. 'Plainly one of you has seen my face before.'

Gully raised his head. 'Many times, my lord! You will not recall – and why should you? – but I was privileged to ride with your guard years ago.'

Prince Enlos peered hard with a baffled expression, then his blue eyes lit up. 'Radath Gully! By all the demons!' He swung one leg over his saddle and slid to the ground. 'Radath Gully! It *is* you! Up off your knees, man! This is a pleasure, a great pleasure!'

Gully rose, Prince Enlos clapped him heartily on the shoulders, shaking his powerful frame. 'It's been a long time! Gully, Gully, my brave and faithful man, it is good to see you! What is your business now, and what brings you here?'

The two chatted like old friends long parted. Sildemund watched slack-jawed, Picadus beside him equally impressed. Sildemund was aware that Gully had at one time served in the Dyarch army, had been a junior officer, a radath, in the cavalry – but that he was on intimate terms with the heir to the throne? This was something new.

'Come!' said Prince Enlos at length. 'We should leave this heartless place. You and your two companions will ride beside me. We can talk as we go.'

At the head of the troops they made their way slowly across the barren plain towards the Dharsoul Road. Gully pointed, 'It was there that we were attacked, my lord. They came from the high rocks. There is a gutted wagon and the bodies of a merchant and his guard upon the road.'

A thin wreath of blue smoke could still be seen above the rocks.

'The brigands have become more daring of late,' growled Prince Enlos as they approached the scene of carnage. 'Until recently they would never have dared come so close to the capital. They kept well to the borderlands in the north. We may have to consider policing the road. Still, I'll warrant there is no one lurking here now.'

The bodies still lay in the road, flies feasting while vultures hung overhead. The wagon was a burned-out husk. The guard who had still clung to life when Sildemund and his companions had been attacked was found now to be dead.

Prince Enlos commanded his men to bury them. Others took up positions in the rocks to guard against the unlikely prospect of the bandits' returning.

'Those you pursued, did they escape?' Gully enquired.

'Our arrows brough a couple from their saddles, but the terrain is difficult for prolonged pursuit. Those men know the land better than any. They can vanish like spectral things.'

Prince Enlos's company contained no prisoners. Sildemund wondered what had become of the bandits that had been shot from the saddle.

They rode on for Dharsoul. Sildemund could barely contain his feelings; this journey had turned into a high adventure more exciting than he could have imagined. To have seen and listened to the song of the hill-ghosts; to have been attacked and almost murdered by bandits, then rescued by the crown prince himself; and now to be riding alongside Prince Enlos at the head of a troop of the Royal Guard!

Prince Enlos leaned across to address Sildemund. 'You are in good company, to have Radath Gully here as your guardian. I take it you are familiar with his exploits?'

'I had thought so, my lord, but plainly I was wrong. Gully has never told me that he knew you.'

'Ah, he is a modest man. Has he told you that he was decorated for his services to me? That he helped save my life?'

'No, sir. Is this true?' Sildemund stared at Gully, who appeared uncomfortable at the turn the conversation was taking.

'It is indeed,' said Prince Enlos. 'You are too young to recall, but perhaps your parents or others have told you of the rebellion here in Dyarchim, ten years or more ago?'

'I have heard, my lord. A band of treacherous nobles turned against the throne. They tried to oust your mother, Queen Lermeone, from power.' Sildemund recalled his father having referred to the event once or twice. There had been rumours of some sort of scandal associated with the rebellion, something involving the Queen. All knowledge of the event had been suppressed though, and plainly it would have been inappropriate to make mention of it now.

'And failed,' said Prince Enlos. 'I was fifteen at the time. Just prior to the outbreak of the rebellion I was sent on a state journey from Dharsoul to Trore, in Ghence. Gully's company was assigned as part of my guard. On the return journey we were attacked by rebel soldiers who lay in wait for us close to the Dyarch border. In the ensuing battle many brave men were killed. We took refuge on a hilltop, but were surrounded by the enemy and unable to escape. For almost two weeks we were trapped there. The enemy assaulted out position many times. Each time we successfully repelled them, but with the loss of good men. We had sent out messengers, but had no way of knowing whether they had been caught by the enemy. In the final days we were reduced to a mere twelve tired and hungry men. Radath Gully was one of those twelve, and with the deaths of my own faithful officers he became my second-in-command. That I can stand here today is testament to his unswerving loyalty and courage.'

Sildemund was spellbound. 'How did you escape?'

'A relief force finally arrived, alerted by a messenger who had managed to sneak through the enemy lines.' Prince Enlos shook his head, his features drawn, 'Too many good men. . . .'

Sildemund looked again in admiration at Gully, who kept his eyes cast down as if embarrassed. Prince Enlos leaned across and slapped Gully's thigh. 'I am in his debt!'

'No longer, sire, if ever it were so,' said Gully, 'which I do not believe, for I only did my duty. But today you have saved my life, and the lives of young Sildemund here, and our friend Picadus, both of whom I love like brothers. It was a stroke of great good fortune that you should come upon us like that, in such lonely wilderness.'

'Fortune it was, indeed,' the Prince agreed.

'What brought you there, sire, if I might ask?'

'I have been engaged upon a mission to Garsh, in Tomia, and am returning now to the capital. Military activity by the Tomian authorities in that region has had the contingent effect of displacing a renowned local brigand, Fagmar the Cursed. Knowing him to be operating in this vicinity I sent out scouts. One spotted your plight.'

'Garsh?' Gully mused. 'I have heard there is military activity there. It is the cultist enclave, is it not?'

'The Revenants of Claine. Aye it is.'

'They have weird beliefs, so I've heard.'

'They are reincarnates, if you would believe their patter.'

'Do they not claim knowledge of some great secret?'

Prince Enlos nodded stiffly. 'Such is their claim. Most consider them to be nothing more than lunatics.'

Gully gave this some thought. 'Word has it that Garsh is currently under siege by Tomian troops. There has even been talk of a massacre there.'

The Prince patted his horse's sleek neck but made no reply.

'But Garsh is in Tomia, sire.' Gully went on. 'I know that at one time the Revenants spread into Dyarchim, but that was long ago. They were exiled to Garsh more than a century ago. I was not aware that Dyarchim held any interest in them now.'

Prince Enlos gazed straight ahead. 'Unfortunately it is not a matter I am at liberty to discuss.'

They rode on, passing more travellers upon the road as they drew closer to the capital. The wilderness gradually gave way to orchards, fields and meadows where workers tended their crops or goats and cattle grazed. The sun was well past its zenith when they crested a gentle rise and saw, in the heat-shifting distance, the mighty Tigrant bending languidly across a green and fertile plain. Spread along its banks, shimmering in the haze at the limit of their vision, could be discerned the walls, domes and towers of the great river city of Dharsoul.

7

AFTER A RESTLESS and uneasy night Meglan was up as the first glimmer of dawn washed the dark low in the eastern sky. Of her two guards, Jans was asleep in his blanket beside the embers of their campfire, while Eldan, who had the watch, sat nearby with his back to a boulder. Meglan saw from his posture that Eldan also slumbered. She shook him roughly – 'Wake up, make yourself ready. We ride immediately!' – then went to Jans and roused him in a similar manner.

They led the horses out onto the road, Jans and Eldan chewing on tack and hurriedly swigging water from their sacks. Meglan gently rotated her head to ease the stiffness and tenderness of her neck, the result of Skalatin's attack on her the previous day. Jans and Eldan confirmed that her throat bore livid bruising, more pronounced than earlier. Her chest and shoulders were also painful, obliging her to move gingerly.

Meglan glanced back along the way in the direction of Volm. It was light enough now to see a layer of thick grey cloud spread across the sky above the city; Volm itself was not visible, being obscured by intervening terrain. The sea glittered way off in the distance.

Meglan thought of her father, Master Frano, alone in his bedchamber, probably still sleeping. Or would he be awake, concerned about her? Almost certainly he would be aware by now that she had gone. She felt a pang of immense guilt for leaving him. He was less than an hour away. Her breast heaved. *Oh, benevolent soul of Yshcopthe, keep him well!*

She mounted Swift Cloud. 'Let us go!'

She made off at a brisk trot. The two men quickly climbed to their saddles and spurred their mounts that they might not fall behind.

Within minutes Fate dealt them a blow of cruel irony. Eldan's horse stumbled on a rut in the road, and wrenched its leg. Cursing, Eldan was forced to halt and dismount. As Meglan seethed with impatience he examined the animal. He looked up, shaking his head grimly.

'She's lame. She won't be carrying me anywhere for a couple of days.'

Meglan vented a scream of exasperation. 'Do the gods themselves conspire against us?'

Her emotions surged in her breast. Eldan said, 'The nearest posting-house is several hours away. Volm is closer. Do you wish to return so that I might hire another horse?'

Meglan shook her head. 'Go! Make your way back to Volm as best you can. We will continue without you. Go straight to my father. Tell him I am well and will return to him very soon.'

With that she wheeled Swift Cloud around, and with Jans as her sole guard set off again for Dharsoul and Sildemund.

For Master Frano the daylight hours passed without great event. He had woken early and asked for Meglan. Upon receiving the news of her departure he had merely nodded to himself. He had known she would go. He had known, too, that he was powerless to prevent her. He feared for her, and for Sildemund, upon whom he had laid the burden of the mysterious red stone.

Frano questioned himself, his motives, his reasoning in acting the way he had. It was too late to regret this now, of course; what was done was done. But he recognized that, however unwittingly, he had become the agent of a great misfortune which was affecting not only himself; but others, close to him. Master Frano felt the weight of a great and profound sadness descending upon him. Deep within him was the growing fear that he would never set eyes on either of his two beloved children again.

He might have risen that day and exercised a little in his room, testing his injured leg. But his mood was such that he felt no inclination. Neena brought him food and drink. He ate alone, without enthusiasm. Two guards remained at all times outside his door. At least one other, he knew, was stationed within the house. Master Frano half expected that Captain Gosbedah would return with more questions, but he didn't. At some point, though –

probably after darkness had fallen – Frano did not doubt that he would be paid a visit by Skalatin.

His mind recalled the events at the secret grotto where he had discovered the stone. Why had he not listened to Edric then? He saw again Edric's mutilated corpse. He imagined poor Dervad, his chest cavity filled with shattered glass and shards of broken pots. The images haunted, mocked, accused. He saw Skalatin hovering over him, felt again the pain as his hand was crushed in Skalatin's murderous grip.

He railed against himself for what he perceived now as his irresponsibility and greed. He should have returned the stone to Skalatin immediately! Dervad might still be alive, and he, Frano, fifty crowns the richer. True, he did not have the stone when Skalatin first demanded it. But he could have let Meglan go after Sildemund to bring him back immediately, as she had suggested doing. Better, rather than risk Meg's safety he could have sent a rider who might have caught Sildemund before he reached Dharsoul. Had he followed that course, might Sildemund have returned by now, or early enough to effectively prevent the terrible events that had ensued? It was possible, Master Frano acknowledged gravely, but unlikely. So his excuse was valid, he did not have the stone. But Frano knew that at all times he had clung to the hope that he might make more from the stone than Skalatin – or his client – had offered.

He waited in a suspense of helpless fear, tormented, half-sensing something of what was to come.

From outside his room the sounds of the street filtered through the open window. Bustling during the day, growing quieter in the torrid afternoon when many folk slept, then rising again to a low hubbub as evening drew close. He could see, through the window, the roofs and upper floors of the city, framed by a gap between the two buildings opposite. He observed the slow passage of shadows as the sun moved imperceptibly across the sky, heard the cries of gulls, saw the light change gradually on domes and minarets. The low hills in the distance were misty blue. He wondered unceasingly about Meglan, dear sweet Meglan. Where was she now? How did she fare? Was she safe?

And Sildemund, of whom he was so proud. He was surely now at Dharsoul, or close. What would he find there? Was he, through his very possession of the red stone, imperilled? Had he been prevented by some means from even reaching the capital?

Master Frano lay, his body still. His heart beat unnaturally fast, his thoughts raced. The night drew down.

Neena came and lit the candles in his room. She bathed and dressed his injuries, then returned with his evening meal: a broth of barley and vegetables, then spicy meat with cracked wheat and warm doughbread pancakes, and a flask of robust red wine. She scolded him, for he had barely touched his midday meal.

'Do you wish me to sit with you? You have been alone all day.'

'No, Neena, leave me please. I wish only to rest.'

He waited, noting familiar sounds within the house, waiting for those which would signal the arrival of his visitor. A rap at the door downstairs? He had not previously been aware of Sakalatin's knock. No, probably the first indication, if he strained his ears for every nuance of sound, would be Neena's footsteps as she shuffled to the front door, then her laboured return upstairs. She would knock at Frano's door and announce the visitor. Or would Skalatin simply march straight up without waiting to be announced?

Frano heard the scrape of a foot outside the door. He started nervously, then relaxed: it was only one of the guards shifting his position. There was a muted chink and accompanying light thumps downstairs, but that would be Neena going about her normal business, or perhaps another guard. Beyond the window a dog bayed. Master Frano caught the distant strain of a male voice, rough and basso, raised in spontaneous song.

Later came sounds of revelry from the tavernas and pleasure-houses. Frano grew impatient with the strain of waiting. He could not relax, nor sleep, nor get up and walk. His leg and hands pained him and there was a fierce, relentless throbbing behind his eyes. He wanted no more. He could not bear this tension any longer.

He was aware, quite suddenly, of a movement at the window. A shadow, a dark blot, obscuring the dark that was already there. It came soundlessly, no warning scuff or scrape of a body scaling the wall.

Silent as a phantom, Skalatin stepped down into the room.

With two strides he was at the bedside.

'Where is it?' He was garbed as before, in a dark burnous,

hooded, his face hidden. His voice had the rasping, scowling quality that Frano had come to detest and fear.

Frano was at first too shocked by his entrance to respond. Recovering from the shock he felt himself outraged. He would not speak to Skalatin – not yet. This man, this *creature*, had murdered Dervad and Edric. Likely he had come here now with murderous intent.

'*Guards!*' Frano called. His voice shook. It sounded feeble, but it carried beyond the chamber, for the door opened and the two armed men stood there. Seeing Skalatin they drew their short-swords.

Skalatin spun to meet them, and emitted a scoffing, rancorous sound. He stepped swiftly across the room and punched the first guard hard in the face. The man cannoned backwards as if hit by a ram, knocking his companion off balance.

Skalatin reached out and seized the second guard by the throat, dragging him into the bedchamber, lifting him off his feet, wrenching, twisting, squeezing. The poor man gurgled, his feet kicking. Gripping the guard's sword-wrist so he could not strike back, Skalatin shook him with terrible strength, dropped him then struck him with a powerful backfist, breaking his neck.

He tossed the body aside. The first guard was rushing back in, blood pouring from his nose and cheek. He lunged with his sword at Skalatin, but there was insufficient room for swordplay. Skalatin had moved neatly aside. The guard's elbow struck the doorjamb, deflecting his blow.

Skalatin took his sword arm, yanked him inwards, swung him around and hurled him at the wall. As he crumpled in a daze Skalatin leaped upon his back, put his knee into the man's spine and grabbed his chin. He wrenched up and back. There was a sickening, tearing sound and a click. Skalatin released the lifeless form.

He wheeled back, and laughed at the sight of Master Frano, half-sitting in his bed, white-faced with terror, clasping his dagger in one bandaged hand.

'Again, old fool? Again?'

Frano let the dagger drop. Skalatin came close and bent towards him. 'Do you have it for me?'

'I – I have sent for it! Believe me, I will have it!'

'That is not enough!' Skalatin thrust himself angrily erect. He strode to the door and kicked it shut. He paced the length of the room, once, then returned to the bedside. He took a deep, glottal breath. 'I warned you. The price. Plainly it was not enough.'

'I am trying! I'm doing all I can, believe me!'

'What does it take?' Skalatin hovered over him, menace in every atom of his presence. His voice dropped to a loathsome purr. 'Where is she?'

'Who?'

'The malkin. The love-ly child.'

'Meglan?' Frano shuddered. The very way in which Skalatin spoke the words filled him with shock and disgust.

'Aah, Meg-lan,' Skalatin lifted one leg and climbed onto the bed, straddling Frano's waist once more. He reached down and took the lapels of Master Frano's bedshirt, drawing him towards himself. Frano was powerless to resist. Again he found himself gazing into those cold, dark eyes, recoiling at the stench of Skalatin's breath.

'Whe-re is lov-ely Meg-lan?'

Frano shook his head but his voice was trapped in his throat.

Skalatin thrust him back against the pillows and sprang from the bed, snarling, 'I will find her!'

He swept from the room. Frano heard his footsteps descend. There was a cry, then shrieks downstairs, the clatter of something falling, the noise of a scuffle. A male voice yelled out loud, and was abruptly curtailed.

Master Frano half-rose to try and get out of bed, then froze. He stared, stupefied with horror, at the two bodies on the floor of his chamber. Was this a terrible dream?

The shrieks resumed below. Short, repeated screams and sobs. He knew it to be Neena's voice, intermingled with the berserk snarls of Skalatin. He tried to drag himself from the bed. He heard heavy, forceful footsteps returning, their pattern confused, as though something of some bulk was being dragged or impelled up the stairs.

He sat rigidly, too frightened to move.

The door flew open and Skalatin marched back in, hauling poor, sobbing Neena by her grey hair, which he clasped in one fist. He stood near the end of the bed. 'I don't find the malkin, but this will do!'

70

'No! Leave her, please! She has done nothing! She has no part in this!'

'Where is the stone?'

'I told you, I have sent for it! It will be here soon!'

Skalatin spat in fury. He raised his arm, and Neena, who had been forced to her knees by the pressure of his hand holding her head down, was suddenly hoisted high. She screamed, clawing in agony at his hand, the tips of her toes no longer touching the ground.

'*No!* Please!' Master Frano implored. '*Please!*'

'Where is lovely Meg-lan?'

'She is gone. To bring you the stone. Truly!'

As he spoke Master Frano was visited by the shocking image of Meglan in Skalatin's grasp. Was he condemning her by his words? No, for Skalatin did not – could not – know where she was. In confusion and terror he spoke again, desperate to ensure Meglan's safety. 'We will leave the stone somewhere! Tell us where! Anywhere you wish! It will be put there for you!'

'Gaaah! You do not learn!'

Skalatin's unencumbered hand shot out and around. With horrific speed it punched into old Neena's frail chest. Even as it moved Master Frano glimpsed something clawed, pincered, which seemed to take the place of fingers. The monstrous hand burrowed effortlessly into Neena's flesh, tearing tissue and smashing bone as she hung, twitching and kicking in her death throes.

Skalatin withdrew his bloodied hand, clutching her still palpitating heart. There was the sound of something liquid slithering to the floor. He released her body and pulled aside his mask. He held the glistening organ and its writhing, rubbery tubes, red, purple and bluish, up before his face. Frano stared in horror at that face, saw its peeling, rotting skin, its fleshless gums laid bare by a lipless mouth. Things seemed to move in those gums and within the mouth; tiny wormy things with a life of their own. Frano saw the long yellowed fangs that lined the pitted jaws, the ropy greyish tongue that flicked out to lick the old woman's vitals. He bit into the wet flesh and tore a great gobbet free. He chewed and swallowed, eyeing Frano, relishing his horror.

'*Gaaah!*' Skalatin flung the heart away. It smashed glutinously against one wall, splattering blood and slime in whiplike trails, and rolled to the floor. He spat pieces of meat from his mouth. 'That one is no good!'

Skalatin stood over Frano, his features contorted into an obscene grin. And even as Frano stared the face began to change, moulding itself into new shapes. Suddenly it was Neena's face gazing at him from beneath that dark cowl. Neena smiling benevolently, except for the eyes which held an expression of bone-chilling evil. Even the body beneath the burnous had altered to take Neena's form.

Frano stared, at Neena who stood before him, to Neena whose violated corpse lay upon the floor, and back again.

'Where is love-ly Meg-lan?' enquired Neena's voice.

'Please! *Please*. We will bring you the stone.'

Skalatin/Neena's head shook slowly with a mocking smile. 'Ah, no matter. I will find her. I will find the stone.'

There was a sudden movement of Neena's shoulder. Master Frano gagged as something plunged deep into his chest, then there was a searing, tearing, explosive pain as that obscene limb foraged inside him, seeking his heart.

As the world retreated, all strange in a haze of red and shiny white, the last thing Master Frano's eyes beheld was old Neena, leaning her face close to his, holding up the pulsing muscle that he knew had been drawn from his chest. And Neena, opening wide her mouth, turning back to Skalatin as she did so, eating Frano's still living heart.

PART TWO

8

'SOMETHING IS GRAVELY wrong. I am worried.' Sildemund stared at Picadus's still form slumped at the foot of a taverna wall. Quick, amber-coloured ants scurried across the dry ground close to where his hand lay.

Sildemund sat with Gully upon a cracked wooden bench in the shade of an arbour of vines. They had had a long and exhausting day, and were resting, taking cool mint tea at the taverna which was situated in a tiny square set away from Dharsoul's busy, dusty market streets. Sildemund was growing despondent. His efforts to discover something of the provenance and value of the mysterious red stone had so far been fruitless.

Gully nursed a sore hand. He too looked down at Picadus, who was blind drunk and who sported ugly swellings and contusions about his mouth and nose and one cheek.

Earlier Picadus had forced a fight with some foreigners in another bar. Gully had had no choice but to step in to extricate him, for it was plain that Pic was up for a brutal beating. Gully and Sil had managed to calm the fray and remove Picadus – but Gully had been obliged to throw several effective punches before his point was taken.

He shook his head. 'I have never known him like this.'

'Is it a sweetheart, Gully? Has he left someone behind at Volm, someone he wished to be with, whom we know nothing of? Or has he perhaps been betrayed in love? Is that it, do you think?'

'If either of those things were so I would know. Pic and I have been friends for many years. We have few secrets. That is not the cause of his misery.'

'Then I feel that his mind is diseased.' Sildemund's brow puckered. He waved away a wasp that had settled on the rim of his tea bowl. 'One other thing has struck me. Gully, might he have fallen under a spell? The hill-ghosts we saw the other day . . . could they have influenced his mind?'

'That thought occurred to me, but I recall that Pic was brooding afore ever we encountered the hill-ghosts. Remember when we left the caravanserai, Pic took no breakfast. And later at the inn, again he hardly ate, and drank little too. And besides, we did not come close to the hill-ghosts.'

'But we heard their song.'

'Yes, *we*. Neither you nor I are affected.'

'Who is to say that Pic does not have a greater susceptibility?'

Gully shrugged. 'It is one possibility, aye. But my feeling is that it's the wrong one.'

Sildemund was silent for a while. Another notion had begun to form in his mind as he recalled the conversation between Meglan and his father before he left Volm. Meglan believed the stone could adversely affect people; Master Frano had not been wholly convincing in his efforts to deny the possibility. Sildemund wrestled with his feelings. On the one hand he wished to express the thought to Gully, but he recalled his father's caveat that he should make no mention of the stone to his companions. Troubled, he maintained loyalty to Master Frano and kept the thought to himself, saying, 'What can we do? In this condition he is useless to us.'

Gully gave a mirthless grin. 'Worse than useless, he is a hindrance. When we were under attack on the plains he scarcely lifted a finger. He was in a dream. And now, drinking to his cups and brawling. . . . This is not Picadus.'

They called for more tea. The evening was drawing down. Sildemund felt the weight of responsibility settling heavily upon him. This was his expedition. He was in charge, entrusted by his father. But things were not going well.

It had begun auspiciously enough with their entrance into the city the previous day. At the head of a company of Dyarchim's elite knights, riding beside the crown prince of Dyarchim himself, Sildemund could not have hoped for a more encouraging beginning. He was exhilarated, heady, filled with a sense that he himself must be dreaming, but knowing that he was not.

He had stared at the city as they approached. The high red walls, built of imported stone, contrasted spectacularly with the yellowish earth of the region. As they drew close to the city gate a fanfare had blared. Sildemund had watched as soldiers ran from the gatehouse to clear the milling crowds. A guard of honour formed, lining both sides of the street as the prince's company cantered in. The soldiers stood at stiff attention, lamellar tunics gleaming in the sun.

The people of Dharsoul gave voice to loud cheers, waving as their prince rode by, or standing and watching in awe. Prince Enlos had smiled, lifting his hand from time to time in acknowledgement. He did not slacken his pace. The troop rode on, clattering up the wide way that led away from the central markets and commercial areas.

There was a minor incident at this point. A woman, clad in tattered garments of red and brown, broke suddenly from the crowd and rushed towards Prince Enlos. Her arms were raised and she was shouting something, though her words were not easily made out.

Soldiers were upon her on the instant. They dragged her back to the roadside. Enlos had been obliged to swerve his horse slightly, but was otherwise unaffected.

The woman was without a weapon, and plainly had no intention of seriously harming the prince. Sildemund stared at her, wondering what it was all about. She was still yelling, hands high, even as she was dragged back. He caught some of her words: 'You have not listened! Even to your own! — must not be allowed to perish!'

What was it that must not be allowed to perish? The word was unfamiliar and unclear, but he thought it might have been 'Claine'.

Sildemund recalled the exchange earlier in the day between Prince Enlos and Gully. Mention had been made of the Revenants of Claine, but the Prince had cut the conversation short. Sildemund's thoughts went to unknown Garsh, located somewhere in the wilds of Tomia. He had heard only the vaguest tales concerning the strange religious sect based there.

And then the incident was forgotten. The prince's company cantered on, the woman disappeared from sight, the crowd cheered the louder. The troop veered, and passed beneath a colossal stone arch. They entered the royal mall, red-paved, dividing wide, formal gardens, and flanked by lolling palms and a blaze of flowering shrubs. The mall led up a long, even slope to the massive barbican and gates of Dyarchim Palace, the home of the royal family. More fanfares rang out from atop the mighty, crenellated walls. Tall, iron-clad gates, set at the head of a fortified ramp, swung open.

Sildemund glanced questioningly across at Gully. Ought not they to be taking their leave of the royal party now? Within moments they would be within the palace walls. Surely Prince Enlos would give some signal, indicating his wish for them to go their own way? But Gully just smiled, keeping pace with Prince Enlos, and Prince Enlos looked askance at a Sildemund and called, 'Join me, please. Bathe and refresh yourselves, then we will enjoy a modest collation.'

Sildemund gazed up at the soaring red walls and the magnificent towers, turrets, cupolas and domes of the palace rearing behind them. The company rode up the ramp, through the barbican gate, along an enclosed causeway which took them through a fortified inner gate, and entered the first court.

Prince Enlos led them to the foot of a short flight of steps at one side of the court, where he dismounted, signalling for Sildemund and his companions to do likewise. Grooms came at the run to lead their horses away. The company of Dyarch knights rode on for barracks and stables.

Prince Enlos sprang nimbly up the steps and led the three across an ornamental garden to enter the main wing of the palace itself. He talked with Gully as they went. Sildemund stared in wonder at the splendour into which he had entered: high, twisting marble columns, ornately carved pillars and sweeping staircases; fabulous statues, opulent furnishings and ornaments; vibrant frescoes and mosaics, rich tapestries and drapes; dazzling windows in every shade of stained glass; high, vaulted, decorated ceilings. Elite Guards were stationed at doors and in corridors, equally impressive in glistening armour, colourful silk capes and masks. It was a feast for his eyes, a drug for his mind, for he had never seen its like.

Behind him Picadus's eyes were downcast, finding nothing to attract his interest.

Prince Enlos came to a halt outside an arched door of oak planks and wrought-iron straps. 'Here are my apartments. Refresh yourselves, then return here and we will eat and drink together. Have you made arrangements in the city? Where do you stay?'

'We have made no arrangements as yet, my lord,' replied Sildemund. 'We will be seeking a modest hostelry somewhere close to the commercial quarter.'

'Excellent! You shall stay here, in the guests' wing. You will be my honoured guests.' Prince Enlos beckoned a steward. 'This fellow will take you to your rooms. Wash, bathe, as you see fit, and I shall see you here anon.'

They were taken to a set of communal chambers elsewhere in the palace, set on the third level, overlooking a pleasant courtyard. Again, Sildemund was taken aback by the sheer opulence. Magnificent paintings were mounted upon the walls, the pantiled floor was carpeted in the richest rugs. The ornaments were of precious metal or finest glaze, encrusted with fabulous stones. He stepped out onto a wide balcony. The city of Dharsoul lay revealed before him.

The focal point of the city was the waterfront. The numerous quays jutted out into the mighty Tigrant, which glistened, dark and reflective, a hundred small boats and barges studding its slow, shiny surface. From the quaysides the labyrinth of twisting, angling streets that were the souk and commercial area stretched chaotically back. Some were dark shadowy slots, others, touched by the sun, were bright, their colourful awnings visible even from this distance. The city covered four low hills, upon one of which sat the palace. It was built mainly of red or whitewashed stone, though many of the roofs and domes had been painted in other bright hues.

'You are a well-connected man, Gully,' said Sildemund as Gully came out to stand beside him. 'And a man of secrets! I had no idea, nor I believe has my father, that you have such intimate acquaintance with the Prince. Why have you never said?'

Gully's eyes took in the magnificent vista. 'The occasion never arose. It is years since I have seen Prince Enlos. Had not fortune thrown us together today we would probably have passed our lives without ever meeting again.'

Sildemund was curious. 'What were the circumstances behind the rebellion, Gully? Was there not some supposedly shameful incident involving the Queen?'

Gully lowered his voice. 'No one knows. There were many scurrilous tales, too many to relate, and probably none factual.

79

Certain members of the nobility tried to despoil the Queen's name, claiming some improper conduct on her part. But I know nothing of it. Whatever it was, it is long in the past. And this is seditious talk! Come, let us make ready.'

They bathed in a sunken marble tub large enough to contain a dozen bodies at the same time. The water was scented with linden and orange blossom and they were attended by palace maidens with perfumed soaps and oils. When they came to dress again they found that their travel-stained clothes had been removed and new garments set in their place: light gowns of finest white cotton, baggy pantaloons and soft slippers. A steward arrived to escort them to the Prince's chambers. Picadus, who had found the energy to bathe himself, had curled up naked upon his bed and now refused to budge.

'You cannot spurn the Prince of Dyarchim!' protested Gully indignantly. 'We are his guests! It is the grossest insult! What is the matter with you?'

'I am weary. I wish to rest.' Picadus turned his face to the pillow and would speak no more.

Sildemund took Gully's arm. 'We must make excuses for him, explain that he is unwell. It is perhaps best this way. As he is, he would make incongruous company.'

Disgruntled, Gully could only concede.

Prince Enlos had changed into a long robe of deepest blue, bordered in regal gold, with flared, scalloped sleeves. His dark hair was combed and plaited, and he looked fresh and invigorated. He expressed regret upon learning of Picadus's condition, which Sildemund described in terms of a physical sickness. 'I noticed as we rode that he seemed a lugubrious fellow. Plainly, if that is not his normal posture, he has been struck down by some gloomy affliction. Shall I have my physician attend him? He is a miracle-worker, an expert in ailments of body, mind and spirit.'

'You are most kind, my lord,' Sildemund replied, 'but we believe that, at least for the present, Pic's most pressing requirement is rest. Perhaps if he is fevered in the morning we might take advantage of your generous offer.'

'By all means. But at least let me have a servant deliver food and drink to him. That way, should he wake and discover an unexpected gnawing in his belly, he will find himself well catered for and have no cause to accuse me of niggardliness! Now, come, be seated. Take wine, eat your fill, and let us talk.'

They ate, aromatic spicy lamb on a bed of semolina, served with side dishes of yoghurt and cucumber, marinated chickpea sauce sprinkled with wild parsley, flaked herb potatoes, olives, diced scallion and a crisp green salad. Then came juicy pink charcoaled prawns, squid in yellow bean sauce, oysters stewed in golden ale, crayfish with rose sauce and almond milk, and fragrant steaming rice. Tangy iced sherbets followed, and fresh dates stuffed with soft cheese, then figs, pomegranates and oranges. All was served with a variety of elegant and distinguished wines.

Gully and Prince Enlos regaled one another with recollections of past adventures as they ate. The wine flowed abundantly and the tales took on legendary dimensions. A fine storyteller, Enlos later revealed himself to be an accomplished lutenist. When they had done eating he took up his instrument and they joined him in stirring ballads and poignant laments, then bawdier songs of camp and tavern. The evening progressed and Sildemund, who had planned to spend the hours in the pursuit of his father's business, quite forgot about the red stone and Kemorlin and the other people Master Frano had commissioned him to seek out.

Then, abruptly, Prince Enlos brought the merriment to an end.

He put aside his lute and stood, clapping his hands together. 'My friends, this has been a rare and thoroughly enjoyable evening, but regrettably I have other duties. Join me tomorrow evening, if you will. If it is at all possible I shall introduce you to my mother, the Queen. But for now, I must bid you good night.'

Sildemund blinked uncomprehendingly, his senses befuddled by too many intoxicants. Prince Enlos seemed to have dispatched his gaiety like throwing off a cloak, as though it had been an act, as though the food, the wine, the companionship had had no real effect. He was perfectly polite now, but formal and precise.

A servant appeared to escort them from the Prince's apartments. Groggily, Sildemund and Gully rose and took their leave. Sildemund's head was spinning. He was flushed with wine, and moreover was still trying to convince himself that his ears were not deceiving him. Had Prince Enlos truly said what he believed him to have said? That he, Sildemund, was to meet Lermeone? Lermeone, Dyarchim's revered Silent Queen! She who had ruled Dyarchim for thirty years! The firm, benign sovereign who by sacred decree might never publicly utter a word, whose sage thoughts and intentions were revealed via mystical connection and divine interpretation! Could it be so? Was he truly to stand in the same hallowed space as she?

They made their way back to their chambers. In a corridor they passed a young man accompanied by three armed guards. He was well attired in an elegant green robe and floppy, crushed velvet, brimless hat. He was heading in the general direction of Prince Enlos's apartments, though whether that was his destination it was impossible to divine.

As they passed, the man halted briefly to give a courteous bow of his head. It would strike Sildemund later, when his mind was less befuddled, that there was a tenseness in the soldiers' faces, and that their hands hovered nervously about the pommels of their short sabres as the stranger stopped.

The stranger was of no great stature, but bore himself with dignity and élan. His glance, as they passed, was keen and penetrating; his gesture, though understated, carried a flourish. There was a slight smile on his lips. Sildemund was struck by his appearance. His eyes were deep green, his hair light brown. His skin was quite pale and he sported a finely trimmed beard and moustache. He was certainly not Dyarch, and Sildemund guessed him to hail from the north. Sildemund marked him down as a personage of some authority, yet curiously, while the stranger was accorded respect by his escort, it seemed to Sildemund that he was in fact under guard.

They passed on. In their apartment they found Picadus asleep. Food lay untouched on a silver platter upon a table close to his bed. The hour was too late for Sildemund to engage constructively in any business in the city, and he was in no fit state to do so anyway. He promised himself an early start as he undressed, then fell upon his own bed and knew nothing more until morning.

9

SILDEMUND AWOKE WITH a dull pain in his temples and a
squeasiness in his gut. But mindful of his promise to himself the
previous night, he set to in earnest to complete his father's
commission. With Gully and the gloomy Picadus he departed the
palace and set off for the souk and commercial district. There he
would seek out Kemorlin, in the hope that he could inform him
as to the value and provenance of the red stone.

The souk was a teeming, throbbing hive, a maze of noisy
streets and smelly, shadowed alleys, interspersed with small
crowded squares. Everywhere were shops, booths, stalls.
Vendors stood beneath gaudy awnings, surrounded by their
wares, striving to outdo one another with loud proclamations of
the quality, beauty and cheapness of the myriad goods on sale.
Beggars, sharps, whores and entertainers vied for business; old
men squatted in shaded alcoves, smoking shugweed through
ornate water-bowls and staring with vacant smiles into a world
that had no true existence, yet which was infinitely more
comforting than that in which they had passed their lives.

On two occasions Sildemund spotted women garbed in the red
and brown tatters of the woman who had dashed out in front of
Prince Enlos's horse the previous day. Their rags, it appeared,
were a uniform of sorts, identifying them – so he believed – as
members of the Revenants of Claine. The second of these women
was addressing a small crowd of curious onlookers, and
Sildemund paused briefly to listen. The woman shouted in
earnest, something about 'forgotten words of the ancestor' and
'protecting she who protects', then emotive pleas for clemency
and intervention in Garsh. It was hard to make out much, so
busy and crowded was the street, and she was being mercilessly
heckled by her audience. Someone threw a rotten persimmon,

which struck her on the breast, spilling its seeds and flesh.

Sildemund was uncomfortable. He was being jostled, forced to move one way then the other. He gave up and moved on.

He asked at shops and taverns for the whereabouts of Kemorlin, whom he described in the way his father had described him, as a man knowledgeable in rare stones, gems and ancient artifacts. At first he gained only blank looks and shakes of heads. Then a woman in the doorway of a cloth store nodded in recognition. She pointed to an alley, scarcely more than a crack between buildings, where a stony way twisted steeply upward. She shouted something about 'the square of the Martyrs.'

The three entered the alley and climbed. They came to a shadowy passage above which ragged blankets were strung to form a canopy. Rickety walkways had been constructed, linking the buildings on each side. Water seeped between mouldering stones, a filthy brown colour, and a rank stench tainted the motionless air. They followed the passage, bending to avoid the canopies, stepping over drunks in doorways, avoiding crowds of children who appeared shrieking from nowhere and ran past them, endeavouring to relieve them of their purses.

Presently they broke out into bright sunshine on another teeming market street. Sildemund enquired again, was directed up the street. They pushed through the crowds and came to an intersection of six ways. A small crowd had gathered around a fellow garbed in white, wearing the badge of the Mabbuchai, the famed orator-poets of Dyarchim. The man's lips moved intermittently, though Sildemund could hear no sound. Sildemund looked about him for indications of where the six ways might lead, but there were no signs.

'This is hopeless,' he exclaimed crossly, wiping sweat from his brow. 'We are lost and getting nowhere.'

They took refuge between the columns of a massive portico, and Gully beckoned to a half-naked boy standing nearby. He spoke to him briefly, then turned back to Sildemund. 'He will be our guide, for a few coins.'

'Gladly.' Sildemund addressed the boy. 'Do you know the home of Kemorlin? Can you take us there?'

The boy nodded and held out his hand.

'When we get there you will be paid,' said Sildemund. The boy set off into the maze of side streets.

In due course he brought them to a large, walled villa set in a secluded area just off the main thoroughfares of the souk. The villa had been painted in shades of pale orange. Bright bougainvillea tumbled over the walls, and oleander and other flowering shrubs brightened a gravel courtyard where water played from a fountain. A dog, pink and hairless, was stretched before the villa's scrolled iron gate, its hide scabbed and ribs almost bare.

'Is this Kemorlin's home?' Sildemund asked.

The boy nodded vigorously, and grinned, holding out his hand. Sildemund paid him and he ran off.

There was a bell-pull set into a recess on a pillar beside the gate. Sildemund gave it two good tugs and heard a distant tinkle from somewhere inside. A few moments passed and an elderly woman appeared in a doorway on the far side of the courtyard. She was big, grey-haired and brown-skinned, swathed in black. Dark, lumpy veins were prominent around her ankles. Her gait was slewed, as though to walk caused her pain. She halted at the head of a short flight of orange stone steps and called shrilly, 'What is it?'

'I seek Master Kemorlin.'

The woman half-raised a bulky hand and made a tired, dismissive motion. 'He is not here.'

She turned as if to walk away.

'When will he be here? It is important that I speak to him.'

'Kemorlin? Who knows? Later, perhaps, or tomorrow. Kemorlin is Kemorlin. He comes, he goes.'

'Can I make an appointment to see him?'

'Only Kemorlin makes appointments to see Kemorlin.'

'That's a lot of help,' Sildemund muttered, aside. 'How do you make an appointment with a man who is not available to make the appointment with?' He tried again. 'Can I call back?'

The woman might have shrugged, but her shoulders seemed too heavy to lift. 'If you wish.'

'I will return after midday. Please tell Master Kemorlin that I called – Sildemund Atturio, of Volm. I seek his advice on a rare item. I will pay. Please tell him that.'

The old woman nodded. 'As you will.' She hauled herself back into the house.

Sildemund gave a sigh. 'Well, I have other names: tradesmen in the souk, a learned professor at the university. Let us try them before returning here.'

They made their way back to the souk. Gully found another fellow eager to act as guide. Indeed, there was no dearth of them. A substratum of the community survived, it appeared, by guiding foreigners through the city's chaotic muddle.

At Sildemund's request their new guide, a painfully thin youth with a filthy eyepatch, took them first to the premises of a lapidary in the souk. Sildemund went in, leaving Gully and Picadus to await him on the street. He had not revealed to them the nature of his business and, always mindful of his father's words, had kept the red stone from their sight.

The lapidary was fascinated. He spent long minutes examining the stone, only to profess himself clueless. The few hints he was able to provide matched approximately the information given to Master Frano by the Volm lapidary, Jerg Lancor – though Sildemund knew nothing of this. In regard to provenance or value the fellow could not begin to guess, and Sildemund stepped back into the busy street with a feeling of disappointment.

He had one other name, which he thought to try before returning to Kemorlin's villa. The name was known to their guide, and he led them without hesitation through an impossible labyrinth of grim alleys and covered ways, thrusting aside beggars and urchins who approached asking for alms, to burst out eventually upon a long flight of crooked steps where the shop Sildemund sought was located.

Here Sildemund had an odd and unsettling experience.

He entered the shop, a cramped chamber, dusty and dry, piled high with stones, crystals, vases, pots, vials, talismans, amulets, effectuaries and other paraphernalia. The man he had come to see was named Zakobar. He sat in one corner on a stool behind a wooden counter. He was thin, small of frame, old – perhaps ninety years – garbed in a long green gown. His hair was wispy white, falling to his shoulders. He had a narrow, slight-boned face with a long, uneven nose. Nearby another man, younger by some forty years, worked attentively with a file, shaping a piece of marble in a vice. His face and build bore some resemblance to Zakobar's, and Sildemund took him to be his son.

Zakobar was busy with a tall, twin-handled glazed vessel which rested before him upon the counter. He was glueing a broken chip onto the vessel's rim. He glanced up briefly as Sildemund approached, but maintained his concentration on his work.

'Young man, there is something I can help you with? You wish to buy a gift for your sweetheart? I have precious stones and rare jewels, guaranteed to charm the heart of any girl. Or a talisman, perhaps, to ward off banes cast by jealous lovers.'

'Neither, sir. I have come from my father, Master Frano of Volm, to seek your advice.' Sildemund pulled the red stone in its cloth binding from his satchel. He placed it upon the counter and unbound the cloth. 'Can you tell me anything of this?'

Zakobar glanced at it, then glanced again. He ceased his work with the chipped vessel and leaned forward to stare intensely at the strange red stone.

'Where did you get this?'

Sildemund found himself staring down at the crown of the old man's head, with its sparse white hair and pink scalp, flaked with yellowing skin.

'My father brought it back . . . from a trading expedition to Ghence.' For reasons he was not entirely clear of Sildemund did not wish to reveal the truth of how the stone had been acquired.

Zakobar's thin mottled hands were exploring the smooth surface of the stone. 'Extraordinary. . . . ' His voice was faraway, as though he spoke only to himself. 'What a strange thing . . . .'

Quite suddenly Zakobar's hands ceased their motion. He bent his torso forward across the counter, stiffly, supporting his weight upon his elbows. His arms and thin shoulders trembled. He thrust himself back, groping for his stool. Sildemund stared in shock. Zakobar's face had turned blue. His eyes bulged in their sockets. He breathed in laboured gasps.

His knees buckled and he fell with a crash to the floor, knocking over the stool.

The younger man rushed across. 'Father!'

An elderly woman appeared from a back room, drawn by the noise of the falling stool. When she saw Zakobar her hands flew to her mouth and she gave a strangled shriek.

'Fetch the doctor!' the younger man commanded. The woman rushed from the shop with cries of distress. The man found a cushion which he placed beneath his father's head. Zakobar lay motionless, his eyes staring at the ceiling. His son looked up at Sildemund. 'Sir, do you know anything of medicine?'

Sildemund shook his head.

'Then I am sorry, I must ask you to leave. You understand . . . .'

'Of course.' Sildemund quickly bound the stone and stuffed it back into his satchel. He was ushered to the door, which was closed and barred behind him as he stepped out into the street and rejoined his two companions.

Unnerved, Sildemund instructed their guide to take them back to the house of Kemorlin, for although they had left it only recently they would never have found it again without assistance. The villa was as before, only the hairless dog had departed its sleepy station before the gate. Again the old woman brought herself out to the head of the steps.

'He has gone,' she replied flatly to Sildemund's enquiry.

'Kemorlin? Do you mean he has been here in our absence?'

'Briefly, yes.'

'And where has he gone now?'

Again the shrug, which came more from a movement of her head than her shoulders. 'He does not tell me.'

'Do you know when he will be back?'

'Sometime.'

'Did you tell Kemorlin that I called earlier?'

'Yes.'

'Did he say anything?'

'Yes.'

'What? What did he say?'

'Mm.'

'Pardon?'

'Mm, Kemorlin said "Mm".'

Gully spoke quietly into Sildemund's ear, 'I think she derives amusement from this.'

For the first time Sildemund was aware of the wry twinkle in the old woman's eye, though her face remained otherwise expressionless. 'And he made no suggestion of an appointment?'

She shook her head.

'What should I do, then, if I wish to see him? It is important.'

'Wait. Come back.'

'Do you have any idea how long I might have to wait?'

'None.'

'Thank you,' Sildemund turned away. He spoke to the other two. 'We will go to the university, if our guide can take us there.'

'I have had enough of this!' said Picadus suddenly. 'Traipse here, trudge there! For what? We are getting nowhere!'

'You don't have to come, Pic,' Sildemund replied in an even voice. 'You may return to our apartments in the palace, or remain in a tavern in the town, or do whatever you wish. I release you from any bond, for you are obviously not happy accompanying me. For my part, I am engaged upon my father's work, and I will go now to the university in the hope of furthering it.'

Picadus clenched his jowls, smouldering, but said, 'I will come.'

The university was on the other side of the city, a journey which took almost an hour.

They entered a wide, vaulted reception chamber in which half a dozen scribes and clerks sat at desks set between mighty stone columns, heads bent over ledgers and registers, quills scratching diligently. None acknowledged the arrival of the three. Sildemund approached the nearest, grateful for the cool air of the chamber, and waited politely.

A minute passed. The clerk gave no indication of being aware of Sildemund's presence. Sildemund cleared his throat. Then again. The clerk's quill came to rest. He looked up, twisting his head and squinting, one eyebrow raised. His back and neck remained bent over his work. 'What is it?'

'I seek—' began Sildemund.

'Wait over there,' said the clerk, with a darting gesture at a bench set against the opposite wall. He returned to his work.

Sildemund and his two companions crossed obediently to the bench and sat down and waited.

And waited.

After what seemed like an age a new fellow entered the chamber through a door in the eastern wall. He carried a pile of thick black ledgers stacked to his chin. These he distributed to the workers at the desks.

He was about to leave when the last clerk, the one Sildemund had spoken to, signalled to him and whispered something in his ear. The two looked across the chamber at the three. The new man straightened and approached Sildemund, Gully and Picadus. He appraised them down a thin, crooked nose, his small hands clasped over his abdomen.

'You wish something?'

Sildemund stood. The man took a small step backwards. 'I would like to speak to one of your learned professors, Ractoban by name I believe, whose expertise lies in Lore and Arcane Science.'

'Professor Ractoban is unavailable.'

Sildemund passed a hand across his brow. 'Is it possible to make an appointment?'

'In what connection?'

'I am Sildemund, son of Master Frano Atturio of Volm. My father seeks the professor's advice on an object that has come into his possession.'

'Your name means nothing to me. The professor is a busy man.'

'I realize that. Nevertheless I would consider it a great honour and a boon if he would deign to allow me a brief audience. I will, of course, offer suitable remuneration.'

The clerk turned upon his heel and walked straight-backed to the desk of the scribe. He opened a drawer and took out a large, leather-bound book. He returned to Sildemund, studying the open pages of the book.

'The earliest I can fit you in is in the afternoon of the fourth day of next month. The hour of terce.'

'Next month! But I am only here for two days.'

The clerk gave an emotionless smile. 'Then I'm afraid I am unable to be of assistance. Good day.'

His book made a dull slap as it was closed. He turned and was gone, returning the book to the desk then marching stiffly from the chamber via the door through which he had entered. Sildemund stood where he was, lost for words.

Gully rose from the bench and moved up to his shoulder. 'Come, Sil, it is well past midday and my belly rumbles, as does yours. Let us eat somewhere and ponder our difficulties.'

They left the university and paid off their guide, confident that they could hire another as and when the need arose. Taking a carriage they made their way back to the centre of the city and there repaired to a taverna. They had not eaten since breakfast, and the sun was now well advanced in the afternoon sky. So they dined well and for a while took their minds off their frustrations with a flagon of strong, dark ale.

Now it was that Picadus chose to make trouble. He had eaten little, but drunk more than the other two put together. Raising the ale flagon to refill his mug, he discovered it empty. Without a word he rose, flagon in hand, and made for the bar.

The taverna was enjoying good trade. A couple of tables, which lay between Picadus and the bar, were attended by clientele from Dyarchim and elsewhere. Picadus chose to ignore the fact that the tables created an obstacle in his course. Rather than make his way around them he simply stepped up, first onto one, then down to the floor again, then up onto the next.

The customers at the tables gaped, too dumbfounded to respond upon the instant. Picadus lurched on obliviously to the bar.

Conversation at the bar was boisterous. Many of the customers were foreigners. A group of three, who Sildemund later discovered to be Khimmurians in the employ of a travelling merchant, stood directly in Picadus's path. Picadus barged into them, spilling their drinks, elbowing them rudely aside. He raised his flagon and hailed the serving wench.

The Khimmurians took exception. One grabbed Picadus by the shoulder, jerking him around, and demanded to know what he thought he was doing. Picadus gave him a blank stare, then shoved him hard in the chest. The Khimmurian stumbled backwards and fell over one of the tables.

His two companions launched themselves upon Picadus. He struggled like a man possessed, dropping his flagon and lashing out with both fists.

Both Gully and Sildemund rose, knowing they had little choice but to intervene. But Gully pushed Sildemund forcefully back into his seat, then leapt across the room. He grabbed one of the Khimmurians and threw him aside, crying out, 'Stop! He means no harm! I will take him away!'

The Khimmurian whom Picadus had knocked across the table was back on his feet, charging with fury into the fray. Gully tried to wrestle him to the floor. A second man leapt on Gully's back. Gully threw him, but by now the taverna was in uproar. Strong as he was, Gully found himself forced to use his fists. Two or three men felt the force of his blows before a space cleared around him.

Gully grabbed Picadus by the scruff of the neck, red-faced and panting with exertion. He roared out, 'He is sick! He means no harm! Let him be! I will take him out!'

It might have made no difference, but the landlord was on the scene now, with three or four burly henchmen hefting cudgels.

'Good landlord. I apologize for my friend,' breathed Gully. 'He is feverish and cannot control himself.'

The landlord, bulky and not a happy-looking man, eyed the two of them, 'And what of the damage? Look – a broken table, cracked mugs!'

'I will pay for the damage!' It was Sildemund. He held out his purse, tipped coins into his hand and thrust them at the landlord. 'Will this suffice?'

The landlord eyed the money and nodded. 'Now begone.'

Sildemund spoke to the three Khimmurians. 'Here, we are not hooligans. I offer you apology on my friend's behalf. Please, take this to pay for the drinks that were spilt.'

He tossed them coins, then he and Gully hauled Picadus out, for he was too drunk or dazed to walk without support. They half-carried him down a couple of alleys to a square where they laid him to rest outside another taverna, took up places on a bench and ordered mint tea.

Gully gazed up at the sky, where the sun had shed something of its fierce white haze and was sinking lazily towards the horizon. For a long time they remained immersed in their thoughts, neither speaking. Eventually Gully said, 'We should return to the palace to greet Prince Enlos, and who knows, perhaps gain an audience with the Queen.'

Sildemund gave a doleful nod, a welter of troubled thoughts in his brain. He wondered again whether to make mention of the stone. He felt he owed it to Gully to do so, and he would have welcomed his opinion.

'Gully . . .' he began.

'Aye?'

Sildemund was reminded again of his father's last words to him. He shook his head. 'It is nothing. You are right, we should leave.'

Gully rose and stretched. He took the earthenware jug which

had contained their tea and emptied its slops onto the ground. He strolled to the middle of the little square, where there was a fountain. He swilled the jug, then filled it with cold water.

Returning, he tipped the lot over Picadus's head.

Picadus came to with splutters and curses.

'Come, lout. We are leaving,' Gully growled.

Exiting the square Sildemund thought to note a familiar street. 'Gully, if I am not mistaken this place is but a stone's throw from the home of Kemorlin. I will try one more time. Will you join me?'

He led them along a narrow side alley and in short order found himself to his satisfaction outside the orange-shaded villa. The hairless dog had returned to its lethargy before the iron gate. Sildemund rang the bell, but no one answered. He tried again, and again, but there was no response. Eventually he gave up.

A few minutes later, as they made their way out of the souk in the direction of the royal palace, they found themselves by sheer chance passing the crooked steps where Zakobar's shop was located. Sildemund quickly darted up the steps, thinking to enquire after the old man's health.

The shop was closed. Sildemund swallowed. The door and window had been festooned with the heads of dried sunflowers. This was a sign of mourning in Dyarchim. Death had visited the house of old Zakobar.

10

PRINCE ENLOS RECEIVED them again in his chambers in the early evening. Picadus did not attend, as previously. Upon returning to the palace, mumbling and moaning, barely able to walk, he had collapsed onto his bed and fallen into a deep slumber from which they made no attempt to rouse him.

'You really ought to have him looked at by Doctor Artolo, my physician,' said the Prince. 'Your friend's gloom seems profound, and Artolo is accustomed to dealing with the spiritually stricken as with those smitten by bodily disease or injury.'

Sildemund felt deeply ashamed. He wondered whether Prince Enlos knew anything of the brawl that afternoon. Upon reflection it seemed unlikely, and he saw no gain in raising the subject. But if Doctor Artolo were to visit Picadus he could not help but notice the bruises and cuts, and would surmise something of their cause. Within Sildemund there was conflict, feeling that his – albeit unwitting – activities might cause embarassment to his royal host. 'You have done so much already, sire. Picadus is simply under a mild fever, I am sure, and will quickly recover. You have been more than generous, and I am greatly in your debt, but I would not wish to impose upon you further. I thank you sincerely for everything. Tomorrow we will remove ourselves from the Palace and take up lodging in the city for the duration of our stay.'

Prince Enlos dismissed the sentiment with a flutter of the hand. 'Nonsense, I will hear nothing of it. You are my guests, and every convenience of my house is yours. And, with your permission, Artolo will attend your friend this evening.'

Sildemund could not refuse. He bowed his head. 'Thank you, sire.'

Enlos spoke in an undertone to a servant, then gestured towards the dining table. 'Now, come, eat, and tell me of your day.'

Another fine meal had been set upon the table, though tonight the wine was less in evidence. 'You shall attend a brief audience with my mother,' Prince Enlos revealed, in explanation. 'Her Presence will be announced in due course, when we have dined. She is anxious to meet you – though I have not revealed to her your precise identities.'

Sildemund gawped at him open-mouthed. *She*, the Queen, was anxious to meet *them*? It was a politeness, of course. Yet the fact that Enlos had even bothered to say it, let alone actually arrange the audience, was a gesture of highest courtesy.

They ate, and Enlos enquired again as to the events of their day and the progress of Sildemund's business. Sildemund was reluctant to complain, yet his spirits were not high after the day's disappointments and he had no taste for pretence. 'Alas, I am not making the progress I had hoped, sire. The persons I had wished to see here in Dharsoul are elusive, to say the least. One seems never to be at home, and his staff lacks any facility for arranging an appointment; another will not see me for a month, by which time I shall be long gone; and a third was taken ill and died as I was about to speak with him.'

Prince Enlos arched an eyebrow. 'That is unfortunate, and how disheartening.' He chewed thoughtfully on a mouthful of spiced capon. 'Perhaps I can be of assistance. I am the Crown Prince, after all, my influence is not inconsiderable. Who are these persons you seek?'

Sildemund repeated the three names.

'In the latter case, of course, even I can do little,' said Enlos. 'My powers do not extend to raising the dead, and I assume you have no desire to discourse with a corpse. Most tragic, though. And unhappy timing as far as your concerns are affected. But these other two scoundrels, Kemorlin and Ractoban . . . they are known to me.'

He raised his hands and clapped twice. A steward stepped forward. Prince Enlos spoke briefly into his ear and the man withdrew.

'They will be with us before our meal is done,' said the Prince.

Sildemund stammered his thanks.

They talked on, about this and that, though the tone was more subdued than the previous evening. Sildemund's and Gully's thoughts were on their imminent audience with Queen Lermeone, and Prince Enlos seemed a touch preoccupied and less given to spontaneity.

In due course a footman entered and spoke in an undertone to the Prince.

'Show him in immediately!' commanded Enlos. 'And when the other blackguard arrives, show him in too.'

A bald, dumpy man, about fifty years of age, entered, glancing hesitantly from side to side. He wore a russet-coloured surplice embroidered in gold and green, over baggy green pantaloons. A wide red cincture bound his ample waist. His face was plump and round, with flaccid rubicund cheeks, small eyes beneath pale brows, and a small, thin mouth. His eyes darted quickly over the occupants of the room before coming to rest upon Prince Enlos. He took three short steps forward and dropped to one knee.

'My Prince! I am humble before you.'

'And scornful behind!' muttered Enlos. 'Up, Professor Ractoban, and be done with your fulsome scraping.'

The man rose. 'Sire, I have been summoned into your revered presence without prior notice. In order that I might be of service to you I flew here as swiftly as was possible within the bounds of human endeavour. But I know not the reason why I am called. I trust I have not displeased you in any way?'

'Who knows what you've been up to, Ractoban? No doubt much would displease me were I to be made aware of it. But beware, for while there are certain things I may not know, there are many more that I do. And you cannot be sure which are which. My loyal agents penetrate every den, every lair, every seething centre of "learning". Be assured that they bring to my ears notice of all those who might preach subversion or unrest.'

'Subversion! Unrest!' spluttered Ractoban. 'My Prince, if you have received reports linking myself with any such activities, I can assure you that they are false! Most manifestly and utterly false! I am your most loyal servant, sire, as you must surely know. And the devoted servant of your revered and beneficent mother, also.'

He licked his lips with a quick pink tongue, and his eyes flickered uneasily over Sildemund and Gully. Plainly he wondered as to their identities.

'You are an educator, Ractoban. That is a position of great

responsibility. Remember that.' Enlos stood with his hands upon his hips, his feet firmly apart. His expression was grave, yet his blue eyes held a glimmer of sardonic humour.

'Be assured that I do, sire. At all times the weight of my responsibility rests uppermost in my thoughts.'

'Good. Now, I have called you here for assistance.'

Ractoban brightened, linking his fingers before his portly belly. 'It is always a pleasure and a privilege to serve you, sire. I am yours to command. How might I be of service now?'

'My good friends here tell me that they applied to you today at that nest of perfidy that you have the gall to term a university, and were informed that an audience with you could not be granted for another month.'

Ractoban threw open his hands. 'Sire, I know nothing of this! I am a busy man, as you will appreciate, but if your honoured friends had mentioned that they came at your behest my clerks would have interrupted me upon the instant. Be assured of that! I would have attended them immediately.' He turned to Sildemund and Gully. 'Good sirs, did you mention Prince Enlos's name to my assistants?'

Sildemund shook his head. 'I did not.'

'Then my sincere apologies, but we could not have known.'

'Ah well, no matter. You are here now – as are they,' said Enlos. 'The coincidence is apposite. They seek your advice.'

Ractoban made to address Gully, taking his age as indication of his senior station despite Sildemund's having responded to his previous question. But before he could speak the door opened to admit another attendant.

'Master Kemorlin, sire.'

Kemorlin strode in, an imposing figure in his late-middle years, somewhat taller than average, solidly built, with long grey hair held back from his face by a pair of jewelled clasps, one on either side of his skull. He wore an ankle-length robe of deep umber pigment, and sandals. A variety of fabulous rings adorned his fingers, and around his wrists were bracelets of precious metals fashioned with glittering gems. He entered frowning, with an air of distraction, tugging at a flowing grey beard which fell to his sternum.

Kemorlin halted three paces before the Prince and bowed. 'Sire!'

Straightening, he acknowledged Professor Ractoban with a slight nod of the head. His prominent dark brows furrowed more deeply. His gaze alighted momentarily upon Sildemund and Gully before returning to the Prince.

'Ah, Master Kemorlin, you arrive at a convenient moment,' said Prince Enlos. His voice was flat and almost brittle.

'I came as soon as I was summoned, my lord. How might I be of service?'

'My two friends, here, have spent the day endeavouring to meet with you, but found you unavailable. They seek your advice.'

Kemorlin turned to the two. 'In what capacity, good sirs?'

'I – I am not entirely certain, as I am not informed precisely as to the nature of your professional skills,' said Sildemund, a little intimidated by Kemorlin's commanding presence and penetrating gaze. 'My father, Master Frano Atturio of Volm, was advised to seek you – and Professor Ractoban – out in the hope that you might be able to provide information that has so far eluded us in regard to an unusual item that has come into his – my father's – possession.'

Prince Enlos gave a cold chuckle. 'The nature of Kemorlin's professional skills. . . ? We know his many "skills" full well, do we not? Kemorlin styles himself a master alchemist, a mystic, savant, mage, Dream-walker and a host of other titles too numerous to recall. He extorts a high price for his services, which by all accounts are not always given to success, so that some are moved to call him a charlatan and hoaxer.'

'My lord,' protested Kemorlin stiffly, 'the mysterious arts in which I have immersed myself and to which I have dedicated my entire life are unpredictable, without known limits, and beyond the ken or utility of ordinary folk. My clients are made aware, before ever they engage my services, that success cannot be guaranteed. You know this.'

'But your fees are guaranteed. Succeed or fail, you demand the same price, in advance.'

'The materials of my trade are rare and expensive; they are consumed in the endeavour, regardless of its outcome. My training has been long and hard, and many of the tasks I undertake involve no little risk to myself. I charge what I consider suitable and fair. My profit margin, I do assure you, is virtually negligible.'

'Perhaps so,' replied Enlos. 'Still, negligible though it may be, it has been sufficient to make you wealthy beyond the grasp of most men.'

Kemorlin stood proudly. 'I believe I am unique in my talents, sire. At least in Dyarchim. Folk from far and wide apply to me for my services. It takes a grand toll. I have little time for myself.'

Prince Enlos's blue eyes shone, but there was a hardness in them, and Sildemund sensed a tension between the two men. 'Yes, your devotion is legendary. More than a few wives and daughters of wealthy citizens have attested to that fact. I have heard that there are those who have turned to you seeking an end to the woes and afflictions that beset their lives, who subsequently report that your methods can take unusual turns.'

Kemorlin stroked his beard and regarded the Prince sidelong. 'I apply my wisdom where and as best I can, my lord.'

'Hmph!' Enlos seemed for a moment to struggle with himself. He turned away. 'Ah well, be so good then as to apply it here tonight. Young Master Sildemund is in need of your expertise. His gratitude, genuine and heartfelt, will be sufficient payment on this occasion, will it not?'

Kemorlin stiffened. He cleared his throat. 'If that is your wish, my lord.'

'It is.'

Kemorlin faced Sildemund. 'May I see the item you refer to?'

'I will fetch it at once,' said Sildemund. 'If you will excuse me a moment; it is in my chamber.'

He went quickly back to the apartment, a tremor of unease in his heart. He had hoped to avoid this moment: revealing the stone in the presence of Gully and Prince Enlos. Why should he feel such reservation? He trusted Gully implicitly, and the Prince could have no possible self-interest beyond simple curiosity. Indeed, Prince Enlos had demonstrated only affability and a willingness to help.

Still Sildemund felt an irrational sense of foreboding. It was something to do with the stone. It was foolish, but he could not rid himself of it. Deep within himself was the fear, as yet vague and no more than a suggestion, that the moment now impending was going to be the trigger for dire and catastrophic consequences.

He entered the apartment and located his satchel beside his bed. He looked in on Picadus, who slept soundly, his snores sundering the silence of the room. Taking the satchel with the stone bound inside it, Sildemund returned to Prince Enlos's chambers.

A heated discussion was in progress. Sildemund heard the words 'Garsh' and 'Claine' as he entered. Both Kemorlin and Professor Ractoban had their voices raised above normal. Prince Enlos stood before Kemorlin with a challenging stare, and the blood had risen to Kemorlin's swarthy cheeks. Gully stood to one side, making no contribution to the conversation.

Prince Enlos used Sildemund's reappearance to cut the discussion short. 'Ah, Sildemund! You have the item now? Good. Let us see this curiosity.'

Enlos cleared a space upon the dining table. As the others gathered round, Sildemund took his bundle from the satchel, placed it upon the table and began to unbind it. Was it his imagination, or had a discomfiting silence descended? He felt tension, a stiffening between his shoulder blades, but told himself that he was surely only unnerved by the situation he found himself in.

As the red stone was revealed he looked up guiltily at Gully. Gully stared, drawn-faced, at the stone before raising his eyes to Sildemund's. Sildemund could not meet his gaze. He felt he had betrayed his friend by not revealing to him earlier what it was that he carried.

But was it really of consequence? A welter of emotion crowded in Sildemund's mind. Why did he place such importance on this act? It was just a stone, a strange stone. Gully would not have expected to have been informed of the precise nature of Sildemund's – that is, Master Frano's – business. There was no reason, therefore, for Gully to feel in any way aggrieved. And yet . . . the fact remained that Sildemund still had no idea why his father had advised him against revealing the stone to Gully or Picadus.

Into Sildemund's thoughts came the memory of Edric, his strange behaviour upon the initial discovery of the red stone, and his mysterious death in the grotto. He had an image suddenly of the old man, Zakobar, who had died this very afternoon, directly upon setting eyes on the stone. A sudden chill gripped Sildemund's innards. He wondered again about Picadus, who seemed caught in a mounting inner rage, who slept like a man drugged in the apartment upstairs. His delinquent behaviour – it was so unlike him. All this . . . was it connected with the stone? He could hardly doubt that it was.

Sildemund met Gully's gaze and saw mild surprise there, but no trace of accusation. Emboldened, he observed the others.

Master Kemorlin had bent towards the stone, a fierce light in his eyes. His thick eyebrows had drawn together into a puzzled frown. Professor Ractoban's chubby features were likewise moulded into an expression of dubious query. Prince Enlos's face seemed bloodless, all bar the cross-shaped scar on his cheek, which had taken on an unnatural lividity.

Then Enlos produced a stiff smile. 'Quite obviously this is no ordinary stone. Your faces show that it has captured the imaginations of you both. Well then, gentleman, do not keep us in suspense. What have you to say?'

Kemorlin straightened quickly, as though stung. Ractoban likewise jerked out of his entranced state and a troubled look entered his eye. He moved around the stone, not quite touching it.

'Where did you get this?' he demanded.

Sildemund repeated the story he had given Zakobar that afternoon, nervously, for he felt he was on fragile ground. He glanced again at Gully, but Gully's eyes were on the stone.

'And you wish to know . . . what?'

'Where it came from. What precisely it is. Whether it has value.'

Professor Ractoban extended an arm and allowed his fingertips to tentatively caress the stone. 'Cold,' he murmured. 'So cold.'

'It seems to pulse,' observed Prince Enlos, blinking. 'The dark areas, do they move, or am I imagining things?'

Ractoban fixed his gaze upon Sildemund, fingering his round chin. Sildemund withered under his scrutiny. Ractoban put his hand to his brow and closed his eyes for a moment. When he opened them they held a slightly glazed look. He turned to Prince Enlos.

'This is an object of exceptional rarity, that much I can tell you.'

'Tell Master Sildemund, not me,' said the Prince. 'It is his property.'

'Quite. Well, I can say little else at present. I will have to conduct some research before I can divulge more. Even then, I am not sure that I will be able to tell you much.'

Sildemund nodded. Enlos addressed Kemorlin. 'And you, revered Master of Mysteries, what have you to say? It is not like you to remain so quiet.'

Kemorlin ruminatively stroked his long grey beard. 'I too confess myself at a loss, at least for the present.'

'What? You, the great Kemorlin, who has dedicated his entire life to mysteries such as this, you can tell us nothing?'

Kemorlin pressed his beard to his chest, a flash of anger crossing his features. Ignoring the sarcasm, he said, 'It has emanations, of that I am in no doubt.'

'Emanations?'

'Of an unwholesome kind. Do you not sense it, Prince Enlos? Perhaps you lack sensitivity. But does no one else feel it? There is something extraordinary about this stone. I sense it may be an effectuary of sorts, but I can say no more than that at this time.'

Prince Enlos eyed him sceptically. 'It is unpleasant to gaze upon, I will grant you that. But this is disappointing. Can you not be more definite? What of its origin? Its value? Are Dharsoul's – nay, Dyarchim's – two self-professed most knowledgeable intellects so willing to admit defeat?'

'Like the Professor, I believe that with sufficient study I might discover more,' Kemorlin replied. 'Though the prospect has no great appeal.'

'Well, you are uninspiring. Both of you. For this, no doubt, you would under ordinary circumstances have already exacted an enormous fee. I am not impressed. Professor Ractoban, is something the matter?'

Ractoban had taken himself off to one side and had sunk onto a chair. He had turned very pale.

'Forgive me, sire.' One hand rested shakily upon his brow. 'I have come over a little faint.'

'Are you ill?'

'I think not. I will be well in a moment.'

'Take some water. It may help.' Enlos nodded to Gully, who quickly filled a goblet with water and delivered it to the ailing professor.

'Now,' said Enlos after a moment, turning back to Kemorlin, 'what of this? Are we to send Master Sildemund away unsatisfied? It is a sorry thing. And I confess, I too will be disappointed. This extraordinary object, unpleasing as it is to the eye, yet fascinates me. I would love to know more about it.'

Kemorlin was silent, staring ruefully at the stone. Presently he said, in a low voice, tinged with resentment, 'It costs me dear to admit this, sire – as you will appreciate in due course – but I take into account your high regard for your two friends here, and the importance you place upon this elusive information. So I will say it. There is one other person who may be – ahem! – more knowledgeable than I in regard to this object.'

'There is?' Enlos raised a sceptical eyebrow, but his expression was almost mocking. 'To whom do you refer, Master of Mysteries?'

Kemorlin squeezed his beard. 'It is one who is already here, within the Palace.'

'Do you play games, sir? To whom specifically do you refer?'

'Must I speak that name, sire? Can you not divine it?'

'Divine it? It is you, not I, who are the mage, Master Kemorlin. You the majestic delver into the Arcane, the skilled Walker of the Paths That Others May Not Tread. I have no perception of your thoughts.'

Kemorlin made a gesture of annoyance. He tilted his head to indicate the other persons in the chamber. 'You yourself may not wish it spoken aloud.'

'If you are reluctant to speak out loud, I have two ears, into either of which words may be whispered. Whisper then, before my patience cracks.'

Kemorlin stepped close and put his lips to the royal ear. Prince Enlos's expression became thoughtful. He looked aside at Kemorlin. 'You believe this to be so?'

Kemorlin gave a shrug. 'Possibly this . . . *person* may know nothing more than I or the Professor. But – and it costs me dear to say it – if anyone is able to tell us more, it will be he – as you were surely already aware.'

Enlos nodded, concealing a wry smile. 'Then I shall send for him immediately.'

He snapped his fingers. An attendant came forward, received instruction, and withdrew. Enlos turned back to Ractoban. 'Professor, how are you now?'

'A little better, thank you, sire.' Ractoban remained slumped in his seat, but his pallor contained less of the ghost. He swivelled his eyes mistrustfully to Sildemund's stone resting on the table, then away again. 'I do apologise. It came so suddenly. It has never happened before.'

'Oh, tut! No apology is necessary.'

'It is a darkly intriguing thing.' Kemorlin was examining the stone again, but keeping a distance and refraining from actually touching it.

Prince Enlos moved up beside the table. 'I cannot say that I am charmed by it. See how the red shifts to puce and purple. And the pale tendrils upon its surface. And again, as I observe I could almost swear that the black fades and shifts in slow waves across the surface.' He shook his head and looked up. 'Well, it has certainly caught our imaginations, has it not?'

'It was purchased from a foreign trader, you say?' queried Kemorlin to Sildemund. 'Do you have his name?'

Sildemund swallowed. 'Alas, no. The transaction was made by my father. I was not present.'

He was aware that Gully watched him. He felt his cheeks grow hot. He would have given anything to be away from there just then. How he wished he had not mentioned his unsuccessful day to the Prince!

Prince Enlos had moved now to the other end of the dining table and was pouring watered-wine into his goblet. He offered the pitcher to the others but all declined.

Moments passed. The conversation was intermittent. It seemed to Sildemund that the atmosphere grew more charged, but each strove to pretend otherwise. And then came a sudden loud rap at the door.

'Come!' called the Prince.

The door opened and an officer of the Palace Guard entered. He saluted Prince Enlos, then moved to one side and beckoned to an unseen party in the corridor outside. A man stepped in, youthful, pale-skinned and well attired in baggy blue breeches and a puff-sleeved silk shirt of deeper blue decorated with purple lozenges. A floppy blue cap sat atop his head, its soft crown, flashed with purple, falling over one side to his shoulder. Sildemund recognized him immediately. He was the foreigner he had encountered briefly in the corridor the previous evening.

The newcomer swept in with deliberate panache, confident and loosely erect. He paused before Prince Enlos, doffed his cap and performed a deep bow.

'Prince Enlos, good eve. I apologize for my state of undress, but when your messenger arrived I was attending to my toilet, and as the summons appeared urgent I had little time to prepare. I simply threw myself into the first outfit that came to hand. Accept me as I am, therefore, or banish me temporarily, that I might make myself fitting company for a royal sire!'

'You are perfectly presentable as you are,' said Enlos drily. One forefinger had gone to his lower lip and he eyed the newcomer as if unsure what to make of him. At the door three guards had entered and fanned out, hands on sabre-hilts.

The stranger looked about him. His eyes fell upon Kemorlin. 'Ah, good Kemorlin! It has been a long time. How are you? Still struggling to understand the basics of magic? Your skills have developed at least a little, I hope?'

Kemorlin scowled and muttered something incomprehensible. Prince Enlos's eyes shone with amusement. The newcomer saw Ractoban. 'Professor! Greetings! You look unwell. Can I be of assistancce?'

Ractoban shook his head. The newcomer let his gaze settle briefly upon Sildemund and Gully, nodded politely, then turned back to Prince Enlos. 'Have I been summoned into your august presence for a specific reason, lord? I trust you have not invited me to pick over the leavings of the splendid banquet I see spread upon the table here? Alas, I have already dined, a most palatable repast, prepared by your own Palace chefs, I understand.'

'No,' said Prince Enlos a trifle tersely. 'You are here for a reason. At Master Kemorlin's recommendation, I might add.'

The newcomer turned to Kemorlin with an arch smile. 'Really? How kind. How gracious.'

'But first, perhaps you might like to introduce yourself, for not everyone here has made your acquaintance.'

'Certainly.' The man turned to face Sildemund and Gully. 'My name is Dinbig. Ronbas Dinbig.'

Sildemund's look was blank. The man's bearing was impressive, but the name meant nothing.

Prince Enlos had poured wine into a goblet, which he now

handed to his new guest. 'Master Dinbig is from Khimmur, in the north. He is currently sojourning here within the Palace.'

'Sojourning? Sojourning?' echoed Dinbig. He accepted the wine. 'It is not entirely an accurate term, considering that my liberty is more than a little restricted.'

'You are free to come and go as you please,' said Prince Enlos.

'Providing that I remain within my chambers.'

'You have the freedom of much of the wing.'

'As long as I stay in close proximity to my guards. It is a form of freedom to which I am unaccustomed and not enamoured.'

'Ah well, we shall see what is to be seen. But in the meantime I have, as you rightly surmised, called you here for a purpose. Look, sir, if you will, at this strange object resting here upon the table. Cast your eye over it and give us your view.'

The Khimmurian stepped forward, setting aside his wine and twiddling ringed fingers fastidiously. His eyes rested on the stone. 'This is an uncommon object.'

'Pick it up, feel it, if you wish,' said Enlos.

'I would prefer to ascertain a little more about it first.'

He posed the inevitable question as to the stone's origin, and Sildemund uncomfortably repeated his previous answer. Dinbig scrutinized him alertly and Sildemund somehow knew himself exposed.

Dinbig returned his attention to the stone. His light air departed him as he concentrated fully upon the task. His features took on a grave expression. After a few moments he murmured, 'There is great suffering associated with this thing.'

'What do you mean? How can you tell?' enquired Enlos.

'I mean, the stone is connected with pain. It carries an odour of death, of corruption and decay. It has baleful associations. Even now it emanates a powerful and most unsettling aura.' He straightened. 'How can I tell? I am *Zan-Chassin!*'*

He pronounced these last words with deliberate emphasis. Sildemund gave a start. *Zan-Chassin?* He had never before met one of the renowned sorcerer-shamans of Khimmur. They were shadowy figures, respected and in many cases greatly feared.

* See appendix.

'Can you tell us more?' said Enlos. 'Kemorlin has already said virtually as much.'

'Give me a little time alone in meditation, Prince Enlos, and I will be able to tell you more.'

Enlos nodded. 'Very good.'

'It will cost you, of course.'

Enlos opened his mouth to respond, his expression indignant. But as that moment there came another loud knock upon the door.

At the Prince's bidding an under-chamberlain entered. 'Sire, Her Venerated Majesty Queen Lermeone will bestow her presence in half an hour.'

Enlos gave a nod and addressed his guests. 'Master Sildemund, Gully, return now to your apartment if you would attend The Presence. An official will come for you there. Master Kemorlin, Professor Ractoban, I thank you for attending so promptly. You may go now, but further efforts on your parts to discover anything you can of this stone would be appreciated. If you are weak, Ractoban, a carriage can be provided.'

'Thank you, my lord, I have my own.'

'Master Dinbig, you will be escorted back to your chamber. Apply yourself to your meditations. I would wish to learn more about this enigmatic stone before the night is out.'

All bowed to the Prince and left for their individual destinations.

As they returned to their apartment Sildemud could barely contain himself. The idea of being presented to the Queen filled him with trepidation and awe. Simultaneously he experienced grave misgivings, an irrepressible feeling of dread.

It was the red stone. Meglan – and his father – had been right. Almost everyone who laid eyes on it was adversely affected in some way. Kemorlin had detected something unwholesome, a subtle emanation or aura. The flamboyant Khimmurian, Ronbas Dinbig, the *Zan-Chassin* sorcerer, had instantly and unsettlingly reinforced this, associating the stone with death and corruption. Professor Ractoban had all but collapsed moments after inspecting it. Zakobar *had* collapsed, and died!

Picadus . . . Edric . . .

Sildemund's thoughts raced, back to Volm the day before his father had dispatched him to Dharsoul. He recalled the strange disturbance at the taverna in which Dervad had been stabbed in the hand by a stranger apparently seeking Master Frano; and Master Frano himself had been knocked to the ground and injured as a direct result of that fracas.

Was the incident also connected with the stone?

Sildemund felt panic begin to rise within him. *The stone must surely hold malignant properties!*

He fought his fear, thinking again: But what of me? I have had adventures, yes, and come perilously close to death. But I was rescued by Prince Enlos, no less! And now I dine with royalty. Dignitaries, scholars, master arcanists are summoned to render their services to me without charge. No, this is good fortune. There is a mystery surrounding this stone, that cannot be questioned. But I have not suffered, nor Gully. Such a glut of misfortune has fallen upon others, but it must be coincidence, for surely were the stone to affect one, it would affect all?

Moderately calmed by this thought he followed Gully into the suite of chambers in which they were lodged. Picadus was on his bed, half-sitting groggily, his look befuddled and morose. 'W'as'appnin?'

Gully strode over to him and shoved him back. 'Lie down and return to sleep, you dog-mannered thug. It is the middle of the night.'

Picadus, knowing no better, did as he was told.

New garments had been laid out for them. This was formal attire; crisp white trousers and tunics with braided loops and studs, and white cloth sandals.

'Are we to change into these clothes to attend the Queen, Gully?' Sildemund asked.

Gully, already stripping, nodded. 'That would be my guess.'

As he dressed Sildemund said, 'Gully, when I returned from fetching the stone, I caught the end of a conversation. You were talking about the Revenants of Claine, weren't you?'

'Not I,' said Gully. 'But Master Kermorlin raised the matter with Prince Enlos, remarking that he had seen more of them in the city recently.'

'I noticed some today. Remember, we stopped and tried to listen to one? I thought they were forbidden to leave Garsh, is that not so?'

'For generations they have been incarcerated there. Garsh has become almost an independent state, so I believe. Now it appears some are free, roaming at will, in Dyarchim as well as Tomia.'

'Why were they incarcerated?'

Gully shrugged and shook his head. 'It was long before my time.'

'You say they claim knowledge of a great secret.'

'So it is said.'

'Do you know what it is?'

Gully gave a grin. 'If I knew, it would not be a secret, would it?'

'But what are they, Gully? Are they magicians, a priestly sect? Do they have a known message, a creed? Who, or what, is Claine?'

'Truly I know little of them, Sil. Until we encountered the problems at the border three weeks ago I had barely heard previous mention of them, at least not for many years.'

'Then what was said tonight? From what I saw and heard, the discussion was heated.'

'It was hardly a discussion. Kermorlin seems unhappy at the knowledge that Revenants are free in the city. Professor Ractoban also expressed some concern. Prince Enlos was plainly uncomfortable. He seems especially uneasy with Master Kermorlin. But little was said, I suspect because I was present. As soon as you returned Enlos closed the matter.'

'He was returning from Garsh when he saved us from the bandits.'

Gully nodded, fastening the studs of his tunic.

'And when you asked him then about Garsh, he declined to speak of it. Then yesterday, one of the women in the crowd, a Revenant, rushed out at him as we entered the city. What do you think it's all about?'

'I do not know, and I do not enquire, such matters are of state, Sil. They are not the business of the likes of you or me.'

Sildemund was pensive for a moment as he attended to his dress. 'The Khimmurian sorcerer is a curious fellow. What do you make of him?'

'Aye, he is a mystery. I do not know what to think. His position is ambiguous, that much is sure.'

'Do you know much of the *Zan-Chassin*?'

'Little. People, when they speak of them, do so in guarded voices. Their reputation is—'

He got no further. The door opened and a palace official entered: stiff, formal, in a uniform of vermilion satin, crowned with a brimless, tasselled hat of the same hue bound with streamers of deep primrose. His face was drawn in a taut, haughty expression, his lips puckered, chin high. He observed the two of them cursorily down the length of his pointed nose.

'I am Quidpin, Senior Under-Assistant to the the Sacred Fellowship of the Supreme Haruspices of the Royal House of Her August Majesty, Queen Lermeone. I am to escort you to the Hall of Receiving. I was informed that you are three.'

'Two,' replied Gully. 'Our companion is unwell and regrettably cannot join us.'

'As you wish.' Quidpin swivelled upon his heel and made for the corridor with a swift, prim step, seeming to walk almost upon his toes. Sildemund grabbed his satchel containing the red stone, hardly aware that he did so, and with Gully followed the Senior Under-Assistant from the chamber.

'You are aware of the protocol?' said Quidpin as they passed along the corridor. He phrased the words so that they were simultaneously statement and enquiry.

Sildemund glanced uncertainly at Gully. 'Er, no.'

'You will under no circumstances give utterance in the Presence of the Royal Personage,' said Quidpin. 'Unless, of course, you are bidden to do so by the Illustrious Majesty, or the Prince or one of the Supreme Haruspices – which is thoroughly unlikely. The Majesty will, it goes without saying, not speak or acknowledge your presence in any way. Such is the Sacred Law. Her thoughts, should she desire their dissemination, will be communicated by the Supreme Haruspices. You will on no account approach the Queen. You will remain upon your knees in the places allocated to you. When the August Majesty enters you will bow your heads and will not gaze upon her person until bidden to do so. When the audience is done you will again bow your heads until the Majesty has departed. Is everything understood?'

'Yes. Quite. Except . . .'

Quidpin shot him a sidelong stare, indignant and disdainful, as though his requiring more information than that provided was something quite beyond the bounds of acceptability. Sildemund persisted nevertheless. 'I wondered, as it is already evening, what is the reason for this Audience? Surely it cannot have been convened for us alone? Does Queen Lermeone not normally conduct her meetings during the day?'

Quidpin's eyes narrowed and his mouth puckered further, as though he had sucked a particularly bitter lemon. He raised his head, and for a moment closed his eyes as he walked. 'Her Beneficent Majesty bestows Her Presence in accordance with the Law. The hour after sunset on the fourteenth day of Salmas is a designated time. Of course The Presence has not been convened for you alone! You are not a pertinent factor in any way. Remember this, and do nothing to bring attention to yourselves.'

They passed without further conversation along seemingly endless passages, through arcades and galleries, and came at last to a great bronze double door. A pair of sentries of the Palace Guard, armoured and masked, stood motionless before it. They held ceremonial glaives, beaked and fluked, which were tilted to bar access. Quidpin spoke a word; the guards brought the weapons erect. Quidpin stepped forward and pushed upon the doors, which swung inwards, slowly, making no sound.

They entered a spacious hall, set with rows of velvet-upholstered padded mats which were arrayed in precise rows across a floor of grey-and-white mosaic. Occupying the front rows were half a dozen or so persons, kneeling upon the mats, garbed in the same white attire as Sildemund and Gully.

Beyond these was a low, wide dais. A second, smaller dais rested a little way back upon this, where a throne of Barulian whitewood was positioned, intricately carved and ornamented with precious gems and jewels. On the floor immediately in front of the throne was a complexly segmented circular design in red, blue and black, figured with glyphs and symbols. Brightly coloured standards were ranged along the rear of the double-dais. Along the walls and at the sides of the dais Palace Guards stood at semi-rest.

Sildemund spotted Prince Enlos talking with a man in white and a masked officer at the front of the hall. Quidpin began to lead Sildemund and Gully to one side, but Enlos saw them and beckoned. He strode forward to greet them, and spoke to them in hushed tones. 'Be seated here, a short way back. Has the Under-Assistant instructed you in the protocol? Good. Did you by any chance bring the red stone with you?'

Sildemund nodded with sudden anxiety. Why had he brought it? Was he in breach of the rules?

But Enlos was pleased. 'It may interest the Queen.'

He was gone. Sildemund and Gully self-consciously took their places. It was plain that the others in the Hall were dignitaries or city or palace officials. The two felt out of place. Quidpin was nowhere to be seen.

Prince Enlos took up a position on the first level of the dais, kneeling on a mat and facing the throne. A few moments passed; hurried whispers passed between those kneeling on the mats, then a pair of heralds marched forward from the rear of the dais. Each held a long spiralled horn, hung with the Dyarch royal standard. They tipped horns to lips and blew out a shrill fanfare.

The guards snapped to attention. The dignitaries in the front row placed their hands flat upon the floor before them and inclined their heads and torsos. Sildemund and Gully did likewise, though Sildemund could not prevent himself from guiltily raising his eyes.

From one side of the dais he observed two men enter in long purple robes and high conical blue hats with pendent, fringed ear-flaps. They walked reverently towards the throne. Each held in his hands a shallow wicker bowl.

The two seated themselves, one on each side and a little in front of the throne. They placed their bowls beside them at the edge of the circular floor design. These two were the Supreme Haruspices, highly-schooled mystic priests whose role was to interpret the thoughts of their mute sovereign, Queen Lermeone. The wicker bowls contained petals of rare gentian and crimson hesperis flowers, the agents by means of which the Queen and her Haruspices communed. Long ago, in more barbarous times, the bowls would have contained the entrails of sacrificial victims. Over centuries the guts of animals gradually came to supersede those of humans, and these in turn had eventually been replaced by other agents. Later refinements resulted in the more recent introduction of petals, the use of which had endured for longer than any living person could remember.

Under-Assistants walked forward upon their knees, bringing small wooden trays holding quills, ink, a soft-bristled hand-brush and sheets of vellum. These they placed upon the floor beside the Supreme Haruspices, then withdrew.

'All hail the Queen!' announced a herald loudly.

There was absolute hush as Queen Lermeone entered. She was tall and erect, clothed in a long gown of pure grey broadcloth. Her age was about fifty years. Her hair was grey, bunched at the neck. Her face held an expression of regal impassivity, the mouth set, downturned at the corners. The jewelled crown of Dyarchim sat upon her head. The only sound was the slow swish of her heavy gown sliding across the floor as she approached the throne and seated herself.

The heralds, bowing low, departed the dais. The members of the audience now knelt erect. One of the Haruspices spoke. 'Our Gracious Queen is here to benefit those assembled with Her Pressence, in the name of the common good and the sacred heritage of our beloved nation, noble Dyarchim. Bring forth your petitions, that Her August Majesty may apply her sage wisdom to your concerns.'

An Under-Assistant moved on his knees to the fore of the lower dais. One of the half dozen white-clad men at the front of the hall rose, bowed deeply, and approached the dais. In his hand he held a rolled manuscript bound with blue satin ribbon. This he passed into the hands of the Under-Assistant.

The Under-Assistant, on his knees, rotated and made his way to the edge of the second dais. From here he was able to hand the manuscript to one of the Haruspices. The Haruspex untied the ribbon, unfuried the manuscript and examined its contents in silence. He then passed it to the second Haruspex, who likewise scanned it, then turned and gave it into Queen Lermeone's hands. The Queen read it in silence then placed it upon her lap and gave a nod.

The first Haruspex raised his basket so that Queen Lermeone might dip her pale hand into it. She drew forth a cluster of gentian petals, inclined her body forward and let the petals fail upon the segmented circle of the floor before her. Now the second basket was proffered. The Queen took hesperis petals and repeated the process. She sat back, unmoving. The two Haruspices leaned over the petals, intently studying the pattern of their fall upon the circle. Their scrutiny lasted two or three minutes, during which time they each took a quill and a sheet of vellum and hastily scratched notes.

With a nod they signalled to one another that they were done. Each took up his brush and with studied, ritual motions swept the petals from the circle. They put aside their tools and sat erect once more. An Under-Assistant came forward with a short-handled, broad-headed besom and brushed the petals fully away from the circle.

The first Haruspex spoke. 'Your petition has been accepted. Her Majesty has viewed it and communicated her verdict in full and proper observation of the Sacred Law. Her official answer will be delivered to you tomorrow, signed and certified with the Royal Seal.'

The petitioner before the dais bowed low once more. He took three steps back and departed the hall.

This process was repeated with the remaining persons assembled at the front of the hall, four men and two women. Each petitioner was received and dealt with in like manner. The ritual took a little under an hour in all, and throughout that time not a word was spoken by the Queen. Sildemund's legs, confined in the kneeling position, grew increasingly painful. He longed to stretch them but dared not for fear of breaching protocol.

At last all was done. The petitioners had gone, leaving only Sildemund and Gully as audience. Now Prince Enlos spoke.

'Mother, my Queen. I beg your ear.'

The Queen settled sombre grey eyes upon him and gave a slow nod. Her face showed no expression, though Enlos's tone and term of address had eased the formality of the proceedings a little.

'Mother, I mentioned to you yesterday that I had renewed acquaintance with an old friend. Do you recall Gully, Radath Gully, who fought so bravely at my side and helped save my life during The Treachery?'

A small frown of concentration formed briefly on Queen Lermeone's brow, then vanished. A lightness came to her features. She gave another brief nod.

'Two days ago fortune brought Radath Gully and I together again. He has returned with me to Dharsoul. He is here now, with a companion. I would present him to you, if that is your will.'

Again the slight nod. Prince Enlos turned and called to Gully. 'Gully, come forward, please!'

Gully rose, stiff and awkward. He made his way towards the first dais and bent before the Queen.

Lermeone surveyed him for long moments. Her eyes held a glow and it seemed that the tightness at the corners of her mouth had gone, so that her lips no longer drooped. Indeed, she almost smiled.

The two Haruspices, eyeing Gully, turned to regard the Queen. They lifted their wicker bowls. Queen Lermeone took petals from each and let them fall upon the circle. The Haruspices bent over them, nodded to one another, and carefully brushed them away. The first spoke.

'Radath Gully, Her Beneficent Majesty expresses her extreme happiness at setting eyes once more upon the man who saved the life of her only son and the heir to the Dyarchim throne.'

Gully shifted uncomfortably. He glanced nervously from the Queen to Prince Enlos, then to the two Haruspices. Prince Enlos spoke up. 'I think Gully wishes to speak.'

Queen Lermeone gave a nod of acceptance. In a halting voice Gully said, 'Your Majesty, I am greatly honoured to be in Your Presence again. But I am unworthy of your praise. I did what any loyal soldier would have done, and no more.'

'Ah, Gully, you understate the case,' Prince Enlos chided gently. 'You greatly endangered your own life to preserve mine. Lesser men would have deserted. Many would have been pleased to hand me to the enemy to save their skins. You stayed at my side and fought on, with but a handful of others, even though death seemed your most likely end.'

'Death is unquestionably my end, sire, as he is everyone's,' Gully said, discovering boldness in levity. 'But on that day he was before his time and was sent home empty-handed.'

'Ha! That's how it was, Gully! You're right! We beat him, Old Master Death, did we not?'

Prince Enlos gave a laugh. He ushered Gully back, not to his place beside Sildemund but to the first row of padded mats where the petitioners had formerly knelt. Then he spoke again to the Queen. 'If I may, I would introduce Radath Gully's companion, Mother. A young Master Sildemund Atturio, from Volm. He has something I would like you to see. I and others are intrigued by it.'

Queen Lermeone gave her imperious nod. Enlos signalled Sildemund forward. Sildemund rose, his heart in his mouth. His legs were numb from kneeling; he was barely able to walk. Keeping a tight grip on his satchel he somehow made his way to the dais and performed an awkward bow.

Prince Enlos spoke a few more brief words of introduction, then: 'Master Sildemund, will you allow us to see the stone?'

'Of course, sire.' Sildemund took the bound stone from the satchel. He held it out, uncertain to whom it should be proffered. 'Your Majesty.'

An Under-Assistant advanced on his knees across the dais. He took the bundle and kneel-walked towards the second dais. He laid the stone upon the floor before the Queen and her two Haruspices. At a signal from the Haruspices he unbound the cloth. The stone was revealed, large, purple-red, with its black shadows and yellow-white filaments.

The Haruspices inclined their upper torsos to inspect the stone. At the same time there came a queer sound from above them. All eyes turned to the Queen, for she had pushed herself up and back, half out of the throne. Her face was a shocking sight. It was contorted into a fearful grimace, her mouth open, lips trembling, her eyes transfixed by the sight of the exposed stone. That she should show emotion was profound and disturbing in itself. That her reactions should be so uncontrolled and forceful was un-expected beyond belief.

But there was worse to come.

Shuddering, the Queen raised a finger and pointed at the stone, still pressing herself back as if repulsed by it.

And then she spoke.

From the mouth of Dyarchim's Silent Queen, whose voice had never been heard in public, came words, strangled and hoarse, delivered in a near-hysterical tone: 'It is the Heart! *You have brought the Heart of Shadows!'*

12

FOR LONG MOMENTS nobody reacted. The event was unprecedented. Even the rigidly disciplined Palace Guards could be seen to shift uneasily, casting troubled glances from behind their masks.

Stunned silence reigned, until Enlos leapt suddenly to his feet and barked an order: 'Clear the Hall!'

Instantly four Guards ran forward and seized Sildemund and Gully by the arms, marching them briskly from the Hall of Receiving. Outside they released their grip, but stood tensely, and Sildemund understood that he was not free to walk away.

An officer appeared, tautly polite. 'You will be escorted back to your chambers.'

Two Guards marched with them through the Palace to their apartment. Sildemund wanted to speak, was bursting to do so, but the Guards' presence was inhibiting.

The Queen had spoken!

The stone!

What was it? *What had happened back there?*

Sildemund's thoughts were a whirl. The moment they reentered their rooms and the door slammed shut behind them he wheeled on Gully. 'What is going on, Gully? What does this mean?'

Gully strode to a seat, running his hands through his long fair hair, and thrust himself down, shaking his head. 'More than I am able to contemplate just now.'

'Is it of such great consequence that Queen Lermeone spoke?'

'It is.'

'The Sacred Law forbids her from ever voicing her thoughts?'

'That is it.'

'Something struck me, back there in the Hall. If the Queen

cannot speak, or even physically demonstrate her opinion in any way, what would happen if the Haruspices misinterpreted her thoughts, by error or deviousness? She cannot refute them, can she? So no one would know.'

'That is a sacrilegious thought, Sil.'

'But it is true, Gully, isn't it? Queen Lermeone is our sovereign, yet it is the Haruspices who speak her mind.'

'Maybe so. Just now that is the least of our worries.'

Sildemund gave a start. 'Gully, I have left the stone! In the confusion I forgot all about it.'

'Damn the stone!' snapped Gully, thrusting himself to standing.

Sildemund was absorbed in his train of thought. 'She knew it, Gully, Queen Lermeone knew the stone. She called it the Heart of Shadows. Do you know that name?'

Gully stepped forward, his face a mask of tension. He took Sildemund by the shoulders and shook him fiercely. 'Sildemund, you have not taken in what has happened here tonight! Think, lad! The Queen *spoke*! What does *that* mean?'

Sildemund stared at him, nonplussed. 'The Law— The Sacred Law forbids her to speak in public.'

'Yes, upon pain of death!'

'Death?'

'That is the mandatory penalty.'

'For the Queen? No, it cannot be! She cannot be executed, surely? For those few words?'

Gully gave a great, exasperated sigh. He turned away. 'Sil, you have still not grasped it, have you?'

'What? Gully, what are you saying?'

'The Queen spoke, aye. And for that she faces death. But who was there? Who witnessed her words?'

Sildemund shrugged. 'Prince Enlos, the Palace Guards, the two Haruspices, a couple of Under-Assistants. . . .'

'And who else?'

'There were no others, besides us.'

'Precisely! Us!'

Sildemund shook his head in confoundment. 'I do not follow you, Gully. What are you saying?'

'I am saying this: if it be known that the Queen has spoken in public her life will be forfeit. That is the Law. *If it be known!*'

'You mean that if none of us who were present ever speak of this event, then Queen Lermeone will be spared?'

Gully gave a sharp, cynical laugh. 'Sil, you have the body of a man, but you view the world with the eyes of a child. Listen again: *if it be known* that she has spoken, she will die. But do you think that the powers that rule Dyarchim will allow that to happen if there is a means to avoid it? No! Of course not! They will instead take the necessary steps to ensure that it can never be known.'

Sildemund stared long and hard at him, and his voice, when it came, shook. 'You mean . . .'

'Prince Enlos, and I would imagine the Haruspices, are above reproach. The same would go for the loyal Palace Guards, though some may yet be deemed unreliable. They will die. The Under-Assistants too, almost certainly.'

'But what of us?'

'We, too, Sil. This is what I have been trying to tell you. We have witnessed what we cannot possibly ever witness. The choice is between us and Dyarchim's Queen. That is, there is no choice. We will never leave this Palace. Go to the door and see for yourself. There will be guards outside. For what we have witnessed we are condemned to death.'

13

MEGLAN SQUATTED AT the river's edge, replenishing her empty water-flask. The clear water over her hand was cool and refreshing. She capped the flask then took a rectangle of cloth, soaked it and applied it to her face. She stared out across the Tigrant's shining surface, deep in thought, seeing nothing. Close by, her horse, Swift Cloud, sank her muzzle into the water, taking long, deep draughts.

Meglan glanced back up the bank. Her remaining companion, Jans, was silhouetted against the harsh yellow sky, staring into the far distance. He stood with his hands upon his hips, one leg before him. The stance was stiff and unnatural.

'Come down and get water, Jans.'

These were the first words she had spoken to him in almost an hour.

Jans shifted his position slightly but did not look at her. 'Aye, I will.'

He was embarrassed, Meglan knew. And affronted. She had been angry with him and had said things she now regretted. Jans had only been doing his job, she accepted that now. His words and his actions had been wise in the circumstances. But, it seemed so long that they had been stuck here, unable to move on. Jans refused to advance any further. Meglan could barely keep still, so great was her frustration at the situation she found herself in.

She stood, putting her hand to her neck. The flesh was too painful for all but the lightest touch. Her throat was swollen and sore, her shoulders and back stiff. It hurt to swallow. Earlier Jans had told her that the bruises left by Skalatin had blossomed into myriad colours.

She climbed the bank to the roadside, stood for a moment, then put a hand on Jan's arm. 'I'm sorry. I lost my temper, and I shouldn't have. You were right. I just . . . Oh, everything seems to be going wrong!'

Jans glanced at her, his craggy face begrimed with sweat and dust, then looked down at his boots. 'I would not have stopped you if there was any other way, Mistress. But it is too dangerous to go on alone.'

Meglan nodded resignedly. 'I know it.'

She turned away so that he would not see that her eyes had filled with tears.

They were on the western edge of Dazdun's Despair. They had been in this spot since meeting earlier with a caravan of three wagons travelling west. The caravan was driven by a Hanvatian silk merchant accompanied by several mounted guards in their saddles. They seemed only half-conscious and bore bloodstains and marks of battle.

The merchant pulled the first wagon to a halt as Jans and Meglan rode up.

'Greetings!' said Jans.

The Hanvatian nodded wearily and spoke in a listless voice. 'Greetings, travellers. Where are you bound?'

'Dharsoul.'

The man shook his head. 'You would be well advised to change your plans. Dharsoul was my destination too, but the road is held by brigands led by Fagmar the Cursed. I have been forced to turn back.'

'Brigands, on the Dharsoul Road?' Jans gave a low whistle. 'How is that?'

The merchant shrugged. 'Fagmar's operations are well known further north, around the Tomian frontier. The Tomian military have been active in force around Garsh and the border, forcing the brigand south. Now he harries the road here. Look! I had fifteen good fighting men. We were attacked today, at noon, and now only eight are fit for their saddles. Three others lie severly wounded in my wagon; four are dead. And I have lost a wagon to the bandit.'

'Dharsoul will not tolerate this for long,' said Jans. 'There will be a force on its way even now, I would guess, to arrest or eliminate this Fagmar and his gang.'

'Word is that they were put to flight only yesterday by a company led by Prince Enlos himself,' replied the Hanvatian. 'They were operating further east then, closer to Dharsoul. It seems that the Prince has achieved nothing more than to drive them further this way.'

'How close are they?' asked Meglan.

'Two hours or three hours distant, in the heart of the Despair.'

'It is possible that they harry only merchants carrying valuable goods. Perhaps a pair of travellers with nothing to offer might pass unmolested.'

'That is a foolish and dangerous thought, young woman,' the merchant said sternly. 'One as enchanting to the eye as you would be a rare prize for men such as these. Take my advice, go no further. I have said as much to a pair of wayfarers we encountered some distance back. They, if they have sense, are now returning somewhere in our wake. Until the road is made safe by troops it will offer no passage for any unaccompanied by a strong military guard.'

He clicked his tongue and urged his horses forward. The wagons rumbled on. The guards, exhausted and demoralized, had hardly glanced at Meglan. Now they rode slowly past, eyes low, men whose spirits had abandoned them.

Meglan and Jans sat for a few moments in their saddles, gazing into the hot, empty distance.

'I must go on,' declared Meglan at length. 'I have to, for my father.'

'No, you must not. You heard what the merchant said. It would be foolhardy.'

'I must!' she dug her heels sharply into Swift Cloud's flanks and gave him rein. But Jans threw out a hand and seized her wrist, holding her back, so that Swift Cloud snorted and pranced but advanced only a few short steps.

Meglan screamed. 'Let me go! Jans! How dare you!'

'I cannot.' Jans maintained his grasp on her wrist.

'You need not come. I will carry on alone.'

'No! It is not safe.'

'You are disobedient! How dare you lay hands on me! *Let me go!*' Furiously Meglan lashed out at him. The horses nickered and shifted in alarm.

'I'm sorry, Mistress.' Jans leaned across, slipped an arm around

Meglan's waist and hauled her from the saddle. He let her slide to the road, then leapt down from this own mount. He grabbed Meglan as she ran again for Swift Cloud.

'Mistress, I will not let you go!'

Meglan struggled like one possessed, her anger intensified by the pain of her bruises. 'You are dismissed! Leave me now! Immediately!'

'Mistress Meglan, you hired me to protect you, and that is what I will do to the best of my ability. I cannot let you go on. We will wait here and hope that others come along this way. We will travel on with them.'

'No! I have to go. If you are so cowardly, stay behind. I do not need you! Go! You are no longer in my service!'

'Mistress, I am bound to protect you. Equally my duty is to your father, who has been a good and generous employer over many years.' Jans released her, sensing that she would not run again for her horse. 'If I let you go on now, knowing danger, I will be failing in my duty both to him and to you. So we will wait – or return to Volm if you wish.'

She glowered at him, seething with anger, but her first impetuousness had passed. She felt herself caving in. Her thoughts went to Sildemund. What had been her brother's fate? Had he reached the safety of Dharsoul, or had he fallen into the hands of the brigand, Fagmar? Whatever the case, she had no hope now of bringing the red stone back early.

She thought of her father, Master Frano, waiting, wondering – so she believed – as to her fate, worrying about his two children, fearful of Skalatin's return.

Had Skalatin returned yet? Almost certainly. How would Master Frano have fared? There were guards in the house this time, Meglan reassured herself. Skalatin would not have resorted so readily to violence.

She looked back down the road. What should she do? Such misfortune, to be standing here, unable to advance. She felt that the gods were against her. But should she go back?

She shook her head. Her entire effort would have been for nothing. The stone was the focus. That was what she had come for, that it might be returned to Skalatin. She had to go forward, to find Sildemund. And if – she swallowed – if something had happened to Sildemund on the road . . . if he had become parted from the stone . . . If that had happened, then she, Meglan, would have no choice but to continue the search until she found it.

But how? It could be anywhere! And by then it would be too late in any case.

What was she to do?

Her heart hammered painfully. She felt herself about to be overwhelmed by the conflict of emotion in her breast. She reminded herself that she did not know what had become of Sildemund, and that she was allowing herself to imagine the worst. She was aware that Jans stood before her, watching her, and she was suddenly both angry and ashamed at her behaviour.

Meglan went to the side of the road and sat down upon a rock, her head in her hands. There was nothing for it, Jans was right. She could only wait. But stubborness and pride precluded her doing the right thing now, which was to apologize.

Time passed. Neither of them spoke; both were embarrassed by their fight. No one came along the road. Jans let his horse wander down to the riverside to drink.

Soon it would be evening. Meglan fretted that they would be forced to spend the night here. What if no one came at all? Was word already out that the road was unsafe? It could be days before troops arrived. Meglan began to think desperately again. But she calmed herself as she went to the river and filled her flask, then climbed the bank and made her peace with Jans. And Jans pointed along the road into Dazdun's Despair. 'A cart comes. Two people, I think. This must be the pair that the merchant spoke of.'

In the heat-haze Meglan made out a dark blot, a single horse plodding towards them, hauling a cart.

'Watch them, Mistress Meglan, while I get water.'

Long before the cart reached them Jans was back at Meglan's side. The cart's two passengers were wrapped in hooded burnouses to ward off the hot sun. Meglan and Jans mounted their steeds to provide them with better vantage.

The cart drew close and halted. The passengers were a man and a woman of fairly advanced years. He was of small build, pinched, almost emaciated, with a thin pasty face, protuberant brown eyes, a dark fringe of hair beneath his hood and a dark, greying frizz of beard. His companion was equally thin, with a long body and limbs. She wore a ragged brown skirt beneath her burnous. She seemed deformed about the head, which was broad and compacted. The lower half of her face pushed forward to resemble a short blunt snout. Her eyes were round and bright, set well back and far apart. The mouth was wide and thin, the nose so flat as to be hardly more than two flaring nostrils at the fore of the face. There was something ophidian in her look.

'Hail, fellow wayfarers,' said the man. 'We wish you a very good afternoon. Do you travel to Dharsoul?'

'That had been our intention,' Meglan replied.

'I would caution against it. There is trouble upon the road.'

'We have heard as much. Thieves and bandits, is that not so?'

'It is.'

'Were you molested? You appear untouched.'

'Ah, we were fortunate,' replied the man, his eyes darting over Meglan. 'We met a merchant from Hanvat who had come under fierce attack. He had barely survived, and had lost men and goods before being forced to turn back. We debated our best course, for we have goods to sell in the souk at Dharsoul. We go there every two months; it is our main source of income and it will cause us hardship to miss it. But plainly we could not continue, so we are returning home. But what of you?'

'We have met the same merchant and on his advice have advanced no further. We waited in the hope of meeting others with whom we might band together for safety, but none have passed.'

'And it is unlikely that any will, at least today. If you consider, anyone setting out along this road will also have met the Hanvatian and will have been discouraged. Your wait is futile.'

Meglan nodded, feeling suddenly foolish, and silently berated herself. Neither she nor Jans had thought of this. The couple on the wagon conferred briefly in muted tones, then the man spoke again. 'Our home is no great distance from here. Will you not join us? The day is almost done; we can provide you with a meal and a place to sleep for the night. Tomorrow, who knows, you may fare better in your travels.'

Meglan glanced around her briefly in indecision, then replied, 'You are most kind. Thank you. We will accept upon condition that you let me pay you in coin for your hospitality.'

'Such things can be discussed at the proper time. Now, let me make introductions. I am Gaskid; this is Dame Inonna.'

'And we are Meglan and Jans.'

'Then, good Meglan and Jans, let us be on our way.'

They moved on, and after they had travelled about half a mile Gaskid drove the cart from the road onto a barely visible track that made off into the wild. Progress was slow, since the ground, baked hard by the sun, was rutted and untrodden. They were obliged to make long detours – or so it seemed to Meglan – around rocky outcrops or to avoid deep pits and gullies. The cart groaned and rumbled as though it ached, and seemed ready to fall apart at every next bump, but somehow it held together.

Meglan grew concerned at the extent to which they were penetrating into the arid wasteland of Dazdun's Despair. The sun was low, the sky a haze of colour. She glanced over her shoulders, trying to determine the way back to the road, but no way was apparent and their tracks left scarcely any impression on the ground.

They entered a narrow gulch overshadowed by high, vertical rock walls. Slowly Meglan grew aware of a strange sound; a female voice, chanting in a low, uneven pitch. The voice seemed to intone words in a specific tongue, though none were familiar to her. It was some moments before she identified the source of the sound; it came from the cart.

She moved closer, edging Swift Cloud alongside the cart. She saw that Dame Inonna had her eyes closed and was making slow, fluid motions with one hand held before her as, from between her lips issued the unusual chant.

Gaskid noticed Meglan's proximity, and smiled. 'Do not worry. Dame Inonna is gifted. Her song wards off the malicious spirits that inhabit this place.'

Dame Inonna became silent; the cart rolled creaking on. They emerged from the gulch and rounded a small rocky spur. Before them, at the edge of a grove of dark cypresses, stood a low cottage built of whitewashed stone, bounded by a stone wall and makeshift white picket fencing. A couple of stone outbuildings were set against the wall.

Dame Inonna turned in her seat to Meglan, her wide, thin lips stretching into a smile. 'There. All is well.'

At the back of the cottage Meglan saw a cultivated area, planted with corn, sunflowers and a few ranks of vines. Closer by were eggplants, tomatoes, strawberries and other vegetables and fruits. Chickens scratched in the dust and from somewhere Meglan heard the bleating of goats.

Jans and Gaskid stabled their horses, Gaskid providing them with hay and water, while Meglan went indoors with Dame Inonna. The interior of the cottage was rudely furnished, though kept spick and span. It seemed that the couple lived as peasants. A large wood carving of a serpent dominated one corner, and Meglan noticed snake motifs decorating several bowls and pots.

Dame Inonna lit lamps then busied herself preparing mint tea. Meglan went to a window and looked out. The light was slowly fading. Fruit trees grew in a small orchard close beside the house. Beyond were the cypresses casting long shadows onto the barrenness of the Despair.

'This is an unusual spot,' said Meglan to Dame Inonna. 'Lush and fertile, it seems, in a region that elsewhere bears no growth.'

'We are fortunate to have found it. It affords a modest but fair living.'

'You live entirely off the land?'

'More or less. We even make a small profit from surplus produce. There are rare herbs and flora growing here that are not known to grow elsewhere – at least, not within Dyarchim. And minerals too. Dharsoul's apothecaries and alchemists are pleased to purchase these from us in such quantities as we can provide.'

'You would perhaps be wise to keep such information to yourselves,' said Jans, who had just entered with Gaskid. 'You give us your confidence, knowing nothing of our characters. Are you not concerned that we be felons who would think little of murdering you and taking control of your harvest?'

Dame Inonna gave a throaty chuckle. 'The income derived is modest, certainly insufficient to tempt anyone intent upon wealth. Furthermore, my plants require specialist attention. Only one with an innate affinity, schooled over a lifetime, as I am, could hope to rear and harvest such plants successfully. As for the minerals, they are hidden, and to the untrained eye, unrecognizable.'

'Yet someone might still leave here intending to return with such a specialist.'

'Few visit; none have ever returned,' said Gaskid. 'This place is not known, nor is it easy to find.'

As the dusk gathered they sat down to a supper of rice and vine leaves stuffed with spiced minced goatsmeat, with pimentos and salad, followed by fruit and goat's cheese, and accompanied by a strong beer brewed by Gaskid. When they had finished and the table had been cleared Dame Inonna remarked, 'Now, child, I note the bruising about your neck. It looks sore, and such a sad blight upon one as pretty as you. Will you let me examine it? I can relieve it for you.'

Gaskid leaned forward and winked. 'Inonna has the gift. Put yourself in her hands and you will be made well.'

Meglan's discomfort was acute and she unhesitatingly gave her assent. At Dame Inonna's word she seated herself upon a stool near the window, within the light of a pair of lamps, and loosened her tunic at the neck. Dame Inonna placed herself beside her and applied light fingertips to her bruised skin, stroking it in relaxing, soothing motions.

'The flesh is deeply hurt,' she said in a quizzical murmur. 'What has happened? The marks suggest a murderous attack.'

Meglan had her eyes closed; Inonna had the healer's touch, her expert fingers seeming to draw out the pain. But at her question Meglan felt a spasm of unease and was at a loss as to how to reply.

'Ah, no matter,' said Inonna. 'It is not my business.'

Her fingers continued their light strokes, kneading with infinite tenderness, working knowingly upon the flesh of Meglan's throat and neck, beneath her chin, onto her shoulders and breastbone.

'It is extensive,' observed Dame Inonna. 'I have an embrocation which will encourage the anger to depart. One moment.'

She left the room and after a short space returned holding a fat clay jar plugged with cork. 'Now, let us be rid of these cruel contusions which so disfigure your beauty. Here, removed your tunic. Do not worry about Gaskid seeing your breasts, nor your companion, either. They can turn the other way. In fact, Gaskid, bring out your counterboard and dice and engage Jans in a tournament while I banish the pain that grips Meglan's flesh. Look, Jans yawns! We are poor hosts, who have bored him so quickly!'

Meglan was self-conscious at first, but the men complied, seating themselves at the table where they had eaten, with their backs to the two women. Meglan slipped the tunic from her shoulders and breasts. Dame Inonna watched her with a bright, unblinking gaze. 'So pretty,' she said.

She had uncorked the jar. A fragrance touched Meglan's nostrils, lightly pungent, delicately perfumed, distant. It evoked thoughts of faraway places where Meglan had never been, seemed to stir wistful memories which she could not quite bring to consciousness. She gazed at Inonna's strange face, which expressed so much yet gave little away. Dame Inonna scooped an opaque bluish substance from the jar with two fingers. She moved to position herself behind Meglan.

Meglan felt the soothing touch of her cool, oiled fingers again upon her neck. She felt herself relax, all tensions flying from her body as the embrocation penetrated her skin and Dame Inonna's fingers plied their gentle magic. Dame Inonna hummed in a low voice to herself, a slow, hypnotic chant, lacking melody or fixed rhythm, but which in itself was as comforting as her touch.

Meglan closed her eyes; her head lolled back against Inonna's shoulder. She slipped easily into a blissful half-slumber.

Time ceased. She floated in a dreamy somnolence beyond conscious control, suspended perhaps for moments, perhaps an age. It would never end; she never wanted it to. She was adrift in infinity's ocean, warm and slumbrous, beyond harm, beyond pain, beyond concern, sublime. Nothing could be the matter. Until somehow, penetrating her languor came a far-off, unwelcome twinge, a barely apprehended sensation of discontent. Something was not quite right.

Even before her eyes were open she sensed the change, subtle as it was. Dame Inonn's fingers still stroked and caressed, but their touch had a different quality. Lightly her hands moved upon Meglan's breasts, just touching, exploring, moving away, returning. The touch was pleasurable: Meglan both wanted it to continue and felt that it should not. It was not as before: these were caresses, not healer's motions. Without invitation they had gained an intimacy of a specific kind. They were no longer innocent.

Meglan opened her eyes. The first thing she saw was Gaskid's face, close. His eyes, fixed upon her breasts as Dame Inonna stroked and massaged them, almost bulged from his neck. Meglan stiffened and recoiled, pushing away Inonna's hands and covering her nakedness with her arms.

'Ah, child, do not be alarmed.' Dame Inonna's voice came huskily, close to her ear. 'Gaskid requires instruction in the healing, that he may pass on the goodness to others. He learns through observing me.'

'Yes. Yes. I observe. I learn the way.' Gaskid flicked an eager tongue over his lips, his face flushed and gleaming. His bony hands shifted in agitation upon his knees. He pressed his thighs together.

Meglan pulled up her tunic to cover herself, and rose from the stool. Only now did she see Jans, who was slumped across the table, his arms asprawl. 'What has happened to Jans? Jans! Jans!'

'Your friend had too much to drink,' said Gaskid, who had drawn back.

'He only had two tankards full. It was not enough to put him to sleep like that. I had one, and was hardly affected. Jans! *Jans!*'

'He cannot hear you, my dear,' said Dame Inonna, still at her back. 'He will not wake before morning.'

'You have drugged him?'

In sudden fear Meglan reached for the dagger at her belt. She drew it forth, taking a step back. At the same time Dame Inonna stepped around into her view. Meglan gave a gasp. Dame Inonna's skin had taken on a mottled green hue, marked with a clearly defined pattern of zig-zagging black. Her face, too, had changed shape. The whole lower part protruded further forward into a broad, blunt muzzle, nostrils at the fore, the mouth a wide, thin, lipless line. The eyes were yellow and revealed nothing human.

'Don't be afraid, my child. We mean you no harm.'

Meglan stared wildly from one to the other. 'Come no closer!'

'My dear, we will not hurt you.'

'Then why do you— what *are you*?' Even as she framed the words it hit Meglan that Dame Inonna's transformation had caused her to resemble nothing more than a huge snake.

'She is Inonna, the gifted one,' replied Gaskid. 'She is Inonna, Queen of the Serpents. She heals; her counsel is prophetic; she comprehends the workings of the universe and the meaning of all things.'

'I want to leave!'

'You would be ill-advised to do so,' Dame Inonna said. 'There are things out there, most especially at night, which would harm you. And you would be alone; your companion would not be able to aid you.'

'The risk can be no greater there than here.'

'Believe me, my dear, you have nothing to fear from us.' Dame Inonna made a motion as if to step towards her.

'Come no closer! I will kill you!'

'You cannot kill me. But think, my child. Had we intended you harm, would we have allowed you to keep your dagger that you might menace us? And think again. Have I not helped you? Are you not healed?'

Meglan had forgotten her bruises. She put her free hand to her neck, applying careful pressure. She felt no pain. Gingerly she moved her head, shifted her shoulders. Still no discomfort. She swallowed: the soreness in her throat had gone.

At Dame Inonna's instruction Gaskid produced a mirror framed in white wood decorated with a carved serpent design. He offered it to Meglan, holding it tightly in his shrivelled hands. Nervously she accepted it and glanced at her reflection. The bruises and swellings had vanished.

She fought back her bewilderment, struggling to find words. 'This— this is—,'

Dame Inonna smiled – inasmuch as her distorted face could be said to be capable of forming a smile. Her serpentine appearance was in fact diminishing. The mottled pattern on her skin was fading. She was becoming human again.

'How have you done this?' asked Meglan, agog.

'She has the gift,' Gaskid said.

'Meglan, put away your dagger and I will explain everything,' said Dame Inonna. 'I will not harm you. Had I wanted to I could have done so already, could I not?'

It was true, she had had Meglan at her mercy. But what of Gaskid, who had ogled her so? Meglan grew hot and angry. And Inonna's caresses, grown so intimate?

Meglan's eyes alighted again on Jans. *What was happening here?* A renewed terror threatened to rise, but she fought it back. Wholly unnerved she sheathed her dagger, sensing that it would not protect her.

'Explain, then.'

Dame Inonna waited, gathering her thoughts, then began. 'As a young girl I lived with my family in a small village some distance from here. One day, while working in the fields, I was bitten by a poisonous serpent. I should have died, but I did not. Immediately after receiving the bite I began to feel odd, weirdly light, buoyant. My perceptions became acute; the air about me seemed alive, full, abounding with discordant noise. I lay upon my back, my eyes closed, yet I could see things. Visions confronted me. Later, when I returned to normal, my parents could not believe it. They took it as a sign that I was somehow different, set apart from others. Over the ensuing weeks they plied me with other poisons. Again I was unharmed, but again found myself in that strange, heightened condition of unusual intoxication. And I found I could speak the language of snakes, and of some other animals. They imparted to me secrets, knowledge of hidden things. I gained insights, I was able sometimes to see into the future, I had knowledge of the past, and learned that the body I now occupied was but a temporary vessel. I had lived before and would live again. I discovered the healing gift; certain techniques of what you would term magic were made known to me. It was a great gift: the wisdom of serpents is little known. But I discovered also that I was changing. My skin, my appearance, my nature. I was becoming something other than human.'

Dame Inonna paused, her eyes downcast, and stared for sometime into a private distance. 'In time I was driven away from my home. I was a freak, and despite the benefits I could provide, the people were afraid of me. Upon the tail of fear comes hatred. I could not stay, for fear of my life and the lives of those I loved.

'The serpents brought me to this place, which is protected. There is a convergence of rare energies here. Here I discovered the secrets of administering the rare plants, the minerals and compounds that have gathered in this extraordinary domain. I have lived here ever since.'

Meglan watched her with a puzzled frown. 'I still do not understand. Your story is fascinating, extraordinary, but what has it to do with me?'

'Nothing. Except that I needed you tonight. No, you have nothing to fear. Be calm. I am still changing, you see. The gift I received makes demands upon my greater self. I am one with serpents, but they take from me. They draw me to them. Gradually I become one of them. I fight against it. To delay the process I need to spend time in the company of people, that I may take a little of their human essence. But I am a freak, shunned by all but Gaskid. I take something of him, but he suffers through my dependence. That is why he is as he is. He would give me all, for he is devoted, but that I will not let him do. Nevertheless, the fact that we are together, without others, means that Gaskid is continually giving of his essence in order that I might retain my humanness. Every two months we take our goods to the souk. There I mingle with the crowds, touching where I can, receiving the human essence in infinitesimal doses from each person I come into contact with. They are unaware. I take so little from each that they are not diminished. But it strengthens me, enables me to survive. Now, as you know, we were prevented from going to Dharsoul by the bandits. I don't know what will become of me.'

Meglan had tensed again, her heart beating wildly. 'What are you saying? Have you taken something from me? My— essence? What have you done to me?'

'Again I say be calm, child. I have not harmed you. I have taken your pain, both physical and spiritual. It is as much a part of your humanity as any other aspect of your person. You have suffered nothing – indeed, you have gained. And I have gained. It has been a reciprocal exchange. I thank you.'

In bewilderment Meglan's eyes went from Dame Inonna to the strange little man, Gaskid, and back again. Inonna smiled her ophidian smile. Meglan said, 'But you— touched me. Without my consent you became intimate.'

'I apologize. I absorb your pleasure, your pain, any aspect of you. It is what I crave, the sustenance I need to retain my humanity. But as I have said many times, I would not have done you harm. And if you will allow it, I would take more from you tonight. It will restore me. In return I can be of great assistance to you.'

'In what manner?'

'When I took away your hurt I sensed certain things. I think that you are an unusual young woman. You are greatly troubled. I have a feeling also that you may be in great danger. If you will allow me to know more, I can help you. I can counsel you on the most advisable course you should take. In addition I may be able to bestow upon you something that will help you through the troubles that lie in wait for you.'

'What must I do?'

'First of all sit here with me, place your hands in mine, tell me briefly something of what oppresses you and allow me to share your mind for a moment.'

'That is all?'

'That is all that is required for me to help you. If you will help me in return I ask only that you lie with me this night, that I may take something of you in order to restore something of myself. But you need not say yes. I will take nothing if you do not wish it. And this is not a trade. Give me your hands now and I will freely help you in any way I can. Tell me of your father and brother, who so occupy your thoughts and for whom you feel such concern. I ask for nothing in return.'

Meglan stared hard at her. 'You know?'

'Little. But come, sit with me, take my hands, allow me to see.'

Meglan hesitated just a moment, torn with conflicting emotions and fears. All this was so strange. She was frightened. But to know something of Sildemund and her father. If it might be possible. . . . There was really no decision to be made. Meglan placed the ends of her fingers in Dame Inonna's hands.

Immediately she felt a warmth, like a subtle breath in her veins. She allowed herself to be seated before the snake-woman, gazing into her otherwordly face. Dame Inonna closed her eyes. 'Tell me what troubles you, and hold an image of your father and brother in your mind, that I may see them also.'

'My brother Sildemund – my twin – has been sent to Dharsoul on an urgent mission for my father. I went after him, without my father's consent. Something he carries is greatly needed by my father. I had hoped to bring him back more quickly than he would otherwise have come. But I am thwarted, I am afraid. What has become of Sildemund? Has he been murdered by bandits? Is he in Dharsoul. . . ? And my father, Master Frano, is frail and ill at home in Volm. I feel that I have deserted him, yet I really had no choice. And now . . . I don't know what to do. Should I continue on in hope of finding Sildemund or return to comfort my dear father?'

Dame Inonna remained seated for some time, her eyes closed. Her grip tightened spasmodically from time to time around Meglan's fingers. Beneath their lids her eyes moved back and forth. Once or twice she winced, as with pain or shock. When she opened her eyes her look was troubled, but she stared into space as if seeing nothing around her. She said 'Sildemund has been attacked by the bandits, but he is safe. He is in Dharsoul now. It is confused. I see him and two companions with Enlos, the Crown Prince. But all is not progressing well. I sense difficulties – and more lie ahead.' She shifted her bleary gaze a little. 'Your father. . . .'

Dame Inonna straightened on her seat. Her face was suddenly very grave. She stared unblinking at Meglan. 'Ah. . . . No, I see.'

'What is it?' said Meglan anxiously. 'What do you see? Has something happened?'

'No. I am sorry. The vision was a little blurred for a moment. You should go after your brother. He needs you. You should find him and remain with him to do what has to be done.'

'But what of my father? What do you see?'

'You chose the right course in leaving. There was nothing you could do to help your father by staying with him, and there is nothing to be gained by returning now to Volm. Be sure of this. You should not go back. *You must follow Sildemund!*'

Dame Inonna released her hands. 'There is danger, more so than I first perceived. Something . . . I could not make out. Child, you are involved in a hazardous mission. Do not return to the Dharsoul Road.'

'But how then will I reach Dharsoul?'

Dame Inonna inhaled deeply and pensively. 'There is a way, through Dazdun's Despair. It is not an easy way. It twists and winds, and is invisible to normal eyes. It is known as the Invisible Path, or the Serpent's Path. It is not a fast route, but as long as you do not wander from it it will take you to Dharsoul.'

'But if it is invisible, how will I find it?'

'A moment.' Dame Inonna rose and shuffled to the corner of the room where the large carved wooden serpent stood. She opened a small chest, removed something and came back.'

'This will show you.' She held out a small model of a snake, half the length of her little finger, cast in silvery-white metal with tiny opaque white-gems for eyes. 'Treat it as precious. Its head will always point in the direction of the Serpent's Path.'

Meglan took the little snake. Dame Inonna looked wan. Meglan sensed that the effort of her vision had drained her.

'You are willing to do this, to help me further?'

'In any way I can.'

'But in return I should lie with you tonight?'

The snake-woman shook her head. 'I said, I would make no demands. There is no trade. I give you my gifts freely.'

Meglan closed her fingers around the snake talisman. 'Your talent is too important to be allowed to die. You have aided me; let me then give my gift, if it is of use to you. I will lie with you if it will restore you.'

Dame Inonna smiled, bowing her head slightly. She held out a hand. 'We should retire now, child, for my energy is low.'

At the door to the next room Dame Inonna halted, one hand resting upon the wall. 'Tomorrow you will not recall me, nor this place. It is our protection. You will know what you need to know. Take care, then. Be alert. I have sensed a shadow on your track.'

'A shadow?'

'A presence, dark and hateful.'

Meglan shuddered. Dame Inonna clasped her hand in both of hers. 'Your quest is more important than you know. Whatever may befall you, as long as you are physically able do not relinquish your task. You remain in my thoughts. I wish you well.'

14

Meglan dreamed.

A voice spoke to her from a distance, raised so as to be heard over the soughing of a dark, warm wind. The speaker was unseen.

'Do not stray from the Serpent's Path, not even for a moment. It will lead you safely to your destination. The Serpent reveals the way.'

The wind grew in volume. Meglan was buffeted, could hardly stand, was lifted off her feet and carried from the earth, up to into darkness, helpless as a leaf in a storm, then down, down, rolling over and over, no sense of direction, drawn into a void, closing all around her, absorbing her, fear was all she knew, hurling her into the unknown.

She opened her eyes.

She closed them again, tight, quickly, stabbed by light, piercing, shifting off and on without rhythm. She jerked back her head, opened her eyes; the dazzle passed.

A monstrous sight confronted her. A head, filling almost her entire vision, armoured in hundreds of small scales coloured in bright shades of red, gold and white. A huge wide maw hung half-open, showing twin rows of pointed white teeth and moistly glistening pink gums. A purple tongue was curled into a compact ball within. From snout to crown ran a row of horny barbs, and on either side of the broad skull a big, globular, pale blue eye bulged, round and heavily lidded, slowly blinking, swivelling, each independent of the other.

Meglan gasped, on a reflex thrusting herself away. The world focused into its proper perspective. The armoured monster became a lizard, no larger than a rat. At her movement it flipped around and darted away, spatulate feet raising tiny spumes of dust. It vanished into a cranny in a clump of rocks.

Dazedly, Meglan sat up, pushing her long auburn hair from her face. She saw that she was in the shade of a tall cypress, in a grove of cypresses. The dazzle was the low morning sun, pushing sudden beams through the aromatic green foliage, dappling the earth. Jans lay nearby, his head upon a rolled blanket. He appeared to be sleeping. Their horses were tethered to a bush a few paces off, close beside a small spring.

Meglan leaned back against the trunk, confused. She did not know where she was.

'Jans! Are you awake?'

Jans stirred, opened his eyes, blinking. He sat up. 'Mistress Meglan.' He peered about him. 'Where are we?'

'I don't know. I – ' She looked out beyond the trees onto an arid landscape of blasted yellow rock which stretched to the horizon. Bare, ragged hills, scarps and declivities characterized the land, scarred with deep rifts and gullies, wild upthrusts of rock, and here and there growths of hardy scrub. The sky was pale azure shifting to glaring yellow, without a cloud to be seen.

Slowly Meglan stood. 'Jans, do you recall how we got here?'

Jans shook his head.

'Have we slept here all night?'

'I don't remember, Mistress. The last thing I recall, we were at the roadside, waiting. There were bandits. . . .'

'Yes. And then. . . .' She stared about her. 'Where is the road?'

Jans gave a shrug and rubbed his eyes. Meglan walked to the horses. Their saddles and bridles rested on the ground close by. She checked her saddlepack; nothing had been removed. Within she found a package containing rice-cakes wrapped in leaves, bread, preserved meat and other comestibles which she was sure had not been there the previous day.

'This is all strange,' she murmured to herself, and walked back through the cool shade of the trees to the other side of the grove. The same harsh landscape confronted her, baked by the sun, bearing away endlessly in all directions.

She put a hand to the back of her neck, slowly rotating her head to ease a tension there. Now she recalled her bruises. There was no pain.

'Jans, am I marked here?' she said, turning as Jans moved up beside her.

139

Jans stared, not quite believing. 'There are no bruises. Your skin is unblemished.'

Something moved, glinting in the sunlight, at Meglan's wrist. She saw a tiny metallic, globe-eyed snake dangling on a leather thong. She stared at it for a moment, trying to remember. 'This is not mine.'

Meglan lifted the snake and placed it on the palm of her hand. An image flickered briefly in her mind. She touched fingers to brow, closing her eyes, trying to recall the image, to build it into something more meaningful. But it had come and gone. A single, isolated picture remained, perplexing her.

'Jans, do you remember a cottage here, at the edge of this grove? White, surrounded by an orchard, vines and many different crops.'

Jans looked vague. 'I recall nothing.'

Meglan took off along the line of the cypresses, convinced that somewhere here the cottage must lie. She had gone almost full circle, and found no indication of a cottage or anything associated with one. But something now brought her abruptly to a halt. She took a step back, her heart beating wildly, staring at the thing that rested upon the ground before her.

'Jans!'

Jans ran up from between the trees.

'Look.'

He stared in the direction she pointed, and his jaw dipped. The thing was long and approximately cylindrical in shape, made up of thousands of tiny, semi-diaphanous hexagons, like scales. It was as delicate as a spider's web, but dry, friable, thinner than paper. Its colour was predominantly a translucent greenish, mottled, with a black zig-zag, diamond pattern along its length. Except for the fact that four long protrusions branched off the main body, like fragile sheaths for limbs, it resembled nothing more than the sloughed-off skin of a gigantic serpent, complete with head and eye casing.

Meglan stared at the empty head. It was like a snake's, yet not. Some quality of otherness, even a suggestion of humanness, imbrued the dead expression of the face. Again, something almost came to her consciousness, something profound, disturbing, poignant, which she could not grasp. Without knowing why, she felt tears welling behind her eyes.

'We should leave this place,' said Jans. A breath of a breeze shifted the skin slightly, causing it to give off a dry, barely audible whisper.

Meglan tore her eyes away, struggling with emotions she could not identify, rising unfathomably from the deepest core of her being, a place she had never reached before. She gazed out into a distance. 'Yes, but where to?'

The serpent reveals the way!

Her eyes were drawn back to the snake-skin, then to the talisman dangling at her wrist. Her brow furrowed. She took the tiny snake again and placed it in the palm of her hand. Then she began to walk out from the trees, slowly, into the full glare of the sun. She had covered perhaps a dozen paces when the little snake, with no help from her, began to swivel upon her palm.

Holding her hand steady before her Meglan changed direction, moving the way the snake's head now pointed. As she did so the little talisman shifted again, pointing in its original direction. Meglan stopped, nodded to herself. She walked off sharply to the left. The snake turned again, so that its head pointed in the direction she had previously followed. She stood for one moment, feeling the sun beating hard upon her.

Meglan began to walk back, thoughtful. She had lost sight of Jans for a moment, but as she came closer she saw him watching her curiously from the edge of the trees, his hands on his hips.

'I know the way,' she called.

The route was laborious and slow, the pace dictated by both terrain and Meglan's need to keep her eye upon the little snake talisman which guided her. She found she could safely leave it suspended upon its thong, which was preferable to holding it in the flat of her palm. The snake kept its head pointing always in a specific direction, altering from time to time as the invisible pathway looped and twisted, bearing them on deeper and deeper into the untracked wilderness of Dazdun's Despair.

Midday came and went. The sun was indiscernible, lost in a sheet of glaring white, blazing down mercilessly to parch the earth. The tortured landscape shimmered and blurred as if striving to escape the inescapable, offering no comfort and scarcely any shade. Yet despite the obvious heat, unrelieved by all except the merest infrequent arid breath of breeze, neither Meglan, Jans or the two horses suffered severely. It seemed to Meglan that they were partly shielded, which caused her to wonder whether the Serpent's Path, through some strange, unknown property, formed an unseen barrier which fended off the harshest effects of the surrounding environment.

Early in the afternoon they came upon a spring which bubbled out of the side of a low rise. Rushes, clumps of strong green grass and a few bushes grew around it, which seemed further evidence that the Serpent's Path was a route that offered survival to any who knew how to tread its invisible course.

They paused to rest and eat while the horses drank from the spring and cropped the grass. Meglan expressed a fear that had been growing within her throughout the morning: that the Serpent's Path might be leading them further from civilization, deeper into this no-man's-land, aimlessly on towards some end of which they knew nothing.

'Where is Dharsoul? How can we know where we are bound?'

Jans squinted at the sky, then into the distance. 'I have been trying to answer that question to my own satisfaction. Calculating from the movement of the sun, I would say that Dharsoul lies somewhere in this direction,' he pointed. 'The Dharsoul Road will be that way, south. We have swung to a position something northwest of the city. At some point I would expect this path to veer, then, towards the south or south-east, if it is to carry us to the capital.'

'We have covered so short a distance,' said Meglan glumly, looking back the way they had come.

'Aye, it's slow going.'

She put aside her food, finding she had little appetite. 'Do you estimate we are far from the city?'

'It is impossible to say, for we do not know from where we started out. Had we been upon the road, unmolested, we could have reached the city within a day or a day and a half. I am assuming that we remain north of the Tigrant still, for the Despair does not extend that far south. The closest I can estimate is that we are within two to three days of Dharsoul, if the route remains fairly direct. If the terrain forces long detours. . . .' He shrugged and pulled a rueful face. 'Who can guess?'

Meglan drained her flask and went to the spring to replenish it. 'We should move on.'

Squatting beside the water she looked back again along the way they had come. She shielded her eyes, squinnying, and stood, leaving the flask on its side at the water's edge to fill itself. 'Jans, look.'

Jans rose and stood beside her. Their slightly elevated position afforded them a view over many miles. Jans stared in the direction Meglan indicated. 'Do you see anything, right over there, in the far distance?'

Jans shook his head. 'Only barrenness and heat-haze. What did you see?'

'I don't know. I thought something moved across the land, quite rapidly. It was far away. I may have imagined it.' As she spoke Meglan experienced a sudden chill along her spine. She shivered, wondering where it could have come from. The day was so hot, yet this was raw, as cold as ice. It came and was gone in hardly more than an instant, but in that instant its touch penetrated her to the bone.

They watched for some moments more, but nothing was evident. Presently Meglan shrugged, albeit uneasily. 'Come. Let's be on our way.'

They had crested the rise and were nearing its base on the other side when Meglan remembered: 'Jans, my flask. I was filling it it at the spring. I must have left it there.'

Jans began to turn his horse.

'No, wait here. I will go. There's no point in two of us returning. In fact wait with Swift Cloud. It is as easy for me to cover this short distance on foot.'

She dismounted and handed Swift Cloud's rein to Jans, then made off to the spring. The flask was as she had left it, lying in the water. She picked it up and capped it. Standing, she was about to return to Jans when something made her look again back the way they had come. A dark shape was approaching, some sort of creature; she could not tell what it was. It bore down towards her at great speed.

Meglan stared in sudden fear, in indecision, trying to make out what it was that ran so unnaturally fast. The beast was a couple of hundred paces off. It was large, but she could not define its form. It came in long bounds and leaps, almost skimming over the rough terrain, moving with dogged intent. It was making straight for her.

Meglan glanced back, Jans and the horses were out of sight beyond the lip of the rise. There was not time to reach them before the creature arrived. Her heart hammered. She was in danger, she sensed it urgently.

Had the creature seen her? She could not tell. Was it possible that it was making for the spring, not her, in order to drink?

That seemed just plausible. Meglan was in no doubt that she should hide. She glanced around. A jagged slab of brown rock just a few paces away offered some cover. She looked back to check the creature's approach. She glimpsed a dark shape descend like a fleet shadow into a hollow. It was almost here!

She ran, head low, and threw herself behind the rock. On the lee side the rock was fissured, creating a shadowed nook into which Meglan pressed herself, curling her legs beneath her and drawing forth her sabre.

Only a moment later she heard the rapid scrabble of feet upon the rubbly earth somewhere close to the spring, and a panting breath. The creature slowed its pace. There was silence, then less frantic but equally menacing movement; the intermittent shift of a stone.

Her heart pounded, thundering in her ears, its noise seemed so great she thought it would give her presence away. She could hear nothing now. She wondered what the thing was doing. Was it drinking? Would it leave when it had slaked its thirst? She wanted so much to look; the silence, the not-knowing, was unbearable. But she dared not move even a hair's breadth.

She heard a breath, and a soft, prowling footfall. So close! The creature was on the other side of the rock!

Meglan gripped the hilt of her sabre tightly with both hands, ready to thrust out at anything that moved. She almost choked upon her fear. Something about this unknown, unseen creature terrified her more deeply than she could explain. She held her breath, praying to all the gods that the thing would move away.

What was it? What was this demon that had arrived so suddenly?

And then she heard another sound, something familiar and yet so shocking, so utterly unexpected as to impel her into a new intensity of terror. Her innards contracted, her whole being trapped in a cold, silent shriek of disbelief, of both denial and horrified acceptance of what she faced. She felt, with that dreadful sound, that she had been entered, violated; that something was ravaging her to her very soul.

On the verge of madness, in a waking nightmare, she was yet conscious that from somewhere within her came a whisper, a command, a warning: *Do nothing. Do not move, or you will die.*

The sound she had heard was a voice.

The voice was human; at least, it formed human words. It wheedled, coaxed, purred, its pitch ascending and falling in tones of quiet fervour, obscenely playful. Meglan had heard that voice before, had hoped never to hear it again. And the words it spoke, the way it spoke them, make her retch through her terror.

'Meg-lan? Where is love-ly Meg-lan? Love-ly, love-ly. Love-ly Meg-lan.'

Skalatin!

Meglan forced herself to utter stillness. There was a sudden, soundless movement on the ground before her. A shadow had appeared, spindly, grotesquely misshapen. *He was above her, on the rock!*

'Beauti-ful chi-ld. Come, pretty Meg-lan.'

She heard the scrape of claws upon the rock. The shadow swayed slowly from side to side. It was not human in form. Not Skalatin. Then what. . . ? With a swift movement it was gone.

Meglan listened, her heart in her mouth. No sound. Then, yes, a stealthy footfall, off to her right, around the angle of the rock. She pushed herself even further back into the nook, impossibly, for there was nowhere to go. The rock pressed into her flesh, but her fear numbed all recognition of the pain.

Go away! Go away! Go away!

'Oh, love-ly. Oh, pret-ty. Meg-lan, Meg-lan.'

Skalatin stepped into view.

Or rather, some*thing* stepped into view. It was Skalatin, but something other, too.

He was on all fours. His head pushed forward and up, his snout testing the air. He was part-human in form, yet resembled a huge, hideously deformed hound. The arms and legs were long, ropily muscled, sinewy and powerful. The back was arched, the feet clawed and padded. The skin was pale pinkish, rough, covered in a patchy layer of sparse brown fur.

Skalatin's head was turned slightly away from Meglan; she could not see his face. The sight of him, almost a man, almost a vile, unnatural beast, was a blasphemy.

'Meg-lan? Meg-lan?'

Even as she watched Skalatin began to change. The clawed feet bulged and stretched, the body filled out. He stood erect, naked. His head turned. He looked directly at her.

Meglan stiffened, bracing herself, rendered mute by the sight of that face. The flesh was almost gone; what remained was decayed, greenish, flaking. The bone beneath was pitted and rotten, the gums crawled with worms, the tongue was a dark purple writhing mass. And the eyes . . . she remembered those depraved, infinitely cold, dark eyes, whose stare reached into her as though to corrupt her to the core.

Skalatin was just feet away.

'Meg-lan?'

He still peered curiously, still sniffed the air. His malevolent gaze failed to focus upon her. It shifted. He took another pace forward. He was so close, almost touching! He moved again, but off at a slightly oblique angle from Meglan.

'Meg-lan? Love-ly, love-ly. Where?'

He could not see her!

Why? How? He had gazed right at her. She had caught the foetid stink of his breath. Yet he had not seen her!

Unbreathing, unmoving, Meglan was suspended in a new dimension of horror and disbelief. He was playing a game! At any instant he would wheel around, leap upon her and wrench her from her hiding place, do with her whatever it was he wanted to do.

But no, Skalatin continued to move away, still seeking, his head turning from side to side. He still repeated her name, over and over, in that horribly intimate way. Now he was ten paces off; now twelve.

He halted. He turned. Meglan froze. But Skalatin merely uttered a sound of disgust. As she watched he dropped to all fours. His form altered again to become the obscenely disfigured hound of moments earlier. With a swift, sudden movement he bounded away.

Long moments passed. Meglan dared not move. Presently a long, shuddering breath escaped her lungs. Her muscles slowly unlocked the tenseness that, unconsciously, had turned her whole body as rigid as bone. Painfully she eased herself a little way out of the nook. She craned her neck to peep over the rock. She half-expected to see Skalatin standing there with a gloating, evil grin. But there was no sign of him.

She crawled further out. Her limbs had started to tremble violently. She began to sob, great wracking motions of lungs and gut, the release of pent-up terror. She fell forward onto her hands and knees. As the convulsions passed she sank onto her belly, utterly exhausted.

She would have lain there, too weak to move, but into her mind came a new fear: *Jans!* Had Skalatin found him?

At the same time she realized her stupidity, sprawled upon the dusty ground, wholly vulnerable. Skalatin might be prowling nearby. He could return.

Meglan scrambled to her feet. Her legs still shook. She made off as quickly as she could towards the spot where she had left Jans and the two horses. Her head was swimming, she was almost delirious, but rising through her emotions now came a feeling of anger which imbued her with a new strength and a sense of determination.

She came around a low bluff. A figure rose up before her. She fell back with a gasp, shielding herself with an arm, then gave a cry of relief. It was Jans, who was running, half-crouched, his face pale and set. He grabbed her and drew her behind the rocks.

'You are safe, Mistress!' Jans was breathing hard. He peered around the rocks into the desolate distance.

'What is it, Jans? What is the matter?'

'I was worried for you. I saw something, a beast of some kind. I feared you had been attacked.'

'Where did it go?'

'Away. That way. It moved so fast.'

'I saw it. I don't know how it didn't see me.'

'I too thought I had been spotted. I was not hiding, and the horses were conspicuous. It passed fifty paces away. I thought it looked directly at us, yet it neither slowed nor altered its course.'

'Perhaps it is only looking for me,' Meglan muttered through pursed lips. But she was wondering, Why? It's the red stone Skalatin wants. Why is he following me? *And how is it that he did not see me?*

Jans looked at her curiously. 'You? What do you mean?'

'It was searching for me. It knew my name. I have met this monster before.'

'You have met it before?' A nervousness entered Jans's gaze. 'Mistress, what is happening? What is the reason for this journey we have undertaken?'

Gods, Meglan thought, what right had I to involve others in this? I should have come alone.

She reasoned to herself that she could not have anticipated Skalatin's coming after her, nor this enforced detour due to the brigands upon the Dharsoul Road. Jans was a bodyguard, well paid for his services; but even so, the perils they now faced were enormous. She could not expect so much of him.

'Jans, this creature, I don't know what it is. It can change its shape – I have just seen it do so. Previously it has taken the guise of a man-thing. He calls himself Skalatin. He has menaced my father. He is evil, this I know without a shadow of a doubt. Master Frano has something – a strange red stone – which apparently belongs to Skalatin, or to some person whom Skalatin represents. I am coming to believe that this second person does not exist. It is Skalatin who covets the stone, for what reason I don't know. Father sent my brother, Sildemund, to Dharsoul with the stone, to try and find out more about it. Later Skalatin made it clear that he will go to any lengths to regain the stone. He has murdered Dervad, and Edric too, I think. He assaulted my father and myself. I left, to reach Sildemund and have him return the stone to Volm without delay. I believe father is in danger as long as the stone is kept from Skalatin. But now, for some reason, Skalatin has come after us – after me.' She put her fingertips to her brow, frowning and shaking her head. 'Yet he found me and did not see me. I don't understand.'

From the thong around her wrist the little snake talisman swayed to and fro before her eyes. Meglan watched it, a grain of an idea forming in her mind. She stood quickly.

'Jans, wait here. Watch me.'

Meglan walked away slowly, out from the direction from which she had come. She observed the snake talisman, and shifted her gaze from it to Jans, who watched with a vexed expression. She had gone perhaps ten paces when the talisman turned as if with its own volition. She felt the heat upon her. She took a couple more paces and looked back.

'Jans, where are you?'

'Is this a game?'

Meglan's heart beat fast. 'No. No game. I cannot see you.'

She was staring at the place where Jans had stood. She could see the rocks, the ground . . . but Jans was not visible. 'Are you hidden? Are you behind a rock?'

'I have not moved. I am here, looking at you.'

'Do something. Move. Wave your arms. Something vigorous.'

Now she made him out, a blurred, vague figure, frantically waving.

'Now stop.'

The movement ceased. Jans was invisible again.

Meglan strode back. Within three paces he had come clearly into view.

'It is the Serpent's Path! It protects us. It makes us invisible to any not on it. Go, stand where I stood. Can you see me?'

Jans walked out towards the spot where Meglan had been, watching her over his shoulder as he did so. At a certain point he stopped, and gaped. 'Mistress, you have gone.'

'I am still here, Jans. It is as I said: we are invisible upon the Serpent's Path. Now come back, before you are seen.'

Jans rejoined her quickly. Meglan thought hard: why had Skalatin not seen her? He had been so close. It must have been sheer luck. Skalatin, in stepping past the rock where she crouched, had taken himself off the Serpent's Path. Perhaps only by inches, but it had been enough. He had not seen her. Had she hidden anywhere else, anywhere at all, she would have been lost.

'We will be safe as long as we remain on the Path,' she said.

'Aye, and as long as Skalatin does not join us on it.'

'Jans, I'm sorry. I should never have brought you on this journey. But I did not know the danger. I had no way of knowing what would happen. Now I would gladly say to you, "Go, for there is no reason you should subject yourself to this. Leave me, and I will not think the worse of you." But . . .' she spread her hands, 'we are lost.'

Jans gave a wry shrug. 'Aye, are we lost. I cannot go, other than with you. But if the circumstances were different, that would still be my decision, rest assured, Mistress. I will do all I can to help you. Come, we should not waste time.'

15

THEY RODE ON, slowly, ever-watchful, ever cautious, into the Despair, which seemed without end. There were no signs of human habitation, barely any indication of animal life bar an infrequent glimpse of a wild goat, or the bleached bones or desiccated cadaver of some unfortunate beast. It was as if there was no other world, as if nothing existed but the bare rock, dust and shimmering heat of the Despair, stretching on forever.

They were overcome with the monotony of it, the sheer desolation. Their eyes constantly searched the landscape, hungry for relief, an indication of life, any kind of reassurance that they had not been cast into a dead and irredeemable land. At the same time they feared that the one thing they might see would be that which they dreaded most – the fleet, demonic form of Skalatin.

The glare of the sun was merciless, but they were at least protected from its terrible heat as long as they remained upon the Serpent's Path. They pushed on, sometimes dismounting to lead their tired horses over the more difficult terrain. The sun settled, the night gathered; they made camp in a defile beneath the chill wind which sprang up with the darkness.

There was no spring here. Both Meglan and Jans gave up precious water from their flasks so that the horses might at least take a modicum of fluid. Neither voiced their thoughts, but it was on both their minds that there might be no water on the way ahead, that the Serpent's Path might yet be taking them to their deaths.

They lit no fire, for fear of attracting that which they did not want. They ate food from their packs, hardly speaking, then Meglan took first watch while Jans curled up beneath his blanket on the hard earth, and slept.

With the first yellow-grey light of dawn they moved on. After about three hours, to Meglan's relief, the snake talisman turned towards the south, and while still winding and twisting, held generally true in that direction. Meglan's spirits began to rise; this was what Jans had predicted if the path was to take them to Dharsoul. She sat forward in her saddle now, eagerly scanning the horizon for the first glimpse of the city's towers and minarets, though she knew within herself that it must still lie a long way off.

They came upon a tiny rill, from which they replenished their flasks and let the horses drink. Then onward again.

Meglan's thoughts took on a wild aspect, almost mad, tumbling over each other as she struggled to find a way out of her predicament: *Skalatin wants the stone; he is following me. I will lead him on, yes, that's it! Have him follow me to Dharsoul. Find Sildemund. Then, when Skalatin comes, give him the stone. Then go. That's all he wants. We will be safe then. It will all be over.*

But she didn't believe it. There was something in Skalatin, something about the way he had touched her at home in Volm, the way he had looked at her, spoken to her, assaulted her; the way he had followed her (how?) across Dazdun's Despair, searching her out, speaking her name in such a brazen, loathsome, lascivious way . . . Even if he was given the stone he so coveted, she did not believe that would be the last she saw of Skalatin.

It was during the afternoon that Meglan saw the vultures circling in the sky ahead. She had seen them once or twice before, tearing at any tatters of flesh that still clung to animal corpses. But this had been carrion, dead for some time; the birds had been on the ground, and few in number. Those she saw now were in a mass. And the fact that they remained airborne implied that something still clung to life on the way ahead. Meglan felt apprehension mount in her breast. She told herself that it was probably nothing more than a dying animal, yet she felt no easier. She gauged the position of the birds. If the Serpent's Path did not alter course she would find out soon enough what it was that had summoned them.

They came upon the sight about half an hour later. The corpses of two wild goats lay upon the earth, freshly slain, their blood seeping into the dust, glistening brightly in the sunlight. A third goat, a ram, was alive but bleeding profusely, with one leg broken and obviously in a very weak condition. It was this survivor, the ram, that was keeping the big birds at bay. About a dozen or so vultures had descended, flapping and squawking about him and his two dead females. Head down, the ram was charging the vultures when they came too close. But he stumbled, and was often on bloodied knees.

Meglan and Jans observed from their horses, about twenty paces away. Few vultures were in the sky now. Sensing the ram's ebbing strength, they crowded the two corpses, squabbling over the flesh. The big ram stood for some moments, panting, head low, watching the birds, but he made no renewed charge. His legs folded and he sank onto his belly. A pair of vultures ventured close. He tossed his head, scaring them back, but could manage nothing more.

Meglan scanned her surroundings nervously. 'What can have done this?'

'A lion, perhaps.'

'A lion would kill only one, and then would have eaten. And those are not wounds inflicted by a big cat.'

'It is impossible to tell from here. I'll take a closer look, and put that poor creature out of his misery.'

'Be careful. You will be off the Path.'

'Whatever was here has gone now, I think. I will only be a moment.'

Jans urged his horse cautiously forward. Meglan watched as he approached the fallen goats, waving his sabre to frighten off the scavenging birds. He dismounted, stood before the two corpses for a moment, then turned to the ram. A vulture, braver than the rest, had alighted on its rump and was tearing at its haunch with its powerful beak. The ram had barely the strength to raise its head. Jans stepped across, bringing his sabre high. Meglan closed her eyes.

Jans remounted and made to return. He could not see Meglan, so approached at a slight angle. Entering the Path he turned towards her, pale-visaged.

'It's a grisly scene. The two goats' ribcages have been torn open. Their hearts are gone.'

Skalatin!

'That is how he kills,' Meglan began. Something caught her eye. A movement, a shadow, beneath a rock a little distance away. Her heart thumped. She strained her eyes, peering hard. She could see nothing now. Had she imagined it?

No! There it was again! Or were her eyes playing tricks? There was a hot skittering wind, raising dust in swirling clouds, and the air was addled with the heat, giving the impression of motion where perhaps there was none.

'Jans, keep absolutely still. Do not move a muscle.'

She still could not tell. She stared, blinked, stared again.

Then she saw it again. Her eyes had not betrayed her. Another movement. Something of bulk shifted beneath a low overhang of rock. A body of some kind, concealed in a natural pit scoured by wind and sand.

Meglan felt her terror rise. The thing moved once more, sliding forward. From the darkness came Skalatin.

He was on all fours, though in his mock-human guise. He rose erect, peering in Jans's direction, his head tilted to one side.

A moment passed and he took four loping steps forwards, then stopped, continuing to stare at Jans, though plainly he could not see him. Slowly his dreadful gaze shifted. He stared directly at Meglan. She thought she'd been seen, then his eyes moved away, back, his head cocked quizzically. He took another step.

In a moment he will step onto the Path! Then he will see us both!

She did not know what to do. Jans, seeing the fear in her eyes, turned his body to look in the direction she faced. Skalatin's eyes rested on him.

'Don't move!' whispered Meglan.

Skalatin twisted his head a little more. Had he heard her? He seemed confused.

His vile mouth opened. 'Meg-lan? Pretty, pretty? Where are you? I know you are here.'

Meglan sat, breathless.

'Meg-lan? Where is my heart?'

His heart? What was that? Did he mean her? Was he employing some obscene form of endearment?

Meglan shuddered. Skalatin took another step, slightly to the side. He could only be inches from entering the Path. She half thought she caught the taint of his breath.

'Meg-lan? My heart? You stole my heart. Give it back, love-ly chi-ld. To Skalatin. Give back my heart.'

Meglan's mind worked feverishly. Her thoughts flew back, to her father's study just a few evenings earlier: her first sight of the red stone. Immediately upon seeing it she had been struck by its resemblance to a heart. Cold, hard, bloody. A heart turned to stone. The very sight of it had chilled and disturbed her, and filled her with a sense of unutterable sadness that she could not explain.

'Meg-lan? Sweet Meg-lan?'

This is why he has come after me! It is no endearment. He believes I have the stone!

Could she make use of this knowledge? How? There was no time to think. Skalatin was moving closer.

A wild impulse came to her. 'Jans, stay here! I will draw him away. Don't stray! I will come back for you!'

Before Jans could respond she had drawn her sabre and dug her heels hard into Swift Cloud's flanks. Skalatin heard her, and saw her movement, but could not respond quickly enough. Swift Cloud surged forward, slamming into him. Meglan struck with her blade. She felt it bite into his flesh, drew it free, saw Skalatin knocked back hard onto the ground, heard his dismal roar.

She did not cease her pace, her instincts telling her that no blow she might inflict would kill or even seriously incapacitate her foe. She drove Swift Cloud on towards the rocks from which Skalatin had appeared, aware of the sun's full blast upon her back. Not daring to look back, she invoked the fabled Enchantress Yshcopthe to give her strength, give her the moments she needed to gain an edge.

He would pursue her. That was what she wanted. Her plan was to draw Skalatin away from the Serpent's Path, then, before he saw where she had gone, to vanish back onto it. Skalatin could not find the Path, except by hazard.

The vultures rose in a squawking, flapping cloud. She urged Swift Cloud through them, thinking they might prove a hindrance, however minor, to Skalatin. Almost at the outcrop of rocks she risked a glance back.

Skalatin was on the ground, rising onto all fours, staring after her as she fled. His form was changing. He was becoming the swift beast-hound that she had seen earlier. She could not outrun that, she knew.

She swerved around the rocks. The ground rose a little. She

154

glanced at the snake talisman which swung wildly at her wrist. Its head pointed forwards, slightly to her left. She was out of sight of Skalatin. If she could just find the Serpents Path. . . .

She bent low, head to Swift Cloud's neck, desperate, terrified. They entered a path of scrub. The head of the talisman turned. She veered Swift Cloud in the new direction, up again, over hard rock. She looked back. A dark form sped like an arrow from the rocks behind her. It raced forward, then swerved a little, then halted. It came no further, but stood, turning its head from side to side.

Meglan breathed a shuddering sigh. She was invisible! She brought Swift Cloud to a halt, fearful that the sound of their flight would betray her. Skalatin stood twenty paces away or less, watchful, angry, but not looking at her.

With a powerful thrust he bounded up the side of a leaning rock, climbing to its crest. His form altered again. He stood tall, staring about him.

Slowly Meglan walked Swift Cloud on, wanting to put as much distance as possible between her and her foe. She did not think Skalatin's hearing was particularly keen, and the wind favoured her. With care she would not be heard. Her intention was to break from hiding again somewhere up ahead, draw Skalatin on further, then once again return to the sanctuary of the Serpent's Path. When she had drawn him far enough away she would double back, to collect Jans.

She entertained two immediate fears: that Skalatin might inadvertently stumble upon the Path, and thus see her; and that he would discover her tracks. There was little she could do to prevent the former, except hope. As for the letter, the ground was hard here, the wind was shifting any dust that lay, and again, she did not think that Skalatin utilised particular tracking skills. Somehow he had followed and almost found her, as though by some terrible unnatural sense, but when it came to actually pinpointing her he seemed reliant on no more than normal human senses.

The ground rose a little more steeply. Her view of Skalatin was obscured by boulders. She watched the snake talisman carefully. Through a gap between the rocks she looked down again. Skalatin was still upon the rock. She reached the lip of the slope.

Now she could see Jans. He sat patiently upon his horse where she had left him, a solitary figure in a menacing wilderness. A little way off the vultures feasted.

Stay there, Jans! I will lead him away and come back to guide you.

Her eyes swept the plain below, then back. With a sudden shock she realized that Skalatin had left his rock. She could no longer see him. Where had be gone? Had he spotted her? Did he ascend unseen in her wake?

She looked around, back down the way she had come, back across the wasteland. Then she saw him – and knew her mistake.

Skalatin had moved back to the place where she had originally left him. He was slinking past the feasting vultures. He moved up beside the Serpent's Path as she watched. Jans had seen him, was sitting motionless upon his horse, watching him.

Meglan wanted to scream. She saw, hopelessly, what was about to happen. She would have urged Swift Cloud forward, raced down to intervene, but already it was too late. Skalatin, with a stealthy, questing gait, padded forward. He was so close to Jans. He had to be upon the Path!

Yes! Meglan sobbed out loud. Jans drew his sabre at the precise moment that Skalatin wheeled, with shocking speed, and sprang. Jans had no time to strike. Skalatin was upon him, leaping high to grapple him from the saddle. The tussle was savage and brief. Jans was thrown like a doll to the hard earth. He had no chance. Dazed, he tried to lift his head, but Skalatin was on him again.

Meglan stared in mute horror. From this distance she could not see precisely what occurred, but she did not need to. She saw the dreadful motions, saw the blood blossom from Jans's mutilated chest as Skalatin plunged his hands into the writhing body, drew something forth, bowed his head to gnaw rapaciously at his prize.

Oh Jans! Oh Jans! Oh Jans! Forgive me!

She remained transfixed, her eyes refusing to be dragged from the terrible scene. Tears poured down her cheeks as she berated herself over and over. Then a red heat rose before her, an overpowering hatred directed at the monster who sat below, sucking the blood from his fingers. All she could think of was to urge Swift Cloud into action, launch a futile attack upon her tormentor.

There is nothing you can do! Leave now, or you will die!

She fought down her rage. An attack upon Skalatin would gain her nothing now, would simply play into his hands. Jans was gone: nothing would bring him back. That was the one simple, brutal fact of it. She had to think now solely in terms of self-preservation.

With this thought came the recognition that she was in full view of Skalatin should he turn now and look her way. Her vision was blurred with tears, but she turned Swift Cloud away, walked over the crest of the slope and out of Skalatin's field of view.

As she descended the other side she reassured herself through her grief and anger: Skalatin did not know the Serpent's Path. There was little doubt that he would wander off it, probably almost immediately. She would be invisible once more.

And safe?

He would pursue her, of course he would. She was far from safe. But she was hidden.

She made herself look at the snake talisman at her wrist. Part of her wanted to discard it, tear it off and throw it away into the wasteland. She wanted to give up everything, turn around, go back and give herself to the fiend.

She fought it. She fought the agony of remorse and self-recrimination that threatened to tear her apart. She rode on, weeping softly.

What now?

Sildemund. Her goal had not changed. She had to find Sildemund and the red stone.

The barrenness of the Despair spread all around her, unpitying, arid as the heart that she pursued. Swift Cloud bore her slowly on. Somewhere, Dharsoul. She glanced back from time to time, fearful, alone.

16

'BUT YOU ARE a hero of the Realm, Gully! You saved Prince Enlos's life. That carries weight, surely?'

For the fifth or sixth time that evening Sildemund voiced the same, strained protest, a plea for Gully to somehow assert himself to acquire their unconditional release. And for the fifth or sixth time Gully responded with the same weary, resigned reply.

'Not in the light of what we have witnessed here tonight, it doesn't. Not at all.'

They were still in the luxurious guests' apartment provided for them by Prince Enlos the previous day. The cruel irony of their situation was not lost on Sildemund: held in splendour, until death.

Outside the night was a velvet blue-black. Through the windows could be seen the lights of the city. The river was a phosphorescent haze, here and there reflecting the lights. Distant sounds of revelry drifted up on the air from the tavernas around the souk and entertainment district. Dharsoul, as evening descended, had come alive.

Sildemund paced the room, then halted. 'How will they do it, Gully?'

Gully, seated, passed a hand across his jaw. He glanced up at Sildemund, wondering how to soften the blow, then acknowledged to himself that there was little point. 'It will be without ceremony, I would imagine. Knives or swords, our bodies quickly disposed of. It will be as though we never existed.'

'You must do something. You must try. We cannot even fight!'

Earlier, soon after they had been returned here from the Hall of Receiving, a squad of masked guards had entered and removed their weapons and many of their personal possessions.

'I will appeal to Prince Enlos if the chance arises, of course I will,' said Gully. 'But it will do no good. Enlos is powerless in this instance. Not even he can defy the law when the price is so high. It is us or the Queen, remember. That's the fact of it. No choice.'

'There has to be some way!' Sildemund resumed his pacing, agitated, a knot of fear in his gut, and presently halted again. 'When will they do it?'

'Tonight, almost certainly.'

Sildemund gave a groan. 'Just because we heard her speak? Is it so important?'

'You know that it is.'

'Yet when Queen Lermcone's father was sovereign, he spoke without restriction. He made speeches, addressed his subjects, conferred in person with whomsoever he chose. I know it, my parents told me about King Hirun. The Supreme Haruspices played a different role then, a lesser role. They advised, gave counsel. They were not sole interpreters of his thoughts or wishes. Is that not so? Why is it different for the Queen?'

Gully shrugged. 'Because she is Queen; a woman. The Old Texts declare that woman knows not her own mind, nor may she trust her own words. Sovereign, scullery maid or whore, it is the same. Our Queen's intentions must be divined by infallible means.'

'It is absurd.'

'It is the Law.'

'She does not rule, Gully. That's the truth of it. She has no actual power. How can she be called sovereign?'

Gully fidgeted uncomfortably. 'Dyarch Law decrees that in the absence of a male heir the eldest daughter of a sovereign becomes eligible to accede. Certain conditions apply by rote. It is not for us to argue; it is above us. And it can serve no end to protest the matter now.'

Sildemund sighed then strode to the window, as if seeking a way out there. But there was no escape. They were several levels above the ground. In the courtyard below sentries had bloomed like nocturnal flowers; his thoughts had been anticipated.

Picadus, who had awoken soon after their return and hauled himself morosely from his bed, sat scowling on a divan. 'Why me?' he growled. 'I had nothing to do with it. I didn't hear her speak. I shouldn't have to die with you.'

Sildemund turned on him, angrily at first, but his emotion was tempered by the realization that what Picadus said was true. He had not been there; he was condemned to death by association, because he had heard Sildemund and Gully talking of what had occurred.

'You shouldn't have told me! You should have let me get out of here before you said anything!' Picadus slammed his fists down hard on his thighs, his face darkening. 'I don't want to die!'

He thrust himself to his feet. Gully likewise rose, and placed his big frame in a position between the two of them. 'Steady, Pic. It does no good. We're in the same situation together, like it or not.'

Picadus glowered, twitching. There was a sudden loud noise at the door. They turned as the door was thrown open. Four masked guards entered and fanned out to either side.

The three men stared, no words to say, sensing the worst. In the flamelit corridor outside a shadow loomed, grew, diminished. Into the chamber strode the flamboyant Khimmurian, Ronbas Dinbig.

He was garbed as before, in blue and purple, but minus his hat, revealing a full head of pale brown wavy hair, elegantly coiffed, long at the sides and trimmed in a neat fringe across the forehead. He halted before the three men and performed a short, polite bow, then turned to the guards. 'Would you be good enough to wait outside?'

The guards filed out and drew the door shut behind them. Sildemund, finding his voice, said, 'You exercise a surprising degree of authority, sir, for one who is not here of his own free will.'

'They are soldiers,' replied Dinbig, as though that explained all.

'And you are in their custody – at least, that was my understanding.'

'Unhappily, that is so. Nevertheless, I gained Prince Enlos's word that I might speak with you privately. It is he they obey, not me. Now we should talk of important matters. There is much to be discussed, and my time is limited.'

'As is ours,' said Gully, without humour.

'Quite so. You are haggard, and at each others' throats, I see. If I might point out the obvious, it is a fruitless way to spend one's twilight hours.'

Sildemund was lost for a response. Picadus's shoulders heaved, his breath seethed. Gully said, heatedly, 'And how would you suggest we spend them?'

'In calm and reasoned thought. Surely you see that there is nothing to be gained by squabbling among yourselves?'

'Reasoned thought?' Gully's voice shook. 'Sir, do you mock us?'

'Not at all.'

'Are you aware of what has happened here tonight?'

'I am.'

'Yet you expect us to indulge in calm and reasoned thought?'

'It is surely preferable to bitter argument? Who knows, cool reason might yet suggest a way out of this predicament?'

Gully was firm. 'There can be no way out.'

Dinbig put a hand to his chin, scanning the three of them. 'Hmm, plainly cool reason does not lie naturally with you. It had not struck me until now, but seeing the three of you, most particularly this bruised and battered fellow,' (he indicated Picadus) 'I am drawn to wonder. Tell me, are you by any chance the thugs who set upon my men in a taverna earlier in the day?'

Sildemund's jaw fell open. 'Your men? The foreigners?'

'Quietly relaxing, by their account – which experience encourages me to believe – when they were set upon by a Dyarch madman and his two companions.'

'With respect, sir,' said Gully, 'the brawl was not intentional on our part. Pic, here, got a little overexcited. Blows were exchanged, but we calmed the situation and left as quickly as we were able.'

'And paid for all damages,' added Sildemund.

'Yes, that accords with my men's version.'

'I apologize unreservedly,' Sildemund said.

Dinbig grinned. 'Unnecessary. My fellows enjoyed the sport.'

Sildemund scratched his head, confounded by the Khimmurian's manner. 'Master Dinbig, are you aware of the *full* circumstances of what happened here this evening?'

'I believe I am, yes.'

'Then you know that we are condemned without trial, simply for having heard the Queen speak?'

'That is the information related to me by the crown prince, yes. He is greatly saddened by the fact, but can perceive no way out of it. If word were to leak out that the Queen has spoken, she would perforce be executed. Enlos would of course gain the throne, but he has no desire to do so under these circumstances. And the scandal, the political embarrassment, would have far-reaching effects for Dyarchim. The incident, therefore, must be erased. It has not happened.'

'But it occurs to me that you share our predicament, is that not so? As you know what has happened, you, like us, cannot be permitted to depart with that knowledge intact.'

'I am fully conversant with the facts, and with the law and its immutability. But let us leave that aside for a moment. I have come here to speak of more important things.'

'More important things!' blurted out Gully, hard put to contain himself. 'What can we possibly be expected to deem more important than our own lives?'

Dinbig fixed him with a level gaze. 'You have no wish to die, that is to be expected. But believe me, your lives and mine are of no consequence in the light of the issue we have to confront. That Queen Lermeone spoke is scarcely of relevance now; it is what she spoke *of* that is all-important. I refer to the red stone that you showed me earlier.'

'That stone!' muttered Sildemund. 'It has brought nothing but misfortune.'

'Precisely. And the misfortune has scarcely begun.'

'She called it the Heart of Shadows.'

'The Heart of Shadows. . . .' Dinbig pursed his lips. 'Would that it were not.'

'What have you discovered about it?'

'Not as much as I would wish. It is a baleful object of immense antiquity, apparently referred to in Dyarchim's Old Texts. It was believed to have been a fabrication of myth or lore, never to have actually existed, or if it had, to have been lost or destroyed before history ever dawned. Queen Lermeone knows more, I am sure. She has received unique schooling in the understanding of the Old Texts. Her knowledge is being elicited from her at the present time. That she was the only person capable of recognizing the stone for what it is suggests much. I have learned one or two other facts about it, and have concluded without doubt that what you have brought here is reason for profound concern.'

'How have you learned these things?' enquired Gully. 'Earlier you could tell us almost nothing about the stone.'

'I am *Zan-Chassin*. Now, I have some questions to put to you, particularly with regard to how you came upon this stone.' He looked directly at Sildemund, who averted his eyes. 'Your father bought it from a trader in Ghence, you say? Forgive me, but in the light of what I now know I find this unlikely.'

Sildemund wrestled in awkward silence with himself. Gully turned away and with a grim visage seated himself on the divan. Presently he said, 'Tell him, lad.'

'We found the stone,' said Sildemund.

'Found it? Where?'

'In the wilderness. It was a legitimate find. The stone was buried, hidden. It was sheer chance that we stumbled upon it. It was in a sealed cave; it hadn't been entered in decades, I would say, even centuries.'

Dinbig tilted his chin, assimilating this. Sildemund looked to Gully for support. Gully nodded. 'It's as he says. No one had been there. We were digging out a rabbit that had gone to ground. We found the cave by accident.'

'And the stone was in there? Just lying on the cave floor?'

'It was hidden,' said Gully. 'Behind a false wall. Again it was chance more than anything that led us to it. We'd searched the cave, hoping for treasure, but found nothing. We were on the point of leaving when I found the false wall.'

'And the stone was behind it. Was it protected in any way?'

'It was inside a kind of cage structure, sunk into the rock itself. It took some freeing.'

'But you freed it, and then left?'

'We camped overnight, and moved on the next morning.' Sildemund looked troubled. 'One of our number was killed.'

'How?'

'Edric had been acting strangely ever since we entered the cave,' said Gully. 'He seemed deeply afraid of something. Got quite hysterical. We put it down to Blue Estuary Fever, which he'd suffered from a while earlier. But in the morning, without telling anyone, he went back into the cave. Master Frano found him in there, dead.'

'Were there any particular circumstances to his death?'

Sildemund shrugged. 'My father said it looked as though he had fallen onto a sharp rock. It had pierced his chest. None of us actually saw the body.'

Dinbig nodded thoughtfully to himself. 'Tell me, how did you come to be in this place?'

For a moment neither spoke. Gully expelled a big breath. Dinbig produced a smile. 'Come, now, I am a merchant, too. In fact, I am acquainted with Master Frano. I am fully conversant in the means and methods by which we ply our trade. You were carrying contraband, is that not so? And the border posts were being rigorously checked. I know it, for I was picked up there myself, and brought back here.'

'You were arrested for carrying contraband?' said Sildemund. 'Normally a fine is imposed. There is an agreement. . . .'

'Aye. Certain persons had other reasons for wanting me in custody in Dharsoul – but that is another story. Let us stick with yours. The controls were unusually severe; you took to the wilds to avoid them. Even so, it's a harsh and dangerous land, most especially with wagons. You were fortunate not to have come unstuck.'

'I know the region well,' Gully said. 'I was able to guide Master Frano safely to the Volm Road.'

'But this place, where you found the stone, had you never come across it before?'

'It was not directly on the route I followed. But I was warned of a landslip which necessitated a small diversion. It was there that we came upon the grotto.'

'Warned? By whom?'

Gully shrugged. 'A fellow traveller at an inn.'

'What was his name? Can you describe him?'

'He did not give his name. He approached me, just for a moment, to pass on the advice. I hardly saw him. He wore a traveller's hood and scarf.'

'Why was there so much activity at the border, Master Dinbig? Do you know?' Sildemund asked. 'We heard different stories, of murders, an escaped criminal, of trouble around Garsh. They say it is under siege by Tomian forces. But why would that affect traffic at the border?'

'I am not entirely certain. But there were murders in the region, yes. Particularly gruesome by all accounts. One of the victims was a Tomian border guard. Money was stolen. And there is concern over Garsh and its inhabitants. Revenants have been appearing in villages and towns all over Tomia, and now in Dyarchim, preaching their message to any who will give them ear. Officially they are banned from leaving Garsh. The Tomian authorities have moved to prevent further excursions. I understand there has been bloodshed, though I don't have details. I am not sure what it is all about, but I am concerned at what is happening there. Most particularly because I now believe there may be a link between Garsh and the strange stone, the Heart of Shadows, which you have inadvertently brought to Dharsoul.'

'What sort of link?'

'Until I know more, I would prefer not to say.' Dinbig's eyes rested upon Picadus, who had seated himself again, his face pale, his eyes upon the mosaic floor. 'Your companion does not look well.'

'He is not like himself,' said Sildemund in a murmur. 'I wonder whether it might be the stone. Others have suffered after coming into contact with it. You saw Professor Ractoban – and you perceived something unwholesome about the stone as soon as you set eyes upon it. Yet neither Gully nor I seem affected.'

Dinbig nodded. 'It is likely that some persons will be more susceptible to its influence, just as there are those who are sensitive to the aura of magic where others feel nothing; those to whom spirits manifest which are unseen by most; those who are haunted by feelings they cannot identify, a deep sense of the world's sadness, of life's unutterable mysteries, to which others are oblivious. We do not know why this is, just that it is.'

'Then are we free of the stone's influence?'

Dinbig hesitated. 'A man who does not sense magic will yet not deny its effects; one who is cursed sees not the agent of the curse, nor knows the curse itself, except in its manifestation.' He slowly shook his head. 'We have here something foul, something profoundly and utterly evil. Over time it will wreak its havoc upon all with whom it comes into contact, I scarcely doubt. I do not know what is to be done about it. I will go now to speak with Prince Enlos and the Supreme Haruspices; perhaps the Queen has divulged something more.'

'And what of us?' asked Gully.

Dinbig paused. 'I do not know if there is anything I can do. I am sorry.'

'You are not walking gladly to your own death, I am sure of that,' declared Sildemund. 'If you can somehow bargain your own way to freedom, can you not speak for us? After all, we are guilty of no true crime.'

'The truth is that "freedom" now, as you might imagine it, does not have the appealing ring that it formerly possessed. The Heart of Shadows has changed that. Such is its nature as to corrupt all things. Believe me, it might be preferable to die tonight than to be let free upon the course that this stone sets. I will speak for you, but the law is the law, and I have no power over it. And in the unlikely event that I am successful, you will not thank me for it. The consequences that would then lie before you may be little better than the fate to which you have been condemned tonight. We shall see.'

Sildemund studied him coolly. 'Your role in this business raises many questions in my mind, Master Dinbig.'

'Would that I had no role! I am not here by choice.'

'Yes, both prisoner and honoured guest, it seems. An unusual combination. How is it?'

Dinbig spread his hands. 'It is a complex affair. To explain all will take time, of which we have little. For now, we should surely concentrate upon immediacies.'

He turned, walked to the door, nodded politely, and left.

Sildemund stared impotently at the closed door for some moments, then said, 'If it is true, Gully, if we are sentenced to die, I will fight. Unarmed I may be, but it will never be said of me that I gave up my life willingly. If there is no other way I will leap upon a guard and take his blade. If I cannot escape then I shall die, but others will go with me.'

Even as he spoke he knew the hopelessness of his words, and felt the fear, the coldness, deep inside as he contemplated the awful prospect of his death.

Gully had seated himself upon the divan again, his eyes upon the floor.

'Are you with me, Gully?'

Gully raised his head and looked at him, then offered a grim smile. 'I am with you, Sil, for what good it may do.'

THEY PASSED WHAT remained of that night and the whole of the next day confined in their apartment. Food and drink were brought to them at regular intervals by servants accompanied by guards, but they received no other visitors. The day was interminable; they knew nothing of what went on beyond their door. Their tempers were frayed and they were hardly able to eat.

A little before dawn of the following day the guards returned. Sildemund, Gully and Picadus had barely slept in all that time, though Picadus had taken himself off some while ago to lie in smouldering silence upon his bed. Following Dinbig's departure late the previous night Gully and Sildemund had exchanged few words. There was nothing to be said. They shared the same fears, the same tenuous hopes, but no thoughts that they might express could change the outcome. They waited, then, as the day passed, the evening came and the candles burned low, absorbed in their thoughts, enduring another night that was both an endless suspense and a too brief flicker which came and was gone in an instant.

In the silence of the pre-dawn the soldiers' marching steps became audible from far away: at first a faint tattoo, muffled and distant, becoming louder, reverberating along empty corridors. Sildemund listened, his heart in his mouth, recognizing the sound for what it was, and prayed that it would turn away, diminish into another distance.

But the footsteps came on. Sildemund's eyes met Gully's in the candlelight. Gully's face was grey, lined, mirroring his own, he knew, expressing everything.

The sound became a thunder, hammering off the cold stone slabs: *rap, rap, rap!* It filled Sildemund with terror, became all he knew, a heartless beat, matching the thunder of his own heart.

Then it ceased, directly outside their door. In its wake was a ringing silence, louder than the noise had been. Involuntarily, both Sildemund and Gully had risen to their feet, and now Picadus emerged from his bedchamber and stared, haunted, at the apartment door.

The latch shifted and the door swung open. An officer of the Palace Guard stepped smartly inside, followed by two soldiers. More filled the corridor.

'You will come with me.'

They were marched through the torchlit palace, back, Sildemund reckoned, towards the Hall of Receiving. Faceless sentries, motionless as statues, were the only signs of life within the endless corridors; the entire place was silent but for the ominous drum of their own marching feet.

At a certain point they were joined by a second squad of guards coming from a passage a little way ahead. With them was Ronbas Dinbig. He glanced aside and nodded as he stepped into the main corridor, but his expression gave no indication of what might lie in store.

They followed close behind this second group, and at length were brought to a halt in a small gallery before an arched portal. The guards waited. Sildemund, a hollow fear in his gut, succeeded in sidling close to Dinbig, and whispered falteringly, 'Are we condemned?'

The Khimmurian gave a minimal shrug. 'I do not know. I reasoned long and hard. Prince Enlos was not hostile to my argument, but the Supreme Haruspices maintained a wall of resistance. Their decision has not been made known to me, but I feel there may be little cause for optimism. So much is at stake, as they perceive it. My feeling is that we are to be informed now, but it may be little more than a preliminary to execution. Still, it will be interesting to meet the Queen at last.'

'You have never had an audience?'

Dinbig shook his head. 'I have been presented with the opportunity on numerous occasions in the past, but I was concerned that she might inadvertently mutter some aside, clear her throat, sneeze or otherwise give utterance and bring about my premature end. I have therefore always made excuses and declined the honour.'

Sildemund stared sidelong at him, wondering at the character of a man who could summon humour when facing death. Or did Dinbig know something he didn't? He was an enigmatic fellow, Sildemund acknowledged. Ostensibly debonair, but many-sided. Guileful, certainly. Quite an unknown quantity. He was a prisoner here, but what precisely were the conditions of his confinement? He was accorded respect, comported himself with an air of confident authority and command, was wholly at ease with his predicament – or so it appeared.

There was intrigue here, and Sildemund doubted that he would ever know the full story even if he lived beyond the next few hours. But that Ronbas Dinbig was a personage of some status he could not doubt. A sorcerer of the legendary *Zan-Chassin*; a man of knowledge; an international merchant of influence; official emissary on behalf of his liege and nation, the semi-barbarian kingdom of Khimmur in the north. And what else?

Sildemund found himself a little awed and unsettled by the man. He was not sure that he could trust him, yet in the matter of immediacies he had little choice. Dinbig professed to share their predicament and their impending fate, but though he, Gully and Picadus might die this morn, Sildemund somehow could not imagine that this charismatic young man would join them.

He was being eyed coldly by the officer of their guard, and he conferred no more with the Khimmurian. But standing now in silence, waiting, the horror of his situation suddenly rose to engulf him. He looked around him at the guards. There were more than a dozen, elite fighters all, well armed. He recognized the inevitability of his swift and bloody death were he to attempt to put into motion his declared plan, to fight. Despite himself, Sildemund began to tremble violently. He felt suddenly alone in a callous, hostile universe. He stepped back, on wobbling legs, and involuntarily let out a sobbing breath.

He became aware of strong hands taking his arms, holding him up, for his legs threatened to give way. He turned to see Gully, a strained smile of support etched upon his gaunt features.

'I don't want to die, Gully.'

'Nor I, lad. But if it is to be, we must face it with courage.'

Sildemund shook his head from side to side. 'No. No. Not like this! It should not be!'

Gully took him in his arms and embraced him hard, blinking back his own tears. Then Sildemund was aware of another hand laid softly upon the back of his head. He looked around and saw Dinbig standing close.

'Stay your fear,' said the Khimmurian gently. He withdrew his hand, and as he did so made a small gesture with his fingers, at the same time briefly mouthing words that made no sound.

Sildemund ceased trembling. His mind no longer raced and the full flood of his terror was dispelled. He straightened, embarrassed at his outburst, but in control of himself. He looked at Gully and saw that though he remained grim-countenanced, the haunted, leaden glaze of his eyes had given way to a more characteristic glimmer. Picadus, too, stood straighter, looked less surly, and was glancing about him as if alert to his surroundings for the first time.

The Khimmurian, Ronbas Dinbig, stared straight ahead. Sildemund looked at him curiously. Something had happened, but he was not sure what. Before he could give it further thought the portal was opened from within and they were ushered through.

They passed into an austerely furnished reception chamber where Prince Enlos was in hushed conference with the two Supreme Haruspices. All three wore tense expressions, and dark crescents beneath their eyes evidenced lack of sleep. Behind them Queen Lermeone sat in stiff silence upon a carved beechwood chair. A pair of Palace Guards stood at alert before her.

The officer guarding Sildemund and his companions saluted. His men ranged themselves along the walls. Ronbas Dinbig bowed deeply; Gully sank to his knees and made his obeisance, and Sildemund and then Picadus followed suit.

'You may rise,' said Enlos solemnly. 'Come forward.'

He indicated with stiff movements a place where they should stand, in a row, before himself and the Haruspices. He was plainly discomfited and unwilling to meet their gaze, most particularly in Gully's case. The cross-shaped scar upon his cheek was dark against the pallor of his face.

'We are faced with a most difficult problem,' he said. 'It is more complex than you may realize. I have passed more than a night and day striving to reach a satisfactory solution. My position is impossible.'

These last words were spoken in utterly downcast tones,

accompanined by a hopeless shaking of the head. He raised his eyes now, looking at Gully, as if pleading to be understood and forgiven.

Sildemund struggled with himself, found his courage, and spoke. 'Allow me to speak plainly, sire. You are saying that we are condemned to death, is that not so?'

Enlos swallowed. 'I have argued that there should be a way around this – to no end. The Supreme Haruspices are the arbiters of law; I am powerless in this matter.'

'But we have done no wrong.'

Enlos dropped his gaze. 'I know it.'

Sildemund looked at the two nameless Haruspices. They returned his gaze. He thought, *yes, you wish it this way, that you may retain control. It is you who are the true rulers of this nation, and you will employ any means to maintain that power.* He quivered with anger, despising them, then boldly addressed the Prince once more. 'Prince Enlos, Gully here is a hero, by your own admission. He is a former soldier in the Queen's army, loyal and brave, who saved your life. Does that mean nothing?'

Enlos's face was written with anguish. 'By the gods, do you think I do not know it?' He strode to Gully, clasped his upper arms. 'Gully, Gully. I wish . . . I wish. . . .' He turned away, too overcome for words.

Sildemund spoke again, this time appealing directly to Queen Lermeone. 'Sacred Majesty, this man saved the life of your only son. Is he—'

'You will not address the Queen!'

Both Haruspices spoke as one, their complacent expressions giving way to sudden indignation. The guards before the Queen stepped forward in offensive stance, their glaives angled to strike at Sildemund. Queen Lermeone herself sat unmoving – but not unmoved. Her face betrayed her, for she could not wholly conceal her emotion.

Sildemund saw it. *She wants to speak, she wants to intervene!*

He felt Gully's hand upon his arm, heard his taut whisper, 'Quiet, lad, or you will surely die right here and now!'

One of the Haruspices spoke, addressing Sildemund directly. 'Your fate is not a matter for debate; the law is unequivocal. You are condemned to die, that the Realm may continue undisrupted under our Beneficent Majesty's just rule. Consider this: your death is a contribution to the peaceful continuance of the Dyarch way. You are honoured.'

Sildemund glared at him, speechless. The Haruspex continued, 'You profess innocence, but the evidence is to the contrary. You brought evil into our midst. Through your irresponsible actions we are pitched into profound crisis. The evil has yet to be dealt with, but the immediate crisis can be overcome. Give your lives gratefully, then, for you are privileged.'

'*Pah!*' Picadus made a sound of disgust and spat upon the floor. He glowered at the two, then suddenly lunged forward with an enraged bellow, his features twisted, fingers extended to seize the throat of the Haruspex who had spoken.

He achieved barely three paces before being brought down by a guard, who struck him on the back of the head with the butt of his glaive. He was sent sprawling across the floor.

'Remove him,' commanded the Haruspex, unperturbed. Another guard ran forward and Picadus was dragged limp and senseless from the chamber.

At this juncture Ronbas Dinbig lifted a hand to his mouth and pointedly cleared his throat. 'Prince Enlos,' he said, stepping forward, 'am I to take it that hours spent in discussion with you were wasted? Did my argument carry no weight whatsoever?'

'To my mind your argument was persuasive,' replied Enlos. 'The Haruspices view it in another light, however.'

The first Haruspex shook his head. 'Your argument is untenable. The law permits no variance.'

Dinbig began to pace back and forth before him. 'But my researches – and I believe, the information you have yourself elicited – reveal that this is an extraordinary circumstance: the Heart of Shadows unearthed and brought to the capital, with all that that implies.'

'We will take appropriate steps.'

'This event is written in the Old Texts. You are disregarding the revelations of antiquity.'

'Not so. We are obeying the Law.'

'Blindly!' Dinbig's voice rose, taking on a new timbre. 'You know that there exists no precedent for this circumstance.'

'That is irrelevant.'

'I say that it is far from irrelevant. I believe you are making a serious error of judgement. You will do your nation a most grave injustice, and if the Old Texts are correct, will suffer long-term consequences. The wiser course is to wait and learn the fullest picture. Then consider.'

'That cannot be done.'

'What constructive end can be served now by taking the lives of these men?'

Upon the words 'these men' Dinbig threw a particular emphasis, and swung his arm in a deliberately exaggerated manner to point at Sildemund and Gully. All eyes automatically turned to regard the two men. Sildemund's own gaze was fixed upon the charismatic Khimmurian, and he saw now what no other did. He saw the fingers of Dinbig's free hand form an elaborate gesture, and Dinbig's lips shape silent words which followed immediately upon his speech. He saw that Dinbig's eyes settled for a moment with a strange intensity upon the second Haruspex, who had so far made no vocal contribution to the debate; and it was towards this man that his fingers gestured.

Sildemund watched the second Haruspex now. A curious frown briefly furrowed the man's brow; he compressed his lips in thought.

And Dinbig continued to declaim, striding animatedly back and forth, and it was upon this Haruspex that he focused his words: 'You *know* that these men might yet serve you, and their country. You *know* what has happened here was preordained: *The Heart of Shadows will be brought to the capital by the unknowing.* The event has been foretold! And you know the course that the Heart has to follow. Act unwisely and you may precipitate the very crisis that you seek to avoid.'

The second Haruspex seemed troubled. His gaze flickered from Dinbig to his colleague, to Prince Enlos, then to the mute Queen Lermeone. Dinbig said, 'Where is the Heart now?'

'It remains where it was left, in the Hall of Receiving,' replied Prince Enlos. 'No one has touched it.'

'Aye, and no one should.'

Enlos nodded. The two Haruspices eyed Dinbig, one with resentment, the other with uncertainty.

'Do you doubt that it is so?' challenged the Khimmurian. 'Then go, yourselves. Take up the Heart and bring it here!'

The second Haruspex bent his head to his colleague, to confer in muted tones. Seeing this Dinbig allowed himself a taut smile of satisfaction. He stepped close to Sildemund and murmured. 'You may not thank me for this.'

Sildemund was not sure what had happened, or what the Khimmurian meant. But he sensed a subtle but significant change in the situation. One of the Haruspices spoke again, and Sildemund's heart leapt, then, as quickly, plummeted.

'We will review our decision. The Queen shall make her judgement.'

If they pass it to the Queen, they will still interpret her decision to fit their own ends. She cannot gainsay them, and even if she could, she can only rule against us, for to do otherwise would be to condemn herself!

He stared for a moment at the Queen, wondering at the state of mind of this woman, nominally powerful yet in truth plainly impotent, who throughtout her adult life had not been permitted to speak her mind, who was conditioned to believe that anything and everything that she might consciously think or feel was worthless and unreliable, and that her true wishes should necessarily be interpreted by others.

She may not speak, upon pain of death. Even were she to speak, her words would be judged invalid. She is helpless. She has been reduced to the level of a cipher, nothing more.

We are dead.

He glanced at Dinbig, who was stroking his whiskers in contemption, his eyes also upon Queen Lermeone.

One of the Haruspices motioned to the officer of the guard, who strode briskly from the chamber and was heard to bark an order in the passage outside. Moments later underlings hurried in carrying a pair of shallow wicker bowls filled with petals, two hand brushes on trays, quills, ink and vellum sheets, and a large slab of white marble, square in shape, upon which was figured a complex circular design, the same as that drawn upon the dais in the Hall of Receiving. These articles were placed carefully upon the floor in front of the Queen, and the underlings scurried out.

The ritual of divination was carried out as it had been two evenings earlier in the Hall of Receiving. The two Haruspices took their places before the Queen. One spoke, briefly, in high ceremonial terms, outlining the character of the dilemma, praying for guidance, invoking the inner wisdom of the Sacred Sovereign who sat above him. The Queen listened, her eyes bright, her face revealing the tension within her. Sildemund noticed Dinbig, who had withdrawn unobtrusively to one side. His eyes were closed as though he were in some kind of trance.

The petal bowls were raised to the Queen. She dipped a hand into each and let the petals cascade onto the circle below. The two Haruspices bent forward to make their interpretations. Their inspection lasted for the customary two to three minutes, but Sildemund noted the creases upon their brows and the darting glances they exchanged. Their quills scratched the vellum with a vague hesitancy, and he had the impression that they were looking to one another for cues. He looked at Dinbig again. The Khimmurian's eyes were open now, his gaze intense, focused upon the pair, and his lips were moving, very slightly, but repetitively, as though reciting a silent chant.

In due course the Haruspices sat back, their spines straight, but failed immediately to take up their brushes to sweep the petals from the circle. Again they looked at one another with uncertainty. They examined their notes, exchanged them, pored over them for some moments longer, then at last took up their brushes and with resigned motions cleared the circle. One of them now addressed the waiting men, his tones clipped.

'Our August Majesty has seen cause for reassessment. It appears that circumstances of which we were formerly unaware may exert an influence. We will adjourn.'

Sildemund felt a surge of elation, *Reprieved!* Regarding Queen Lermeone he saw the tension slip from her shoulders, her features relax. *She had wanted to hear those words!*

The guards came forward to lead them from the chamber. They filed out, passing Prince Enlos, who raised his eyes to theirs, a trace of a jubilant smile compressing his lips. Sildemund glanced across at Dinbig. He was bowed, seemed dazed, almost exhausted as he fell in between the guards.

They were escorted back to their apartments, where they found Picadus barely conscious, nursing a sore head. Gully applied a cold compress; Sildemund stood at the balcony window, anxiously watching the sun rise over the city as the Palace slowly awoke. An hour passed. There were marching feet in the corridor again; the door opened, the same officer entered with two guards.

'Which of you is Sildemund?'

'I am.'

'Come.'

He was taken back through the Palace to the Hall of Receiving. It was empty. He stood with his guards at the back of the Hall. Before him, upon the dais where he had left them, were his satchel and, further back, the purple-red stone, the Heart of Shadows, resting in the soiled, ragged nest of its binding.

The officer pointed. 'Collect them.'

Gingerly Sildemund made his way to the front of the hall, picked up his satchel then stepped onto the dais and approached the stone. Did he imagine it, or did the thing pulse as he drew close? For a second he thought the dark bands upon its surface had shifted, but he stared hard and they did so no more. The stone had taken on a new and sinister aspect now, lying there like a bloated, petrified organ. He was reluctant to touch it, half-thinking he sensed its evil radiating invisibly to clutch and claw at his subliminal self.

He lowered himself onto his haunches, slowly collected the cloth binding and rewound it about the stone. He lifted the stone and eased it back into his satchel, then returned to the guards.

He was taken back through the Palace, but instead of returning upstairs to the guests' apartments, as he had expected, he was led through unfamiliar passages.

'Where are we going?' he asked. The soldiers gave no reply.

They marched on, keeping to the ground level, eventually to emerge into a high-walled service yard. Here a group of horsemen waited. Sildemund halted for a moment, blinking in the bright sunlight, taking in the scene before him.

Prince Enlos sat upon his mount alongside the two Supreme Haruspices. A little further away were Gully, Dinbig of Khimmur and, unexpectedly, the self-professed mage, Kemorlin. They were also mounted. Half a dozen horse troops waited beside them. Picadus, also mounted, was separated from the others and watched by three guards. Sildemund saw his own horse, saddled and harnessed.

To one side was a cart laden with covered baggage and flanked by two more mounted soldiers. Seated beside the driver was one other person. Sildemund looked at her for a moment in surprise. She was aged about thirty, had long, uncombed brown hair, and she wore the red and brown tat of the Revenants of Claine.

'What has happened?' he asked.

'Do you have the Heart?' demanded the Prince.

Sildemund nodded dumbly. Enlos inclined his head towards Sildemund's steed. 'Mount, then.'

'I don't understand.'

The officer of his guard pushed Sildemund forward. In some bemusement Sildemund climbed upon his horse. The company rode slowly from the yard into an outer court. Here a gilt carriage drawn by six black horses waited, its windows draped, with a column of elite Dyarch knights as many as one hundred strong. The carriage started forward as they passed, the knights forming up in their wake.

They proceeded through the outer bailey and barbican, exiting the Palace. More horse-soldiers joined them, some riding in advance, others falling to the rear. Sildemund estimated that their number now totalled more than two hundred and fifty, and looking back he saw baggage wagons trundling behind.

They left the royal mall and trotted down the wide thoroughfare to the main city gate. The gate was open, the way cleared by guards. They passed through, onto the hot Dharsoul Road and the open country beyond.

Sildemund had manouevred himself into a position between Gully and Dinbig of Khimmur. He leaned towards Dinbig. 'Where do we go?'

Dinbig looked weary, a stark contrast to his appearance earlier. Sildemund was convinced that he, through some subtle sorcery, had influenced the minds of the Sacred Haruspices to bring about this change of plan. Now Dinbig barely turned his head to reply.

'To the besieged city of Garsh, in Tomia.'

18

'AND WHO RIDES inside the golden carriage?'
'Who would you expect? It is the Queen.'

'Queen Lermeone?' Sildemund glanced back in astonishment at the carriage glinting in the sun as it rolled along, swaying upon its springs, its wheels churning the dust on the metalled road. 'Why does she accompany us?'

Dinbig gave a twisted smile, raising his voice above the din of the horses. 'Among other things, to avert a conflict.'

'A conflict?'

'We must enter Garsh, which is sovereign territory, besieged by Tomian troops. To do this we must first enter Tomia. We have no permission to do either, and there is no time to obtain such through the lengthy diplomatic channels that must necessarily accompany the transport of a sovereign head over foreign territory. Relations over Garsh are already tense between Dyarchim and Tomia. The Tomians will not welcome our arrival, yet so urgent is our mission that we can under no circumstances be deterred. The presence of Queen Lermeone will leave them in no doubt of the gravity with which Dyarchim perceives the issue.'

Sildemund was not sure that he understood. There was too much to take in, and nothing had been explained to him. 'What of Kemorlin? Why is he here? And the woman upon the cart, the Revenant?'

But Dinbig evidentally wearied of his questions.

'Boy, the dust clogs my throat and I find no joy in shouting over the thunder of hooves. We will stop to take rest at some point; we can talk then.'

With that he pulled his scarf up to cover his mouth and nose and let his horse drop back a few steps so that he rode alone.

Sildemund rode on, his head a welter of thoughts. His group

consisted of himself, Gully and Dinbig, and travelled somewhat separate from the main body. Prince Enlos rode at the head with his troops; Kemorlin was a little way behind, followed by more soldiers. There was a gap then, after which came six troopers, set to guard Sildemund's group. They were placed a good ten paces ahead of Sildemund. Six more rode the same distance behind. Picadus rode behind them, flanked by two troopers with another six behind him. Beyond these was the main force, which included the Queen's carriage, a second carriage into which the Supreme Haruspices had transferred themselves and, further back, the cart which carried the solitary Revenant of Claine.

Sildemund deduced that the red stone, the Heart of Shadows, was the reason for his isolation. Its baleful aura could not be permitted to affect others. He realized, too, that this was a primary reason for his reprieve: he had brought the stone to the capital, he would carry it on, suffering any influence it might exert upon him.

He was overcome with loathing for the thing now, and fearful of it. What was this evil object? What might it be doing to him without his being aware? He glanced back at Picadus, who rode hunched in his saddle with the mien of a man enraged at the world.

Poor Pic, I have brought this upon you, though I am truly not to blame. We are caught up in something larger than we know. Oh, why did we ever enter that grotto?

Sildemund was seized with the urge to wrench the stone from his satchel and hurl it away, be forever rid of it and its insidious influence. He suppressed the feeling, knowing it was impossible, hating the stone even more. The Heart of Shadows was bound to him, and he to it. Whether he wanted ir or not, it had become part of his destiny, had perhaps *forged* his destiny.

The idea dismayed him and sent a chill along his spine. He had never until now considered himself in such a light: that he took part in events which were somehow preordained, that he lived under a numen, that everything he had ever done had somehow been a step along the path that would bring him to this moment.

And beyond . . . ?

He tried to dismiss the thought, but it persisted. Had not Dinbig, only this morning, stated as much? And had not the Supreme Haruspices, in their own manner, acknowledged it? The Heart had led Sildemund to the edge of death, and because of it he was now reprieved. His mind went back over the whole pattern of events through the last few weeks. The way his father's caravan had been diverted from the Tomian border, and had stumbled upon the resting place of the stone; the way he and Gully had been rescued by Prince Enlos; the fortune of Gully's past which had conferred upon them the status of honoured guests in the Royal Palace. Truly it seemed that events had been shaped by some unknown force, bringing him to this. But for what? To what was the Heart of Shadows taking him?

He ached to question Dinbig further, and again found himself wondering about the Khimmurian, who seemed to know so much yet revealed so little. Sildemund clenched his jaw and sighed. He would learn nothing more until they stopped. He endeavoured to give his attention to the journey.

They had come a couple of miles out of Dharsoul. The way was slow: already there was a fair amount of traffic upon the road close to the capital. Troops were engaged in diverting this to the verges on both sides to allow the company to pass. Additionally the pace was dictated by the two carriages and wagons.

The day was growing hot and stifling; the river slumbered, the colour of mud, tinted with a sluggish glitter. Boats plied slowly up and down, labourers bent their backs in the fields on either bank. Some of those closest to the road paused in their toil to stare as the column rode by. At the roadsides merchants, pilgrims, vagrants and a diversity of other wayfarers gazed at the unexpected dazzle of soldiery and royalty, their expressions ranging through blankness and indifference, to awe.

A little way further on, gazing absently across the landscape, enmeshed in his thoughts, Sildemund experienced a queer sensation. His eyes had become drawn to a solitary figure on a grey horse, making its way down a rocky hillside towards the road. The figure wore a burnous and light hose, and was of slight build, almost certainly a woman.

He could make out nothing of the rider's features, but something about her captured his attention. Her posture, the line of her body, the very manner in which she rode as she picked her way carefully down the rubbly slope. And the horse, too . . . . For a moment Sildemund was reminded of his twin sister, Meglan.

The vision was brief. He turned in the saddle to follow the

rider's progress. She had halted to observe the cavalcade upon the road.

Could it be? Of course not. Plainly he was homesick. He felt a poignant stab in his breast. Images of home filled his mind's vision. *My sister, my father, how do you fare? What has happened to you in my absence?* He wanted to weep. *I have let you down.*

Sildemund was taken by a sudden impulse to wrench his horse around, burst free of his guard and gallop from the road to join the rider on the slope. But it was foolishness, he knew it. The guards would not allow him to get far, might even down him with arrows if they perceived any likelihood of his escaping. And even should he make it up the slope, his mad dash would be doomed to disappointment. Preposterous to think that Meglan could be here. Plainly he would find himself before some startled local farmgirl or doxie making her way to the fields or the city. It was just something about her that had brought Meglan's image to mind.

He twisted in his saddle and watched for as long as he was able, until his view of the rider was obscured by a stand of palm trees close to the road. A second before he lost sight of her he saw something else. Another figure had stepped from behind a boulder a few paces ahead of the rider. This one was garbed in a dark burnous, the hood raised.

Sildemund's vision seemed to suffer a distortion. It was probably the heat-shifted air, combined with his mental exhaustion, but in the brief instant that he glimpsed this second figure it appeared to him that it was somehow misshapen, that it was not entirely human.

As the two figures passed from view Sildemund turned back in his saddle to face the way ahead. Tears stung behind his eyes; he squeezed them back. How he wished to be home now, with his family! How he wanted an end to all this!

Late in the morning the company halted to take rest and refreshment at a caravanserai beside the way. Messengers had plainly been sent on ahead to give forewarning of their arrival, for food and drink in the copious quantities required to satisfy such a large body of troops and their horses were in an advanced state of preparation. Dozens of servants rushed hither and thither within the caravanserai walls – Sildemund imagined that the proprietor must have summoned them out of the air, for he could not imagine such a large staff to be typical.

Whatever prior clientele there were had been ushered from the main compound and serving rooms. Awnings had been erected to provide shade, and beneath one of these Sildemund and his companions were placed, away from the others, with guards positioned at a reasonable distance. Picadus remained segregated, his guards at alert beside him.

The proprietor, a fat, round-faced man, fell over himself in his efforts to accommodate the desires of his illustrious customers. With gestures of humility, coupled with puffed-up pride, he showed Prince Enlos and his officers, and Master Kemorlin, inside. The Queen, Sildemund noted, did not leave her carriage. Its drapes remained drawn and it was surrounded by soldiers.

Dinbig of Khimmur was escorted indoors, presumably for discussion with Enlos. A few minutes later his guards brought him out again and he rejoined Sildemund and Gully beneath the awning. They, and the troops, were served mounds of doughbread packets stuffed with spiced meat and salad, with flagons of cool water. As they ate Sildemund found the opportunity to ply Dinbig with more questions.

'Why do we go to Garsh, Dinbig? What is its relevence to the Heart of Shadows?'

Dinbig chewed upon his food, a small frown creasing his brow. He swallowed, raised a mug to his lips, took a long draught of water, then said, 'Have you heard of the Book of the Beginning?'

Sildemund and Gully shook their heads.

'I suspected not. It is perhaps the first book ever conceived, and deals with events that occurred long before history began. It contains within it a myth of the origin of our species, ancient beyond telling. Numerous versions exist – I have come across comparable tales in many different cultures. They vary widely, but certain central ideas, symbols, images can be seen to be common to all. The Book of the beginning contains the earliest version, considered to be the original. It is little known, and be warned . . .' He inclined his shoulders towards Sildemund and Gully, glancing at the guards and lowering his voice. '. . . there is danger in its telling.'

He closed his eyes briefly as if to gather his thoughts, and when he spoke again, his voice still lowered, he seemed to be reciting from memory. ' "*I shall tell you the tale of First Woman, who was created out of the stuff of the Cosmic, born through the divine wish of the universe to know itself and its wonders. She was the first sentient creature. Other creatures there were, but they did not know that they were. They saw, but did not know that they saw. First Woman knew that she was; knew that others were too. She saw herself and knew that she was both within, and embracing, all else.*

' "*First Woman delighted in the world, its beauty and wonders, but she wept at the harshness and pain that its denizens suffered. She walked the land, and through her powers gave life to things that had no life, caused flowers to grow and bloom, brought new species into being, assisted those creatures that knew pain and suffering. But she was alone, and as the centuries passed she longed for the companionship of her own kind. She saw that all things passed in their own time, and knew that her time must one day come. And she grieved, for she wanted her kind to live on, that they might be the guardians of the world.*

' "*So she formed a seed from her pure essence, mingled with rock, water, fire and air, and she gathered this and took it into herself, nurtured it within her wholeness, and in due course Man was born from her loins.*

' "*But unbeknown to First Woman other things had come into being during the time that she had walked the world. Invisible things, dark spirits, daemons, creatures of corruption and mischief. They perceived what First Woman did and they sought to unwork it; before she took it into herself, they touched with their own foul taint this seed that she had created, so that when at last it was born its soul contained a hidden darkness, and its heart was neither pure nor true.*

' "*First Woman and First Man loved, and out of their love were born the children who were the parents of humankind. But First Man was not wise, nor knowing. He coupled with First Woman for joy alone, not seeing that from this act was the race born. When her belly grew big and babies slipped from between her legs, he knew it as a miracle. His love of her grew; he fell down and worshipped her as a goddess; all across the land he erected temples and shrines in her name, for he perceived her as the source of life.*

' "Time passed and his love and reverence began to change. He knew the first twinges of envy, even of fear. First Woman possessed the power of creation and of procreation; he perceived himself as being without purpose, a mere adjunct. Out of jealousy and, later, hatred he sought ways to deprive First Woman of her power, to make it his own.

' "He sewed dissent against her among their daughters and sons, and the progeny of their daughters and sons. He smashed and burned the temples he had erected to her, razing them to the ground, and besought others to do likewise. He erased from the land all traces of her, destroyed her symbols, that none might ever learn of the power she possessed. He eliminated her name and gave their children his own. He decreed that henceforth all progeny should bear the father's name, in honour of himself. In his name he built new temples, that his children and his children's children might worship him.

' "And he coupled with his daughters, and the daughters of his daughters, so that their children were born of his own seed; hence the taint that had been worked in him before he was born was passed on, corrupting the blood of the future.

' "Witnessing all this, First Woman grieved. All had turned against her; she was alone and reviled, her goodness forgotten as the words of her lover spread, poisoning hearts and minds against her. For days and nights she wept, not knowing what to do. First Man, whom she still loved, was yet her enemy. She knew that if he had his way he would destroy her and all her works.

' "She took herself to him one day and confronted him with what he had done. She told him all, explaining his role in the creation of the race, of which he was still ignorant. Hearing this he was at first repentant, but the anger in his heart was too great and made him resent her the more. She saw that it was too late. She said to him, with tears flooding from her eyes, 'I know that you love me and that you wish to love me, yet such conflict is within you that you hate me too. You both desire and are repulsed, want to give and yet are consumed with jealousy; you come close so that, from fear, you can learn to take my power. In truth you remain far away. Your tenderness becomes an instrument that you use to subordinate me. And you truly do not know why you do this. You do not know what you do. You do not know the heart that beats in

184

your own breast. But this heart has turned against me and will never be turned back, for it has gone too far. It lies in deep shadows cast by your own shameful nature.

' " 'We have been lovers; we should have been friends, but betrayed by your own jealous heart you have betrayed me. You have brought impurity to our kind, and have elected to force enmity between us.

' " 'I created you; I gave you my whole heart, that perfection might be born into this world out of our love. You took my heart and I believed you gave yours, but it was pretence, and in truth you held both for yourself. You stole mine and betrayed it, sullying its purity, trying to cloud it with the shadows of your own. Your greed and ignorance has destroyed everything that might have been. I take your heart then, now, in fitting requital, that it may never again be an instrument of destruction.'

' "And she took his heart and left a chasm in his chest which would persist for all eternity. She encaged the heart in bars of rare ixigen metal extracted from flaming star-stones that had fallen from the sky, and these he might never touch. She secretly buried it deep in the bowels of the earth where he would not find it. And she cast First Man from her, believing that, heartless, he must quickly perish, but knowing that for the remainder of his days he would be bound to search fruitlessly for that which had been taken from him.

' "And she was anguished, for it cost her sorely to do this. She took herself away in grief and sorrow, believing that all she had striven for had been in vain. Her children were sullied, and so would be the generations that would follow. She languished alone for a thousand long years, having no further contact with man or beast, until at last she died.

' "But First Man did not die. Even heartless, he lived on. Because of the work of the daemons he became like them, immortal and wicked, given to depravity and lust. He stalked the earth alone, seeking, ever seeking that shadowed heart that had been wrenched from him. To sustain himself he fed upon the hearts of others, and took pleasure in their forms and their pain.

' "And his own heart, buried in the earth, because of the daemonic stuff with which it also was imbued, turned to stone, a stone harder and colder than any stone in the world. Yet still it held to life, a travesty of life, a pulsing, evil, insentient thing, without purpose unless that day came when it could become one again with the hollow creature which sought it.

' "It is said that First Man is still upon the world, daemonic, inhuman, ever seeking his lost heart. His name is Sko-ulatun, and there are folk steeped in darkness and evil who worship him and seek to help him find his fullness.

' "And the name of the First Woman, who is gone forever, was Claine." '

Sildemund was still, pensive. The first name, Sko-ulatun, meant nothing to him, but the second. . . .

'The Revenants of Claine . . .' he said in a low breath.

Dinbig gave a nod. 'Reincarnates, so they claim. The pure progeny of First Woman, reborn again and again over millennia.'

'For what purpose?'

'That is what we go to discover.'

'That woman,' Sildemund nodded his head towards a spot some distance away, in the shadow of the compound wall, where the woman in red and brown rags sat eating alone, a pair of guards nearby, 'what is her part?'

'She was brought to the Palace early this morning, that the Prince and Sacred Haruspices might clearly hear the message that the Revenants of Claine preach. It helped sway them. For the first time they took seriously words that had previously been considered the rantings of lunatics. They saw a correspondence with what has occurred. I will speak to the guards and ask whether she might join us, if you wish.'

Sildemund nodded. Dinbig rose and approached the nearest guard. After a moment the guard set off towards the centre of the compound where the mass of soldiery sat at tables. Dinbig returned. 'He seeks a higher authority. No doubt his immediate superior will require the same, and so on. We may have a long wait.'

'This tale you have told us,' said Gully, 'I have heard something like it, but in the version I know it is First Man who brings First Woman into the world. She it is who betrays him, and is punished, for by her actions the human race is brought down.'

Sildemund nodded. 'I have heard it that way too.'

'That is the official version, the accepted version,' said Dinbig. 'The one I have given you predates yours by centuries. It is deemed subversive and has been suppressed for longer than I know. Its supposed message is considered unfit for the people. Hence I speak with caution. To repeat this tale – in effect, even to know it – is a criminal offence. Take care, then, for I have given you information which could lead automatically to another sentence of death.'

Gully gave a mirthless chuckle. 'How many times can a man be executed?'

'Just the once; but his careless words or actions may condemn others.'

Sildemund watched the Khimmurian, thinking: *yet again you profess to share our fate, for the Prince and Haruspices must be aware now that you have knowledge of this myth. Yet are you condemned because of it?*

Thoughts of the red stone intruded. He slid his fingers unhappily over the satchel at his side. 'So we have disinterred the mythical stone, the Heart of Shadows, and now we take it to Garsh, to the Revenants of Claine. What then? And what of this monster, Sko-ulatun?'

'I can answer neither question with any degree of confidence, for I truly know little,' Dinbig replied. 'Our friend, the Revenant, may be better informed. Of Sko-ulatun I know nothing, but if he exists it is almost certain that he will be on the trail of this stone.'

He looked around him, perhaps hoping for some indication that his request to interview the Revenant of Claine had been granted.

'Master Dinbig, what happened this morning, at the Palace?' said Sildemund suddenly. 'You employed magic, did you not? Influencing the Haruspices to secure our release?'

The corners of Dinbig's mouth quivered. 'I was less subtle than I'd thought, then.'

'I was watching; you had already used it to help me, had you not?'

'It was a safeguard. You might have ruined everything – you or your companion, Picadus. He is in a bad way, but as it happened his outburst served to deflect attention.'

'What did you do? How did you change their minds?'

'Would that I *had* changed their minds! No, that is not so simple to do. I merely altered their receptiveness to what was already there. Their minds were closed; clamped shut. I allowed them to open just a little.'

'Then what was it that was already there?'

'The knowledge that this has been foretold. They responded initially to the mere fact that the Queen had spoken. That could not be made public, hence you had to die, ostensibly to save the Queen, but as we are all aware there is the ulterior purpose of maintaining the status quo. If the Queen dies and Enlos accedes to the throne the Haruspices lose their full power. They become advisors and little more. Thus they disregarded at first – or may have been genuinely ignorant of – the greater issue: the fact that the Heart of Shadows has been unearthed. But it is written that the Heart will be brought to the capital by the unknowing. I merely had to alert them – as Queen Lermeone also strove to do – to the connection with Garsh, and make them see the wisdom of letting the unknowing also carry the Heart from Dharsoul before Sko-ulatun can regain it.'

'Then our thanks to you.'

Dinbig raised a hand. 'Stay your thanks. I have not secured your release, merely a short reprieve. As I said earlier, you may not thank me for it. You are on a road fraught with perils, and when this business is done – *if* it is done – make no mistake, your troubles will not be over. The Haruspices are dangerous and powerful men. They will want your lives.'

After a silence Sildemund asked, 'What are the consequences of Sko-ulatun's regaining the Heart?'

'Again, I do not know. The answer may lie in Garsh, if we succeed in entering that place. But for all I know it may no longer exist, its inhabitants may already have been slain by Tomian troops. The Revenants claim extraordinary knowledge, linked, I am coming to believe, with the Heart of Shadows. But Tomia has long been tired of their presence. When Revenants started leaving Garsh to renew their preachings in towns and cities – breaking the terms of their occupancy of Garsh – Tomia became impatient. An official delegation was sent to Garsh to speak with the elders of Claine. Last night, in conversation with Prince Enlos, I learned that upon reaching Garsh these delegates were murdered. It goes against the creed of Claine, yet is apparently true. Hence the siege which, as I say, may already have terminated in violence.'

'And Kemorlin, why does he accompany us?'

'Ah, that is yet another facet in this strange affair. But it is a tale too involved to repeat now.'

Sildemund had another question, which was to ask again exactly how Dinbig came to be involved in all this, and what precise part he played. But the *Zan-Chassin* had risen to his feet, muttering something about talking to Prince Enlos, so for the moment no more was said.

19

FOR THE REMAINDER of that day Meglan had plodded on across the scorched desolation of Dazdun's Despair, lost, in her mind, bereft, with barely the will to keep her eyes on the serpent talisman which oscillated at her wrist. The sky glared; the land was an unbroken waste behind a film of heat-haze.

Over and over again she railed at herself. Jans was dead. She shed tears of grief, of mute anger and utter self-pity. She knew fear of the beast that pursued her, who might be anywhere; and another fear that she might be lost, that the serpent led her false, that she might never emerge from the Despair.

A curious thing occurred to her – she had thought about it more than once; Skalatin had followed her across this wasteland. How? Through the welter of her concerns came a sudden horror. She raised her wrist, stared at the gleaming metallic serpent dangling there. *Did it give her away?*

She fought the impulse to tear it off and fling it from her. It could not be. It was the serpent that kept her safe, guided her along the Path. But might it perform a dual function? From where had it come? She cast her eyes about her wildly, then: No. *Why would it bring him to me, then keep him from me? It wouldn't make sense.*

Nothing did make sense.

The image of Jan's mutilated body rose to torment her; stretched in the sun, surely picked at by vultures now. She saw the monster squatted upon it, the obscene vision of what he did. She cried out in anguish, then silenced herself, knowing that sound could expose her to her enemy.

But she should have gone back – that was the least she could have done – to bury poor Jans. No! No! She forced herself to accept the truth; to have gone back would have been a fatal mistake. Indeed, that might well have been Skalatin's aim.

The thought failed to ease her tortured conscience.

Swift Cloud bore her steadily on, her sole constant, her one source of comfort, her link to life, her past and all she held dear. She spoke softly in the filly's ear, hugged her neck, stroked her long silvery mane and sleek grey flank.

Night came and Meglan took refuge in a hollow. She lit no fire and was without appetite. Nor was she able to sleep. It was a moonless night, too dark for her to attempt to move on. She sat huddled in her blanket, tense, jumping at every tiny sound; the close skitter of a lizard, the shift of wind-blown sand or tiny particles of rock tumbling between stones, and once, the harsh, ear-splitting cry of some unknown night-bird which hovered unseen in the sky overhead.

Midway through the next morning she discovered that she had lost her way.

She did not recall how long it had been since she had last looked at the serpent talismen. Lack of sleep, the days enwombing heat, the gentle, uneven rhythm of Swift Cloud's careful step . . . it had all combined to lull her senses. Her eyelids grew heavy, too heavy to bear, and closed. She slumped in the saddle, then jerked awake. Seconds later, despite herself, her eyes closed again. It was so comforting, nothing could harm her now. She slipped back into welcoming half-sleep, even while a voice within her warned that this was the one thing she must not do.

How long did she doze? She could not tell. A vague feeling of unease penetrated the levels of her slumber, worked through her unconsciousness then became, suddenly, a pitch of alarm which snapped her back into dazed wakefulness.

At first she did not know what it was that was wrong. She stared around her, disoriented; nothing appeared to have changed. Yet she felt different. The heat was terrible. Her skin burned.

Her skin burned!

Meglan turned her face to the sky. It blazed blinding white, the sun invisible. It was the heat, fiercer than she had ever known, except . . . except upon those two occasions when she had left the Serpent's Path – at the beginning of her journey with Jans, and then more recently, when she had burst from the Path to flee from Skalatin.

A mere glance at the talisman confirmed her fears; the little serpent faced back the way she had come. In her lack of vigilance she had wandered off the Serpent's Path – how far back? Now she was exposed upon the plain.

She brought Swift Cloud around, her heart pounding, the hairs between her shoulder blades crawling, and moved back in the direction in which the serpent's head pointed. Watching the talisman, she still glanced around her, fearful of a dark, moving blot bearing down upon her at unnatural speed, or a shadow that was more than it seemed, a thing that metamorphosed into the foul form of Skalatin.

She had covered less than one hundred paces when, to her relief she felt the terrible heat diminish. After a couple more paces the serpent swung completely around upon its axis.

Meglan sat for a moment, stilling her heart, reassured in the conviction that she could no longer be seen. But then a new fear hit her. She turned her eyes again to the talisman, her brow creasing in perturbation. The serpent faced to her rear, the way she had come.

She turned once more, stepped Swift Cloud back. At the third step the heat slammed upon her back. The serpent swung around.

Meglan moved to the side; the snake's head remained aimed at the one point. She walked Swift Cloud towards that point, moved out of the heat, kept walking, crossing the Path until she entered the heat again. The talisman had reversed itself.

Her heat sank. She knew now, and looked about her despairingly, hopelessly, filled with a sense of bitter betrayal. She was nowhere. She had reached the end of the Serpent's Path. It had brought her this far across an arid wasteland, and then abandoned her.

For long moments she sat motionless in the saddle, no longer caring that she could be seen. Moments passed. Perhaps because of the unbearable sun, perhaps through a self-preserving instinct, she moved Swift Cloud back onto the Path. She felt suspended; her mind no longer seemed to function. She was at a loss what to do. Go back. . . ? There was nowhere to go. Remain here? She would starve eventually, if Skalatin did not find her first. But all around her there was only shimmering waste.

Ahead, in the direction she had been travelling when she dozed in the saddle, the land rose steeply to a long ridge, its slopes made liquid by the heat-maddened air. Meglan judged it to be southwards. She had no other choice. Wearily she prompted Swift Cloud on, moving out into the burning land, becoming visible again to any who might watch.

The ridge was further away than she had thought. After half an hour's laboured travel it seemed scarcely any nearer. But she kept her focus on the ragged blur of the high land; it was her one hope, that she had not been run false, that beyond that ridge there might be something other than arid wasteland, some indication that she was returning to the world.

The ground began to rise, gently at first, then at a greater cant. Meglan dismounted and led Swift Cloud, navigating the ascent by long traverses, pausing frequently for breath, until eventually she broke out onto the crest of the ridge.

A road ran along the ridge, stretching from north to south. Beyond it, below her, were trees. Green trees, a small stream twisting between them across a flat plain. In the further distance were fields planted with maize, durra and other crops, bounded by low stone walls and irrigation ditches. She saw sparse ranks of vines, olive, pistachio and peach trees, as well as firs and cypresses. And at the limit of her vision, dotted here and there among the trees, were four or five little white cottages.

Meglan passed that night upon the flat roof of the cottage of a family of peasants who worked for a local landowner. Despite her exhaustion sleep was intermittent. She woke frequently, dreaming that Skalatin had found her, was climbing the wall or the stairs, was crouched upon her, feeding on her flesh.

In the morning she replenished her stock of rations and water, and paid the good folk with coin from her pouch. She followed their directions, carrying on across country, and topped a rise some hours after setting off, to see, far in the distance, the hazy, shimmering towers and domes of Dharsoul.

In due course Meglan found herself descending a long rubbly incline, at the foot of which, across a small bare pasture, was the road which led to the capital's main gate. There was some activity upon the road; soldiers were clearing travellers to the sides to make way for a large company of knights and mounted troops coming from the city. The troops made an impressive sight; Meglan stopped to watch as they passed by. She estimated two hundred or more, their brightly hued banners fluttering in the hot air. She wondered about the identity of the rider at their head, who was flanked by a personal retinue of magnificently bedecked knights. She supposed him to be a noble or dignitary of no minor stature. Further to the rear came two gilt carriages, and at the tail were baggage and support wagons in some number.

Dust rose in dense, pale clouds behind the cavalcade, obscuring the view beyond. Meglan was afflicted with a strange longing. Her thoughts had gone to Sildemund, her twin brother. She turned her eyes towards the city, which rose now less than a league distant beside the great Tigrant river. Somewhere among the teeming mass which dwelt and laboured behind those great red walls her brother must be. How would she find him?

She did not know that Sildemund had ever reached the city, though for some reason she was convinced that he had. Within her a small voice, an echo from some unknown source, seemed to speak, telling her that Sildemund had been to the city, was with the crown prince, but that not everything had gone well. Why was she so certain of this? She searched her mind, seeking a memory that would not come.

Meglan looked back at the great cavalcade. She was suddenly uncertain of her goal. Before she could attempt to analyze her feelings she was interrupted. A shadow had moved on the slope before her. Skalatin came out from beneath a massive rock.

Swift Cloud nickered in alarm and took several slithering steps backwards. Meglan fought with her panicking impulses; to try to flee or to charge forward again and knock him from her path? She sensed that neither would work.

'Oh, Meg-lan, my sweet malkin. At last.'

He appeared hideously disfigured, neither the fleet-footed creature that had pursued her across the Despair, nor the man-fiend who had entered her father's house. But the voice was the same, that wheedling, coaxing, mocking voice, rising and falling constantly from plaint to purr. She shuddered at the sound. Her own voice shook as, fighting for time, she forced herself to respond. 'What do you want? Your heartstone? I do not have it.'

Skalatin took a step forward and raised a hand as if to take Swift Cloud's rein beside the bit, but the filly shied, so he merely stood there with his hand elevated at shoulder height, skeletal and discoloured. The fingers curled and slowly extended. At their tapering tips Meglan saw curving, brown claws.

'Meg-lan, Meg-lan, why did you run from me, pret-ty?'

Meglan could not answer; her voice caught in her gullet. It struck her that Skalatin showed no sign of any wound from her sabre-stroke.

Skalatin's voice took on a harsh, grating quality. 'What have you done with my heart?'

'I've told you, I don't have it.'

Skalatin suddenly snatched the rein beside Swift Cloud's muzzle. The horse tried to pull back, but he held her, casually, with no apparent expenditure of strength. In the shadow of his hood his mouth formed a travesty of a smile. Meglan felt the filly trembling between her legs.

Skalatin brought his other hand around to touch Meglan's calf. He let the tips of his fingers run up to her knee. She stiffened, rebelling at the touch, overcome with fear and revulsion.

'I have come here to find your heart, so that I can return it to you,' she said, the words tumbling out. 'As soon as I find it it is yours. I want no payment.'

Skalatin regarded her for a moment, but seemed now distracted. He turned his head to look back over his shoulder at the cavalcade passing upon the road below.

'My heart,' he said. There was a queer, questioning tone in his voice. 'You have my heart.'

'No. You are wrong. I am seeking it. It is in the city. I will find it and give it to you.

He turned back to her. 'Give it to me. It is mine.'

Meglan nodded. 'That is what I will do.'

His hand had gone from her leg. Now he released the rein and gazed back once again at the disappearing cavalcade. Meglan sensed a change in him, and was not sure what it was. He still menaced, that could not be doubted, but something else had his attention. He moved away a couple of paces, continuing to gaze intently at the road. For an instant Meglan thought again of trying to break away, make a dash for the road and the city. But there was no safety there. Not anywhere. Somehow, harrowing and distasteful as it was, she had to work with him if she was to survive.

Skalatin's head turned towards Dharsoul, then back to the

distant cavalcade. The last of the troopers were almost out of sight now. Skalatin was muttering to himself, words that Meglan could not make out. A breeze fluttered the dark folds of his clothing.

'Let me get it for you, Skalatin. Let me find it and bring it to you.'

Skalatin turned back as though suddenly recalling her presence. Yet he seemed unwilling to dismiss the company on the road. With a distant air he said, 'I will come with you.'

The thought appalled her. 'That is not a good idea, is it? You will be conspicuous. You are a creature of the shadows, whereas I must move in daylight, talk with people, perhaps in their homes. Your presence would cause alarm.'

Skalatin stood close again; his head was almost against her thigh. He upturned it and she caught a glimpse of the face beneath the hood. She turned away, unable to look. A whiff of his noxious breath reached her nostrils and she gagged; she felt its vaporous warmth upon her thigh, even above the sun's heat.

'I will wait, then,' said Skalatin, and Meglan breathed with relief. 'You will bring to me here my heart. Do not try to deceive me, pret-ty Meg-lan. I can find you.'

She nodded. 'Yes, you can. How? How do you find me?'

She knew that he smiled again – if such a face could really be said to smile – though she did not look. 'I have your essence,' he said.

'My essence?' His words shocked her, and seemed to touch something deep within her, prodding at a memory she could not recall.

'I took it into me. At your home, when we touched. I breathed you in. Love-ly child. So-o pret-ty. Part of you is already mine.'

Meglan choked back her revulsion and the red hot anger that urged her to lash out and strike him. Instead she encouraged Swift Cloud forward, pushing past him, saying, 'Let me go, then, that I can bring it to you the sooner.'

'I will be waiting, love-ly, love-ly Meg-lan.'

She stood in the wide court inside the main city gate, wondering which way to go. The crowds milled, folk of all kind, making their way to the city centre, to places of trade or entertainment, to family or friends or perhaps, unknowingly, to enemies. Others passed the opposite way, leaving Dharsoul for the fields or further destinations. Meglan took herself off to one side, in the shadow of a tall building out of the jostling crowd and the hard heat of the sun.

She had names, gleaned from a conversation overheard between her father and brother as Sildemund had made ready to depart Volm: Kemorlin was the first name and, she believed from her father's emphasis, probably the most important. But she knew nothing of him, had no notion of where he lived or worked. Similarly with the next name, Zakobar.

There was another, called Ractoban, a professor and administrator at the university of Dharsoul, and this seemed the most logical place to begin. She could find the university with little difficulty and was hopeful that the professor might also have knowledge of the other two.

Meglan found a stable behind an inn where, for a modest fee, she was able to leave Swift Cloud to be fed and watered. A word with the ostler put her on course for the university, and she set off without delay.

In due course she found herself in the vaulted and columned reception chamber where scribes and clerks worked at their desks. Not one looked up at her entrance. She approached the first desk. 'I wish to speak to Professor Ractoban.'

For a moment the clerk's quill continued its journey uninterrupted across the page of the ledger in front of him. Then it halted. The man lifted his head. Small, dull brown eyes looked Meglan up and down, seeming to have difficulty in accepting what they saw before them. Narrow lips twitched and an affronted expression clouded the man's lean features.

'What did you say?'

'I wish to speak to Professor Ractoban. Is he here?'

'That is not possible.'

'It is important. I must.'

The clerk looked her insolently in the eye and said, quietly accusing, 'You are a woman.'

Meglan stared him down, narrowing her eyes. 'I am quite aware of that.'

A supercilious smile formed on the clerk's thin lips. 'The professor does not entertain women here. In fact, do you not know, the professor finds no pleasure in women at all.'

Meglan's ire rose. She spoke through gritted teeth. 'I have come here neither for pleasure nor entertainment. It is business that I have with the professor.'

The clerk cast an arch glance at his colleagues who, Meglan now perceived, had ceased their work and with schoolboy smirks were observing the exchange. She was the butt of their scorn and it made her the angrier.

'It is one and the same,' muttered the clerk, and bent back over his work.

'It is not,' seethed Meglan. 'I have urgent business. I must see the professor.'

'You are a woman,' the clerk repeated, now matter-of-factly, his eyes upon his ledger. He held his quill poised above the page. 'And even were you not, you would find the professor unavailable. He is a busy and important man. He does not concern himself with the likes of you.'

It was too much. Her temper would not be contained. Her sabre flew from its scabbard and she brought the flat of its blade down with a deafening *slap*! upon the desktop. The sound reverberated off the stone walls of the chamber. The clerk jumped in his seat, spilling purple ink across the page.

Meglan brought the blade up, its tip an inch from the man's throat. 'He will concern himself, or it will be your blood that next colours the book!'

Every eye in the place was glued to Meglan, but the peak of her temper had passed and she knew her mistake. Two guards whom she had not previously been aware of were advancing upon her, pikes levelled. She drew back, quickly sheathing her blade, raising her hands in an open, conciliatory gesture, praying for a way out. She tensed involuntarily as her flesh anticipated the penetration of the cold, brutal pike-tips.

The clerk, white-faced, had risen and stepped back out of her reach. He was adjusting his robe with fluttering, nervous hands.

'To the cells!' he ordered, his voice breaking.

Desperately, Meglan protested. 'No! I am sorry, but you don't understand! I have to see the professor.'

The guards took her roughly by the arms and proceeded to march her off.

'I am seeking someone! Sildemund Atturio of Volm! He came here to meet the professor!'

'Halt!' commanded the clerk, a sudden, unreadable look upon his features. His face, which had flushed momentarily, was being drained of blood again. 'Who did you say?'

Meglan sensed a change in the atmosphere of the chamber. The other clerks were regarding her with new interest. 'Sildemund. Master Sildemund of Volm.'

The clerk seemed suddenly very ill-at-ease. He gestured irritably at the guards to let her go. 'You— you are from the Palace?'

Meglan was nonplussed, yet saw her advantage and seized the moment. 'I come on very important business.'

The clerk became flustered. The guards withdrew to the shadows. 'Madame, why did you not say? We—I didn't—Forgive me, please! You were right to have drawn your blade. Quite right. Yes, you should have struck me down; you had every right to. I am so sorry. Please, be seated a moment.' He called to a colleague to bring a chair. 'Madame, one moment, please. I shall fetch the professor immediately.'

He hurried from the chamber. Meglan seated herself, bemused, upon the chair provided. All heads were lowered once more; not one dared cast a glance at her.

She sat tall, enjoying the triumph, yet astonished that the mere mention of her brother's name could engender such a dramatic about-turn. *Sil, what have you been up to?*

Scarcely moments had passed before the door through which the clerk had exited flew open again and a plump, bald, flushed-faced fellow in a long lilac robe trimmed with vair rushed into the room, trailed by the troubled clerk. The newcomer's eyes found Meglan and he hastened towards her, arms spread, beaming obsequiously and bowing from the waist almost before he had reached her.

'Madame, my apologies. I hope you have not been inconvenienced. I am Professor Ractoban, at your service. I am delighted to welcome you to our university. Please, allow me to escort you to my office where we can converse in private. Can I offer you something? An iced cordial? Wine? Tea? Some biscuits, fruit?'

'Water will be fine, thank you,' said Meglan.

Professor Ractoban aimed a meaningful nod at his clerk, who signalled to someone else who made off to comply. Ractoban made an expansive gesture. 'This way, if you will.'

Meglan was ushered from the chamber, along a short corridor, up a flight of stairs to a comfortably appointed office on the first level. A servant entered just behind her, carrying a salver holding cups, a pitcher of cold water, another with iced raspberry sherbet, numerous dishes and small plates heaped with biscuits and cakes, fresh figs, dates and sliced watermelon. As Meglan seated herself these were arranged upon a low table before her. The professor was at pains to attend to her comfort, urging her to eat and drink her fill. She gratefully accepted the sherbet, found it delicious and refreshing. Then, discovering herself hungry, she took biscuits and figs.

'Now, how might I be of service to you?' enquired the professor, seating himself upon a divan opposite her. He made to recline, then changed his mind and remained erect, a little stiff. 'You were enquiring after the young Master Sildemund Atturio of Volm, I understand? I was privileged to make his esteemed acquaintance only two evenings gone. In the company of our beloved crown prince, no less! Of course, I am honoured to see Prince Enlos on a frequent basis, both as friend and counsellor in a number of areas in which I hold expertise.'

'You saw Sildemund? Was he well?'

'On, very well. Hale and hearty. Yes. A most engaging fellow – I took an instant liking to him. Destined for distinction, if I am not mistaken. You remind me of him, as it happens, is there a family connection?'

'He is my brother.'

'Ah. Mmh. Well, I am pleased to say I was able to assist him, and Prince Enlos too, in a professional capacity.'

'In what way, might I ask?'

'I was called upon to offer an authoritative opinion upon a certain artifact which Master Sildemund has in his possession. It was fortunate that I was on hand, for no other had been able to provide information on this exceedingly rare article.'

'You refer to the red stone, I presume, Professor?'

'Indeed, the red stone!' Ractoban seemed relieved that Meglan knew of the stone. She had the impression he was ever more ready to take her into his confidence.

'What, then, were you able to tell Sildemund and the Prince about the stone?'

'Ah,' Ractoban raised his hand to his mouth and coughed delicately. 'It is an unwholesome thing – that much I detected immediately. An object of immense age, which radiates an intangible aura of quite unusual intensity. At Prince Enlos's behest I have spent hours in the university library and archives during this past day and night, researching this stone. In fact, that was the task I was engaged upon until just a few moments ago, when I was informed of your presence. I came immediately, of course, for I am most happy to be of service – please do make that plain to the Prince, if you would.'

'Of course. But the stone. . . ?'

'The stone. Yes. It is referred to, I am now virtually positive, in certain ancient writings.'

'Really?' Meglan sat forward with sudden eagerness. 'In what way?'

The professor became guarded, a little embarrassed. 'Madame Atturio, forgive me, but regrettably I cannot pass on that information without written authority from the Palace. Do you have such?'

'No.'

'Then . . . please understand. It is Prince Enlos's commission that I am engaged upon. If I can help in any other way?'

'Is my brother still at the Palace, Professor?'

'Why, no. As it happens, news reached me just a short while ago that he departed Dharsoul early this very morning – with the Prince and full entourage, I believe.'

Meglan recalled the cavalcade she had seen upon the road. 'Departed? For where?'

'For Garsh, in Tomia, so I am told.'

Her heart sank. So close. To have come this far and then to have unwittingly watched Sildemund ride by. She stood, knowing that she had no choice but to leave now for Garsh, wherever it might be. 'One more thing, Professor. Do you know of a man called Kermorlin? Master Sildemund also had business with him.'

Ractoban frowned darkly and spoke with resentment. 'Kermorlin, yes. My understanding is that he also rides to Garsh in the same company.'

'And Zakobar?'

'I knew of him. Sadly, he has passed away.'

20

BACK AT THE inn by the city gate Meglan forced herself to eat. A little fresh salad and grains soaked in herb oil was all she could manage, for so agitated was she that her stomach rebelled at almost every mouthful.

She had to face Skalatin. Briefly she considered the possibility of trying to elude him, perhaps leaving the city by another entrance, but to what end? She had to follow Sildemund to Garsh, and to use any route other than the most direct would prolong her journey by days. And Skalatin could find her anyway: he had taken her essence.

She shuddered. He was out there just beyond the walls, waiting for her to bring him the heartstone. Or had he followed her into the city after all? He could be watching her even now from some concealed nook.

How would Skalatin react to her failing to deliver the stone? Could she make him believe her?

Her mouth went dry; the food caught in her throat as she fought down her terror.

Meglan thought back, recalling the cavalcade that morning in which Sildemund had almost certainly ridden by before her eyes. She thought about the way Skalatin had also been distracted as it passed on the road below them. Was it possible that he had half-sensed something? The presence of his heart? Its loss as it was borne away from him?

He had been confused, just briefly, she was sure of it. A vague, desperate idea began formulating in Meglan's mind.

She settled with the landlord for her food and drink, then went outside to the stable at the rear. She hired a fresh horse, a roan mare, somewhat aged, but strong and of an easy disposition. With sadness she left Swift Cloud in the hands of the ostler, paying him well for her care and promising to return for her as soon as she could. They grey filly had borne her steadfastly over the past days, but she needed rest now and Meglan could not take the time to wait for her to recover her strength fully. She prayed that she would be able to fulfil her promises.

Meglan rode from the city, and before she had covered a league was met by Skalatin, who appeared from among a clump of palms next to the road.

'You do not have it, pret-ty malkin.'

Meglan shook her head. 'It is no longer in the city. I know where it has been taken, though. I am going now to find it.'

She steeled herself, half-expecting his fury, his violence. But he remained perfectly still and said, in a quiet rasp, 'Where?'

Her nerve almost left her. 'I will not tell you.'

Skalatin's shoulders rose a little. His clawed fingers flexed at his sides and he leaned towards Meglan. The taint of his breath reached her and she recoiled. 'You will tell me, love-ly Meg-lan. Or I will feast.'

She was in no doubt of his meaning, and she felt sick with fear. But she had gone too far to pull back now. To do so would surely condemn her on the instant to the fate Skalatin spoke of. She clenched her teeth, shook her head once. 'I am going, Skalatin. I know where to find your heart – it is a long way from here. But I can retrieve it for you.'

She wondered at the truth of this last statement. She knew nothing. But all was bluff anyway. She was fighting to stay alive – for a few more hours, a few more days. And what would be the ultimate cost? In effect her proposal was to lead Skalatin to her brother. She prayed she could get the stone from Sildemund and pass it on, without risking Sildemund's safety. Would that be an end to the matter? She did not believe it could be, but she had to try. She would have sacrificed herself now if she had believed it would save Sildemund, but she did not believe it. Skalatin would find the red stone, somehow, just as he had managed to find her. Paradoxically, it was in this that her one hope lay.

'I can find my heart.'

She nodded to herself. 'Then do so.'

'You do not know what I can do.'

'I know enough.' She faced him down. 'Kill me, then, if that is what you want.'

Skalatin seemed almost to vibrate with tension, and the intensity of the glare from those dark, inhuman eyes turned Meglan's blood cold in her veins. But he made no move, and she took courage. More and more she was becoming convinced she was right. Skalatin might be able to find the heartstone, and it was plainly vital to him. *But so was she!* She could not say why, but he had pursued her when he could have directly pursued the heart. Perhaps he had genuinely believed she carried it, but there was more than that. He was unwilling to let her go. He wanted both her and the heart together.

She prompted the roan forward. 'I am going, Skalatin. You must follow, if that is what you want.'

There was a cart approaching, drawn by a scrawny white ox. It was the only traffic visible on the stretch of road they occupied. An old man and woman sat at the fore, dressed in peasants' tat.

They looked across at the two as they drew near, and smiled at Meglan as she made to pass.

Meglan heard a growl at her back, low and guttural. She swivelled in the saddle. Skalatin was striding the road's width, bounding up onto the cart. With one hand he seized the old man by the hair and yanked him erect.

'No!' Even as Meglan screamed she saw Skalatin plunge his other hand deep into the man's thin chest, bringing forth a fountain of dark blood.

The old woman gave sudden vent to hysterical shrieks. She rose, trying to strike Skalatin, then turned rigid with shock as she saw what he held. Skalatin turned to her, discarding the body. But his eyes went to Meglan as he feasted upon the heart.

He stood erect before the old woman. His form began to change. She screamed, pressing her hands to her head as she found herself once more facing her husband, whose corpse also lay convulsing across the sideboard of her cart.

She made to escape. Skalatin roared. He turned again to face Meglan, letting her see how perfectly he had assumed the guise of the man he had murdered.

He pounced.

Meglan saw no more. Even as the old woman's shrieks were cut short, as Meglan heaved, voiding the contents of her stomach onto the road, as hysteria took her, she dug her heels into the roan's flanks.

Skalatin paid her no heed, intent with his business upon the cart. She screamed at the roan, driving it to frantic flight, that she could be borne away up the deserted road.

PART THREE

21

S ILDEMUND GAZED OUT across the valley, the wind ruffling his hair. He focused beyond the troops encamped upon the valley floor, past the great mangonels and ballistae erected higher up the slopes, and the hundreds of infantry dug in among the trees and rocks. He concentrated upon the town that hugged the upper reaches of the hill, its battered stone wall snaking around its circumference, following the line of the land. It looked almost defenceless.

Garsh was completely invested. Sildemund could not imagine anyone entering or leaving the town without the knowledge of the Tomians.

From time to time he glimpsed signs of life behind the walls: tiny figures moving along narrow streets, or a solitary figure appearing for a few brief moments upon the parapet of the wall. Their appearance bestowed an odd sense of normality upon the scene. White tufts of clouds moved overhead, at peace in a clear blue sky, further belying what was passing below, for in the town the people were believed to be starving.

Behind Sildemund a blue pavilion had been erected upon a level area of grass. Within, Prince Enlos and the Supreme Haruspices were locked in talks with the commander of the besieging Tomian force, Count Draith, a nephew of the king, Lalvi III. The Dyarch sought entrance to Garsh; the Count, plainly uncomfortable with this new circumstance, withheld his sanction. His orders were that none should enter or leave the town, save under conditions of full surrender by the inhabitants. Faced now with Dyarchim's most illustrious and persuasive personages he was thrown into dilemma. The situation was without precedent; to offend such persons risked serious and far-reaching consequences. Yet his mandate was clear, and the circumstances under which he would defy his sovereign did not exist.

Count Draith took some solace in the knowledge that help was on its way. With the arrival of the Dyarch company at the border earlier a Tomian messenger had been dispatched at speed to Pher, the Tomian capital. Officials of highest rank, conceivably even royalty, would now be making for Garsh. Count Draith expected their arrival within a day.

But the Dyarch were reluctant to wait.

The journey to Garsh had passed without major event. At the intersection on the Dharsoul Road, where the northern road led up along the edge of Dazdun's Despair, fifty Dyarch horsetroops had left the main force. They, Sildemund learned, had been assigned the task of policing the road and dealing effectively with the Tomian brigand, Fagmar the Cursed.

The border had been reached a day later. There was some hold-up as the Tomian guards pondered their predicament. Faced with the commanding presence of Prince Enlos, who impressed upon them in no uncertain terms the urgency of his mission, they could arrive at only one decision. Indeed, they were not slow to acknowledge that there was no choice. Enlos was in no mood for debate or wrangle. Subtly but certainly he made it plain that his force *would* pass, legitimately by preference, but by other means if necessary; and the Tomians lacked the manpower for armed resistance.

So they employed delaying tactics for as long as was reasonably possible, prolonging formalities while sending out riders to both Pher and Garsh to inform relevant parties of the Dyarch ingress.

Fifteen leagues' more travel through lonely back-country had brought the Dyarch company to Garsh. It was a godforsaken place, set in harsh hills far from anywhere. When the Revenants had been exiled here almost a century earlier the town had long been uninhabited by all but ghosts and wild animals. They had worked diligently to restore the old town, had planted crops in the thin soil of the surrounding slopes. They lived peaceful, self-sufficient lives in accordance with their creed, and troubled no one. Until now.

By Ronbas Dinbig's account the problem had begun to re-surface a year or so earlier. Revenants were appearing in diverse towns and villages, in contravention of the statutes established long before by the Tomian government, which forbade them from stepping beyond Garsh and its immediate environs.

In times past, before their incarceration in Garsh, the Revenants had roamed freely. They preached at will, gathered followers, lived as they would. There were reincarnates among their number, and as their influence gradually spread the authorities in both Tomia and Dyarchim grew concerned. The Revenants preached no political dogma, professed no interest in the other religions of the region, nor attempted in any way to affect or interfere with the running of the state. But they claimed a secret, which they would not disclose, and more seriously, the ability of their elder members to be reborn at will gave them the status of godlings. Their potential to stir the people could not safely be ignored, and it was felt that they should be controlled.

'About two centuries past,' Dinbig told Sildemund, 'Tomia took the first steps. It established a register of all individuals who claimed the ability to reincarnate. Seventy-four names were recorded. Most hailed out of Tomia, but a good number lived in Dyarchim, and a few others in March.

'Once this was done new laws were brought in to limit the movements and activities of these Revenants. Any considered to be seriously in breach would be arrested, banished to some remote corner and forbidden from ever again manifesting in the flesh.'

The Khimmurian's eyes twinkled. 'It was quickly seen to be ineffective, of course, for how in Moban's name do you prevent a person being reborn? Tomia resorted to more extreme measures – as did Dyarchim. Revenants were tortured in an attempt to extract from them their great secret. Again, to no effect. The secret was known only to their leader, whose identity was itself unknown.

'Then came disappearances and murders, ostensibly random killings by thugs, but plainly the work of the Tomian secret police. This quickly became a political embarrassment. After all, the Revenants were an innocuous folk and had committed no real crime. More importantly from the government's point of view, death was itself as ineffective as banishment. For again, what is achieved by executing someone who is almost immediately going to return elsewhere in other flesh?

'Banishment en masse seemed the most logical answer. It at least went some way towards solving the problem by putting all the

Revenants in a single location where they might be monitored and prevented from mingling with the populace. So the Revenants and their non-reincarnating followers were rounded up and removed to ruined Garsh. They were forbidden to leave or to reincarnate elsewhere.

'Next Dyarchim argued that it would make sense for their Revenants to be also removed to Garsh. Tomia resisted initially, seeing such a move as elevating their problem while neatly relieving Dyarchim of its own. There followed a long period of wrangling. Eventually a compromise was reached which kept both sides happy. Tomia agreed to accept Dyarchim's Revenants, for a yearly stipend and certain other concessions. Thus it has remained to this day.'

'But now the Revenants defy the law,' Sildemund remarked.

Digbig nodded. 'Something seems to have alarmed them, given them sufficient cause to risk themselves to put out warnings to the people.'

'Warnings about what?'

'I am not absolutely sure, but I suspect it is not entirely unconnected with the contents of the leather satchel which rests against your hip.'

Forewarned by the messenger from border control, the Tomian commander, Count Draith, was waiting with an appropriate contingent when the Dyarch company arrived before Garsh. A tall, dark fellow, somewhat heavy of build, of saturnine character and in his young middle-age, he greeted them with polite formality and escorted them in person to an area suitable for their encampment. He then took Prince Enlos and others to a vantage point where they could survey the town.

'How many inhabitants are within?' enquired Enlos.

'About four hundred.'

'I understand that they are in the main civilians, including women, infants and elderly; and lightly armed?'

The Count acknowledged this with a stiff nod.

'And non-violent, also. Your besieging force appears particularly massive for the containment of such an unthreatening adversary.'

'They profess non-violence, my lord, but you are forgetting that important officials were murdered here. And the threat to my men comes not so much from within as from without. I came originally with a more compact force. We suffered attacks from local brigands led by Fagmar the Cursed. I was obliged to call up extra troops to put him to rout. He has gone now.'

'Yes, into Dyarchim.'

The commander ground the ball of one booted foot into the soil, uncomfortably. 'Nevertheless, the risk remained that he might return, so I kept my men here.'

'Do you perceive a link between the brigand and the activities of the Revenants of Claine?' asked Dinbig, who stood beside the Prince.

'It is possible.'

'But unlikely, I would have said.'

'Fagmar's strikes against us aided the cultists.'

'Possibly. Though ultimately it has surely only exacerbated their position?'

Count Draith declined to comment. Prince Enlos, shielding his eyes against the sun, said. 'We received reports of a massacre; I was more than concerned that we might arrive to find the town razed and every last soul murdered. It is with relief that I see that that is not so, yet the reports cannot have been entirely un-founded.'

The Tomian commander plainly wished he could put himself elsewhere. 'There was an incident. I had agreed through negotia-tion to permit some of the elderly and infants to leave the town. It was a delicate business, for they cannot be allowed to go free. Any one of them might be a reincarnate. But I gave my word that they would be taken into protective custody, that they might be spared the harshness of the siege. The main body refused to budge from the town, but they allowed about forty out. We held them temporarily in a stockade until it could be decided what to do with them.'

Count Draith fell silent for a moment, his eyes searching the sparse grass before his feet. Prince Enlos gazed at him with an unblinking eye. 'And what happened?'

The Count exhaled a deep breath. 'It would appear that some of the old folk had taken it into their heads that they might be robbed. Not that they had much of value. But some, at least, possessed a few coins, gold or silver. To save these they swallowed them before leaving the town. The following day a couple of guards spotted an old man examing his faeces and extracting coins. They fell upon him, disembowelling him in the hope of recovering more. Before it could be stopped word had got around that the Revenants had bellies filled with gold. The soldiers . . . You can imagine. . . .'

'How many dead?'

'Seventeen.'

'Is this normal mode of behaviour among the Tomian army?'

'It was an unruly element, not regulars. The men have been here a long time. They are bored. But I offer no excuse. It was a shameful incident. Those responsible have been executed.'

'I am glad to hear it. I trust there will be no recurrence?'

'There will not. The irregulars have been assigned other duties.'

'Of what ages were the seventeen?'

'Most were elderly men and women. Three small children also.'

'But none of in-between ages? Youths, or adults, for instance?'

'As I have said, it was only the elderly and very young who came out.'

Prince Enlos nodded to himself and exchanged a meaningful glance with Master Kemorlin, who stood close by. He addressed the Count again. 'How do you intend to extricate the remaining Revenants from the town? Will you storm it?'

'That will not ultimately be my decision. It depends upon the patience of King Lalvi. We have cut off access to the fields, so the town has no food supply. Their storehouses may be well stocked, however, it is possible they could hold out for many months and still be better fed than my own men.'

'And water?'

'I have blocked the main supply to the town, and bored down to cut off two streams which may or may not feed wells within the walls. But who's to say there is not another underground supply?'

'It could be a long investment, then.'

'I am awaiting orders.'

Enlos stared with a sombre expression across the sun-struck valley. 'We must enter this town.'

'That is not possible, sir.'

'It must be made possible.'

'My orders will not allow—'

'Then I must persuade you otherwise. Come, let us speak at greater length in conditions of privacy.'

It was then that they took themselves off to the blue Tomian command pavilion.

Sildemund was under guard and had virtually no contact with anyone other than Gully and Dinbig. His earlier request, that he be permitted to speak with the female Revenant who had accompanied them, had been denied. He assumed the Heart of Shadows to be the reason for his closer confinement. He noted the tension on the faces of his guards. They would not know what he carried, but it would be evident to them that he was a most important charge. And he recalled Dinbig's caveat; that though he was important now, while this business was being resolved, his reprieve would be short. A time would come, possibly very soon, when he would relinquish the Heart of Shadows. Then his life would be forfeit; the Supreme Haruspices would make certain of that. He wondered whether any of these guards had been given specific instructions.

In the centre of the Dyarch camp was a round, white pavilion, heavily cordoned by elite masked troops. Within, unseen, Queen Lermeone sat, awaiting events. Sildemund looked around him at the pavilions, white and blue, the many tents, the lonely hills, the isolated town, the soldiers of two nations gathered in force. He was overcome with a sense of displacement. He should not have been here. He had been cast into a role for which he was wholly unprepared, a player in contingencies he did not understand.

The wind rattled the canvas of the tents. Evening was closing in. Watched by his guards Sildemund made his way back towards his own shelter to rejoin Gully.

'Gully, we have to escape,' whispered Sildemund as they lay beneath their blankets late in the night. Neither had slept.

Gully lay with his hands cradling his head, staring up at the starlit sky. 'Very well. It sounds a fine idea to me. Let's be off.'

'Don't make fun of me, Gully. We have to do it.'

'Escape is easily said, less easily achieved. Do you think I have not considered the same? It is impossible.'

'There has to be a way. We are going to die if we don't. We have become pawns now, moved around the board to play a necessary part for the present, but ultimately a threat to the Queen.'

'Aye, and it's our own Queen, Sil.'

'There lies the immediate peril. We are without allies. But perhaps also there lies our hope.'

'What do you mean?'

'I'm not sure.'

He lay for a long time in silence, his thoughts chasing each other around in his brain. Eventually, though he did not think he would, he slept.

The morning brought an overcast with light drizzle and mist. Sildemund was up early and discovered, when he and Gully attempted to take a stroll up the slope to stretch their limbs and regard the besieged town again, that their movements had been restricted. They were confined to the immediate area of their tent. No explanation was given. Food was brought for them, but otherwise, they were left kicking their heels.

The sun rose higher, pushed through the overcast, dispersing the drizzle and slowly burning off the mist. From the blue pavilion Sildemund observed a figure emerge and make its way across the encampment towards them. As it drew closer he recognized Dinbig of Khimmur.

'There has been a development,' said the Khimmurian, seating himself before the two of them. 'Late yesterday evening King Lalvi arrived from Pher.'

'The King of Tomia!' exclaimed Sildemund. 'He is here?'

'It appears that when news arrived at Pher from the border, giving notice of our ingress, King Lalvi deemed the situation important enough to come in person. It is not wholly surprising, all things considered.'

'Is he prepared to allow entrance to Garsh?'

'It is tense in there,' Dinbig nodded towards the blue pavilion. 'Negotiations have been going on since the small hours. There is tremendous reluctance on Tomia's part to allow access. Lalvi is not a patient man. He is suspicious also. He favours storming the town and killing the inhabitants.'

'But – as you have already pointed out – that would solve nothing. The Revenants will simply be reborn elsewhere.'

Dinbig nodded. 'Lalvi is not a man given to deep thought or easy temper. He seeks an immediate end to what has become a personal irritant. With our arrival he perceives the situation as exacerbated.

His proposed solution, though short-term, would at least relieve him of the problem for a few years.'

'Can he be stopped?'

Dinbig gave a shrug. 'Enlos is a skilled negotiator, with more than one card up his sleeve. He is also unlikely to back down now, whatever the cost. His presence, and that of Queen Lermeone, place King Lalvi in an awkward position – one that he would have preferred to have avoided. There is intrigue here, believe me. And conflict, if all else fails. We shall see what we shall see.'

'Did you employ magic, Dinbig? Upon King Lalvi, to "open his mind"?'

'By good Bagemm, no! Lalvi has knowledge of certain minor magical techniques, and has a counsellor in his company who has received a deal of schooling himself. The risk of their detecting anything I might invoke is high – very high.'

'Was that not also the case at Dharsoul?'

'The Sacred Haruspices know little of the kind of magic I employ. There was a risk of detection, but it was small.'

'What of Kemorlin?'

'Kemorlin was not present when I utilised my skills, you will recall. Even had he been, he has no particular bent. He is alert, but little more. Though he pretends otherwise, he knows as much of true magic as you do of politics.'

'He is a charlatan?'

'A trickster, in more ways than one.'

'Then why is he permitted to practise?'

'Enlos does not like it, as you may have perceived. But Master Kemorlin is wily. He has certain talents, a clever tongue, and has worked himself into an extraordinary position in the courtly hierarchy. When it serves his ends he is able to wield a subtle but effective influence.'

'Dinbig, what *is* your part in this?' Sildemund asked. 'You said previously that certain persons had a reason for wanting you in custody, yet though you are undoubtedly not entirely a free man, you exert authority nevertheless.'

'My part has been foisted upon me through your arrival and the arrival of the Heart of Shadows. Prior to that I was merely passing an unplanned sojourn occasioned by the interest of Prince Enlos and Master Kemorlin.'

'I don't understand.'

'It is not a simple tale to tell. Still, perhaps there is time now.' The Khimmurian took a draught of water from his flask and wiped his lips. 'I first came to Dharsoul on a trading mission some years ago. I had recently succeeded in opening a trade route from Khimmur, to the southern lands. Khimmur, as you may well know, had a reputation for barbarism and a mistrust of foreigners. It was, with some justification, considered unsafe by foreign merchants, and thus avoided. By opening up Khimmur to trade, guaranteeing safe passage as far as was reasonably possible, I gave access between the south and the northern nations, most notably Kemahamek. There are tentative plans to build a bridge over the great White River into Tanakipi later on, which will further extend trade to Pansur, Miragoff and elsewhere. It has proven a lucrative and highly successful venture, if at times fraught with problems.

'Upon one of my early visits to Dharsoul I met and loved a woman. Her name was Epta. She was young and beautiful. I was uninformed of certain things about her, such as the fact that she was intended to be betrothed to the young Prince Enlos. She did not tell me, for she had no desire to marry him. Nor did she, or anyone, tell me that her father was Kemorlin.

'Kemorlin had great ambition for Epta, seeing her marriage as a means to tremendous power and influence in court. The discovery of our liaision placed me in a most delicate position. Prince Enlos, in a fit of rage, tried to murder me with a sword. I am no swordsman. Still, by an exceptional stroke of luck I succeeded in fending him off long enough for Palace Guards to intervene and save my hide. In fact – and I marvel at it still – I drew first blood, my blade etching that neat little cross-shaped scar that you see today upon his cheek! Don't ask me how I did it, for I don't know. But to this day Enlos is convinced that I am an expert bladesman, and that I toyed with him when I might have taken his life!' Dinbig paused and shook his head in wonder.

'Why were you saved by the Palace Guards?' Sildemund enquired.

'At the behest of the Haruspices, who were perspicacious enough to understand that the nation's potential new wealth, occasioned by the opening of the new trade route, would be instantly turned to dust were the route's Master Engineer to be slaughtered within the Dyarchim Royal Palace. And as it happened Enlos acted out of pride and a need to restore his personal honour only, for he had no great interest in Kemorlin's daughter, and was in fact in love with another – though he quickly tired of her, too. So are our hearts ever the instruments of forces greater than we. The affair was hushed up, and in time Enlos and I came to know a mutual respect, if not exactly friendship.'

'What of Epta?'

'There is the sad part. She had become a political embarrassment, and equally an embarrassment to her father, whose most major ambitions were now thwarted. She was sent away. Kemorlin, it must be said, would have had me assassinated had he been able. But I was alert, and he was, moreover, made to understand that my death – for the reasons I have just outlined – was quite unacceptable to the court. There is a curious factor involved in Kemorlin's tale, which I cannot go into now. It provides him with a place in the scheme of things, but simultaneously makes him exceptionally vulnerable. He has been permitted to grow wealthy and influential, to do almost as he wills, but he could, by a single blow, be brought to ruination, and he knows it. He must tread carefully.'

'But why were you arrested at the border. Dinbig?'

'In order that I might understand that I am not immune to the law. I cannot be permitted to rise above my place. It is a charade, really. I am disrupted a little, held in custody on no reliable charge, then released. It has happened before. In truth, Enlos and I enjoy one another's company. We both understand the necessity of the game. And on this occasion Enlos, aware of my information-gathering abilities, had hoped to learn something of what was behind the trouble at the border. As it happens, I knew scarcely more than he.'

'This is a strange tale,' observed Gully drily.

'Aye, and it is but the half of it. But now, I note activity at the blue pavilion.'

They peered across the field to the great tent, now lit by bright sunshine. Sure enough figures were emerging. Sildemund thought he saw Prince Enlos among them. Dinbig was nodding to himself. 'I would guess that a decision had been made.'

22

A QUAD OF DYARCH guards tramped across from the blue pavilion to where Sildemund, Gully and Dinbig waited. Dinbig rose to greet them.

'Ah, good men, I see by your faces that you are the bearers of bright good news! We are to be released, is that not so? Given full and proper recompense for the inconveniences we have suffered, and set upon our way with a full military escort to protect us through these wild and dangerous lands! This is welcome news indeed! Worthy of celebration!' He turned to Sildemund and Gully, smiling broadly, his arms spread, 'Come, let's gather our belongings and be off!'

The captain of the guards addressed him tersely, without humour. 'You are asked to report to Prince Enlos forthwith – sir. And you . . .' he looked at Sildemund and Gully, 'make ready to move.'

'Where are we being taken?' asked Sildemund.

The soldier ignored him and strode across to confer with the guards around Sildemund's tent.

'My good man,' said Dinbig, stepping over to him. 'My young friend here has just asked you a question. Have the courtesy to answer him, would you?'

The captain turned slowly, straightening, his expression sour. Dinbig returned him a smile of airy innocence. 'His question was perfectly reasonable under the circumstances, was it not?'

The captain seemed to have second thoughts. The challenge faded from his eyes. 'I have not been told where you are to be taken,' he said sullenly aside to Sildemund. 'Merely that you are to be ready to leave.'

He scowled at Dinbig, but was unable to hold his gaze.

'Thank you, sir,' said the Khimmurian. 'That is all that was required of you.'

He grasped the captain's arm and steered him away, out of immediate earshot of his fellow soldiers. 'I trust you will take it upon yourself to ensure the wellbeing of my friends while they rest under your aegis?'

The captain indignantly thrust forward his chin. 'I follow the orders of my superiors.'

'Quite so, and quite proper. However, remember I am a magician. I would not be pleased to learn of the mistreatment of those whom I hold in high regard.'

The firmness left the captain's jaw; he eyed the Khimmurian with unease.

Dinbig leaned closer to his ear. 'A hex upon any who offend me is a simple matter. The Chant of Perpetuity's Itch, for instance; or Rutholt's Curse of Flaccidity. Even graver; an Assignment of a Tormenting Wisp; an Insidiate Discomfort; a Visitation of the Qinkulc; a Notule of Scampering Dementia. . . .The possibilities are virtually without limit.'

Dingbig lifted a hand and performed a complex gesture with his fingers. The captain took a sharp step back, alarm upon his face. Dinbig displayed a broad smile. 'Do not fear, captain, I jest only. Unless sorely tried I would not do these things, though I am able. Go about your business now, in your best manner, without concern and with my blessing.'

He turned, still smiling, and nodded to Sildemund, then made off across the field to locate Prince Enlos.

Sildemund and Gully gathered and packed their few belongings. Their guards dismantled their tent and took it away. Their horses were brought and tethered close by. Across the encampment there were signs of activity. Masked Dyarch knights had formed up on horseback outside the white pavilion where Queen Lermeone waited. Others were in attendance before Prince Enlos's command tent, and the tents of the Supreme Haruspices. Closer by Sildemund saw Picadus seated glumly upon the ground, watched tensely by guards. He waved, but Pic's eyes were fixed upon the grass.

Perhaps an hour passed, and then Dinbig returned. He pushed between the guards and squatted at Sildemund's side. His air of levity had passed. 'It is as I had thought. King Lalvi was persuaded as to the urgency of the matter. He has given his permission for a limited company to enter Garsh. We will be among that number. The next step is to persuade the Revenants to grant us entrance. They will be suspicious.'

Sildemund felt a crawling nervousness in his gut. He ran a hand over his satchel. 'The time must be almost upon us when I shall relinquish this hateful stone. Paradoxically, when I do I shall also be signalling an end to my usefulness in this affair. Gully, Pic and myself will no longer be of account. Our lives will be forfeit.'

The Khimmurian's face was grave, but he made no immediate comment. Sildemund looked at the sky, then back. 'And yours, Dinbig? You share the same knowledge as we, yet are you condemned to the same fate? I do not believe so.'

'You are correct in that. Much as they would be rid of me, they cannot. I am too important. Dyarchim will not risk the loss of trade with the north; nor the hostility of Khimmur which my death as a foreign emissary would incur. Wealth is power, my friend. It is everything. Remember that, if you should live beyond this day. All laws may be broken by wealthy and powerful men. It is a fact, nothing more nor less. There is no virtue in poverty, and let no fool ever tell you otherwise.'

'You are surely susceptible to "accident"?'

'Indeed, upon the road, far from Dyarchim — for they would scarcely risk it within their own borders. But it is unlikely that the Haruspices will go to such lengths. The road is dangerous anyway. I am cautious and experienced. What is one more hazard among the many? And besides, I am *Zan-Chassin*.'

Sildemund nodded. The powers of the *Zan-Chassin* were unknown and the subject of much debate, but few would willingly subject themselves to their unwanted attentions. The attitude of the captain of the guard an hour earlier had been a perfect demonstration of the power of their reputation. After a pause, lowering his voice, Sildemund said, 'I will take you into my confidence, then; we intend to escape.'

'Good.'

'Will you help us?'

'If I can. What is your plan?'

'We have none.'

'As I thought.' Dinbig scratched his whiskers and stretched his jaw. 'Your chances of success are remote.'

'They are no worse than the prospects we already face.'

Dinbig kneaded his chin pensively. 'Do as you think best. For my part I would do nothing before we have entered Garsh – *if* we do. I do not think there will be any opportunity before then.'

'And within?'

'Who knows what may ensue? There will be interesting exchanges, that I guarantee. But for you . . . you are surrounded by enemies.' He shook his head. 'You must remain alert. Stay close to me if you can. Now, Prince Enlos has appeared. I must join him.'

As Dinbig departed the captain of Sildemund's guard re-appeared. Sildemund and Gully were ordered to mount their horses. A troop of Dyarch soldiers flanked them. They were led across the field to wait beside the track which wound towards Garsh.

In due course they were led forward to join a group consisting of Prince Enlos, the two Haruspices, Master Kemorlin, Dinbig and several knights. Picadus was close by, as was the female Revenant who had travelled with them from Dharsoul. An ornate palan-quin, its windows draped, was borne by eight attendants and surrounded by masked guards. This Sildemund supposed to contain Queen Lermeone.

Almost immediately the group moved off along the track. Sildemund, Gully and Picadus, with their guard, brought up the rear. Further down the track another group joined them, comprising about thirty Tomian knights plus footsoldiers to the number of perhaps, fifty. At the head of this group rode a huge, bluff figure clad in silvered lamellar; King Lalvi.

They proceeded on down into the valley, passing the main Tomian encampment, then began the ascent towards beleaguered Garsh. As they drew closer they came upon Tomian troops dug in on the slopes beside the road. The incline grew steep, steeper than Sildemund had guessed when viewing it from the far side of the valley. The stone curtain wall which encircled the town, though worn and in places beginning to rot and fall away, yet presented a formidable obstacle. To a considerable extent it augmented natural, sheer walls of rock, making it virtually impossible to scale and too lofty to batter. The slopes were rugged, allowing few channels for assault. Garsh would not be an easy location to take by storm.

They arrived at the edge of an attenuated plateau, about seventy paces from the town's fortified main gate. Before the gate Sildemund saw four Tomian knights on horseback. They appeared to be in conversation with a guard or guards manning the gatehouse and wall. After a few moments he realized that one of the knights was familiar: it was Count Draith.

Presently the Count and his knights withdrew from the gate, turning their horses about and trotting over to the main group. He conferred with King Lalvi. Prince Enlos joined them, and then the Revenant was called forward. Moments later Enlos, Count Draith and the Revenant, accompanied by four knights (two Tomian and two Dyarch), rode to the main gate.

'They use the Revenant to plead their case,' murmured Gully. 'She will perhaps be more effective at persuading her own people to allow us ingress.'

Sildemund looked around him, then back down the track, his thoughts on escape. It was impossible. Too many guards were positioned at his rear. Even should he break through them, where would he go? The one route was back into the valley, running the gauntlet of besieging troops and the Tomian camp below.

He turned and saw Dinbig's eyes upon him, a slight, quizzical frown upon his brow. Sildemund shrugged. The Khimmurian raised a cautioning finger, then returned his gaze to the group at the town gate.

Presently Prince Enlos and the others returned. Sildemund was able to urge his mount forward sufficient to allow him to hear most of what now passed.

'The elders are willing to speak to us,' said Enlos to King Lalvi and the others. 'To that end they will open the gate. But there are conditions: we may be no more than ten in number, with a maximum of six guards accompanying.'

'Unthinkable!' exclaimed King Lalvi. 'They are more than four hundred! We would be defenceless!'

'We enter, remember, not for conflict but for peaceful resolution,' replied Enlos.

'As did my previous delegation, all of whom were murdered.'

'I have raised that matter. The Revenants claim the incident was not what it appears.'

'Death is death. It was served upon my people. There is no illusion.'

'They insist there is a story to tell.'

'They seek to save themselves.'

'It might yet benefit us to listen to what the Revenants have to say. And might I remind you again, sire, of the full and intricate scope of this matter, of the level of our interest and the possible ramifications.'

King Lalvi seemed to falter slightly at this. 'Are there other conditions?'

'That the remainder of our retinue return to the valley floor before the gate is opened; and that, once within, we relinquish all weapons.'

At this King Lalvi raised loud and vehement protest. He was supported by the two Supreme Haruspices who argued that they could not permit their two royal heads of state, and themselves, to enter such a place unprotected.

'Consider,' said Prince Enlos, 'even were we armed we would be but sixteen in number, easily overwhelmed should the Revenants wish it. Unarmed we are hardly more vulnerable. But I negotiated a compromise. The six guards may retain sabres and shields; you and I, sire, but no others, may carry a single dagger at our belts.'

'This is preposterous!' declared the King angrily. 'I am having terms dictated to me within my sovereign territory!'

'The situation is without precedent. I am willing to accept the conditions, as, I have no doubt, is my mother, the Queen.' He stared levelly at the two Supreme Haruspices, daring them to challenge his decision. They exchanged uneasy glances but raised no further protest. Prince Enlos addressed the King again. 'If you prefer, sire, you may remain outside.'

The King shifted in his saddle, clearly uncomfortable with the concept. He hummed and hawed, then said, 'What of your prisoners, whom you deem so important to this mission? They must have a guard!'

Enlos, unhappy with the word 'prisoners', said, 'I have discussed that. Their guard may accompany them through the gate where they will then be escorted by Revenant troops. The guard will also be permitted to wait there, inside the gate, for our return.'

Hearing this Sildemund felt a surge of hope. He was to be put into the hands of Revenant guards, who had no claims upon his life. He glanced at Dinbig, but the Khimmurian was intent upon the exchange between Enlos and King Lalvi.

The Tomian King had found cause for further demurral: 'Thus you have the advantage of as many as ten more soldiers than I.'

Enlos suppressed a sigh. 'I anticipated your feelings, as have the Revenants. The Dyarch guard will consist of four men only, and may be accompanied by Tomian troops to an equal number.' Enlos turned to the others. 'Who else will accompany myself and the Queen? Master Dinbig? Master Kemorlin? You are under no duress.'

'I would not miss it,' said Dinbig drily, and Kemorlin pressed his beard to his chest and gave a stiff nod.

Enlos regarded the Supreme Haruspices, who also nodded their acquiescence. He then approached Sildemund and Gully. 'In truth, you have little choice but to enter this place. I regret that it is so.'

He turned away. 'Come, then, let us waste no more time.'

The main retinue returned down the winding track to the valley floor. The group rode the short distance to Garsh's gate, then all dismounted, passing their steeds into the hands of a pair of grooms. Queen Lermeone's paladin-bearers set her paladin down and she stepped out to stand alone, regal and vulnerable, wearing an ankle-length pale blue robe with hood and full veil, so that her entire face was obscured. Three masked guards immediately fell in around her, and the paladin-bearers departed. Three Tomian knights formed King Lalvi's guard.

There came the sound of a weighted bar being raised, then the gate swung open with a groan of complaint – not fully, merely sufficient to admit them. They entered a paved ward with cobbled streets which led off to left and right in the shadows of the wall, and ahead, flanked by tall buildings, running into the town's heart. There were people here, as many as sixty or seventy, their faces curious, all garbed in tatters ranging from brown through to varying shades of red. Most were armed, with swords or axes or field implements. Many were plainly trained fighters, their weapons supplemented by shields and armour of padded or boiled leather. A few had breastplates. A surprising number were women, and none evinced obvious signs of malnutrition.

As the gate closed six fighters marched forward, headed by a woman. She bowed curtly, then demanded, 'Where are those under guard?'

Prince Enlos nodded towards Sildemund, Gully and Picadus, and indicated to his men to move aside. The six Revenant fighters surrounded the three men. The woman spoke again. 'You will relinquish all arms, bar those agreed upon. These soldiers will remain here.'

This was done. A larger body of Revenant defenders fell in around the group. A litter was brought for Queen Lermeone, into which she climbed. The female Revenant took a position ahead of Prince Enlos and King Lalvi. She gave a signal and they began the march into the town.

The way took them uphill along a crooked street to a wide, sett-paved square. At the centre was a well set before a tall composite statue in green bronze, featuring heroes and phantasmagorical beasts locked in mortal combat. Revenants lined the square, as they had the street along which the group had approached, their faces taut and inquisitive. Casting his eyes upwards Sildemund saw bowmen upon rooftops. There existed no opportunity for escape here, and besides – despite what it might mean for him – he was more intrigued to be present at the imminent meeting.

They left the square via an angled way which took them into a cloistered court. A wide flight of stone steps at one end delivered them to a lower yard at one side of which was a tall, solid building of unadorned, streaked grey stone. They approached this, to confront a timbered portal. The female Revenant leading them hammered upon this three times with the pommel of her sabre. The portal opened and they filed through, to find themselves in a chill, gloomy passage. Following this they turned down smoothworn stone steps, entered another passage, descended yet more stairs and arrived eventually at a wide double-door. Through this they were admitted into a spacious chamber, almost a hall, lined with dark stone columns like the trunks of vast petrified trees. The chamber lacked natural light and was illuminated by hundreds of candles set in candelabra and torchères which hung from the low, vaulted ceiling, or were mounted upon the walls and columns, or merely stood free upon the stone floor. Flues in the walls and ceiling permitted egress for the candle-smoke, but even so the atmosphere was thick and warm.

At the opposite end of this chamber waited the Elders of the Revenants of Claine.

They were three in number, all female, but only one was of advanced age. She, the crone, sat behind a long table of heavy, dark wood. Seated at her left side was a much younger woman, aged between twenty-five and thirty; at her right was young girl of perhaps twelve or thirteen years, hardly more than a child. The shifting, ethereal, smoky light made it difficult to distinguish their features in any detail.

The group was permitted to approach to a point some fifteen paces or so from where the Elders sat. Queen Lermeone's litter was set down upon the floor. Armed fighters, more than half of them women, stood in a double row before the Elders. Others occupied the natural alcoves between the columns.

The crone spoke. 'Who is King Lalvi?'

'I,' replied the Tomian king, standing tall.

'Why do you persecute us?'

'It is not persecution. You have broken the bonds of your confinement.'

'Out of necessity!'

'I have no evidence of that. I see only your persistent refusal to conform to the law, and the brutal and unprovoked murders of the officials sent here to meet with you.'

'The followers of Sko-ulatun are responsible for those murders, not we,' replied the Elder. 'They infiltrated our ranks, and deliberately brought about this situation.'

King Lalvi blinked. 'Sko-ulatun?'

'First Man!'

'Where is Sko-ulatun?' asked Prince Enlos loudly, stepping forward.

The Revenant frowned. 'Who is it that addresses us?'

'I am Enlos, crown prince of Dyarchim.'

'Ah, Prince Enlos. Welcome. We understand that your mother, the Queen, is also among this party?'

'That is so. Now I ask again, where is Sko-ulatun?'

'Seeking. He was here. We held him, but he escaped. He seeks what he has always sought. We have tried to warn you, but you had no ear to listen. Perhaps he has already found it.'

Enlos glanced across at Dinbig, then Sildemund behind him,

then spoke again to the Elders. 'It is true, we did not listen because we did not believe. Now we would listen, if you will speak.'

The Revenant crone shifted in her seat. 'And what of us? Are we to die, here, for defying your laws?'

'You must tell us your tale so that fair and proper judgement may be made.'

'Our tale is simple. We are the Revenants of the Great Mother, Ancestress of us all. First Woman, Claine, whose spirit resides in all her many daughters. We exist to ensure that the disaster whose seeds were sewn millennia ago when Claine was betrayed and eventually brought low by Sko-ulatun, does not come to pass. Claine saw what Sko-ulatun did, and she took his heart and buried it where it could never be found, believing that he would perish. But he did not. He has searched ever since. Only a few among us knew where it lay.'

'You knew?' said Enlos. 'All this time, you knew the resting-place of the Heart of Shadows?'

'Within our ranks it is known. It is part of the secret we live to keep. The location was known to one of us, and the knowledge was passed on with each rebirth. We have always known, too, that Sko-ulatun would infiltrate our ranks with his own followers in the hope of discovering the secret.'

'Did he ever do so?' enquired Dinbig, bringing himself to the fore.

'Only recently. But it is true that his followers have been among us and have forced us to ever greater diligence in the custody of our knowledge.'

'And recently he discovered it? How? And if it is so, why does he not have the Heart now?'

'Do you know that he has not?'

'I know little,' said Dinbig. 'I am here in the hope of learning more, and of providing help if I am able.'

'Who are you?'

'I am Ronbas Dinbig, Realm Adept of the *Zan-Chassin* of Khimmur.'

The ancient Revenant sat back and surveyed him. Her two colleagues inclined their heads towards her and they conferred in whispers, the girl-child apparently on an equal footing with the other two. Then she said. 'We know of your ways. You gather knowledge; you endeavour to manipulate forces you know little of.'

'In order that we might extend the boundaries of knowledge.'

'Perhaps, but beware that you are not the ones who are manipulated.'

The Revenant spoke portentuously, and Sildemund watching Dinbig, thought to see a fleeting, uncharacteristic shadow pass across his features, as though her words had, for an instant, disquieted him.

'You were speaking of the Heart, and of Sko-ulatun,' prompted Prince Enlos.

The Revenant nodded slowly, her old eyes leaving the Khimmurian to address all assembled. 'Thousands of years ago there were changes in the land. There were great eruptions and upheaval. Mountains and uplands that had never before existed were pushed up into the world. Others vanished. Forests, rivers, lakes were swallowed by the earth, others were formed. Cities were destroyed, thousands upon thousands of people lost their lives. No one knows the cause. Some believe it was brought about by the violence of the Enchanter Wars; others that it was the will of the Great Moving Spirit, Moban, expressing dissatisfaction with his Creation; others hold that it was underground gods warring. . . .We can but wonder. But in this upheaval the secret place where rested the Heart of Shadows was thrust to the surface – in your land, Prince Enlos: Dyarchim. The place was remote and uninhabited, which was fortunate, for none knew of the event, nor were likely to suspect anything of the secret that the new land contained.

'But the one among us who held the secret knew – and knew also the danger that Sko-ulatun might now detect the Heart. And so that knowledge was at last shared among select members of our Hierarchy, that we might decide the most appropriate action to take.

'We recognized that the greater danger might lie in our trying to move the Heart to another location. After all, there was nothing that would ordinarily have drawn Sko-ulatun to such a place. Even should he go there and discover the Heart, he could not touch it. It was protected with pure ixigen, which he cannot tolerate. It remained hidden within a cavern, undetectable to the normal eye.

Thus, as Sko-ulatun, or at least his followers, were known to be among us, we left the Heart where it was.

'We placed a permanent vigil over that place. One of us dwelt there at all times, living as an anchorite. At the slightest indication that Sko-ulatun might have gained knowledge of the secret of that place, we were ready to act.'

Sildemund, listening intently, thought back to their discovery of the grotto where they had found the Heart of Shadows. It was Picadus who had pointed out the ancient, almost invisible foundations of a building, long gone. Sildemund recalled brief discussions over who might have lived there, and why. He looked across at Picadus now, but Pic stood stiff, with blazing eyes fixed upon the three Revenants at the table. If he had heard what had just been said it plainly had not aroused his interest.

'That is, until you imprisoned us here! continued the Revenant, her voice suddenly harsh. She jabbed a gnarled finger at King Lalvi and Queen Lermeone. 'With that one blow you deprived us of the ability to guard the Heart properly.'

'You speak of events that took place more than a century ago,' replied King Lalvi. 'We are not responsible for the acts of our ancestors.'

'You are as guilty. You have done nothing to repeal the law. You have kept us here, refusing to hear us, and when we have tried to break free you have persecuted us. You are fools who know not what you do!'

The King bristled at the insult, as did numerous members of the Dyarchim entourage. But they held silence, constrained by their circumstances.

Prince Enlos spoke. 'You said you held Sko-ulatun here.'

The Revenant nodded. 'By a stroke of luck he came to us after our incarceration. He believed, correctly, that we had the secret of the whereabouts of the Heart of Shadows. He believed that if he could mingle with us he would discover it.'

'You did not know him?'

'Not at first. He was disguised. He is a shapechanger, do you not know? He feeds upon living hearts and can assume the form, or a foul mixing of forms, man or beast, of any whose heart he had devoured. It causes him discomfort to do so, and he must reassume his own form after a limited period if he is to avoid permanent

assumption of that guise. But it is an effective means of concealment. Think: he could be you, he could be I. No one would know.'

The Revenant smiled to herself. The assembly exchanged
uneasy glances.

'How, then, did you discover him?'

'We suspected something, for his behaviour drew our attention.
We watched him – watched the person he had become. One night
he was observed re-forming himself. We laid a trap then, tricked
him into entering a dungeon deep in the rock beneath this place,
and there imprisoned him. We held him for many years. He
escaped a year ago. We had grown slack. Sko-ulatun's followers
were among us. We believe one sacrificed herself that he might
take her form and walk free.'

'A year ago,' said Enlos. 'That is when your people began to
reappear.'

'To give warning, though of course you refused still to listen.
And more recently, with the coming of the troops, we have striven
to impress upon you how vital it is that we, the followers of Claine,
be allowed to go free.'

'But Sko-ulatun did not find the Heart, did he?'

The Revenant frowned. 'You seem so sure.'

'I merely enquire.'

'Sko-ulatun discovered the Heart's resting-place, but he could
not touch it. He had to find another who would do it.'

'One of his followers?'

'No. He would place trust in no one, save perhaps a handful of
those who have been fully inducted into his way. Their induction
requires an infusion of the daemonic stuff that drives him, and that
in turn makes them vulnerable to ixigen. So his problem was to get
someone to this lonely locale, that they might disinter the Heart
for him and remove it from its cage. Equally he had to prevent our
intervention. The murders of the Tomian delegates sent to reason
with us was the means he used to achieve that.'

'And the murders at the border. . . .' mused Dinbig.

'Sko-ulatun. He made the border virtually impassable, in the
knowledge that some, at least, would have reason to avoid it and
thus travel overland.'

Dinbig looked across at Sildemund and Gully. 'At Dharsoul you
mentioned a man who gave you advice at an inn.'

Gully nodded, his face pale and lined. 'Aye, I see now that we were guided to that place.'

'Who was the man?'

'As I told you, I did not know him. The exchange was brief and he kept his face hidden. But the information he gave me ensured that we would pass by the place where the hidden cave lay. He emphasized also that that was a suitable spot to rest up overnight.'

'Gully, you have not spoken of this before!' hissed Sildemund.

Gully shrugged. 'It seemed of no importance.'

The Revenants were staring intently at the two. 'Are you saying that the Heart was found?'

'Aye,' said Gully. 'We found it.'

'And removed it?'

'Aye.'

For a moment they scrutinized him in stunned silence. 'And did Sko-ulatun gain it from you?'

'He did not,' said Sildemund. 'But he followed us, that is certain.'

'Did you take the Heart from its cage?'

'My father did, when we arrived home at Volm. He tried to do it in the cavern, but the metal was inflexible. Yet when he came to try it at home it almost fell away in his hands.'

'Ixigen possesses uncommon properties. It briefly undergoes transformation when subjected to varying levels of temperature. Bringing it from the cool of the cave would have had that effect. For a short time it would become malleable, then set again. It is unfortunate, nay, catastrophic, that your father discovered this. Where is the Heart now?'

Sildemund looked nervously at Prince Enlos. The Prince nodded. Sildemund felt sweat break out upon his brow. *He was here! He was about to relinquish the Heart of Shadows!*

He turned imploringly to Dinbig. The Khimmurian also gave a nod, and Sildemund knew that he had no choice. If he did not speak up, another would. He took a deep breath, clutching his satchel in both hands. 'It is here.'

The three Revenants sat forward as one, their eyes upon the satchel. 'Bring it forward!'

He did so, taking the bundle from the satchel and laying it upon the table before the three. Carefully he unbound it, and laid naked the purple-red stone.

233

The Revenants rose from their seats. They stared down at the stone which now – there was no mistaking it – pulsed. The shadows upon its surface rippled. *It was alive!*

The girl-child looked at the other two, her young features set in a questioning frown.

'Take them away!' the crone shouted. The guards strode forward, weapons drawn, to throw a cordon around the company.

There were loud protests, from Enlos, King Lalvi and the Supreme Haruspices.

The Revenant threw up her arms. 'You will be lodged in chambers. We must consider what is to be done. Go peacefully and you will suffer no harm. This is too important. You do not know what you have done. Go now, leave us!'

They were surrounded and outnumbered. To fight would have been hopeless. Sildemund glanced back at the vile stone lying upon the table. Again, he was sure, it pulsed, like a living thing. The Revenant guards pushed forward, bustling them unceremoniously towards the door. Reluctantly they allowed themselves to be marched from the chamber.

23

MEGLAN HAD RIDDEN until common sense, driving through
her hysteria, brought her to the realization that if she did not
cease she would exhaust the roan mare. Skalatin had not pursued
her, at least not immediately. He had no need, for he could find her
now at will. In a brazen display of contempt he had chosen to stay
behind and amuse himself upon the cart.

His behaviour was that of an immature man, she tried to tell
herself as she slowed to a halt – it somehow helped to fit him into a
human category. He could not bear to be bested by me, but nor, as
I suspected, would he harm me. So he committed his violence, not
upon me, but upon others, innocents, purely to assert his power
over me.

*But what is his power? What is it that both protects me from
him and yet makes me his victim?*

She stroked the hot shoulders of the panting horse and looked
back down the road. She realized she was trembling. Again her
mind was filled with the horror of what she had just witnessed. She
closed her eyes, shaking her head, crying to herself as she tried to
free herself of the vision. Memories of the dreadful events of the
previous days came crowding in upon her until she felt, again, that
she would be driven to insanity. But she willed herself to be calm,
recalling her mission, and focused her thoughts on the journey
ahead.

The roan's breathing had returned to normal. Meglan urged her
into a brisk trot. Sometime later they came upon a caravanserai
and Meglan stopped briefly to take water and let the mare drink
and rest. Questioning a serving-lad she learned that the royal party
had passed through earlier in the day.

Towards evening Meglan found herself approaching the intersection with the northern road which led to the Tomian border.

For several leagues the landscape had consisted of little more than wilderness, all signs of civilization diminishing the further she rode from Dharsoul. She had seen no one on the road for some hours, nor were there fields, farm animals or other signs of cultivation to give reassurance of a human presence. The loneliness of it oppressed her. She felt vulnerable, ever conscious of Skalatin padding unseen somewhere in her wake. Far from calming her, the knowledge that he would not do her harm – at least, not yet – began to make his presence almost more menacing. He followed her, with certainty, a dark and malevolent shadow, his intentions unknown.

Did he lack the ability to locate the Heart without her? Was that all it was? The questions went round and around in her head.

She came upon a chilling sight. At the side of the road in a low pass flanked by boulder-strewn elevations was the burned-out hulk of a wagon. Meglan recalled that bandits were operating in this area.

She felt a momentary disorientation. How had she learned of this? She cast her mind back and remembered meeting a merchant and his guard returning along the road closer to Volm. The merchant had told her of the brigand, Fagmar the Cursed, who was attacking traffic upon the way.

She had been with Jans then. Poor Jans. Her eyes stung as she remembered. They had clashed because she had wanted to proceed. Loyal Jans had physically prevented her from continuing, arguing that to do so would mean almost certain death. Now she lived, and Jans was dead.

She closed her eyes. Through her grief a vague unease tugged at her consciousness. There was something else, she was certain of it. A fog obscured her memory. After meeting that merchant, what had happened? They must have left the road, though she had no recollection of doing so. She simply recalled finding herself on the edge of a grove upon the Serpent's Path.

The Serpent's Path.

Meglan opened her eyes and stared at the little talisman that dangled at her wrist. From where had this come?

She was startled suddenly by the sound of a voice.

'*Halt!*'

A man had stepped from the boulders ahead. Meglan's hand

went to her sabre-hilt. Then she saw another, and realized that several more watched from the rocks above the road. They were soldiers; Dyarch. She gave a sigh of relief, then tensed again, for soldiers need not mean safety, particularly for a young woman alone.

'Where do you go?'

'North.'

The soldier beside the road eyed her over his dustguard and shook his head. 'It is unsafe.'

'I know – Fagmar the Cursed. But I cannot stop.'

'You are alone?'

She nodded.

'Come with me, please.'

She dismounted and, leading the roan, followed the soldier. Further up the road, close beside the intersection, was the Dyarch camp. Sentries eyed Meglan with interest as she passed between them. She looked straight ahead, ignoring coarse calls and whistles. The trooper led her to a large tent in the centre of the camp, outside which stood two guards. 'Wait a moment.'

He entered the tent, then re-emerged moments later, holding aside the flap. 'Please enter. I will take your horse.'

Having little option, Meglan entered. Within she was received by a Dyarch officer, the commander of the troop. He was a tall man, aged about thirty, with dark, receding hair and smooth olive skin uncommon for a soldier, even one of aristocratic breeding. He received her politely, offering her wine and fruit, which she declined.

'Where precisely is your destination?'

'Garsh, in Tomia.'

The commander raised an eyebrow. 'Garsh?'

'I follow the royal party which rode there earlier today. They did, did they not?'

He did not answer her directly. 'What is your purpose?'

'I seek someone who rides with the royal company.'

He surveyed her coolly. 'Who?'

'My brother.'

'Your brother? What is his name?'

'Sildemund Atturio of Volm.'

She could not discern from the man's expression whether the

name meant anything to him. He appraised her a moment longer, then said, 'You cannot advance beyond this point.'

'I have to. It is vital that I catch them.'

He shook his head. 'I am detailed to police this region, to rid Dyarchim of the brigand, Fagmar the Cursed. Until that is done the road is unsafe. I cannot allow you to advance.'

'Do you have the legal authority to prevent me?'

The commander smiled to himself. 'You are a young woman, travelling alone. I require no legal authority.'

Meglan fought down her resentment. The commander watched her carefully. 'Listen, evening is drawing down, you would be unable to continue before morning anyway. Rest overnight in the safety of our camp.'

'And tomorrow?'

'You may return to Dharsoul.'

'No. I cannot return.'

'You are a fugitive?'

She shook her head. 'It is imperative that I find my brother and the royal company. You must escort me to them.'

The officer laughed. 'Of course. I will abandon my duties here, disobeying my liege, leaving innocent wayfarers to the mercy of the brigand, and escort you wherever you wish. Should we depart now, or after dinner, do you think?'

Meglan felt her cheeks grow warm. She turned briskly to leave. 'Then I give you my thanks, but must decline your offer.'

The officer stepped swiftly across to put himself between her and the tent-flap. 'You have not understood, or perhaps you are deliberately obstinate. I cannot let you leave here tonight. But come . . .' He extended an arm to embrace her lightly. 'There is room enough in my tent for two. I shall have food and more wine brought. Let us while away the evening hours in pleasurable diversion.'

His arm had tightened a little, moving from her shoulder to her waist, and he steered Meglan towards the rear of the tent, where lay a light mattress with cushions and a blanket.

'Sir, I thank you, but it is my preference to sleep alone, beneath the stars.'

'Then by all means do so – later.'

The commander, without force, pushed her down onto the

mattress. He unbuckled his belt, then knelt, easing her back until they lay side by side.

'Sir, I do not want this.'

'Ah, but you will, you will.'

He was leaning over her, gently but firmly pinning her down. His lips sought hers. She turned her head away. His mouth travelled on, over her cheek, neck, shoulder.

Meglan protested. She strained against him, but he ignored her. One hand loosened her tunic, moved to her breast. He pressed himself upon her and she felt his hardness against her belly.

'No. Please. I do not want this.' She tried to push him off but was helpless against his ardour and his strength. Though he was not rough he overpowered her effortlessly, and her anger mounted that she should be obliged, by the mere fact of brute strength, to submit to his desires.

He was fumbling at her belt. She ran her hand down and drew forth the dagger that was still sheathed at her waist. Her other hand she pushed between the two of them and he, mistaking the gesture, rolled back, smiling.

'That is better. You see, I told you you would want it.'

Meglan unfastened his trousers and exposed his swollen manhood. The officer leaned back, cradling his head with his hands and lifting his hips for her. Meglan rose to kneeling and slipped the dagger between his thighs.

A small frown formed on his brow at the unexpected pressure of the cold steel. Meglan prodded hard.

'Make no move or you will lose your balls.'

His face registered shock, then a fire lit his eyes. She prodded again, and drew the blade across his sensitive flesh. 'Believe me, the blade is keen. I can take the joy from your life with a single stroke. Keep your hands as they are!'

His body was tense. She saw an unaccustomed nervousness enter his gaze.

'I could have you killed,' he said.

'But before your men reach me I will have deprived you of your most cherished possession. Can you contemplate a life without them?' She pressed the flat of her blade against the base of his rapidly detumescing organ.

'What is it you want?'

'Simply what I asked for: the right to continue my journey unmolested.'

His lip curled, but he nodded once. 'Go, then.'

'I am not so easily gulled. When I remove this blade you intend to grab me, or have me arrested.'

The officer said nothing, ever-conscious of the cold metal on his flesh.

'Let us talk a moment,' suggested Meglan. 'It is plain that you give little credence to the tale I have told you. But what if it is true? What if I have vital news to take to Prince Enlos, via my brother, and you actively prevent me? How would that look when the truth is told? How will that affect your career prospects? It is a long shot, of course, but can you really afford to take that chance?'

'There is sense in what you say,' replied the commander. 'But I acted in your best interests. The way ahead is dangerous.'

'My best interests, as I endeavoured to make clear to you, did not include lying with you.'

'I sought only to enliven an otherwise dreary evening with pleasures and diversions for us both.'

'And I made it plain that my choice lay elsewhere.'

'Then I offer you apology. You are a beautiful young woman, and I am a man. But please, take that weapon away. I will not hurt you now.'

Meglan shifted the weapon from his groin; she saw his muscles relax. She kept it before her, aimed at him. 'If you truly wish to serve my best interests, and those of your liege, you will provide me with an armed escort, at least as far as the border.'

'That I cannot do. I am ordered to patrol this area, and I have a limited force. I can spare no men.'

'Do you know the exact location of the brigand?'

'No. He is too wily to stay put in any one place.'

'Does not your area of patrol include the north road?'

'To some extent.' He sat slowly forward. 'May I cover myself?'

Meglan suppressed a smile. 'Aye. It looks silly like that.'

'You are an untypical young woman.'

'I know it. Now, what of it? Can you take me?'

'I must consider. Now, rest. You can stay here, in my tent, if you wish. You will not be touched.' He looked at her long and hard.

She shook her head, and stood. 'Outside is my preference.'

'Very well.' He had fastened his trousers and put his sabre-belt back on. 'I will have someone escort you to a suitable spot.' He grinned sheepishly and motioned with both hands towards his groin. 'And thank you for sparing this. It is precious to me.'

'I don't doubt it.' She sheathed her dagger, wondering whether now he would strike.

He didn't. A trooper entered and in the gathering dusk she was taken to a spot more or less of her own choosing, not far from the perimeter of the camp. She was brought food: a warped tin platter of steaming goats' meat stew ladled from a pot which hung over a campfire. She ate contemplatively, discovering hunger now, and drank a little of the waterered wine that was also brought.

The camp was setting down for the night. Off-duty soldiers gathered in groups to sit and eat their meal. It took no great intelligence to know that they spoke much of her. She saw their glances, even from a distance, but there were no more calls or whistles and, with the exception of the trooper who brought her food, none approached her.

She saw the commander emerge from his tent and stand, hand on hips, gazing across the encampment towards her. For a moment she thought he was going to come over, but after some time he turned instead, bending, and went back inside.

A bright new moon was up, scattering pale light upon the landscape as the sun vanished behind the heights. Meglan considered her position, thinking of escape. She did not believe the Dyarch commander would escort her along the northern road in the morning, nor that he would allow her to continue alone. In fact she wondered what tonight might bring, for she half-expected some kind of retaliation for what had happened in the tent. Though plainly not a brutal man, the commander had been wounded where it most stung, in his pride. Moreover, he must surely be considering what she had said about her mission, and wondering how best to deal with any possible complications.

Meglan had deliberately selected this spot to bed down. Not far off was the makeshift corral where the soldiers' horses were. She had spotted her own roan mare among them. Her thoughts had been upon releasing the mare and making off. She saw now how difficult it would be to reach the horses undetected. Guards patrolled the perimeter, and her horse was without saddle or harness.

She wondered briefly about stealing a saddle, taking it into the scrub then returning for a horse. She acknowledged that she was dreaming. She had no hope of success, and even with a mount it would be foolhardy to continue on alone at night.

Meglan spread her blanket and lay down, her head resting on her pack. The sky had turned to deepest indigo, peppered with stars. Some distance off a pair of sentries stood beside great boulders. She could barely make them out now. As the night encroached they had become vague blotches, fusing with the land. She heard brief male laughter from within the camp, and the cry of a desert owl. Before she knew it she was asleep.

24

SOMETHING WOKE HER, suddenly. She did not know what it was, but a sixth sense told her of danger. She lay perfectly still, peering into the night, her heart thumping hard in her breast.

All was silent. For long moments she lay, her eyes straining in the dark, fearful, striving to discover what was wrong, then wondering whether it was simply her imagination. She realized she could no longer see the two sentries. Had they left their station, or were they merely seated out of sight among the rocks? She was about to sit up, then a brief scuffling sound caught her ear.

It was ahead of her, between her and the place where the sentries had been. She peered into the night, and saw a movement. A blotch, close to the ground. A figure crept forward, crouching low, moving cautiously towards where she lay. Then she saw another, a little off to the side, scrambling forward on elbows and knees. Meglan caught a glimpse of moonlight on metal, and knew they had weapons drawn.

Swine! Son of a devil! She scarcely believed it, but it made sense, of course. The commander had made his choice. What better way of ensuring there was no trouble for him than to have her disappear, with no one the wiser? He knew she had come this way of her own volition, that her journey was unofficial. No one was aware she had come, with the possible exception of the professor at the university, Ractoban, and he would have no interest.

So now the two sentries crept towards her, intent on taking her life. For a brief moment she wondered cynically what bonus they had been promised for this task, then her thoughts were on self-preservation.

Silently Meglan drew her sabre and dagger. She rolled onto her belly, away from the blanket, keeping her eye on the two furtive figures. They seemed to be coming at her obliquely, which struck her as odd. There was hardly the need for such stealth. Whether or not they believed her asleep, they might have made a direct approach. She had no reason to protest, and a single sabre-blow would have taken her life before she had time to understand what was happening, or cry out.

She frowned. She could barely see the second man now. He had gone off to one side, as though to steal completely around her. The first was a matter of five or six paces away, crouching, peering ahead, but not at her.

She lay still, her mind racing. She was among low scrub, possibly out of sight to her assailants, yet they knew exactly where she lay. Why were they circling around her?

The first man moved again – three swift paces forward. Now he was almost past her. She could hear his breathing, and saw that he gripped a knife between his teeth and that in his fists he held a length of garotting wire.

And then she knew.

The men were not making for her. *They were not even aware that she was there!*

As if to confirm her feelings the horses in the corral stirred restively. Meglan glancing across that way, thought to glimpse a darting figure move up close beside the fence. The sentry at this end of the corral was not visible.

Away again to the other side. Another movement. Yes! Two more figures, sliding forwards on their bellies – and a third!

Meglan leapt suddenly to her feet, yelling at the top of her voice: '*Bandits! We are attacked! Bandits! Bandits!*'

She threw herself at the nearest man. He, taken by surprise, swung around at her outburst, but he was crouching and off-balance. Meglan slashed down with her sabre. The blade chewed deep into his neck. She lunged with her dagger and he fell back with a soft sigh.

She wheeled around to face the second. He was half-standing, seemingly confused. She saw the moonlight gleam in his eyes. She leapt away, shouting, knowing she could not confront these men.

And suddenly all was pandemonium. From all around the camp came whoops and cries. The night was filled with charging, moon-illumined shadows.

Aroused by her cries, Dyarch soldiers were beginning to stir from their beds. The sentries – those who had not already been murdered – raced to tackle the brigands rushing down upon them.

A tocsin sounded. Meglan ran on, making for the centre of the camp. A figure loomed suddenly before her and swung at her. She dodged the blow, saw that this was Dyarch soldier.

'Not me, you fool!' she cried. 'The brigands!'

She raced away into me dark and the soldier wheeled to tackle a whooping bandit at her back.

But the soldiers error brought home to her her full peril. In the dark she was as much at risk from the Dyarch troops, many half-sleep, as from the brigands at her back. The situation was too confused. She swerved away, suddenly not knowing which way to go. Somebody came at her with a blood-curdling shriek. She darted to the side, slashing with her sabre, not knowing or caring whether it was friend or foe. Her blade sank into something, then slid free. Her assailant gave a gargled moan. She rushed on.

The night now was a cacophony of battle. Meglan could no longer tell in which direction she was heading. She struck her foot against a rock and fell headlong. As she did so two or three figures rushed past, only feet away.

She climbed to her feet. Someone cried out nearby. She ran, away from the voice. As she did so she heard another sound, one she recognized and which filled her with a cold, crawling horror.

It was an inhuman sound, a frenzied growl, filled with lust, anger and a perversity of joy. Skalatin was among the soldiers, his hateful presence signalled by screams of pain and terror.

Meglan ran on, panting, filled with a new fear, her lungs burning. She dared not look behind her even though she knew that in the moon's spare light she would see virtually nothing.

She ducked into a clump of rocks, scrambled through. The din of battle had receded somewhat, but she ran on, impelled by her panic. Two men fought desperately close by. She smelled their sweat, their fear. She darted away.

Suddenly something huge formed out of the dark in front of her. She had no time to see what it was, or to avoid it. Before she could react the thing cannoned into her with the force of a battering ram. She was slammed to the side, spinning, and smashed sickeningly into the ground. The wind was knocked from her lungs. The world spiralled in a haze of roaring, shattering dark, and her senses left her.

There was a sound more deafening than thunder. Her body failed her. She gasped air into wheezing, tortured lungs, everything turning slowly, her ears ringing, knowing nothing but her terror and a vast, resounding pain ramming across her whole body. After what seemed an eternity she realized that she had sight. But she was paralyzed, feeling nothing but pain, the thunder drowning everything, but huge, blotted forms rushing by above her head. And she was choking, even as she struggled to breathe. She was drawing in a pall of dust. It clogged her throat and nose, stung her eyes and her skin.

Little by little the sensation returned to her limbs. The pain still clamoured above everything, but she felt the hardness of the ground against her spine, was able to move an arm, flex her fingers, draw up a leg. And she breathed, even through the choking dust.

Her first instinct was to move away from those rushing, thundering goliaths that crowded by so close. She knew what they were now; the horses, released from the corral by the brigands and stampeded out of the camp. It was a fleeing horse that had collided with her. Now she was in danger of being trampled to death by the many.

She propelled herself back on her elbows, still unable to stand, until she was protected among rocks. The thunder of the horses hooves diminished, partly because most of the creatures had now passed, but also through her having identified the sound and so reduced its impact upon her senses. In a moment's impulse she tried to climb to her feet, thinking to rush out and leap onto the back of one, ride free of the battle-ridden camp. But her legs would not support her, and her reason told her that even if they had, she could not have ridden bareback. So she lay where she was, tentatively flexing fingers and toes, testing joints, finding to her relief that she had suffered no broken bones.

She knew she could not remain there. Though most of the sounds of battle now came from her rear, she was not yet clear. She rose unsteadily and looked about her. The horses had gone. The dim moonlight showed a flat area before her, and beyond that, perhaps twenty-five paces off, the dark humps of boulders, offering cover. Meglan stepped out gingerly, and with pains shooting through her ribs and shoulder, made for the boulders.

Somewhere just off to her right men were locked in combat. Their grunts and laboured breathing, the clash of their blades, were loud in her ears. She caught a glint of moonlight on an uplifted blade. They were closer than she had thought, but were so intent upon their task that she slipped past unnoticed. She reached the rocks and clung to one, panting, almost fainting.

Rough land extended beyond. Meglan thought to find a sheltered spot some way further out, and there hide up till morning, which was not far off. Already the low eastern sky held faint rumours of dawn. She hoped that by sunrise the battle would be over, the brigands repulsed. She would see.

She limped around the rocks and headed for the black scar of a ravine. But as she stepped out a figure came suddenly from her side and made to grab at her. She stumbled back, swiping with her sabre. She was grabbed roughly from behind. A hand seized her sabre-arm and the first figure took her wrist and forcefully wrenched the sabre from her grip.

She was thrown to the floor, crying out with pain. The two bandits laughed. One leapt immediately upon her, pinning her to the ground. As she struggled he brought her arms up above her head, clasping both wrists with one strong hand. With the other he began to rip at her clothing.

She kicked wildly, but the second man grabbed her ankles.

'Cease!' snarled the one who held her down. She ignored him, struggling as forcefully as she could. He drew back a fist. 'Cease!'

Meglan managed to bring up a knee, catching him on the side of the head. But it was no more than a glancing blow. His lips curled and he raised the fist higher.

She closed her eyes, tensing for the blow. But there was a grunt, and suddenly the pressure on her wrist and ankles was gone. She opened her eyes, in time to see the first bandit being hauled bodily backwards into the air and thrust aside to land upon his rump in the dust.

Another man stood over her, this one massive, barrel-chested. He swung an arm in a wide arc, warding off the other two. 'Back, maggot-ridden cods! Who do you serve? All prizes go first to Fagmar!'

'We were bringing her to you, but she struggles like a wildcat!'

'Bah! Are you bested by a girl? Begone, toad-droppings. Leave us.'

The two brigands made off and the big man, Fagmar the Cursed, bent and, slipping a massive hand beneath Meglan's armpit, brought her to her feet. She stared up into one of the ugliest faces she had ever seen.

Fagmar the Cursed was a freak, a monstrosity. Even in the concealing dark the sight of his face made Meglan shrink. It was as though a powerful hand had taken the lower half of his face and dragged it upwards and to the left, so that the mouth appeared as a slanting, malformed gash high on the left cheek. The jaw was twisted askew, the chin bulging like a carbuncle at an angle beneath the cheek. The whole face was a mass of pimples, raspberry red, weeping, smothering everything, even the lips and eyelids. Tiny eyes were half-obscured between bloated, diseased lids; and the nose, its flesh cracked and fissured, bent to the side midway down, its bulbous tip almost merging onto the mouth. A shock of dark, matted hair fell unkempt below Fagmar's wide shoulders. He stank of stale sweat and urine.

He brought up a hand that could have effortlessly snapped her neck, and tipped her chin upwards, then to one side, then the other, his awful face peering close. 'A prize,' he murmured, his voice distorted by his disfigurement.

'Indeed, a prize.'

He pushed her down so that she fell upon her back again.

'Do not struggle or I will kill you,' said Fagmar as he knelt. 'Alive or dead, it makes little difference to me. I like them live, but the dead are as good while the meat is still warm.'

Meglan's hand found a rock. She brought it up hard to crash into the side of Fagmar's huge head, but he blocked it easily with one arm. He squeezed her fingers around the rock till the pain made her cry out, then took the rock and tossed it away.

'Alive or dead,' he said. 'No more warnings.'

Then another voice spoke. 'The malkin is mine, servant.'

Fagmar the Cursed wheeled his great bulk around. Meglan saw a shadowy figure standing to his rear. She could not make it out, but she did not need to. She knew the voice.

'Master!' Clambering from Meglan, Fagmar the Cursed knelt

upon the ground and abased himself. 'If she is yours, by all means. . . .She is untouched. I did not know.'

'No, you did not.' Skalatin came forward. 'Stand, pret-ty Meglan. Are you harmed?'

Meglan climbed slowly to her feet, the depression of a nightmare settling upon her, from one horror to another. What could be next? She shook her head. Skalatin turned to Fagmar who, having risen to his feet, was a giant beside him. 'It is well, then.'

Other figures were forming out of the half-light, bandits returning from the fray. Some were bloodied.

'How went the battle?' demanded Fagmar of one.

'The soldiers fought well, but we have significantly weakened them. We have lost as many as eight men, though.'

'Master, we should leave immediately,' said Fagmar. At his words the other bandits, recognizing Skalatin, stepped back with respectful, or fearful, bows and murmurs.

Skalatin nodded. 'There is a horse for the lovely chi-ild?'

'Of course.'

Skalatin took Meglan's arm. 'Come, Meg-lan.'

'What do you want with me, Skalatin?' demanded Meglan. Her voice shook; she felt her spirit fleeing her, and fought back bitter tears. 'Why not kill me now and have done?'

'Kill you? Beautiful Meg-lan, I do not want your death. Not yet. That would spoil everything. You must take me to my Heart, you see. And then, when that is done, you are to be honoured.'

'Honoured?'

Ah yes, pretty-pretty. Sko-ulatun has chosen you. You are to be the mother of my children.'

By the time the sun was up they had put leagues between them and the shattered Dyarch camp. From listening to talk among the brigands Meglan understood that the soldiers had been taken almost completely by surprise, not only by the attack itself, but at the amount of men Fagmar had been able to muster. Plainly in recent weeks Fagmar had recruited new followers, thieves, criminals, vagrants from the surrounding regions and beyond – the ne 'er-do-wells of Dyarchim, Tomia and other lands, drawn by his notoriety and the lure of good pickings. Even now, taking into

249

account the night's losses, his band numbered scarcely fewer than fifty. Many of them rode the mounts stolen from the Dyarch camp.

Meglan rode in a state of near-numbness. A cocoon, an emotional limbo, enveloped her, almost protectively, as if to keep her from reflecting upon her wretchedness. She was at the centre of Fagmar's gang of foul-mouthed, foul-smelling dregs, the core of their attention. She kept her gaze averted, not wanting to see how they eyed her, how they leered and winked and made lewd motions with lips and tongues. Fagmar, a misformed giant upon a great grey stallion, rode at the head. And in the wilderness to the side, glimpsed from time to time, Skalatin sped, looking her way, tongue lolling, garbed in the unnatural flesh of his grotesque creature-form.

Through her apathy came anger at the brutal irony of it: Skalatin her protector, keeping her from the lustful attentions of these pariahs!

But protecting her for what? She shut from her mind the image he had etched for her. To become the mother of his dreadful spawn . . . .

She could picture no escape, but she reminded herself that she lived, that Skalatin wished her to live, at least for now, and there, surely, must lie hope. And the journey she now had no choice but to make, in the midst of heartless monsters, was yet the journey, which, albeit coerced by circumstances, she had earlier set out upon of her own accord. To retrieve the Heart from her twin and give it to Skalatin – her goal had not changed.

Skalatin had asked her, in the pre-dawn dimness at the edge of the battlefield, where she was bound. Did he mock her? She half-suspected that he knew, that he toyed with her, but she answered him with half-truths anyway, praying that in keeping something back she might yet be preserving hope for Sildemund, for her father, herself and all others who had become involved in this terrible mystery. She endeavoured not to think of what the ultimate consequences of Skalatin's regaining the Heartstone might be, for she sensed more than ever that his possession of the stone would bring nothing of good.

'The Heart has been taken north,' she had said. 'That is where I am going.'

Skalatin had nodded. 'Where north?'

'I am not yet sure. Perhaps Tomia.'

Was there a swiftly suppressed glimmer of satisfaction in his cold eyes? He asked her nothing more. 'Let me take you safely there, then,' he said.

Now, as she rode, a sudden wild thought came to Meglan. She recalled how, two days earlier, while still on the Serpent's Path making for Dharsoul, she had crossed a road. It had run in a north-south course. It could only be this road.

Was this her salvation?

She kept her eye upon the serpent talisman at her wrist. It swayed, restlessly, pointing in no single direction. But when she crossed the Path it would swing, as it had before, to point along it. And she would become invisible to anyone not also on the Path!

Meglan began cautiously to slow her horse, intending to drop back in the brigand pack. But immediately she was jostled by those behind. One of Fagmar's lieutenants leaned over and slapped the roan hard on the rump, yelling harshly at Meglan, 'Keep up! Don't lag!'

It was ueseless. Downcast yet again, she watched the talisman. It continued to swing as before; she wondered whether they had already crossed the Serpent's Path without her being aware of it. They carried on for an age, and then suddenly she saw its motion arrested, saw it swing determinedly so that its silver-white head pointed to her right. For five of the roan's paces . . . six . . . seven . . . eight . . . then it resumed its erratic sway. She glanced nervously at the men around her, but none showed uneasiness in their gaze or paid her more attention than before. They had seen nothing.

Meglan swivelled upon the saddle and looked back, for now that she was beyond the Serpent's Path those still crossing it should briefly become invisible to her eyes. But none did. She pondered this in disappointment and perplexity. In frustration she ripped the talisman from her wrist and would have thrown it away, but something stopped her. She thought again. Would the Serpent's Path not carry its own protection? At this point, where it crossed a road used regularly by travellers, was it not reasonable to expect that its magical force was suppressed, thus preventing detection by any passing over it?

With this thought in mind she put the talisman in the pocket of her tunic.

The road was deserted all the way to the border. After a few hours of rest they arrived the next day within sight of the Dyarch checkpoint. Fagmar took his men off the road and conferred with Skalatin and a pair of his lieutenants.

The checkpoint consisted of no more than a handful of wooden buildings and a watchtower protected by a timber palisade. Fifteen bored soldiers formed its garrison, with a handful of administrative staff. With the exception of the Dyarch royal party, nothing had passed through for several days.

An attack was launched straightway. Meglan, guarded by three of Fagmar's thugs, watched from a distance as the Dyarch soldiers were quickly overwhelmed and the buildings put to the torch.

She was then brought up, sickened by the sight of bodies, for none had been spared. Fagmar sent a couple of men to reconnoitre the Tomian post, half a mile or so along the road. They returned an hour later to report that the post was manned by twenty or so troops. There were merchant wagons there, some with guards, held up by the usual restrictions. None were heading this way; any intending to enter Dyarchim were travelling further west to cross onto the safer Volm Road. The scouts perceived no great difficulty in overpowering this checkpoint too, with a little trickery, and it was obvious that the pickings there would be considerable.

Fagmar hid ten armed men in a covered wagon. Skalatin, expressing a desire for some sport, joined them, and the wagon was sent forward. Inside the compound the bandits, aided by Skalatin, came swiftly from hiding and secured the main building and gate with little problem. As they fought off the Tomian guards the remainder of Fagmar's force charged in on horseback.

The Tomians offered stiffer resistance than had the Dyarch, and were augmented to some degree by the guards of independent merchants. But those merchants who were able, seeing the way the battle must go, chose to flee, along with their escorts. They were not pursued. The border post quickly fell, and a number of wagons were taken by Fagmar. Survivors' throats were slit and the brigands made ready to move on.

Through the smoke of the burning buildings Skalatin loped up beside Meglan. He was eating something. Small gobbets of flesh depended from his jaw; the sallow meat of his face and gums was wet with blood. Meglan turned away, not wanting to see.

'Now, pret-ty, there are three roads. West towards the land of Ghence, northwards into central Tomia, and, a little way along, a smaller road which leads into the wild hills and eventually the mysterious town of Garsh. Which should we take?'

From the way he said it there was no doubting that he knew.

'Garsh,' she said in a small voice.

'Yes,' he replied.

The brigands sang as they rode, elated by their plunder. Somewhere ahead of them the lonely hilltown of Garsh lay under siege. Tomian and Dyarch troops waited outside its walls. The beleaguered Revenants of Claine had briefly opened its gate to the royalty of both nations, and the fated stone, the Heart of Shadows, had been taken within.

25

A LEAGUE OR SO from Garsh, Fagmar the Cursed took his cutthroat band off the trail and into the hills. They climbed and looped, following no discernible path, but utilising what sparse natural cover existed. It was obvious that Fagmar knew every last feature of this land.

An hour later, from a rocky, wind-scuffed hill, Meglan had her first sight of the town, picturesque beneath a wide, hazy blue sky, and of the troops marshalled before it. Her heart gave a thump. Somewhere there was Sildemund, and somewhere the fateful Heartstone that had brought them both so far, through so much, that had riven their lives, changing them from the innocents that they had been. Uppermost through the welter of her emotion came a sharp pang of regret. It was true: the girl she had been was left forever somewhere far behind. Whatever might happen now, she would never know that person again.

Skalatin crouched beside her, directing her gaze to the fluttering tents of the Tomian force, and those of the smaller Dyarch encampment further back. 'Where is my Heart, Meg-lan? There, or in the town?'

She shook her head. 'I don't know. Truly I don't.'

'Then we must discover.'

He took her hand — she cringed. His was hard, dry and scaly, almost fleshless, and cold, so cold. He walked with her into the lee of the slope to where the huge figure of Fagmar consulted with his henchmen. Seeing Skalatin, Fagmar bowed as low as his over-sized bulk would allow. 'Master.'

'We require a little assistance,' said Skalatin. 'It might be useful to question someone – a soldier perhaps. Will you arrange this for me?'

'Of course, Master. Do you prefer a Dyarch or a Tomian, or perhaps one of each?'

'For the present a Dyarch will suffice, I think.'

Fagmar barked gruff orders and four men set off a pace down the slope. Skalatin took Meglan along a rough track into a gulch, the walls of which were peppered with caves. They entered one. Inside a fire burned. One of Fagmar's men tended a pot in which some unidentified lumps of dark flesh floated in a greasy liquid. Steam rose from the simmering mess, permeating the cavern with an unpleasant smell. At the sight of Skalatin the bandit fell onto his hands and knees.

'Begone,' said Skalatin. The bandit hurriedly removed the pot from the flame and placed it on the ground nearby, then scuttled from the cave.

'Sit, Meg-lan,' said Skalatin. She did so and he took up a position opposite her and regarded her over the low flames. He said no word, but his gaze was unflinching and, beneath his cowl, a morbid remnant of a smile stayed fixed upon his face.

For long, long minutes the silence persisted. Meglan grew uncomfortable. Skalatin did not move so much as a hair. All she could hear was his breathing, mingling with unwelcome intimacy with the sound of her own. The pressure built until she felt she would scream. She realized he was playing with her, and eventually, to break the silence rather than for want of his conversation, she said, 'Who is your client, Skalatin?'

'My client?' His terrible smile broadened. 'Ah yes. Have you not guessed?'

'My guess is that you represent no other. You operate alone.'

'You are wrong.'

'Then who, or what, is it? For whom do you seek the Heartstone?'

'I thought you would understand, Meg-lan. It is for he whom I once was.'

Her brow puckered. 'What does that mean?'

Skalatin chuckled, a low, mocking, bestial sound. 'Aah yes. When I have my Heart I will be whole again. Then I shall be what I was before, when all men worshipped me.'

'Worshipped you?'

'I was alive then!' His eyes flashed. His torso slid forward an inch. 'I was powerful. I ruled. I was a god, the Father of humankind! But Claine was jealous; Claine was mad. She wanted it all. She wanted my children to bear her name, she wanted the worship, she wanted her name, her symbols, to stand over humanity. So she took my Heart and banished me, to suffering without surcease, wandering without end, death, death, death while I yet was alive.' He fell silent, twitching, sunk in bitter reverie, then said in a low, twisted voice, 'I have been a dead thing for so long. I have suffered, Meg-lan, oh how I have suffered. But now I can return. I shall have *Life* again!'

Meglan made little sense of this, but she probed further, hoping for some clue, some indication of how she might keep him from regaining his Heart. 'And what then?'

'Then?' He grinned foully, showing the rotten stumps of teeth and wormy, meatless gums. Leaning towards her he extended an arm, reaching through the flames to caress her cheek with the backs of his fingers. Meglan drew back at his touch, and her eyes widened with shock, for he was indifferent to the fire. 'With Life I shall create Life, love-ly Meg-lan. You shall be my bride. Together we shall begin again the process that was begun, and then curtailed, long ago. From us will be born the forefathers of a new race of men. They will dominate, they will be of me. Sko-ulatun shall be worshipped again! I shall be the Father, a god once more. I shall possess both Life and Death! And you, Meg-lan, are not Claine. You have no power to defy me.'

He withdrew his hand.

Meglan struggled to find her voice. 'Why did you choose me?'

'Why?' Skalatin seemed almost surprised. 'Why? Because you offered yourself, sweet.'

'*No!*' Her anger flared with such ferocity that she almost rose to strike him, though it would have had no effect.

'Chi-ild, you were there. Upon the stairs, remember? You were waiting. Untouched. You had spurned all others. Life held nothing. You looked for something beyond.'

She shook her head, numbed.

'You looked for Death,' said Skalatin. 'And I came. I found you. I saw. I knew.'

'You knew *nothing*!' she spat. 'You just thought, and took. In your heart you are no different.'

Skalatin chuckled again. 'I have no heart.'

'You have no perception.'

256

'You gave me your essence, so that I might never lose you.'

'No! I gave nothing to you!'

'Mmmn.' He stroked his clawed fingers together fastidiously, observing her over the flames. 'I shall take everything from you now. We shall love, when I am whole. My bride. My unblemished bride. Our children shall inherit all.'

She turned away. She sensed Skalatin's hateful smile, knew that he watched her as before, that were she to look she would see the gloating, the perverse jubilation in his eyes. But she kept her face averted, for she sensed that he somehow fed upon her hatred of him.

The silence resumed. He was stronger than her, he controlled it. Again it came to dominate, enclosed her like brittle glass. She felt she would scream. She fought down the need to shatter it, to speak again, then thought. *No! By questioning him I gain, not lose, for I learn.* And she was about to question him further, to ask who Claine was, when a dark shape suddenly blocked the light at the entrance to the cave.

The gargantuan bulk of Fagmar the Cursed lodged there, silhouetted against the brightness outside. 'Master.'

Skalatin stood. 'Come, Meg-lan.'

She followed him out, squinnying her eyes as she entered the daylight. Before them a pair of Fagmar's brigands gripped a young Dyarch cavalryman by the arms. The Dyarch had been stripped of weapons, boots and armour. His clothing was wet and he was bloodied and beaten. His face was grey and contorted with pain. Wide, haunted eyes travelled from the looming figure of Fagmar to Skalatin beside him, smaller but equally shocking, equally menacing. Then the man's eyes fell upon Meglan. He showed a glimmer of surprise, of confusion, and Meglan felt a surge of terrible guilt, for she saw that he looked to her with hope, for mercy.

'This one we picked up by the stream,' said Fagmar. 'Washing his smalls, I'm told.'

'Ah, good.' Skalatin stepped forward to place himself directly before the soldier. 'I hope you will help me.' He turned to Meglan. 'Come here, Meg-lan.'

Meglan stepped reluctantly forward, her legs spongey, a taut sickness in her stomach. She did not want to look at the cavalryman, to see his fear.

'Are you of the Dyarch company that rode here from Dharsoul?' asked Skalatin. The man gave a single nod.

'Who is in that company?'

'The soldier hesitated.

'It will be best for you to tell us,' Skalatin said in a voice that left no doubt of his meaning.

Meglan raised her eyes to the soldier's. 'Tell him, please, for believe me, he can make you. We know already that Prince Enlos is there, and Master Kemorlin. Also three men from Volm. Are there others?'

The soldier shook his head. 'Only officials and troops.'

'They are in your camp now?'

'No. They are in Garsh.'

'Do they carry something? An object, about this size?' Skalatin held out his hands. 'It would be covered, or carried in a casket of some kind.'

'I do not know.'

Skalatin turned to Meglan. 'Who carries it?'

'My twin brother brought it to Dharsoul. I have no knowledge of who its bearer is now.'

'Your brother? Ah, Meg-lan, your father should not have been so greedy. This could all have been avoided.' He turned back to the cavalryman and questioned him further for details of his name, rank, company, the names of his commanders and the commanders of the Tomian force. The soldier was hesitant, but something he saw in Skalatin's face persuaded him to speak.

When he had what he wanted Skalatin spun upon his heel.

'Kill him,' he said to Fagmar. 'And bring me the heart.'

No!' Meglan shrieked. 'Please, spare him!'

She threw herself at Skalatin, clawing at his burnous, but he thrust her off with a growl so that she fell to the ground. The cavalryman's desperate eyes were upon her. 'Don't go,' he pleaded. 'If I am to die, let the sight of you be the last sweet vision that my eyes behold.'

Meglan stood. 'You are brave,' she said. Fagmar's sabre plunged into the man's gut.

Skalatin took Meglan's arm and half-dragged her back to the cave where he thrust her down beside the fire. Moments later the heart was brought on a tin plate. Meglan crawled away to the rock wall. She pressed her head to the cold stone, sobbing as Skalatin noisily took his nourishment. Then she heard a voice.

'Meglan.'

She looked up slowly, stared as a chill spread across her skin, then buried her face in her hands. 'No! Oh no, no, no!'

The young cavalryman rose and stepped around the fire, took her by the arm. 'Come, Meglan. It is time to leave.'

Outside Fagmar handed over the Dyarch's equipment. The cavalryman/Skalatin dressed himself then Fagmar and three of his men led them down towards the place where they had captured the Dyarch. They took one horse, the roan mare, for Meglan. When they were close Skalatin spoke for some moments quietly with Fagmar while the three men kept watch over Meglan. Then the bandits left them, melting back onto the hills, and Skalatin ordered Meglan to mount.

He took hold of her rein. 'We are going into the camp. I have just found you here. You have come from Dharsoul with a vital message for your brother. You must enter Garsh. Say nothing to endanger yourself – or him.'

Meglan stared at him, at that face, the poor, murdered soldier for whom, for a moment, in the brief instant before his life was stolen, she had felt emotions greater than she could comprehend. 'It will not work.'

'We shall see.'

He led her to the track and on at a confident pace towards the sentry post at the perimeter of the Dyarch camp. Recognizing him, the sentries hailed him as he passed. 'Ho; what have we here? What's this you've brought us? A relief from our boredom? But only the one? She will be tired if she is to service the whole camp!'

They laughed lewdly. Skalatin raised a hand in casual greeting, but did not pause in his step. 'A messenger,' he said. 'She must speak with the commander.'

He strode on with purpose towards the central tent occupied by the force's commander, Prince Enlos's deputy, a Dyarch knight named Sir Cantharo. Meglan kept her head down angrily, ignoring the familiar chorus of catcalls and whistles. Arriving before the tent Skalatin ordered her off her horse. He spoke quickly to the guards stationed outside.

'I must see Sir Cantharo. It is urgent.'

Grasping Meglan by the wrist he stepped between the guards before they could react, and entered the tent.

Sir Cantharo was within, seated at field table, consulting with his adjutant. He looked up with indignation, then – his eyes alighting on Meglan – surprise, as the two entered. Before he could speak Skalatin said quickly, 'Sir, I apologize, but I bring the most urgent news. A message for the Prince.'

Sir Cantharo rose, 'What message? Who is this?'

'I discovered her at the edge of the camp.' Skalatin cast a meaningful glance towards the adjutant, and the guard who had come in behind him. 'With respect, sir, she refuses to speak to any but yourself, or Prince Enlos, in absolute privacy. I think you should hear what she has to say.'

Sir Cantharo frowned. 'Who are you?' he demanded of Meglan.

Meglan hesitated, torn, bewildered. What was she to do? She glanced at Skalatin beside her, confused further, for he so perfectly resembled the man he had murdered minutes earlier. Dared she defy him? She would probably die upon the instant. And he would not be stopped. Upon the Serpent's Path her blade had bitten deep into his foul flesh, yet left no mark. He could not be killed, for by his own admission he was already an unliving thing. A dead creature who sought life while somehow clinging to a semblance, a shallow, obscene mockery of it.

In a voice devoid of emotion she said, simply, 'I am Meglan, sister of Master Sildemund Atturio of Volm.'

Sir Cantharo's brows lifted. 'And what is this message you bring?'

'Sir,' interrupted Skalatin, again glancing towards the adjutant and guard. 'I cannot emphasize, these words should not reach the ears of any other.'

Sir Cantharo nodded and dismissed the two soldiers with a gesture. They departed; he turned back to Skalatin. 'And what of y—'

He got no further. Skalatin had already moved. Meglan turned her face away.

Count Draith, commander of the besieging Tomian force, seated upon a folding stool, looking out with concern at the lonely hilltop town, was mildly surprised to have his attention drawn by one of his officers to a group of four people on horseback making their way towards him under Tomian escort. He recognized the first of the four immediately. It was Sir Cantharo, the Dyarch commander. Two of the others were the Queen's cavalrymen. The fourth was a woman, a young woman, rather beautiful, the Count observed as the group drew closer and halted.

Sir Cantharo dismounted and strode to meet him. The two men saluted.

'Might I ask the reason for this unheralded call?' said Count Draith a little warily, his gaze drifting to the young woman on the horse. Sir Cantharo, he vaguely noted, appeared lean and strained.

'There is a new development,' said Sir Cantharo. 'Something so critical that I could not delegate it to another. I must deliver this woman to Prince Enlos immediately.'

'Enlos? I have no way of knowing when he will return from Garsh.'

'Quite so. I must take her into the town.' He took Count Draith's arm and steered him conspiratorally away from his officers. 'Let me explain what I am able. . . .'

Minutes later Meglan found herself ascending the twisting road to Garsh, flanked by a pair of Tomian knights. Before her rode Count Draith and, at his side, Skalatin, still garbed in Sir Cantharo's form.

She racked her mind, seeking to find a way out of this. For they were drawing closer, ever closer, to the Heart of Shadows, which would give perverse life to Skalatin, and be the death of any who tried to stand in his way. But what could she do? Turn to her guards and say: "This is not Sir Cantharo who rides before you, but a monster in his flesh"? She would be deemed mad, and Skalatin would doubtless prevent her speaking again. She had to find a way, but that was not it.

She looked upwards. The high walls of Garsh flowed above her, following the contours of the hill. They were stark against the limpid blue sky. A few strands of cloud were breaking up, passing into who knew where? Upon the slopes Tomian soldiers watched. She felt herself surrounded by enemies.

In short order they arrived upon a grassy plateau across which the road led straight to the main gate of Garsh. To this they rode, observed by the Revenant defenders upon the wall. In a loud voice Sir Cantharo hailed the guards in the gate-tower.

A helmeted head appeared in a crenellation overhead. 'What do you want?'

'Permission to enter. I am Sir Cantharo, appointed deputy to Prince Enlos of Dyarchim. This is Meglan of Volm. She carries a vital message. I am to escort her to Prince Enlos and his company. The information she holds is critical to your situation here.'

'Wait.'

The head vanished. A short while later a small hatch opened behind a metal grille set into the main gate. Another face peered through, this one belonging to a woman, florid cheeked, with long greying hair. 'Explain the nature of this information.'

'That I cannot do, except before my liege and your Elders.'

'How many wish to enter?'

'We two.'

You will be stripped of all arms.'

Sir Cantharo nodded his assent. He climbed from his steed, signalling to Meglan to do likewise. He removed his sword and helmet and gave them into Count Draith's care. 'Perhaps you would be good enough to look after these.'

The town gate groaned upon its hinges as though it ached, opening far enough to permit the two of them to step through. They entered the paved ward within and were immediately surrounded by Revenant guards. Upon an order from their leader, a woman, they stripped Sir Cantharo of his armour. Then in silence they were marched away.

They passed along the same sloping street that Sildemund and the royal company had trodden earlier, across the square and on into the cloistered court. They descended the stone steps and approached the timbered portal set in the high wall of the building on the far side.

It was then that Meglan knew that she had to expose Skalatin, and suddenly saw the means by which she could do it. It seemed so obvious now, yet only minutes earlier she had dismissed it. She *had* to attack him. The very thing that had dissuaded her earlier – the fact that he could not be killed – was what would alert the guards to his deceit. Dealt an obviously mortal blow, he would be revealed, and would be forced to respond.

The dangers were immense. She did not know if the guards could subdue him. From what she had seen she doubted they could. But Skalatin was as close to the Heart now as she dared bring him. Sildemund was somewhere here. She had to find him, make certain that he no longer carried the Heart, for she had no doubt now – if she ever had – what Sildemund's fate would be were Skalatin to find him with his Heart.

All this came to her in a flash as they crossed the sunlit court. Skalatin, as Sir Cantharo, marched before her. Her eyes bored into the back of his neck, detesting him to the depths of her soul. He wore only a light tunic and hose. He was vulnerable, if she could just lay her hands upon a weapon.

There were six guards in her escort, three on either side, plus their leader. They marched with hands on sabre-hilts. Somehow she had to wrest one away.

But it would be suicidal. With a blade in her hands she would have only an instant to strike. The guards would be upon her immediately.

Her palms were sweating, her throat dry. They arrived at the portal. The leader of their troop hammered upon the wood and the portal opened. They filed through, first the leader and two of the guards, then Skalatin, then two more guards. Now it was Meglan's turn to enter. She followed close upon the guard in front, noting that they were stepping down into a shadowed passageway. She saw her chance. As she stepped through she pretended to lose her footing on the step, and fell forward. Deliberately using her full weight she collided with the guard who had preceded her.

He pitched forward, tumbling into another standing below. As he went down, Meglan, virtually upon his back, slipped her hand around the hilt, not of his sabre, but of the smaller dagger which hung beside it. She drew it free.

With a yell she sprang up, lofting the dagger. Skalatin/Sir Cantharo was just in front of her, turning to investigate the commotion. With all her strength she plunged the dagger full into his face, screaming at the top of her lungs: 'Monster!'

She felt the blade-tip crunch through hard, brittle bone, then sink smoothly into the softer stuff within the skull. Skalatin staggered back with a roar, clutching at his face. Meglan had time to see the blood start from his wound, and for an instant she believed she had failed utterly. She had not anticipated blood. Somehow she had thought that the wound would just open the dead flesh, reaveal the imposture.

But blood or not, he would be exposed, for it was a wound which no man would survive.

There was no time for further thought. Instinctively she dropped to the floor and rolled. Her flesh prickled, for she was expecting to be hacked to pieces by sabres. But she came up somehow behind a guard. She pointed, yelling: 'He is not Sir Cantharo! He is a demon called Skalatin! Look, he does not die!'

To her surprise the Revenant guards responded as one. A female voice shouted, 'Sko-ulatun!' – and the guards, sabres drawn, turned upon the figure of Sir Cantharo.

He had wrenched the blade from his face and stood now clenching it, glaring at his enemies, his back against the wall. His bloody features were set in a grimace of fury, his eyes glittering unnaturally, held in the light that stabbed through the open portal. For a moment he seemed of two minds, then a strange smile began to form upon his lips, even as the blood continued to pour down his cheek. He straightened, his body appeared to grow. Indeed, he was changing. His flesh shivered and writhed, gobbets dropping away or re-forming as something else pushed through.

'I am back,' he said in a voice harsh and resonant, recognizably that of Skalatin.

Before he could complete his transformation the guards were upon him. Meglan did not wait to see the outcome. She turned and ran blindly into the half-dark of the passage.

What now? She had alerted the Revenants to Skalatin's presence, but she had to find Sildemund and the Heart, separate them – if they remained together – at all costs. But where should she go? Sildemund might be anywhere in Garsh, but she acted on the hunch, the hope, that he was still with the royal party. It was to Prince Enlos that she and Skalatin were being taken. He could not be far away, surely? Might he be somewhere in this same, massive building?

Numerous doorways and sub-passages led off the passage along which she ran, sparsely illumined by torches set in wall-brackets at wide intervals. Randomly she ducked into one. The howls and cries of combat receded behind her. She hurried on, disoriented, with no idea of where she might be headed. A short flight of steps took her upwards, then left her with a choice of two directions. She went right. Suddenly she heard footsteps, several persons hurrying towards her.

She threw herself into the shadowed recess of a doorway. Moments later a group of Revenant defenders rushed by, presumably to join the fray she had left behind.

When they had passed Meglan came out from her hiding place and moved on, cautious now. She listened at the next door she came to, heard nothing, tried the handle, but the door failed to give. She did the same at the next door, and the next, with similar result. Then, entering another passage, she came to a door that was not locked. She eased it open, then warily peered through the gap.

She was looking into a short corridor. Pale, misty light filtered in through a narrow window, showing another door in the far wall and, in the centre, a flight of wooden stairs descending to the next level. She moved tentatively to the head of the stairs and peered down. As far as she could see there was no one below. She eased past and approached the door, reached forward to turn the iron hoop that was its handle. Before she reached it the ring turned and the door opened.

A young woman stood there, clothed in a short red tunic, hose and studded leather overshirt. Before Meglan could respond she had whipped free the sabre that hung at her waist and advanced threateningly.

'Who are you?' Behind her came others. One . . . two . . . Meglan thought there might be a third.

'My name is Meglan—' she began, but got no further for without warning the woman darted forward, raising her sabre, and brought the hilt down hard in the middle of Meglan's forehead.

Her senses rang with angry, flashing pain. Blind, she was aware that she was reeling backwards, crying out. A massive jolt seemed to spin the world around. She sensed dimly that she had been struck again, that she was falling, then she knew nothing more.

26

SOMETHING WAS WRONG. Terribly wrong.
Sildemund knew it, without knowing how, he could not sit
still. It nagged constantly from the depths of his thoughts, just
beyond conscious reach.

Something was concealed, something had gone out of kilter. He
knew it as surely as he knew that he still lived and breathed.

But for how long might he expect to live and breathe, now that
he had relinquished the Heart of Shadows?

The Dyarch/Tomian party was held in enclosed chambers somewhere within the same complex in which they had been received
by the Revenant Elders. Guards were stationed outside their main
door, and it was plain that, though nominally they were accorded
the status of honoured guests, they had become little more than
prisoners, or perhaps hostages.

Furnishing was no more than adequate, and the chambers were
below ground, lacking windows or grilles through which natural
light, and hence a sense of the time of day, might be perceived.

Straightaway the Dyarch had allocated one of the rooms to
Queen Lermeone, for her exclusive use. She was in there now,
alone and out of sight of the others. Sildemund, Gully and Picadus
had been placed in another, with King Lalvi, Prince Enlos,
Kemorlin and the Supreme Haruspices, plus their guards, occupying the last.

Hours had passed; it was impossible to be sure how long. Food
and water had been brought to them. Gully had cleaned his plate,
but Sildemund's lay untouched upon the floor, for he was too
agitated to eat. Likewise, Picadus had not looked at his.

Sildemund paced the chamber, assailed by the twin certainties:
that there was something vital, dark, mysterious that neither he

nor anyone else had yet perceived: and that his life and those of his two companions were now directly imperilled.

Would the Haruspices risk killing them here, in Garsh, even within this chamber? Or would protocol oblige them to wait? The royal party would not wish to offend the Revenants of Claine. But would the Revenants care one way or the other about his death?

The door opened: Sildemund flinched, and shifted into a defensive stance, for he had agreed again with Gully that if death was coming for them they would fight it to the last. But it was the *Zan-Chassin* sorcerer, Dinbig of Khimmur, who entered.

Is this man our assassin? wondered Sildemund with a jolt.

Dinbig smiled and crossed the room to sit upon the bench from which Gully had just risen. He indicated that the two should join him. Picadus lay curled asleep in one corner.

'Do they plot our deaths?' enquired Sildemund, sitting.

The Khimmurian shook his head. 'They are more concerned just now with the uncertainty of their own predicament. But be sure, a decision will have been made. At an appropriate moment they will strike.'

'In here?'

'Possible, but unlikely, I think. At least for the present.'

'Why so?'

'You may still have a part to play. Until they are assured otherwise they are unlikely to risk losing you.'

'Do you mean I may be expected to carry the Heart again?'

Dinbig shrugged. 'The Revenants' response to the Heart is curious. We are left knowing nothing.'

Sildemund pushed back his nervousness, his fear. He trusted no one, other than Gully, but he sensed openness and genuine puzzlement in the young Khimmurian sorcerer. He could not believe that this man was the instrument of their deaths.

'Did you see the Heart when I laid it before the Elders, Dinbig? It was alive.'

'I saw it.'

'What does it mean?'

'I don't know.' The Khimmurian sat pensively for some moments, then said, 'Tell me once more: when you disinterred the Heart, there was a mark, an emblem of some kind engraved upon the ixigen cage, was there not?'

Gully nodded. 'It was not clear. It had been worn away by ages.'

'I can verify that,' added Sildemund. 'I looked at it in my father's workroom. It appeared like nothing more than a sinuous line, with perhaps another shape behind, but it was impossible to identify. Why? Is it important?'

The Khimmurian slapped his hands upon his knees and pushed himself to his feet. 'I do not know. I am curious, that is all. But if we enter again that chamber where we spoke earlier with the Elders, and if an opportunity arises, try to get a good look at the surface of the table at which they sit.'

He said no more, but bade them a temporary farewell and departed the chamber. Sildemund and Gully sat in silence for a while. Presently Gully said, 'Are you going to eat that?'

Sildemund gazed at the plate of untouched food to which he referred. The meal was basic – mashed grain with some dried vegetables, gone cold now. There was no meat, but the plate was sufficiently full to disabuse them of any notion that the un-habitants of Garsh suffered a serious shortage of food, the Tomian siege notwithstanding.

Sildemund gave a sigh, wondering that his friend could think of his belly in such circumstances. But he shook his head. 'No. Take it if you wish.'

Gully leaned forward and picked the plate from the floor. He took up the spoon that lay at its rim and prepared to eat. Sildemund suddenly placed a hand upon his thick wrist, preventing him from achieving his aim.

Sildemund stared at the food. *There was no meat!*

The thought struck him with a powerful resonance, yet he could not say why. He frowned. Unable to take his eyes away.

'Sil?' Gully eyed him uncertainly. 'Sil? Is something wrong?'

Sildemund turned his eyes to him as if in a daze. In his mind something strove to burst through. He could not grasp it. He shook his head, releasing Gully's wrist. 'No. I'm sorry. Eat.'

He got up and with worried thought resumed his pacing.

A short time later the door opened again. This time a Revenant guard stood there, a female. She beckoned them out. Gully roused Picadus, who came out of sleep swearing and cursing. They filed into the next room to find the others assembled. In the company of their guards they were escorted back to the candle-filled reception chamber.

The three Elders – a term which again struck Sildemund as odd and incongrous – awaited them as before, their fighters ranged before them. The Heart of Shadows rested upon the table where Sildemund had placed it. It had been rebound in its cloth bandages so that its state could no longer be discerned.

The Revenant crone who had spoken earlier addressed them again. 'Honoured guests, we would wish to conclude this matter as swiftly as possible, so that you might return to your rightful places in the palaces of Dharsoul and Pher. Do we have your assurance that we will suffer no further persecution, and that your troops will be withdrawn immediately?'

There were brief murmurs among the assembled, then King Lalvi, thrusting forward his chest, declared, 'You are still in contravention of the terms of your confinement!'

'There should be no confinement!' retorted the Revenant with anger. 'Have we not convinced you of our innocence?'

'You cannot walk free among the people,' Lalvi began. 'Your influence is—'

Prince Enlos interrupted, darting a frown of annoyance at the Tomian King, and turning to the three Elders. 'We have discussed this matter in recent hours. There are one or two points we seek clarification on, but that done there should be no reasons why the siege cannot be ended immediately. We will then initiate discussion in regard to your future and rights, if such is agreeable to you.'

'What are the points you refer to, Prince Enlos?'

'In the first instance, there is the Heart of Shadows. When it came to Dharsoul we quickly understood that we had to bring it to you, who know its full secrets. We came in haste, and as a demonstration of our sincerity and the urgency with which we beheld the situation, placed ourselves at your mercy by entering Garsh virtually unprotected.'

The Revenant gave an arch smile. 'Unprotected but for an army parked at our walls! You suggest we might have killed you here, and it is so, but it would have been in the knowledge that our own deaths would swiftly follow.'

'Ah, but death holds no fear for you,' responded Enlos equally sardonically, 'unlike ourselves, for whom it is unconquerable, summarily cancelling all plans. For you it presents no obstacle.'

The Revenant considered this for a moment. 'It is an inconvenience, nonetheless.'

Enlos grinned. 'Ah, that I might say of Death: "Sir, you are but an inconvenience, an unwanted, but temporary, digression! Away with you, then, for I have had enough of you!" Instead I know and respect Death for what he is. I know he waits somewhere for me, and I endeavour to keep my distance while accepting that he will be drawing closer with each passing day.'

'If you would prefer to meet him on more equitable terms, might I recommend that you join us here, Prince Enlos? Become one of our number; you will discover a new understanding.'

'Is it so simple to cheat Death? I think not.'

'The Revenants of Claine do not cheat Death. Rather, we become acquainted with him, walk at his side, become familiar with his ways. We see that Life is but the obverse of Death: one cannot be without the other. It is the two together that comprise the whole, the phenomenon. Life and Death are one, alternating through an endless cycle, just as you and I sleep, then wake, then sleep once more.'

'Ah, but that cycle is not endless. Death waits somewhere to mark its end.'

'Death waits, but as I say, he need not be what he appears. The Revenants have learned to merge consciously with the whole.'

'Perhaps so, but I say again, it cannot be so simple.'

'Simple, no. One might take a lifetime, or several lifetimes, to acquire the art. But development begins from the moment you declare yourself one of us. Once among us, you will never be lost. The Daughters of Claine protect her children.

'I will give it thought,' mused the Prince. He swivelled to survey his company briefly, and his eyes came to rest upon his mother, Queen Lermeone. Sildemund, watching, saw the Queen make a brief nod.

'Let me return to the matter at hand,' said Enlos, again facing the three Elders. 'We have brought to you the Heart of Shadows, an artifact, plainly, of immense power. What will be done with it?'

'We will ensure that it is kept from he who has sought it throughout time: Sko-ulatun.'

'How will you achieve this?'

'We have the ability, but it is not something we can discuss.'

Dinbig of Khimmur stepped forward, saying, 'In the past, by your own confession, Sko-ulatun has infiltrated your ranks, has lived as one of you without your knowledge. He could do so again, could he not?'

The three Revenant Elders returned him gelid stares. 'We will be ready for him this time.'

Sildemund, listening and observing, frowned deeply. Something . . . something . . . nagging.

There was no meat!

'I am curious,' Dinbig continued. 'Are the consequences of Sko-ulatun's regaining the Heart so much more grave than his being deprived of it? In deprivation, it seems, he is a frenzied murderer, a demon. What will he be when reunited with that which he seeks?'

'Something far worse, believe us! Sko-ulatun seeks Life, for he exists as Death, feeding upon the life of others. Made whole again he will become almost as a man, but with the power of a god. Then he will take his full revenge for the injustices he perceives as having been committed against him. He will do as he did before, turn man against man, woman against woman, child against parent, woman against man. There will be no end to his corruption.'

The blood pulsed in Sildemund's head. He almost had it! Something! Something!

He feeds upon the life of others. . . !

'There is another matter to be resolved,' said Enlos. 'One reason for Dyarchim's close interest in your affairs, as you must be aware, is concern over the welfare of two of your members. They were brought to you at separate times, with emphasis placed on our concern for their wellbeing. We would see them now, if you will.'

The Revenant stared at him with a puzzled expression. 'To whom do you refer?'

'Surely you are aware?'

A new tension had charged the atmosphere of the chamber now, Sildemund looked at the faces of the Dyarch company. On each was etched an expression of deep concern. Master Kemorlin pressed his long beard to his chest, his eyes upon Enlos, then the Elders, with frowning intensity. The three Revenant Elders appeared nonplussed.

'We are not aware, Prince Enlos. Perhaps you would enlighten us.'

'This is most disturbing,' replied the Prince, plainly taken aback. 'When these two were brought here it was on the strictest understanding that Dyarchim held a particular interest in their welfare.'

'Are we to understand from your words that they were brought to us clandestinely?'

'That is so. But documents were exchanged between our officials and yourselves.' Enlos gestured to one of the two Haruspices, who came forward taking from his rope a pair of scrolls. These he unfurled and placed before the Elders. The Elder who had spoken took up the scrolls and studied them. Then a faint smile relieved the grimness of her ancient face and she passed them on to her two younger colleagues. 'Forgive me, Prince Enlos. In such testing circumstances we cannot remember everything. The fact is, I am not one of the Elders with whom your officials would have dealt. She has passed from us. She will be a child among us now, or is perhaps still lingering between rebirths.'

'What of the two wards of whom I speak?'

The Elder regarded the scrolls again. 'A maiden named Epta, brought seven years ago at the age of nineteen; and a babe, with the given name of Lucel, who came to us some twelve or thirteen years ago. I will have the counterparts to these documents delivered, and these two persons shall be brought to you.'

Epta? Sildemund's ears pricked at that name. Epta was the young woman Dinbig had spoken of, Kemorlin's daughter, the lover of both Prince Enlos and Dinbig himself. Then it was here, to Garsh, that she had been exiled. But who was the other, the babe?

The Elder nodded to an armed assistant stationed at the side of the chamber, who turned and departed via a portal set behind the table at which the three sat.

'What is going on here?' whispered Sildemund to Dinbig, who stood now beside him.

'The past is stepping into the present,' the Khimmurian replied cryptically. 'Perhaps we might witness the future being formed.'

There was a period now of growing tension and unease during which no one spoke. All waited. Sildemund craned his neck, standing upon tip-toes in an effort to pursue Dinbig's earlier suggestion, to see what design had been limned or etched upon the top of the table at which the Elders sat. But he could make out nothing. The illumination thrown by the candles did not cast sufficient light, and though in the walls there were numerous flues designed to draw the smoke from the chamber, the air was yet thick and gloomy. It had grown intensely warm. Sildemund's mind worked feverishly – again, so much seemed to be happening that he did not understand. And there was still that something, pushing at his thoughts.

There was no meat! He feeds upon the life of others. . . .

And suddenly he had it! Or thought he had. . . . Cold fingers gripped his gut, as he strove to understand. He stared at the three Revenants before him, consumed with a new and growing fear.

He had to speak! He had to tell someone, for the thoughts that were going through his head now were madness. But he went over them again and again, and each time he could be drawn to only one conclusion.

Dinbig had moved away, thoughtfully stroking his beard, deep in contemplation. Barring Gully there was no one else to whom Sildemund could safely confide his thoughts. He edged close to Gully and whispered, 'We must get away. Urgently!'

He saw Gully's frown.

'Don't question it, Gully. Just help me.' He managed to catch Dinbig's eye and surreptitiously beckoned him across. As the Khimmurian drew close he said, in an urgent undertone, 'The myth states that Sko-ulatun lives upon the hearts of others in order to sustain his own existence, is that not so?'

The Khimmurian nodded.

'And these Elders confirm that he feeds upon the life of others. Yet they held him here, they say, for years. Why did they not let him perish? And what did they give him to sustain him?'

Dinbig stared at him, his face registering unaccustomed shock and bewilderment. Before he could respond the door was flung open. A Revenant fighter rushed in, marching directly to the three Elders without reference to the illustrious company assembled in the chamber. The fighter bent across the table and whispered something. Sildemund became aware of shouting somewhere in the corridors outside the chamber.

The Elders rose as one, and in a curious re-enactment of events hours earlier in that very chamber, commenced to order everyone out. 'Return to your chambers immediately!

Protests this time were more vociferous than before, for the Dyarch, particularly, saw this move as a deliberate and profoundly worrying ploy to disregard the request they had made. But the Revenant guards were pushing forward heedlessly. Their intention was to clear the room. The few Dyarch and Tomian soldiers looked in confusion to their leaders, seeking directions. Prince Enlos yelled indignantly, 'What is this? We protest! What is happening?'

'Go quietly, please, Prince Enlos,' the crone replied, attempting to instil calm. 'All of you. You will be safest in your chambers. You do not understand the gravity of the situation. Sko-ulatun has returned. He is among us!'

There were renewed shouts at this – and more shouting from outside. The guards pressed forward. The three Elders were preparing to leave the chamber; one – the younger woman – had taken up the bound Heart. Enlos, King Lalvi and the others remonstrated more loudly, unwilling to be confined once more in conditions of extreme danger. Sildemund, angry, confused, pushed against a guard who was endeavouring to force him back. Suddenly, close by his side, there was a roar. Picadus, in an explosion of pent-up wrath, had turned violently upon a Revenant guard, striking him hard upon the jaw and knocking him to the floor. As the guard fell Picadus leapt upon him and relieved him of his sabre. In a berserk fury he struck out at another.

Instantly he was set upon by several more guards, male and female. He reeled, madly, bellowing with rage and slashing with the sabre. His position was hopeless: the guards had him surrounded, but so great was his madness as to render him incapable of yielding. He fought, swinging and striking, regardless of the injuries the guards were already inflicting upon him.

'Pic! No!' Sildemund made to lunge forward to help his friend. As he did so a powerful hand came from behind and clamped over his mouth. He was dragged back into the shadows of an alcove at the side of the room, another arm fastening around his chest to keep him from struggling.

A familiar voice sounded in his ear: 'Hsst! This is our chance!'

The hand slipped from his mouth. He twisted his head around. 'Gully!'

'Quiet, or we will be discovered! There is nothing we can do!'

The chamber was in uproar. No one had eyes for Sildemund. Picadus, shrieking like a madman, had taken down two more guards. Three others assailed him. He was streaked with blood. The main body of Revenant guards had moved efficiently to occupy a space between the Tomian and Dyarch royalty and the conflict. They faced Tomian and Dyarch guards, weapons readied, but neither side made a move.

As Sildemund watched, Picadus was struck a blow upon the side of the head. He staggered, blood blossoming suddenly at his temple. His eyes rolled, a great shudder passed through his limbs. A second blade slashed into his chest and with a groan he fell to the ground.

Sildemund felt Gully's strong arm drawing him back, further into the alcove. 'There is a door here.'

In a daze he let himself be pulled through the doorway, which Gully pushed gently shut behind them. They were in darkness. Sildemund leaned against a wall, struggling with himself, while Gully put his eye to a chink in the door. The hubbub outside gradually faded.

'The chamber is empty,' said Gully presently, his voice subdued.

'Pic. Poor Pic.'

Gully took his shoulders. 'There was nothing we could do. Do you think I would have left him, given a choice? It was already too late to intervene. We would have gone down with him.'

He heard the emotion in Gully's voice, knew that he wept. Sildemund nodded, in an anguish of self-recrimination. 'I know it.'

'What now?' said Gully after a pause. 'In the turmoil we have not been missed, but we will be.'

'We have to regain the Heart.'

'What?'

'We have delivered it into the wrong hands, Gully. I'm convinced of it. We must go after it – or I must.'

'I'm with you, lad, you know that. Though I am confused.'

'I, too. But there is no time for explanation.' His eyes were adjusting to the darkness. 'What is this place?'

'A storage cupboard, I think. Look, these are candles – here is oil. . . . There is no other way out.'

'The Elders took the Heart. I think they have gone through

the portal in the far wall, behind the table. That is where we must go.'

'There may be guards still in this chamber.' Gully silently opened the door a crack, peered out, then slipped stealthily through. Sildemund followed. The tall columns reaching into the ceiling rose on either side. Gully crept forward to peer around one, Sildemund did likewise with the other. There were no guards positioned in the recesses to either side, and peering through the gloom across chamber they could see none stationed at the opposite wall. Close to where they stood were pools of blood upon the floor. Bloody footsteps and long smears indicated the dragging of bodies to the main door.

'I would give much for a weapon,' breathed Gully, sweat gleaming upon his face.

Sildemund stepped out warily, then, looking left and right, stole across the chamber towards the portal in the far wall. As he passed the table at which the three Revenant Elders had sat, he paused and glanced down. He saw the emblem etched into the wooden surface: a serpent laid upon a tree. Could it be the same as was on the ixigen cage? he wondered. It was possible.

He moved on, Gully at his side. At the portal he pressed an ear to the timber. He heard nothing beyond, and eased open the door. A stone passage bore off for a short distance, then branched to left and right.

'Which way?' said Gully when they reached the junction.

Sildemund shook his head, listened. He thought he heard faint muffled voices coming from somewhere to the right. He knew he had to pursue, to find where the Heart had been taken. He made off with Gully close behind.

The passage widened, permitting a short stone stairway to lead down to the entrance to another passage, then up the other side to rejoin the way they were on. A carved stone balustrade ran along the narrowed upper passage, linking the two stairheads. The ceiling was much higher here, and daylight filtered in through a wide, mullioned window set in the wall high overhead, though it did little to relieve the overall dimness of the corridors. There was a heavy arched door facing them some way beyond the second stairhead.

Sildemund slipped past the stairs until he was able to look down at the passage entrance at their foot. The feeble light did not extend into the passage, which presented a shadowed hole. Sildemund crouched, peering between the stone balusters, hoping to see further into the passage below. Though it was silent now, he was convinced he had heard something within. A movement, as of something scuffing against the wall or floor; and the sound of breathing. He felt naked and vulnerable. Like Gully, he would have given almost anything to have been in possession of a weapon.

He indicated to Gully that they should explore the lower passage. He crept on, to the head of the second stairway which descended to the passage entrance. Gully was already cautiously descending the first. The stairways were each of a dozen wide stone steps, curving slightly as they descended. On the third step Sildemund froze. There was a movement below, a faint blur of a shadow upon the stone flags. Then the scuffing sound again. From the opening below them a figure stepped.

It was a man, but he came out half-crouching, then straightened. Just for a second Sildemund had the impression of a misshapen body, which seemed to meld into its proper form as it came into view. He put it down to the weakness of the light, playing tricks on his eyes. Then the figure turned towards him and he gave a gasp.

He knew this man. He could not believe it. He knew him well. He was of Volm, and had worked many times for Sildemund's father, Master Frano. Through his astonishment Sildemund gave a smile.

'Jans!'

27

JANS GAZED UP at him blankly.

'Jans, what are you doing here?'

He seemed dazed or drugged or something, his look vacant yet penetrating at the same time. The way he held himself, his movements – was he in pain? Again Sildemund had the fleeting impression of physical distortion, of unfamiliarity. It was as though Jans's muscles, limbs, bones were shifting, modifying themselves, trying to find a comfortable position. But the face was Jans's, and though Sildemund felt half-consciously a frisson of profound confusion and deep unease, he barely assimilated the discordance, so overcome was he with surprise and pleasure at seeing Jans here in this most unexpected of locations.

'Jans, do you not know me? It's me, Sildemund.'

In response Jans's gaze became focused, as though he had snapped suddenly to awareness. His eyes searched Sildemund with an eager gleam. Their expression belied the smile that spread across his face. Sildemund tensed with sudden apprehension.

'Ah, Sildemund. Yes, how are you?'

He began to mount the stairs.

Without knowing quite why, Sildemund backed away a step. From the opposite stairway Gully spoke. 'And I, Jans. I am here, too.'

Jans, who had not been aware of the presence of another, turned to face him, poised with one foot raised upon the second stair.

'Is something the matter, Jans?' queried Gully. 'Do you not know me, either?'

'I do, of course.'

'It is me, your old friend, Edric.'

'Yes, Edric,' said Jans. 'It is so good to see you. I am sorry, I am not well.'

With a flick of his head Gully warned Sildemund away, but Sil was already at the top of the stairway. Jans turned back. 'Sildemund, where are you going?'

Sildemund made no reply. On the opposite stairway Gully was also backing quickly to the top.

'Sildemund, wait,' said Jans. 'I want to talk to you. You have something I need.'

Again he began to move towards Sildemund.

'Sil, he is not Jans!' warned Gully.

Jans cast a mocking look over his shoulder. 'Edric, what do you say? I am Jans, of course I am. Can you not see?'

'I see, yes. I see that you, who resemble and claim to be Jans, are something other. Why else would you believe me, whom you have known for many years, to be Edric, whom you have also known, and whom you know to be dead these past weeks?'

Jans's lips curled into a venomous grimace. Dreadful anger burned in his eyes. He vented a scathing hiss and, spinning, leapt towards Sildemund. As he did so his form began to change.

'Sil, *run!*' yelled Gully.

Sildemund was already making for the arched door at the other end of the passage. The thought loomed large that he should have gone back, along the way they had come, for this door might be locked, and even were it not he did not know what lay beyond. But he heard a blood-curdling snarl at his back and knew there was no way back.

He reached the door, twisted its iron ring. To his relief it gave. He flung his weight against it, half-fell through. As he made to heave the door closed he saw Jans almost upon him. But it was no longer Jans. Vestiges of Jans's features still clung to the face, savage and enraged, bloated, metamorphosing even as Sildemund watched. It was a travesty now, a grotesque, sickening caricature. Snout and jaw were pushing through the flesh, beastlike; naked bone, bloody sinews, muscles and hair commingled in a chaos of derangement.

The body no longer mimicked the human, was half-transformed, a fleet, bounding thing, large and spindly, and in its current state, clumsy. The corrupted remains of hands were still identifiable at the extremities of the forelimbs, which stumbled and skidded as their bone-structure altered.

This was Sko-ulatun, Sildemund could not doubt it.

Sildemund glimpsed Gully in the passage beyond. He was some paces from the stairs, had been making his way in pursuit of Sildemund and Jans. But he was frozen now, for just a moment, seeing what it was they faced. Then he signalled frantically to Sildemund, turned and ran back to the stairs and down.

Sildemund slammed shut the door. As he rammed home the heavy iron bolt to secure it Sko-ulatun cannoned into the other side. Sildemund leapt back in horror. A single blow had splintered the heavy timbers. Within a minute, at most, Sko-ulatun would be through.

'Gully, Gully, keep safe!' whispered Sildemund. Sko-ulatun bellowed in rage, a bone-shattering roar, and pummelled again on the door. Sildemund took consolation that Gully would have time to put distance between them.

The blows upon the door resounded through the stone passages, the door shaking, gradually splintering. Sildemund turned to take stock of his surroundings. He was in a wide corridor, running to left and right, set with statues and columns. There were several doors and side-passages in sight. He made off, impelled by his terror, randomly choosing the third opening, hoping to save himself in the labyrinth of passageways.

He sprinted up a curving stairway, raced along more corridors. Sko-ulatun's hammering had grown dimmer, muffled as stone walls came between them. Now it had ceased altogether. Sildemund halted a moment, panting, listening. Was his pursuer through the door, even now racing after him through the corridors? Or had he abandoned the door, turned around and made off after Gully? Sildemund became aware of the eerie emptiness of the place. He had seen no one since leaving the chamber of candles. It was as if Garsh had been suddenly abandoned.

He pushed himself on. A little way ahead the corridor terminated at another double door. He listened, detected nothing, and opened it cautiously. He stepped into a spacious room, its walls hung with rich tapestries and drapes. Repeated upon several of these was the same emblem, or variations upon it, that he had seen on the table in the chamber of candles: the serpent and tree. There was no one in the room, but in the moment that he entered

Sildemund thought to glimpse, at the edge of his vision, a blur of movement, a swish of red and brown robes, an anonymous figure passing quickly through an arch set in one wall. He would have made straight for the arch, but his eyes fell upon the object in the centre of the room, and he hesitated. A low slab of striated marble was set upon the floor there, and on this was a bundle bound in travel-stained rough cloth.

Sildemund's skin crawled, his innards constricting as he approached the Heart of Shadows. Why had it been left here? What was he to do with it? He stood before it, transfixed. He had to keep it from Sko-ulatun, he knew that. Yet he had brought it to Garsh – had been compelled to bring it – to that end. And now, having delivered it into the hands of the Revenants of Claine, he feared he had achieved precisely the opposite. They had kept Skoulatun here. They had kept him alive! Why? What were they concealing? What were their true aims?

He stared down at the soiled bundle on the slab, the questions spinning in his mind like demented things. He could not think properly. He was alone, more than ever before. He felt that the decision he faced now could be the most fateful he would ever make. There was no one he could turn to, no one to ask advice of.

And there was no time to consider.

He picked up the Heart.

It was cold, but to his surprise it was soft, doughy, fleshlike in its binding. As he held it in the cup of his two hands he felt it move, a sudden palpitation, a vigorous kick, a beat. He shuddered. The thing lived! But its life was cold, inhuman. Its chill permeated the binding as if with mindless intent, penetrating his skin, seeming to crawl into his blood.

Sildemund resisted the urge to unbind it and look within. He pushed the hateful bundle into the satchel which he still carried at his shoulder.

There was a movement across the room, at the arch in the wall. Meglan stood there.

'Meg!' He started forward, startled, stunned, overjoyed, shocked at her appearance, for there was a bright, swollen bruise in the middle of her forehead. She wore familiar tunic and hose, though both were torn. At her waist was a sabre and dagger. 'Meg!'

Then he halted, suddenly deeply afraid. He backed away.

Meglan had her arms open, ready to embrace him. 'Sil, what's wrong?'

He stared about him wildly, his eyes wide.

'Sil! Sil! It's me. It's Meg.' Now she started towards him, but he backed away further, again cursing that he had no weapon, though a weapon, he knew, would be useless against the creature that was Sko-ulatun.

'Stay back!' His jaw was trembling, his leges rubbery; he felt suddenly enervated, defeated by this most cruel of tricks. 'Do you think you can fool me again? First Jans, now Meglan.'

A light of understanding entered Meglan's eyes. 'You saw Jans? Where? Sil, it was not Jans, you know that, don't you?'

'I have the Heart,' said Sildemund. 'Why do you disguise yourself again?'

'This is not a disguise, Sil, my brother, my other half, surely you know me?'

'You can kill me,' said Sildemund flatly. His spirit had fled him. Suddenly he was overwhelmingly tired. The tears started to his eyes. He had no wish to carry on. 'I am unarmed. I cannot fight you.'

'Sil, how can I convince you? I will tell you something. Remember, when we were children—'

'*No!*' He felt a sudden rage, that the intimacy of their shared childhood should be violated by this monster. 'You could know! You could know everything! You adopt the flesh, do you steal the memories, the personality too?'

As he spoke these words the realization hit him, and he almost reeled. The Elders had said it: *Sko-ulatun can assume the form of any whose heart he has devoured.* Jans, then, was dead, the prey of his monster. And if the person, the apparition, which stood before him now was not Meglan, then Meglan too – sweet, beloved Meglan, with all her foibles, her spirit, her life – had suffered the same fate.

It was too much to bear. Sildemund half-staggered; an anguished sob escaped his lips. At his hip he was dimly aware of a chill, forceful pulse. 'There is no need for this,' he said. 'I cannot resist, I have come too far. The Heart is yours.'

'Meglan's eyes brimmed with tears. 'Sil, Sil, Sil. . . . We have

282

both come this far, along separate ways. Now we must go on together.' She was unbuckling the belt at her waist, with its sabre and dagger. Sildemund eyed her, wary. She bent her knees, placed the belt on the floor then kicked it so that it slid towards him. 'Take the blades, Sil.'

'I cannot fight you, even with them.'

'You cannot fight Sko-ulatun, it is true. But Meglan can be slain. Pick them up.'

He did so, uncertainly, drawing both weapons from their sheaths. He held them towards her. She came forward, her arms open. 'Sil, my brother, my love!'

In that moment he knew he could only trust. His longing for her, his longing for truth amidst all this deceit, this obfuscation and terror, overcame everything. He let out an agonized cry. The weapons fell from his hands and clattered to the stone floor. He took her in his arms as her arms tightened around him. Her body was warm and supple, her scent familiar. He embraced her hard, as she embraced him, and together they wept, clinging to one another, kissing one another, too afraid to let go, overcome with a flood of emotion like nothing either had ever experienced.

When at last they drew back Sildemund saw that others had entered the chamber. The three Elders – the crone, the woman and the girl-child – stood before the arch through which Meglan had entered, a number of fighters before them. Sildemund stiffened.

Meglan turned her head, following his gaze, then smiled. 'It's all right, Sil.'

'No, it isn't.' He pointed an angry, accusing finger at the three. 'You work with Sko-ulatun! You kept him here, alive! You fed him living hearts!'

'You have not understood,' declared the Elder, the crone, who had spoken in the chamber of candles. 'Sko-ulatun does not live, he exists in a travesty of life. He is Death incarnate. As such he cannot die, except by particular means. To have deprived him of sustenance would have been to submit him to an exultation of suffering, at the end of which his bodily form would indeed have wasted to nothing. But his essence, his corrupted soul, would have been freed. He would thus remain chained to the world, and would have returned in some other guise to continue his corruption. Our intention was to hold him, keeping him from his Heart, until we could destroy him utterly.'

'But how many innocents were sacrificed to satisfy his craving for life?'

'Many died that he might live on, it is true. It caused us great remorse, but which way would you have it?'

Sildemund shook his head, aghast. 'Remorse? Remorse? What are you? I understand what you say about Sko-ulatun, but to sacrifice the lives of so many others, who have committed no crime, done no harm . . . to murder them in order to sustain him. . . . It places you in kinship with him. You are no better.'

'We are all his kin,' replied the crone. 'He is our first Father and he has corrupted us all. But Sildemund, you cast barbs, yet are you so innocent? Have innocents not died, unnecessarily, that you might live on?'

'This is insanity! What do you say? I have killed no one!'

'You are a flesh-eater, so I understand.'

'Of animals, yes.'

'And you suffer no dilemma, no remorse?'

'There is no question—'

'We disagree,' said the crone forcefully. 'It is our belief that there *is* a question. For each creature that we gave to Sko-ulatun, we suffered. We accept that we took life unnecessarily. It was wrong, we knew it, it was our dilemma. But it was for the greater good. There was no other way.'

Sildemund stared at her with a mounting feeling of deep discomfiture. 'You-you are saying. . . ?'

'Goats, sheep, pigs. Those were the hearts he fed upon.'

Sildemund was struck mute with sudden embarrassment. He struggled wildly for a means to reclaim his dignity. Another thought came, and he blurted out impulsively, 'You killed Picadus!'

'Your friend forced our guards to defend themselves. But they are specially and rigorously trained. They can kill, be sure of that, but it is a last resort. Their greatest skill is in defence. Two died at your friend's hands, but he still lives, he is gravely injured and his recovery will not be swift, but his condition is not thought mortal.'

Sildemund fell back into shamed silence. One hand un-consciously rested upon his satchel, and he felt the sudden, obscene pulse of the vile thing within. Meglan took his free hand in hers and squeezed reassuringly. A young female fighter came forward carrying a belt with sabre and dagger.

'Now that we have established who you are – and what you are not – we give you these. They will not help against Sko-ulatun, but you may take them if you wish.'

Who I am, what I am not. . . . It was something he had not considered. Just as he had been unsure of Meglan, she had been unsure of him. She had tested him, as he had tested her, not knowing that the other was not Sko-ulatun.

He accepted the weapons. The young woman bent to pick up those he had dropped, and handed them back to Meglan. She said, 'We should leave now.'

Meglan nodded. Observing her Sildemund said, 'How did you get those bruises?'

'These?' She indicated the marks upon her body and the torn clothing. 'These were given to me when I travelled here with Sko-ulatun and his followers. This?' She touched her forehead. 'This one was given to me by Epta.'

'Epta?'

Meglan indicated the young female fighter. 'This is Epta.'

Sildemund frowned. 'You are Epta? The daughter of Kemorlin?'

The young woman nodded, but made no comment.

'Your father is here,' said Sildemund.

'I know it.'

He looked back at Meglan, perplexed. 'She gave you this injury? Why?'

The crone behind them spoke. 'We cannot linger here with explanations. Sildemund, you encountered Sko-ulatun in another's guise: Jans.'

'I escaped, but he is in the corridors somewhere behind. And Gully – I am concerned for Gully.'

'As long as Gully keeps away from Sko-ulatun he will be safe – at least for now. Sko-ulatun will come here, following the Heart and Meglan, for whom he yearns. We have emptied this complex, that none might become a victim, for certainly he will kill any in his way. Now we must leave.'

'Where do we go?'

'Just follow,' replied the crone, turning with the others to pass through the arch.

'What of this?' said Sildemund, patting his satchel.

The crone paused. 'The Heart of Shadows. You must bring it.'

28

THEY MADE THEIR way through more empty corridors, feet reverberating on cold stone, their fighters running on ahead to ensure that their enemy was not lying in wait. Meglan glanced aside at her brother as they walked, taking pleasure in the sight of him. Only days had passed, yet both had been through so much: it seemed an age since they had been together. She allowed herself a smile, but full in her mind was the knowledge that there was no time for rejoicing. She feared what they had still to face.

Sildemund was avid to know how Meglan had come to be in Garsh. She had been perhaps the last person he had expected to see and he had still not fully taken in the fact that she was here, with him. In a breathless whisper she told him her story: how she had ridden with such urgency from Volm to find him and bring him back with the stone. She told of crossing the wasteland of Dazdun's Despair, guided by the talisman mystifyingly attached to her wrist; told of Skalatin's relentless pursuit and Jans's awful death. She related how she had arrived at Dharsoul only to witness, unknowingly, Sildemund's departure for Garsh.

At this point Sildemund interrupted, wanting more details, for he recalled the solitary female figure on the hill beside the Dharsoul Road.

'I thought it was you, Meg, then dismissed it, certain it could not have been.'

'Then it most probably was. So close, and neither of us knew it. And yet. . . .' Her face took on a wistful look. 'I thought of you then.'

'And I of you.'

'Perhaps we knew, then, but did not know that we knew.'

'There was another figure, which stepped out from behind a rock,' said Sildemund. 'I caught no more than a glimpse.'

'From *beneath* a rock,' corrected Meglan, recalling with distaste Skalatin's sudden appearance. She recounted how he had waited for her outside Dharsoul, how she had challenged him; and his casual, vengeful act of slaughter of the two peasants upon the road. She told him of the raid upon the Dyarch troops, her capture by Fagmar the Cursed, the ghastly irony of her rescue by Skalatin, who was Sko-ulatun, and how she had finally entered Garsh at Sko-ulatun's side.

'I raised the alarm to expose his deceit. In the confusion I ran. Epta and two others came upon me.' She touched her bruised forehead. 'They struck me down, not knowing whether I was his follower, or even whether I was he. I was brought to the Elders only a short time before you arrived. I was conscious by then and told them my story.'

She looked at him again, but said no more. There were other details she had learned, confided to her by the three Revenant Elders. They had given her a new insight into the role she, and Sildemund, had still to play. It terrified her. To confront Sko-ulatun again. . . . But she had been made to understand that she had no choice.

They were descending a stone staircase which spiralled into the depths of Garsh. The walls changed from decorated stone to natural hewn rock, suggesting that they had passed below street level into the hill itself. At Meglan's prompting Sildemund recounted his own adventures. 'I am still under sentence of death, Meg,' he said, telling of the incident in which Queen Lermeone had identified the Heart of Shadows. 'As are Gully and Pic.'

She frowned. They continued their dizzying descent. Sildemund gave the remainder of his tale, and when he reached the end, said in a low whisper, 'But I am still suspicious. The Revenants left the Heart upon the marble slab back there. Why? I or you might have been Sko-ulatun, they did not know. He could have come in any guise, and taken the Heart. All would have been lost.'

'It is not quite like that,' replied Meglan quietly, but again she kept her thoughts to herself, still uncertain of the things she had been told. Her head ached from Epta's blows, she was sore all over. Her chest and back felt bruised from where the runaway Dyarch horse had smashed into her; and she carried other grazes and contusions from her struggles with Skalatin, Fagmar and the brigands who had tried to rape her. She wanted no more of this, she wanted to lie down and sleep, wake to find it was all a terrible dream. The confrontation she had been told now lay ahead filled her with dread and misgiving.

'Where are they taking us now?' demanded Sildemund.

They had arrived at the foot of the stairs. A short corridor extended before them, its ceiling low and arched. A larger, lighter area, a floor of richly coloured mosaic, opened beyond it.

As they entered this they saw that it was a circular chamber, wide and spacious, its ceiling a huge, spectacularly high dome. Through this, light in a thousand varying hues penetrated to illuminate the floor and walls in myriad bright shades. Such was the play of light and colour that the very air was tinted, so that as one walked across the chamber one passed through a veil of ever-changing tones.

On the opposite side of the chamber reared the effigy of a gigantic serpent, carved in white wood and figured with precious gems. It was set into a tall arched recess so that the colours from above fell at its base but not upon its actual form. At the sight of this Meglan's heart gave a lurch and she stopped short. Her mouth went suddenly dry, her palms damp. The hairs upon her skin began to tingle as she searched her mind, haunted by something just beyond her conscious grasp. She recalled again her journey along the mysterious Serpent's Path, the little talisman she had carried all this way. She stared at the great snake, unable to tear her eyes away.

The old Revenant took her arm. 'Come, Meglan.' She led her on towards the centre of the round chamber.

Sildemund gazed in awe at the great dome overhead. Resplendent, almost incandescent, it yet looked so delicate in its fabulous, multi-hued translucency. An impossible construction, which seemed to his astonishment to be made entirely of stained glass – a relatively uncommon material. He could not figure out how it was supported. Though he could see threadlike metallic struts running along its arch, they looked too frail to shore its weight. By his calculations it defied natural law. He was filled with admiration for the unknown architects who had conceived and created it.

Huge figures gazed down at him, suspended upon a variegated background of leaves, fruits and refulgent, abstract shapes. They stretched across almost the entire dome: an old woman beside a younger one who held a babe to her breast, and beside her a girl-child. At their feet was coiled a great white serpent.

'The three aspects of Claine, the universal Mother, the first Goddess,' said the second Revenant Elder, the young woman, at his side. He had not heard her speak before. Her voice jolted him from his reverie. 'The becoming of youth: the giving and nurturing of motherhood; the wisdom of age.'

'What of the serpent?' enquired Sildemund with apprehension.

'A symbol more ancient than you can imagine. It stands for oracular wisdom, revelation and prophetic counsel. In various forms it existed all across our world as it was before everything was changed. But to discover its true meaning you must search hard. You must look beneath the ruins of all temples and shrines to find the ruins of the original shrines built to Claine; look behind your ancient writings to find texts more ancient still. And the search will not be easy, for most were destroyed utterly, purpose-fully. But that is where you will find the truth, though your law will condemn you to death even for looking. Sko-ulatun and his followers took the serpent, as they took all of the First Mother's symbols, and corrupted it, destroyed it, hid all traces of its original nature. The serpent now is seen as a hateful, slithering, poisonous thing that crawls upon its belly. It is shunned and feared by men and women alike. Sko-ulatun took everything, in his jealousy and his rage, for he could not permit that the Goddess gave life and he did not. He even hid her name and established that her daughters would forever walk in their fathers' shadows, and their offspring would forever bear their fathers' names. He was the First Father and in his vanity believed himself god over all. The society in which you live is testament to this, is it not?'

Sildemund had no ready answer. They stood in the centre of the chamber, directly beneath the high dome, bathed in the splendour of coloured light. The Revenant continued, loss in her eyes. 'It was all through ignorance. Sko-ulatun simply did not know. He believed himself inferior, that only the Goddess was the source of life. Yet all she wished was to share; that was her reason for creating him. Even this he denies; in your texts it is he who gives birth to her. He *is* our First Father, we must acknowledge that, but he has corrupted us all. Even now we are still tainted by him, by the irrational jealousy, the fear and greed that drove him then as it drives him still. It might have been so different.'

The three Elders stood in front of Meglan and Sildemund, and the crone said, 'This chamber is the Temple of Claine. Here is where the battle must be fought. Sko-ulatun will come for you here. We will leave you now.'

Sildemund's blood ran cold. 'Leave us?'

'We will be with you, but our intervention will be minimal.'

'Why? We have brought the Heart to you that might prevent it from falling into Sko-ulatun's hands. We cannot prevent him.'

'Then he will win.'

The three Revenants moved away, their guards accompanying them. Sildemund stood in bewilderment. Meglan reached out and took his hand, 'Sil, we have been long expected. Don't ask me how, but they knew we would come one day.'

'Us? Why? What are you saying?'

'We have been brought to this, Sil. For some reason I cannot fully comprehend. We are twins. Somehow we represent harmony, there is no conflict between us – that is, nothing that could not be resolved. We are one. Something in us is the way it should have been, long ago and always.'

The old Revenant, as she backed away, was intoning words: ' "The Heart of Shadows will be taken by the unknowing to those who claim to know. Two halves shall comprise the twin aspects of one who will be Blessed of Claine, as Claine intended it to be. The Blessed and the Defiled shall meet in the Temple of Claine's Light. There shall the Heart be, and there shall be decided the Light or Darkness of future days".'

'It is us that Sko-ulatun will confront,' said Meglan. 'The Revenant Daughters of Claine can do little except observe, with hope, and – if they survive – record for future generations.'

Sildemund swallowed, stiff with fear and incomprehension. He turned back to the Revenants, but they and their fighters had gone. He did not see where, but assumed there was a hidden door within the murals and drapes which covered the high circular wall. He stood alone with his twin sister beneath the great dome, lit by haloes and cross-slanting shafts of streaming, sparkling light.

'Put the Heart down, Sil. Place it upon the floor,' said Meglan.

He stared at her. 'I don't understand.'

'Just do it. Please.'

Struck by the commanding tone of her voice, he did so.

'Undo its binding.'

He carefully unwrapped the heavy cloth bandage and revealed the pulsing organ.

'Move away now.'

'Meg!'

'Move away, Sil. You can do nothing more. At least, not yet.' Meglan let her eyes rest upon the Heart. Its hue varied from purple to deep murrey, speckled with brighter blood-spots. It glistened, quivered with a semblance of life, streaked with long filaments of yellow-white, untouched, it appeared, by the varied lights that fell upon it. And across its surface moved shadows, their motion unmistakable now. Clouded, umbrageous bands, soot black through dark liver and baleful leaden grey. Their opaque shift was amorphous, undefined, merging and re-merging, mesmerizing and yet repellent; unfading crepuscular shadows.

Meglan shuddered and her brother slowly backed away.

'Meg, what is happening here?'

In answer she raised her hand and pointed to the entrance through which they had come into the Temple. A dark figure stood there, motionless in the shadows of the passage which led from the spiral stairway.

Sildemund gripped his sabre-hilt. The figure came forward, to stand at the edge of the brilliance of coloured light. His voice was a low, menacing purr. 'Ah, Meg-lan, pretty malkin mine. And Sildemund. What a long way we have come. What travails, what unnecessary toils and pains we have suffered. All for my Heart, which you might have given me and profited well had your stupid father only accepted my offer.'

He came a few steps forward, warily inspecting the chamber. Meglan suppressed a gasp of horror as the light fell full upon him. His body was as she had first encountered him at home in Volm: slight, lithe, sinewy, implying hidden strength, swathed in a dark burnous. But the head and face were uncovered, deliberately it seemed, so that he might shock or mock. For his face was that of a baby, chubby-cheeked, big-eyed, both ancient and new, innocent and knowing. The baby smiled, watched them, then the face began to alter. Now Meglan gazed at the old peasant woman whom

Skoulatun had so cruelly murdered upon the cart on the road outside Dharsoul. The old woman displayed a toothless grin, then changed once more. Now it was Jans, smiling, leering, making a lewd gesture with his tongue; now it was poor Dervad. . . .

'Their hearts were good,' said Sko-ulatun, smacking his lips. The face became goatlike. Dark, glittering cold eyes flickered salaciously from Meglan to Sildemund. 'Some were tastier than others. Some were tough, some so-o tender. One or two I threw away, they just weren't good enough. Ah, but they have sustained me, they have brought me here. And now . . .' his gaze fell upon the palpitating organ beside Meglan's feet '. . . now I need no others. I have found my own at last. Oh, it is almost a sadness. I have taken such hearts, for so long, you cannot begin to imagine.'

In a sequence of mere moments his face went through a multitude of changes: a child, a woman, a dog, a young man, a lizard, an old man, a bird, endlessly melding, merging, reforming so that passing features of one became, fleetingly, grotesquely imposed on the next, engendering new forms, impossible creatures of phantasm and nightmare. Then he was Skalatin again, who had come to Volm, malevolence in his shocking eyes, his cadaverous face, lipless mouth, rotten wormy gums.

He came with deliberation towards Meglan, striding quickly through the fabulous riot of light. 'Now I shall take my Heart back, and then – o-oh, pret-ty chi-ild – I shall have you. But first—' he veered suddenly towards Sildemund, his voice rising in a sudden snarl, '*I hunger!*'

'No!' Meglan threw herself between the two of them. 'Get back! Leave him!'

Sildemund, white-faced, his sabre gripped uselessly in his hand, staggered backwards towards the wall and the arch where towered the great snake. Sko-ulatun raised a clawed hand as if to strike Meglan aside, but she stood firm before him.

'Everything you have desired, all you have searched for is here,' she seethed, her hatred of him loud in her shaking voice. 'Everything. But harm him and you will lose me, that I swear.'

Sko-ulatun threw back his head and gave a harsh laugh, his terrible face bathed in emerald, amber and puce. 'How so, love-ly one?'

She had slipped her dagger from its sheath and now turned it upon itself, its tip pressed to her breast. A strange feeling was rising within her, for she did not truly know what she was doing. She felt moved by something she could not identify. Her words and actions came without thought or consideration, as though she acted almost with the impulse of another.

Sko-ulatun eyed her malevolently, and shrugged a shoulder. 'I have told you before, pret-ty, alive or dead, it is of little consequence to me.'

'What of the spawn you wish me to bear? They cannot be born from a corpse. And that is the whole point of your endeavour is it not?'

'There are many others where you came from. You are not special.'

'Then do as you will,' said Meglan, and stepped out of his path. 'But remember, as my brother dies so do I. For we are one.'

Sko-ulatun surveyed her with calculating intent, the tip of his grey, pustulent tongue consulting a rot-ridden pit at the back of his jaw.

'I am your Father,' he said. 'The Father of All. Do you deny me?'

She fought down the nausea these words caused her, the rubbery weakness that threatened her knees. She backed further away, pressing the dagger tip more firmly to her breast. 'I have already said, do as you will.'

'You cannot defy me.'

'Then destroy me, as you destroyed Claine, out of bitterness and your hatred of your own shortcomings.'

'*She* destroyed *me*! Now I have returned and I shall destroy her, forever. I shall destroy you. I shall be what I was, Sko-ulatun, the Creator of All.'

'Alone, your achievements will be negligible and short-lasting. You will perish, for you turn upon yourself. It is yourself that you tried to destroy. You could never be more than half of something greater. That is why Claine brought you into the world. You came from her, to complement her, to become whole.' Again, Meglan wondered at herself, where her words came from.

Sko-ulatun scowled hideously. 'I created *her*! And now I shall become whole again.'

He thrust forward suddenly, past Meglan, bent and quickly gathered up the Heart of Shadows.

Sildemund started towards him, crying out, 'No! Meg!'

Sko-ulatun laughed, clasping the Heart to his breast, enveloping it in the folds of his clothing. His eyes flashed from Sildemund back to his sister. He moved away. 'Ah, Meg-lan, what wonders, what horrors I shall show you. Now you shall see. But first my oppressor shall be destroyed.' He pointed upwards, at the great dome and the three illumined figures. 'Wait, and observe.'

He turned, his body disfiguring, losing the human, becoming something unidentifiable. He passed swiftly across the mosaic floor, a kaleidoscopic shadow, and departed the round chamber.

Meglan sank to the floor, her strength gone. Sildemund ran to her. 'Meg! He has taken the Heart! After all we have done!'

Meglan shook her head, barely able to lift it. 'It is not over yet, Sil. He is coming back for me.'

'Then we must get away, get you away!'

'No. It has to be this way. I can't escape; he knows at all times how to find me. But – I learned this from the Elders, shortly before you and I were reunited – he must come for me when he is whole.' She reached out and clutched her brother's hand. 'Sil, my brother, I love you. Sko-ulatun may take me now, and I may die fighting him. But there is no other way. You and I have played a part in something greater than we can comprehend. I do not know why, just that it is. Whatever happens now, I love you.'

She reached up for him. They clung to each other in a tight embrace, locked in the pain, the incomprehension of finality, both somehow acknowledging that there was no other way.

A flicker. A great shadow momentarily obfuscating the brilliance of coloured light, then a great crash, so loud as to all but burst their eardrums. They stared upwards. Before their eyes the great dome was shattering, splitting into a thousand, a million fragments. The three figures and the serpent of the goddess Claine were rent and torn, cracking into tiny pieces with cacophonous roars and squeals, a sound like discordant demonic music, too loud to bear.

They staggered back. The glass face of the central figure, the young woman with the babe, suddenly exploded inwards in a shower of tortured fragments. Through it, smashing like a missile from a trebuchet through the roof of the temple, came a dark, balled shape. As it passed through, clearing the broken membrane of glass, it began to grow, spreading vast wings to slow its flight, extending cruel talons, unwinding a long cartilaginous neck. Fierce round eyes searched, found the two cowering figures below. The head bent towards them, horny, curving beak opening to emit a shriek which cut through the roar of the shattering dome. His form was monstrous: the head, wings and talons mimicking a gigantic vulture, the body that of a huge, hairless dog-thing with the armoured spine and lashing tail of a great lizard.

He plummeted towards them. As he came the dome in its entirety gave way to the force of gravity and with a sound like tortured thunder began to cave in. A million daggered shards commenced their fall, turning, spinning, a coruscating shower that bent and twisted the sunlight which now dazzled from high above. The Temple of Claine was transformed into a madness of rainbows, of colliding auroras, panicking, darting, warring spectra.

Meglan thrust her brother away. 'Get back, Sil! It's me he wants!'

Sildemund slipped, fell to the ground. The first splinters of glass from the face of the Goddess were striking the floor, compounding the unbearable din as they smashed into more pieces. Reflexively he covered his head with his hands, while knowing that flesh and bone could provide no defence against the lethal rain.

Meglan too threw up her hands to shield herself, sensing that in seconds both she and her brother would be sliced into ribbons. But no glass fell upon her, and she saw that little was falling beside Sildemund. The growing shape of Sko-ulatun, descending towards her, wings spread wide, created a protective canopy.

'Sil, run! Get out!' she screamed. She did not know if he could hear her above the din, but he was on his knees, scrambling forward onto his feet, running bent-backed towards the recessed arch in the wall where the great serpent towered.

Meglan had no time to see more; the dark shape was upon her, talons stretched. She screamed. The talons closed around, squeezing her like a vice. She was thrust away by the sheer weight of Sko-ulatun's descent, then drawn off her feet. She gasped against the pain. Sko-ulatun's head bent towards her, round, hooded eyes wide and triumphant. The talons squeezed harder; the huge wings were reversing their motion, howling as they lifted the body back from the floor, throwing up a deadly storm of splintered, powdered glass.

Meglan strained against the calloused rind of Sko-ulatun's feet, striving to gain a better position that she might draw breath into her lungs. She was drawn up towards the belly as Sko-ulatun rose higher. Now she saw the open breast of the creature, just above her head, a long gash in the flesh. Deep within, half-hidden between lips of torn, glistening pink meat, beat the Heart of Shadows.

'Meg-lan, come. . . .'

Sko-ulatun curved his neck to look upon her. The vulture head had altered. She gazed now into the terrible, vengeful face of Skalatin. Her temples were bursting with constricted blood, she could get no air into her deflated lungs. She was lifted high, borne away towards the sundered roof.

Her vision was a red haze. Consciousness slipping away. She clawed at the pocket of her tunic, desperate. But her hand flapped uselessly, had become a heavy, disconnected thing that obeyed no prompt from her mind. She was lost, drawn into the agony of sound, the roar of glass and blood in her ears, the thunder of pain, the tearing away of all. Everything dimmed. . . .

Sko-ulatun eased his grip – just sufficient to permit her a breath. She hung limply, arched backwards, aware by her returning pain that she was conscious again. The air was cool upon her face. Sko-ulatun still drew her upwards, past dangling glass fragments and the jagged ruins of stone and metal struts around the rim of the destroyed dome.

And she recalled her purpose. Her limbs felt numb and huge, but she forced her arm to work for her, fumbled again at her breast pocket, and at last her fingers closed around the object she sought. She drew it free; the tiny serpent talisman that had guided her across the wasteland of Dazdun's Despair.

From where had it come? She still did not know. But Epta, when she had brought her to the Elders, had shown it to them. It had fallen from Meglan's pocket when Epta struck her down. The three Elders had shown concern at the sight of it. They had demanded of her how she had come upon it, and she could only admit her ignorance. Yet what she had told them had been enough, it seemed. And they had told her then what she had to do.

She looked up. The wound in Sko-ulatun's flesh was no more

than an arm's length away between his great legs, the glistening organ pulsing deep within. Meglan drew back her arm as far as it would go. She filled her lungs and with a great cry thrust forward with all her strength. Her hand, gripping the talisman, plunged into the living flesh. It was slimy, slippery, cold. She pushed harder, bending her torso forward, felt herself enveloped, and the talisman seemed almost to pull her inwards, burrowing as if with a will of its own. She felt the membrane of the Heart give; her hand sank further, into its murderous core. She buried the metal – ixigen, the crone had said – deep into the vile Heart.

A colossal shudder passed through Sko-ulatun's monstrous frame. She felt him lurch wildly in the air, almost throwing her from his grip. An ear-shattering scream rent her eardrums. She saw his head above her, thrown back, the face contorted into a terrible grimace. As she withdrew her arm from his cold flesh, leaving the talisman buried there, she had a fleeting glimpse of the Heart of Shadows. It was shrivelling, wrinkling, withering away within its cavity of flesh. The skin was drawing back, peeling, shrinking. Then the talons released her and she was falling.

She had the impression of the great vulture form slewing wildly against the bright blue-white sky, then the world rolled. Her vision blurred sickeningly. She fell, down, down. . . . A glimpse of green hills, the tents of an army in the valley, the rushing roofs and streets of Garsh; then a face, a woman's face, gazing up at her from far below.

Meglan plummeted helplessly towards that face, realized that it was the face of the goddess, Claine, that it was formed of the mosaic upon the floor of the Temple and could only be discerned from above. It grew larger as she fell towards it. She knew she was crying out, in a delirium of terror, seeing her death hurtling towards her. From her cry, from her open mouth, something sinous seemed to pour. The Temple floor rushed towards, was almost upon her. Certain that she breathed her last, she closed her eyes.

29

IT WAS AN infinity, or merely moments – she did not know how long. She had retreated into the wombworld, the nothingness, the regions of the soul to which consciousness flees when the pains of body and mind become too much to bear. It was non-existence, unknowingness punctuated by fluid visions, dreams, nightmare images which came and then passed, evoking emotions she could not control, taking her into madness and beyond, then casting her back into the nothing. And infrequent lucid moments. A kind of awareness, of one place, a situation, something to which she returned, became a constant to which she wanted to return, wanted to remain.

Familiar, static, recognizable, though she did not yet know it. Into this came a blur. A face, sharpening into focus. A young man, fair-brown-headed, clean-featured. He hovered close, just above her, watching her. His face – she knew it, or should know it. She felt bewilderment, fear of insanity, for she did not know. Her memory raced through a thousand faces, a thousand names, and at last came to rest, reassuring her that not everything had fled.

'Sildemund.'

He leaned towards her. She was pleased, she had his name, his association. She *knew* something. It was enough. Her eyelids fluttered, drawing in the dark veil, obscuring the face, letting her fall back out of the world.

'*Meg!*'

She grasped at the sound as it resounded in the rolling haze of her receding consciousness. It was further proof, something familiar, something cherished. She gathered it, drew it into her, enveloped it, desperate, needing, happy.

When next she opened her eyes he was there again. This time she took in more. Stone wall at his back, a painting, timber beams above her head, light streaming through a window. Sildemund dozed, his head tilted forward, nodding. She watched him for some moments, delighting in the sight of him. He was holding her hand, she sensed his warmth in hers. She knew he was her brother. She squeezed lightly, then again. His head jerked back and his eyes opened, blinking. A big smile lit his features.

'Meg! Meg! You're back!'

The following day she was strong enough to sit up in bed, take vegetable broth and a little watered wine, and talk. Sildemund was ebullient, full of the need to tell her all that had happened. They were still in Garsh. Nine days had passed since she had fought Sko-ulatun. 'I thought you were gone forever, Meg. I looked up and I saw you struggling, striking him, so far overhead. And then you fell. You were certain to be dashed upon the temple floor – and then, an incredible thing!'

'What happened? I was sure I would die, yet here I sit without even a broken bone.'

It was true, she had suffered no physical injuries from her fall. She was in some considerable pain: her ribs were massively bruised, but that was from the grip of Sko-ulatun's talons. No other marks scarred her body, other than the vestiges of those she had already borne. The sickness and coma of recent days, it appeared, had been predominantly mental. She had undergone a massive shock from which her mind had demanded its own time to recover.

'I cannot explain it, I can only tell you what I saw – that is, what I think I saw,' said Sildemund. 'As you fell towards me through the ruined temple roof something seemed to come from your mouth. It was hardly visible, a whitish vapour or mist. It poured from you and curled around you. As I watched it seemed, for a moment, to resolve itself into the form of a huge serpent. It bore you the last short distance to the ground, then dissipated. That is all I saw, but the Revenant Elders wish to speak to you about it. I think they know more, though they will tell me nothing until they have spoken to you.'

'And what of Sko-ulatun?'

'He is gone. You slew him, Meg. I should have warned him, poor thing, for I know you. I, who am no stranger to your wrath, should have told the sorry creature that he would rue the day he ever tangled with you. Still, I doubt he would have listened.'

'Gone. . . .' she dwelt upon the word. 'After so long, is it possible?'

'So much else has been happening, Meg!' declared Sildemund in excitement. 'I have so much to tell you. I don't know where to begin! The siege has ended. The Elders told Prince Enlos and King Lalvi that you had brought them information concerning the brigand, Fagmar the Cursed. You'd told them where he was camped, and that you suspected he planned to ambush the Dyarch force when it left for Dyarchim.'

Meglan nodded. 'I overheard Sko-ulatun and Fagmar talking, just before we entered Garsh.'

'Prince Enlos and King Lalvi returned immediately to their troops. The following morning the Dyarch upped camp. Sure enough, two leagues down the road they came under attack. But they were ready: within their baggage wagons Tomian soldiers were hidden. As they fended off the bandits King Lalvi smote down from the rear. The battle was fierce, but short. Fagmar was captured, and all but a few of his men either captured or killed. Those who did not die on the battlefield were subsequently executed, Fagmar included. His reign, like Sko-ulatun's, is over.'

'And you, Sil, and Gully and Pic. . . . What of you? Do you still face execution?'

'Meg, you will scarcely believe what I am about to tell you! It has all been so extraordinary! A meeting was convened, here in Garsh, between the Revenant Elders and the heads of state of Dyarchim and Tomia. I was permitted to attend, as was Gully. Pic is still too ill to move. He is recovering, slowly. He is in a chamber just along the corridor. He is very weak, but seems to be something of his old self again. It looks as though the Heart has had no permanent effect.'

Meglan nodded. 'And what of this meeting?'

'Firstly it was agreed that restrictions upon the activities of the Revenants of Claine would be immediately lifted. King Lalvi hummed and hawed a little to begin with, but that is his way, I think. He needs to feel that any decision made must be his. Prince Enlos knows how to play him, and he came around quite quickly. Thus Garsh remains the Revenants' headquarters, but they may travel freely within both Tomia and Dyarchim, and are bound only by the normal constraints of the law. This being decided, King Lalvi and his retinue departed the meeting. Now, Meg, I come to the crux of a great mystery. Do you remember I told you as we descended to the Temple of Light, that at a meeting earlier Prince Enlos had asked to see two Revenant members who had been brought here as children? One turned out to be Epta, who is Master Kemorlin's daughter. Her mother, his spouse, apparently died soon after her birth. She came here in secret some years ago after an unhappy liaison with Prince Enlos. So, at Enlos's request, Epta was brought before him and his mother, Queen Lermeone, and Kemorlin. Then the other one, a girl-child who had been brought here as a baby, in far stricter secrecy than that which surrounded Epta, was also announced. Her name is Lucel. You will never guess, Meg: she is one of the three Elders. She is the young maiden.'

Meglan frowned to herself. 'But what is her connection? She was brought from Dyarchim? Who is she?'

'This is what is so extraordinary!' Sildemund shifted on his seat, barely able to contain himself. 'Do you remember, Meg, years ago, when we were still small children, too young to remember, there was a rebellion agains the throne? Dyarchim almost succumbed to civil war.'

'I have heard of it, yes.'

'Gully fought in that war. I did not have time to tell you before, but he was a hero! He helped save the life of Prince Enlos. He was even decorated!'

Meglan gaped at him in surprise. 'Gully? Is this true?'

'It is. Gully is too modest to speak of it. I only learned of it on the road to Dharsoul. We were rescued from Fagmar's men by Prince Enlos. He recognized Gully, and the truth came out! They were like old friends, Meg!'

'Old friends. . . . Yet Gully was still condemned for having heard Queen Lermeone speak? It seems that friendship, even in high places, counts for little in our nation – and heroism even less. But what has this to do with Lucel?'

'I'm trying to explain, Meg. The rebellion came about as the result of a scandal involving the Queen. The details were greatly suppressed so that few people ever knew the real facts. Well, now it is revealed. Queen Lermeone had a child, outside wedlock. She became Queen upon the death of her father, King Hirun, and assumed The Silence. By law she was forbidden from consorting with anyone, even her own husband. He, Prince Ugor, later drowned in an accident at sea. She could speak to no one, other than through the Supreme Haruspices. But, somehow, she established a secret liaison. Certain nobles learned of this, and of the birth of the child. They demanded its life, and the life of the Queen and of the child's father. They were arrested. Their followers then tried to overthrow the throne by force. The rebellion was quashed, though only after fierce and prolonged fighting. Those responsible were executed. The illegitimate baby then had to be spirited away before news of her existence leaked out again. She came here, secretly, to Garsh. The Revenants knew nothing of her origins, only that her welfare was of interest at the highest levels of Dyarch government.'

'Extraordinary. But what of the father? Who was he? Was he executed, or exiled?'

Sildemund smiled. 'Have you not guessed, Meg? The father was Kemorlin, also!'

'What?'

'It's true. After Prince Ugor's death, and with her assumption of rule and of The Silence, Queen Lermeone suffered a profound and prolonged melancholy. There was great concern for her health. Master Kemorlin was called in to render his professional services, for he had a reputation as a healer and alchemist, a mystic and clairvoyant. The Queen, no doubt starved of company, fell under his sway – as, I understand, have many women before and since.'

'But did not the discovery of this liaison carry an automatic sentence of death, at least for Kemorlin?'

'By rights it did. But the Queen forbade it. The details are a little unclear, but I believe she threatened to expose the truth and take her own life if Kemorlin – or the child – were harmed. She was in love with him. Of course, she could never be permitted to see him again, a fact which I believe caused him no great concern. But he was accorded a unique position in society – untouchable, by normal laws. Protected, as long as he spoke no word of what had ensued. He profited mightily, and came to assume a position of tremendous social influence. Meg, I wish you had been there and seen his face when all this came out. I have never seen a man so manifestly eager to be elsewhere.'

Meglan produced a distracted smile. 'So Lucel, then, is stepsister both to Prince Enlos and Epta.'

'That is so.'

'Yet she is a Revenant Elder, even though still a child.'

'By the Elders' acount the babe evinced certain qualities, certain gifts, from the earliest age, which convinced them that her coming was a fateful act. They were, in fact, expecting her. They believe utterly in such things. In the same way they knew that you and I, in some form, would come, as would the Heart of Shadows. Lucel is a Revenant; she has lived many times before.'

Meglan closed her eyes, struggling to take all this in, then: 'But what of you, Sil? That was my question. Surely, you cannot still be under sentence of death?'

'That is what I am coming to. Imagine the scene I was witnessing. It was one of great emotion. Queen Lermeone came forward in tears and embraced her child.'

'Lucel.'

'Lucel, who knew nothing of her origins. And, I should explain, I was confused. Not everything was clear to me, for not everything was being stated. It was Dinbig, standing beside me, who explained exactly what was happening.'

'Dinbig?'

'The Khimmurian sorcerer. The *Zan-Chassin*.'

Meglan stared in disbelief. '*Zan-Chassin?*'

Oh Meg, have I not mentioned him? Dinbig was at Court, in Dharsoul. He is a *Zan-Chassin* sorcerer. He helped us immensely. Without him I do not know whether we would have been here today. He has gone now, alas; returned to Dharsoul to pick up his goods, from there to make his way back to Khimmur. He had hoped to meet you. Two days ago he came to this chamber and applied ritual healing to speed your recovery. But he could not wait any longer. He departed yesterday morning. He is a good man, Meg. I did not know at first what to think of him. He cultivates an air of mystery, quite deliberately, I think. He is an intriguing fellow. I hope we may meet again one day – perhaps at the coronation.'

'Coronation? What coronation?' Meglan's eyes were wide, even more bedazzled by all she was hearing. 'You are advancing in great leaps, Sil.'

Sildemund took a deep breath. 'I am sorry. So much has happened. Where was I? Ah, yes. The Queen held her daughter, the child she had not set eyes on since she was a day-old baby, and she wept. In front of us all, quite openly and unashamedly. And when she was able, still clasping Lucel, she asked for her forgiveness—'

'Asked forgiveness? You mean Queen Lermeone spoke? But I thought—'

'*Listen*, Meg! Let me finish! Yes, she spoke, and the two Supreme Haruspices immediately began to protest. But Prince Enlos stepped before them and ordered them to silence. It was a moment of extraordinary tension. The Haruspices did not know how to respond. Queen Lermeone, addressing Lucel, confessed to her how she had wronged her, told how she had been racked with inner torment ever since, and begged for her forgiveness. Lucel gave it, without hesitation. Then she asked about her father, for she had never known him either. That is when the Queen called Master Kemorlin forward. And he came, utterly embarrassed, and embraced both his daughters. This done, Queen Lermeone turned to us all and announced her abdication.'

'*What?*'

' "I have consulted with the Elders of the Revenants of Claine, here in Garsh" she declared, "and have requested admission as a humble lay member into the Followers of Claine. My request has been accepted, and I shall therefore remain here henceforth, doing whatever I can to restore the name and faith of Claine. I hereby formally announce my abdication of the throne of Dyarchim in favour of my beloved son Enlos." '

'Enlos is to become King?' cried Meglan excitedly.

'In two months' time, in Dharsoul. And we are invited. You, me, Gully, Pic. Not only that, Meg, but we are to be honoured, for our serviced to Dyarchim! Enlos will despatch a retinue to Volm, to escort us personally to the capital!'

Meglan could scarcely believe what she was hearing. She all but pinched herself to make sure it was not a dream. 'But wait, wait,' she put her fingers to her temples. 'What, I ask once more, of your sentence of death?'

'Ah! Immediately upon the Queen's announcement Prince Enlos stepped forward, stating, "And my first decree as King-designate of Dyarchim is that the death sentence visited upon the three men of Volm, Masters Sildemund, Gully and Picadus, be repealed with instant effect. If any dare challenge my ruling let them step forward now and declare themselves and their reasons".

'It was a direct challenge to the Haruspices,' said Sildemund, 'and they knew it. They stood there and fumed in silence, caught like rats in a trap, unable to do anything.'

'But I thought you said the Haruspices are the true rulers, albeit in secret.'

'Only while a woman sits upon the throne, Meg. That is the whole point. Under a king their power is vastly reduced – and in this instance I would wager it will be reduced even further. They are helpless. It has been a brilliant manoeuvre. The Queen could never have abdicated in Dyarchim, for she could never speak her mind. But here, on foreign territory, before independent witnesses, the Haruspices are powerless. I think now we can look forward to profound and far-reaching changes in the Dyarch constitution. When next a queen rules over our nation, I think she will speak with her own voice.'

'This is incredible.'

'I would wager that Dinbig had a hand in all this,' said Sildemund, nodding in agreement. 'I know he spoke long and hard with Prince Enlos in Dharsoul. Enlos was aware of the Haruspices' power, but I don't think he saw the means to overcome it. Moreover, from what I understand he had no particular desire to take the throne. Dinbig must have persuaded him otherwise, and pointed out that by bringing the Heart of Shadows to Garsh, more might be achieved than was immediately apparent. So now Queen Lermeone's life of misery and isolation is over; she is able to function at last, as a woman, as a free-thinking human being. The Revenants of Claine, too, are allowed their own voice. Perhaps it is the beginning of something.'

'Perhaps,' mused Meglan. She felt a tiredness upon her. 'What now, Sil?'

'Now? We leave, as soon as you are well enough. We are going home. We are the only ones remaining. Enlos and his entourage departed three days ago. The Tomians have gone. Garsh is a free town once more. Enlos has left us an escort who will see us safely back to Volm. But now, Meg, you should sleep. I don't want to overtax you with too many wonders.'

He kissed her cheek, then rose. 'I will return soon.'

Meglan lay back, her head a-spin with all she had learned. She lay for a few moments, thinking hard, but her weariness quickly gained the upper hand and very soon she was asleep.

Late in the afternoon she was visited by the second Revenant Elder, the young woman whose name, she now learned, was Iridin. She came in quietly and smiled at Sildemund, who had returned and was sitting beside the bed. Then, seeing that Meglan was awake, she smiled at her and pulled up a stool.

'How are you feeling?'

'Well enough. A little sore; a little confused.'

'You were very brave.'

Meglan shrugged. 'Is Sko-ulatun truly gone?'

'His heart is destroyed, and therefore his ultimate aims are thwarted forever. He cannot contaminate our race with his seed; his spawn will never stride the world. We think he was destroyed also.'

'Think?'

'It is possible that in some form he may live on, lurking in dark corners, never known. If that is so, he will be weak. He will never be what he was. You bested him, Meglan. You, and Sildemund. Already changes are apparent. Remember, you are stronger than he.'

Meglan shook her head. 'There is much I don't understand. How did I survive?'

'That is what I have come to discuss.' Iridin linked her fingers upon her lap. 'Did Sildemund tell you what happened in the Temple?'

Meglan gave a nod.

'I would like to know what your perception of it was,' said Iridin.

'I thought I was going to die. It's as simple as that.'

'We were convinced you could survive. We would never have permitted you to do battle with Sko-ulatun had we not thought that. But in the moment when death was upon you, what was your experience?'

'It happened so quickly. I was falling. I saw the face, of Claine, rushing towards me. I had a fleeting impression of—'

'Yes?'

'It is hard to put into words. I felt that something flowed from my mouth. Sildemund tells me he saw a great vaporous serpent which bore me safely to the ground. I knew nothing of that. It all happened too quickly.'

Iridin nodded slowly to herself. 'Meglan, can I ask you again about your journey here, how you came upon the serpent talisman that you carried?'

'I told you before, I don't know. It is a complete mystery to me. The talisman guided me across Dazdun's Despair to Dharsoul. How I came upon it I just can't remember; nor do I recall leaving the road to enter the Despair. I woke up and found myself there. I have racked my memory again and again, but it is no use.'

'Is there nothing else you can tell us? Nothing at all?'

'Just that . . . close to where I awoke I came upon something strange. A skin, something like that of a huge serpent, lying upon the ground. At the time it filled me with terror.'

'This place, could you find it again?'

Meglan shook her head. 'Not without the talisman, and that is gone now.'

'Yes, that is gone.'

Iridin sat in silent contemplation for some moments, until Meglan asked, 'What happened to me? I think you know something. Tell me, please.'

Iridin drew in a long breath. 'Somewhere in this world we believe there exists a woman who is the embodiment of the spirit of Claine. She is a true Daughter of Serpents, wise, party to ancient magic and knowledge both of past and the future. She may not know precisely who she is; she is probably seen as a freak, shunned by people, and would therefore live alone. We believe you came into contact with her, that she gave you something – the talisman, yes, but something else also, something from within her. Almost certainly she knew something of your task and where you were bound. She helped you.'

'And you want to find her?'

'To welcome her into our community, to bring her back to the world. She may need our help. But—' Iridin spread her hands in a gesture of resignation. '—it is probably impossible. Dazdun's Despair is vast. Plainly she protects herself with magic, and she may no longer be there. We could search forever.'

Iridin rose. 'Be at peace here, Meglan. We hope your recovery will be swift, but that you will not rush to leave us.'

The following day Meglan left her bed. She was reunited with Gully, and visited Picadus in his bed. Pic, though barely conscious and unable to move, seemed to know her and produced a hint of a smile as she sat beside him. It would be weeks before he would be fit enough to leave, but in the meantime both Meglan and Sildemund were anxious to return home to Volm. It was therefore arranged that Picadus would remain behind, to be escorted home by Revenant fighters when he had recovered sufficiently.

Two nights later a banquet was held in their honour, at which they sat at the head table with the three Revenant Elders, Queen Lermeone and Epta. And the following morning they departed Garsh, not without a twinge of sadness. They passed through the town gate to the cheers of the Revenants, riding proudly at the head of the troop of elite Dyarch cavalry provided by Prince Enlos. The valley was empty now, no soldiers waited to storm the ancient hill-town. Meglan gazed around her as they rode away into the Tomian wildlands and headed towards the Dyarch border and home. It was hard to believe all she had been through, all she had achieved. It was hard to believe that it could be over.

She reached across from her saddle and grasped the hand of her brother who rode beside her. 'We have come a long way,' she said.

Sildemund smiled. 'Further than we know.'

A week later they came in sight of the glittering sea and the domes and turrets of beloved Volm in the distance. Meglan felt a surge of emotion; there had been so many occasions in recent days when she had wondered whether she would ever see her home and her father again. She urged her horse into a canter – recalled, for the thousandth time, Swift Cloud, stabled at the inn at Dharsoul. In two months, when they attended the coronation of the young King Enlos, she would reclaim the filly. In the meantime she had gained the assurance of the captain of her escort that, immediately upon his return to the capital, he would personally have Swift Cloud transferred to the royal stables.

The soldiers accelerated to keep pace with her, throwing up a plume of dust in the heat of late afternoon. They arrived at the outskirts of the town. Folk came from their shops and houses to watch as they clattered along the familiar streets. Some recognized them, and waved. Most simply stood, unsure of what to make of the procession.

At last they arrived before the shop and the old house where they had lived all their lives. The windows were shuttered, the door closed. Meglan and Sildemund climbed from their mounts and stood before their home, their hearts full. Half-consciously they took one another's hands, neither quite able to voice their feelings.

As they made to step forwards there was a sound of a latch lifting within.

They waited. The old door opened with a creak of iron hinges. From the gloom within came a familiar figure. He limped forward, leaning on a stick. His leg was bandaged, but the bindings on his hands were gone.

He stopped before them, smiling.

'My children,' said their father, and threw wide his arms. 'Welcome home.'

APPENDIX

The Zan-Chassin

OUT OF THE shamanistic beliefs and practices indigenous to the regions of Southern Lur was born in the nation known as Khimmur a formalised, stratified system of applied ritualised sorcery, called Zan-Chassin. 'Powerful way', 'Path, or Ladder, of Knowledge', 'Mysterious Ascent' are all approximate translations of the term. The Zan-Chassin cosmology held that the universe was created by the Great Moving Spirit, Moban. Moban, having created all, moved on (in certain mystical circles Firstworld is still referred to as the Abandoned Realm). Creation was left to do as it would without interference or aid.

Numerous modes, or realms, of being were conceived to exist within the Creation, not all of which were readily perceived by or accessible to men. In the normal state man realized two domains, the corporeal and the domain of mind or intellect. The power of the Zan-Chassin adepts lay in their ability to transcend these and enter various supra-physical domains, termed the Realms, there to interact with the spirit entities active within them. Emphasis was also laid upon contact with the spirits of ancestors who had passed beyond the physical world to dwell in the Realms beyond, and who could be summoned to an ethereal meeting place to provide advice and guidance to their descendants in the physical world.

Where Zan-Chassin practice differed from that of the shamen of many other nations was in its systematic and quasi-scientific approach. Understanding the nature of the Realms became paramount, resulting in the introduction of a set procedure whereby the aspiring adept, through precise training and instruction, might learn in stages both the sorcerous art and something of the nature of the Realm of existence he or she was to enter, thus mitigating somewhat the inherent dangers. Previously the non-corporeal world had been conceived of as a single Realm of existence. Men had gone willy-nilly from their bodies to encounter with little forewarning whatever lay beyond. The risks were considerable. Many perished or were lost or driven insane by their experiences.

The Zan-Chassin way revealed the Realms to be of varying natures, with myriad and diverse difficulties and obstacles being met within each. Just as normal humans might realise different 'shades' of existence, depending upon the development of intellect, organs of sense, etc., so could Zan-Chassin masters come to know and experience the differing natures of the Realms. Adepts were taught to subdue spirit-entities within each level of experience before progressing to the next, thus providing themselves with allies or helpers at each stage of their non-corporeal wanderings. The dangers, though still very real, were thus partially diminished. Aspirants progressed from one Realm to the next only when adjudged ready and sufficiently equipped by their more advanced mentors.

Nonetheless, over time many of even the most advanced and experienced Zan-Chassin masters failed to survive their journeys beyond the corporeal.

Within Khimmurian society Zan-Chassin proficiency was a key to power and influence. Practitioners generally enjoyed privileged social positions, and indeed the national constitution, such as it was, was structured such that Khimmur could be ruled only by one accomplished in the sorcerous art. A few Zan-Chassin chose the anchoretic life and lived beyond society, but they were in the minority.

To some extent the Zan-Chassin were feared by normal folk, who were much prone to superstition. Their magic was not understood, their ways were somewhat strange and wonderful. The Zan-Chassin made little effort to remedy this, it being expedient in certain circumstances.

Women enjoyed honoured status within the Zan-Chassin hierarchy. The female revealed a natural affinity with the concepts of non-corporeality and spirit-communication which few men were able to emulate. They were equally highly proficient in the exploration and 'mapping' of the furthermost discovered territories of Moban's great and mysterious Creation. Thus the hierarchy remained matriarchal in character, withstanding efforts to reduce the feminine influence.